The New Blue

T. L. Brown

Pink Leather Ink

Books for and about pretty strong women.

The New Blue

Written by T. L. Brown

Published by Pink Leather Ink • Florida

We The Women imprint

For all the young women looking for love with their eyes,
and for themselves in someone else's.

PROLOGUE

If I could punch *Love** in the face I would. I'd give it two black eyes. One for each time I gave it my heart and had it kicked right back to me cold. And blue. Before I flee the scene of my crime I'd give it a good bloody nose for all the times it's held its hand over my nose and mouth and told me to stop resisting. To go quietly. To give up.

As sure as my name is Sidney Shane I'm a tormentee of Love. Love is that lunchroom bully that slaps my food tray out of my hands and then calls me clumsy in front of a crowd. It's that sadistic boss that rides me all week then withholds pay come Friday. It's that all-too-happy-to-do-so security guard in the concert of *coupledom* escorting me from the premises, telling me I'm trespassing as he's tearing up my ticket.

But just when Love thinks that it's emotionally and psychologically slain me—that I've fainted then flatlined—my eyelids move. My lashes twitch. My pulse returns. I'm back.

Resurrection aside, I'm afraid I'm in trouble if what they say is true. If what they say is true about the future being predicted by the past, then my fate, I imagine, has already been sealed.

The past.

What an appropriate place to begin . . .

It all started with that monumental day. That pivotal point that changed everything.

July 23, 2010.

How many twenty-one-year-old virgins do you know? Not many, I'm sure. But there I was, nine weeks before my 22nd birthday giving it up to a man I knew exactly thirty-two days.

His name was Damon. And I can still remember the look on his face. That dark-eyed smirk that said he was getting something he didn't deserve.

But he took it anyway.

The original plan was to save myself for my husband in order to follow in my mother's footsteps. My father is her first and, to this day, only lover. They met when they were nineteen and have been married for almost thirty years. Dad proposed to Mom on their fourth date. She said *yes* on the fifth. I fell in love with that story every time I heard it growing up, and hoped for the same.

But it wasn't happening that way for me. As it pertained to my life, that fate lived only in the *museums* of real romance. And in the lives of a lucky few. Though initially hopeful, I eventually came to feel as if I was kidding myself to think that I would live out my life the way Mom had hers, and that a legendary kind of love such as the one she shared with my father was unrealistic today. Not very many people waited for their wedding day to disrobe. And far fewer bothered waiting beyond the age of consent. Times had changed. People had changed. And in the interim, so had I. I became curious.

Very curious.

I had easily resisted the lure of sex throughout high school, and for most of college, but by the time my senior year rolled around, I was as curious as a cat eyeing a cockatoo! Besides, everyone I knew at the time was getting busy and made sex sound like such a gratifying, self-empowering experience. I *had* to try it. I had been called "good girl", "nerdy virgin", and "Mother Theresa" for too long.

Of course, most people didn't know I was a virgin. The majority assumed based on, not only my age, but my particular choice of fashion and the confidence with which I carried myself that I'd probably had my fair share of between-the-sheets meetings. I guess that just goes to show you can't judge a book by its cover.

But when guys did finally learn about my legs-closed status they all wanted to host the ribbon-cutting ceremony. And to put my panties up on their walls.

But they were only chasing their *own* tails, because, though I was never outwardly cocky about my sexual purity, inside, I knew I was special. I knew that my virgin status made me more desirable to the majority of the male gender.

This was especially the case in high school. Guys worked overtime trying to win me over but they didn't know what they were up against. For they were up against two very powerful opponents, as my popularity and reputation were far more important to me than experimenting with some stupid boy who was sure to run his mouth to the entire school. I'd seen too many pretty girls' beauty tarnished by rumors of their promiscuity. People no longer talked about how cute they were, or even how smart they were, rather how *easy* they were. Their beauty and intellect faded into the background, eclipsed by their smeared reputations. It wasn't fair. But I knew *fair* had no say in the matter. I couldn't let that happen to me. I learned by watching them, even as I entered adulthood, since college guys were silly too.

But before long there was a battle to be had. One between my abstinence agenda and the curiosity that curled its finger and summoned me to test the waters. And when *Chastity*, wearing the white trunks, entered the ring with *Curiosity*, who wore the red, it was destined that only one of them would come out alive.

So there I was, lying on a hard-as-stone twin bed in some guy's hole-in-the-wall apartment, giving my most sacred gift to a person I'd later be tempted to question whether or not cared if I were even awake for it all. It was not an enjoyable experience like I had been told it would be. The pain was almost unbearable. And I think I bled. If pleasure was anywhere in that room, I certainly couldn't find it. Case in point, he acted like he didn't know what foreplay was—or was hoping that *I* didn't. I mean, I was a virgin, not a dummy. I hadn't been hiding under a rock for nearly twenty-two years. I had a general idea of what was supposed to take place in the bedroom, and I certainly wasn't expecting *Ouch!— Ow!!!—You mean it's over now?!* I was expecting that same toe-curling explosion of climactic ecstasy that had been described to me by friends, film, and fiction over the past several years. This was far from it. Instead, I had this guy with a less-than-perfect physique, less-than-fresh breath, and less-than-impressive stamina hovering, heaving, and humping, with me underneath it all.

It lasted seven minutes.

There was no music. No cuddling afterwards. And no profession of love. Seven minutes was all it took to make me the opposite of what I was. Seven minutes erased twenty-two years.

That night I had crossed the point of no return. I couldn't take any of it back—*ever*. As of that moment I was no longer pure and ideally innocent. I could no longer walk into a room with the confidence of knowing that no man present had the privilege of bragging to anyone about having been with me. That comfort was gone. I'd surrendered it all in those few overrated minutes.

And I'd never felt so unattractive in my life.

In the post moments of my experience, not the warmth of afterglow, but *shame* was what I felt. Shame was what eventually rocked me to sleep rather than my lover's protective and appreciative arms, or that magical spark of fulfillment and utter infatuation I was supposed to feel. It was the shame that followed immediate regret. Regret never came so swift. It swept down upon me like an angel of death to a dying man's bedside, descending to witness the demise of my sound judgment and emotional independence.

Shame. Regret. In that moment that was what I felt. But then, I felt a lot of things. I felt embarrassed. I felt cheated. Soiled. I felt like the girl in the Color Purple as I lie there.

I don't even remember him kissing me that night.

CHAPTER 1

Of all the phones ringing in Manhattan that morning mine had to be the loudest.

"*Hello?*" I breathed heavy into the receiver, my brain threatening a migraine.

"Good morning, Butterfly!"

It was Mom. She always made a habit of calling too early. She was a light sleeper. The slightest sound of morning stirring was enough to happily coax her out of bed, unlike myself, who'd probably sleep through a parade right outside my window.

"Good morning, Mommy," I said with untuned vocal cords, then yawned.

"Were you sleeping?"

"No," I fibbed so she wouldn't feel bad. "I was just getting up." I pulled my heavy head up from my pillow and rose in a lip-tugging stretch.

"Oh, good. Well, I was calling to see if you were coming by today. I'm cooking a *surpriiiise* . . ." she singsonged.

Mom was glad that I'd passed on my Syracuse acceptance and decided on NYU instead. That put me closer to her and Dad. They lived in New Rochelle. We'd moved into the beautiful, six-bedroom Colonial home four days into my freshman year in high school, following my father's firm. Dad designed houses, and Mom decorated their interiors. Always a perfect match, together they worked hard to ensure that my older sister and I had the best of everything. We certainly weren't rich, but Chaylene and I didn't know the difference. Christmases and birthdays said otherwise.

Though our upbringing bordered on spoiled, Mom and Dad taught my sister and me to be humble and kind. To share. And to never believe that we "deserved" anything. We weren't even allowed to use the word. Mom said that to say that you deserved something implied that someone else *didn't*. So that word was stricken from our vocabulary early on. But since reaching adulthood it had certainly crept its way back into mine.

Born and raised in Phoenix, we were content, my sister and I, with our wonderful, western lives. But Dad wanted a change for us, so he and Mom decided to move forward with the relocation opportunity my father was presented with. Mom, originally from Louisiana, hated the cold (a hate she and I shared). But that *"cactus climate and sweltering heat"* just wasn't doing it for her anymore she'd say as she spoke of change. I knew better, though. It was less about change, and more about supporting her man. So, New York it was.

Chaylene was *not* happy with the move, to say the least. By then she was a senior in high school and had already established herself as Ms. Popularity. She made a big stink about the relocation and said she wasn't going, threatening to run away. But naturally accustomed to food, shelter, and designer clothing she quickly found herself seated next to me on the plane, giving us all the silent treatment for five hours at 40,000 feet.

Now married with two kids and living in Chicago, Chaylene was living proof that sweet things did happen to sour people. We were never close. I was always unhappy with the quality of our relationship, but she was too busy to care. She had success to distract her. *Love* and success.

Married right after college, Chaylene and her husband, Dennis, had been dating since her sophomore and his senior year at NYU. On her graduation day, instead of attending the commencement ceremony, she and Dennis eloped, denying my parents both the privilege of watching their firstborn graduate, and the joy of witnessing her marry. But again, she didn't care. She'd married the man of her dreams, and didn't care about crushing anyone else's.

Four years into their marriage, my sister and her husband seemed to be as happy as the day they met. He was a corporate attorney, and she, a degree-holding, stay-at-home mom. I always envied her ability to land great men and eventually marry so successfully. What I didn't envy, however, were her flaky friendships growing up. Chaylene never had any real friends. She was always just surrounded by people who were secretly in competition with her. When she got a new skirt, her friends got new dresses. When she let her hair grow long, they got extensions. When she got her braces off, her classmates couldn't wait to go out and buy her smile. I felt sorry for her. To never have any real friends to have your back was horrible.

But now she had Dennis. He was different. He didn't want to be like her, or better than her. He just wanted to be with her. And the two of them were inseparable. If Chaylene brought Dennis over to the house, they were spooning on the sofa. If we had a family reunion, he was operating the grill. They couldn't be apart for even a moment without having separation anxiety. So much so, that one night, in her haste to reunite with him, Chaylene nearly killed me.

"So, what time should I expect you?" Mom asked as I was reluctant to jump up this particular Saturday morning.

"Um . . ." I sat up, looking at the clock. "I should probably be there around three. I have some things I need to take care of before I come."

I didn't have anything to take care of. I just wanted time to kick back and reflect on last night. I may not have had the best tour guide, but the voyage was still a big deal for me. I wanted to reevaluate it in my mind, and couldn't be bothered with jumping up and running out the door first thing in the morning.

"Okay, sweetie. Your dad and I will see around three, then."

"Alright, Mommy."

"I love you."

"I love you, too."

"Drive safely," she snuck in.

"I will."

I hung up the phone and looked at the time. It was 8 o' clock. I'd only been home for three hours. My body felt so weak.

Exhausted, I took a deep breath and fell back into the bed sheets, reminiscing until I nodded back off to sleep.

Finally, a little after one o' clock, I decided to yank myself out of bed. I headed for the bathroom, half asleep, and flipped on the light. The old bulb took its time flickering on. Once it glowed, I unsuctioned myself from the door and dragged over to the sink.

Looking in the mirror, I was trying to determine if I appeared any different. I looked at my eyes. My expression. My body. I didn't notice anything different, but wondered if anyone else would. I began wondering if my mom, who knew I was a virgin and, most likely, proudly shared that information with my father, would be able to tell that there was something different about me.

Will they know what I did last night? Will they be able to tell? I worried, hoping I didn't exhibit any telltale signs of knocking boots, especially around my parents.

I shook off the thought, realizing I was being silly and paranoid.

No way will they be able to tell just by looking at me. Right? I wavered, feeling like the moniker Dee Flower was engraved across my forehead like the Scarlet Letter.

Nooooo, I laughed to myself, feeling foolish for even thinking so. *Besides*—I snatched back the shower curtain—*I'm a grown-ass woman!*

I reached down, turning on the tub's faucet. Out of the silver spout, water poured ice-cold into the oval-shaped basin. As the pipes came to life, I held my hand under the chilly flow until growing traces of warmness began to splash into my curled-fingered palm. Once the water warmed to a temperature I found suitable, I lifted the tiny lever.

While the room filled with steam I closed my eyes for a little while, and began thinking about Damon. Having slept on it, I felt much better. I woke with a certain clarity that the immediate moments couldn't offer me. Suddenly, I felt different about it all. Without so much focusing on the details, I pondered more on its deeper significance and what it could mean for me. What it could mean for *us*.

I walked over toward the mirror again. The mirror that, today, felt brand-new, as if it were just mounted over my sink while I slept, and the old one hauled away. I stood there, eyes lurking low, planning to sneak up on my reflection and catch it within this new looking glass. Steam rolled over and around my shoulders. My heart dipped with anxious excitement at whom I might see.

Slowly, my eyes traveled up from my breasts to my neck, then all the way up to my eyes. They *were* different.

I removed my hair clip, letting my hair fall free, then swept it up with my hand behind my head, turning from side to side, chin up, then down, analyzing myself. Something inside me *was* changed —I saw it. Something in me had either came, or left, thus making me different than before. And I not only saw it, I felt it. I felt the change in me. And I think I liked it.

I released my hair, allowing it to fall loose once again, and smirked at my frosting reflection as thoughts of last night replayed in my head. Removing Damon from the moment was impossible. He *was* the moment. And I realized that he was probably holding back since it was my first time. Maybe I made him nervous, being with a virgin and all. Maybe that was pressure on him. Maybe it was just as awkward for him as it had been for me. Despite the fact that he didn't live up to my preconceived notions about sex, it was exciting being with him. And maybe "it" wasn't so bad after all.

Suddenly, Damon's attractiveness was restored. My mind had worked its way back to wanting to continue exploring a possible long-term relationship with him. We both felt something for one another. He liked me. And, clearly, I liked him. After all, I had dropped my guard (among softer, lacier things) for him for a reason. There had to be a reason for him to get from me what others had not. For me to surrender to curiosity with him, in particular. And now he was part of my history. Perhaps even my Damon to Mom's *Dad*. And to Chaylene's *Dennis*. Like them, I wondered if there could be something special and long-lasting for the two of us. *Sidney and Damon . . .*

✦ ✦ ✦

When I arrived at my parents' house at a quarter to three, my dad was mowing the lawn out front. He was wearing his favorite baseball cap and usual grass-cutting sneakers that saw more mowings than they'd liked.

15

He shut off the mower when he saw me.

"Hey, Sid." He kissed me on the cheek.

"Hi, Daddy." I gave him a hug.

Dad was an average height man with a solid build and, uncomfortably, what women often referred to as "bedroom eyes". Aside from his good looks and mostly-laid back demeanor, he was also the smartest man I knew—professors included. Given his scholastic mind, education was very important to him, and he seldom let me forget that.

"How's school coming along?" he predictably asked. "Are you keeping those grades up?"

"3.8," I boasted.

"Good job, Sid. Your mother and I are very proud of you," Dad said with a look that told me he meant it.

"Thanks," I smiled. "Where's Mom?"

"She's in the kitchen." He wiped the sweat from his forehead, then yanked the mower's chain. It looked like he only had one more patch to tackle.

"Thanks!" I shouted over the loud roar of the mower.

I jogged up the steps onto the porch, and reached for the brass-handled French doors. As I opened them and stepped inside I was immediately greeted by the delicious aroma of Cajun-seafood gumbo. The smell brought back pleasant memories of when, as a child, I would bother Mom in the kitchen and she would make me feel as if I were really helping out, even as I most often made a mess.

Mom loved to cook her famous gumbo, embracing her Creole heritage. It was her number one specialty. She knew I loved it more than any other dish, and promises of its preparation always proved successful at luring me over.

Mom came around the corner wearing a sweet grin as I slipped out of my shoes and dropped my keys and purse onto the console table.

"Hey, Butterfly," she held her arms out and giggled excitedly.

Even though she saw me biweekly, it was always as if it had been years.

"Hi, Mommy."

We were closer than close. Growing up, as all mothers and daughters, we'd had our share of differences, but I knew that she was the only person in the whole world who would ever love me as much as she did.

"How are you?" Mom's back bent as I stood on my tippy toes, hugging her.

At five-nine, Mom hovered a full five inches above me. She was just starting her modeling career, fresh out of high school, when she met Dad. But he was too conservative to have his future wife strut around half naked on some runway in Paris, being the public object of every man's affection, so she quit, never looking back. She said that modeling was short-term, while Dad was forever. I respected her sacrifice. And a sacrifice it was. She could've really had a promising career. She was so beautiful. Drop-dead gorgeous, even. There wasn't a person dead or alive who could deny that. And I was so proud to be her daughter. I may not have gotten her height, but I did get her clover honey complexion and green, gold-flecked eyes.

"I'm good, Mom. Things are great." I squeezed her tight before letting go. "I think I need my brakes done, though."

Mom frowned. "Again?"

"I know," I frowned back innocently, while inside knowing that I was hard on some brakes. But in all fairness, the car was almost ten years old.

"If it's not one thing with that car it's another."

"Tell me about it," I rolled my eyes. "And they cut my hours at the boutique, too," I slipped, wanting to take it back as soon as I'd said it.

Mom's look quickly changed from mildly concerned to worrisome. I knew what was coming next.

"Do you need money?"

"No, Mom. I'm fine. I have a little something saved."

I had nothing saved but a surplus of pride. This week I was flat broke and on a top-ramen-and-tuna fish diet. But I was also dead-set on paying my own bills this last year of college, and had the debt to prove it. Between personal bank loans and Visas, I had everything under control. I figured Mom and Dad were still young and shouldn't have to spend *all* of their future retirement money on me, especially since they were already paying for my education, as well as having paid half my rent for the past three and a half years. What's more, I'd feel guilty taking their money knowing I'd squandered the majority of mine on shoes and clothing every week.

Mom still looked worried despite my *everything's-just-peachy* performance.

"Well, you'll let your father and I know if you need us, won't you?" she asked insistently.

I nodded. "Of course, Mommy. But really, I'm fine."

As far as I was concerned I had things under control. The boutique paid me pretty well. And what I'd already blown this week, I'd easily make next week, reduced hours and all, as my commission was out of this world. But lately I sensed the other employees were treating me funny. Jealous, they began complaining that I was stealing their customers, which was ridiculous. I couldn't help it if customers preferred me over them. They should've put some smiles on those brick-hard faces of theirs.

Nonetheless, I noticed my already part-time hours being slashed nearly in half. I tried not to let it bother me, though. This upcoming semester I was wrapping up for graduation, so working full-time in my major would soon replace my part-time retail position. In fact, I already had a job offer with one of the top P.R. firms in New York City upon graduation. Those broads could have the boutique!

Mom finally took my word that I had a handle on things.

"Alright. Well, come on into the living room and let me show you the new drapes." She tugged on my hand.

I followed Mom into the living room and was immediately impressed by the new, pearl-embroidered, gold-trimmed window treatments. They turned the living room into a queen's quarters. Mom really had a knack for decorating, and was one of the most sought-after interior designers in the borough.

"They're beautiful." I walked over to the window to get a feel. "Where did you find them?"

"In Spain last summer when your father and I went. I've had them tucked away down in the basement all this time. I didn't think I'd ever use them," she wrinkled her nose and shrugged, "but last week, when I started going through some old boxes, I came across them and was once again inspired."

Mom and Dad loved to travel. They were always off "touring the globe", as Mom would say. I was even conceived in Australia, hence my name. Except Mom didn't like the extra *y*. She insisted it was the masculine version, going with the unisex spelling instead.

"I absolutely love them!" I smiled, unable to let go of the satiny fabric that flirted with my fingertips.

Mom smiled at the genuine praise.

I turned to her. "When I get my house, I'm definitely going to hire you."

Mom and I held hands as we walked over to the sofa.

"Speaking of house," she turned to me, grinning, "anyone new in your life?"

How's that speaking of house? I thought to myself.

Mom couldn't resist. She'd been trying to conjure up a potential husband for me ever since my sister married. I think she just wanted to see one of her children walk down the aisle being that my sister deprived her of that. I guess I couldn't really blame her. But that was a sore subject for me lately since I felt like I was nowhere near getting married any time soon. Not with the way dating had been going for me. Sometimes I felt like I'd thrown away my only chance at true love years ago.

Peli was my high school sweetheart. His real name was Alejandro, but we dubbed him *Peli* on the count of the tattoo on his right arm that read *Peligro*—Spanish for *Danger*. But body art aside, he was the sweetest, most generous guy I'd ever met. And he never pressured me about sex. He never even asked. But if I had been ready back then to take that big step, he would've been the one I trusted enough to be with.

Peli and I dated my junior and his senior year. My parents adored him. Voted cutest couple, everyone thought we'd get married and have beautiful bilingual babies. But when he graduated a year ahead of me, and didn't get into NYU right away, he decided to join the service. For one solid year we maintained a long-distance relationship, promising to reunite once I graduated. But when the time came, and he asked me to move to North Carolina where he was stationed, I had to choose between college life and military wife. The pressure of it all pushed me away. I broke up with him, sending back the promise ring he had given me before he left.

Five years had passed and there weren't any more *Peli*s. I wondered if I'd ever get a chance like that again. If I'd passed on my *only* chance. No one had ever touched my heart the way he had. Carefree and confident at that time, I always believed I'd meet my husband in college, just like Chaylene, and move onto a new love story. But now, close to graduation, I had to face the hard fact that it just wasn't happening.

But then I thought back to Damon and last night. *What if we—he and I—could get married?*

Though we may have gotten the order a little mixed up, it still would be a fairytale come true to marry my first.

I could see myself with him, I thought to myself. *I really could. It would be great if . . .*

"Sidney?" Mom broke my fantasy, still awaiting my answer.

With a huge smile that followed a deep, brave breath, I turned to her. "Well, actually, Mom—"

"How are two of my favorite girls doing?" Dad came in and kicked off his shoes.

"Besides Chay, we better be your *only* girls," Mom jokingly threatened as he walked over to us.

"Of course, baby." He leaned over from behind the sofa and kissed her on the forehead.

I had the best-looking parents around. They looked so good together, and weren't shy about showing their affection for one another. But Mom was about as jealous as they came. She'd want to go berserk when other women made less-than-subtle advances toward Dad. But Dad didn't mind reassuring her both publicly and privately that he only had eyes for her. I think he liked the fact that such a stunningly beautiful woman could be so jealous over him. Other women never stood a chance.

Dad leaned over even further this time and kissed Mom on the lips.

I dropped my eyes in my lap to give them a tiny moment of privacy.

"I love you, baby," I heard him whisper.

I looked up for a moment, finding them in a locked gaze.

"I love you, too, sweetheart," Mom whispered back, smiling.

As Dad walked away in search of a shower, Mom's eyes, beaming, followed him to the staircase, then all the way up the stairs. As she watched him, I watched her, her young-looking face glowing with sweet, ripened love. "And don't leave those sweaty clothes on the floor!" she told him before he rounded the corner into the master suite.

Once he'd disappeared she turned to me.

"So, what were you saying?" Mom's face filled with anxious hope again.

I shook my head and smiled. "No, Mom. There's no one yet."

I don't know why I said that. I guess I wasn't really sure where this whole Damon thing was going after all.

"Well, that's okay, sweetie. Your knight in shining armor will come."

Before I'm eighty years old? I wanted to ask, but nodded instead.

Watching my parents made me wonder if something was wrong with me that it had been this long and I still hadn't found what they had. As a full-fledged adult, I knew nothing about love. Only that I wanted to be in it, and wasn't. And as much as my memory referred to Peli when the topic of it came up, we were teenagers, and that was a long time ago. That was a different kind of love. I wondered if I was jinxed. Predestined to be alone. The thought saddened me.

Mom noticed.

"Now, Sidney," she placed her hand on my leg, the simplistic stone in her wedding band gleaming in spite of its size, "don't go feeling sorry for yourself. I know that look. You'll find someone. I promise you." She shook my knee and smiled as my heart struggled to believe her.

"Don't you know that right now—this very moment —that *you* are the only thing missing from someone's life? One day the two of you are going to find each other."

She turned to face me completely. "But in the meantime, Sidney, love yourself the way you would want this person to love you."

My eyes began to water.

"Awww," her look softened, "you're just the sweetest thing. And look how beautiful you are." She cupped my face in her hands. "A man would be a fool not to want to marry you."

I wanted to smile, but couldn't. Mom didn't know what I was feeling inside. She was unaware of the frustration her words really brought me.

"Remember what I used to tell you when you were a little girl?"

I nodded my head, then chanted with her:

"Sidney Simone. Sidney Simone. Has a strength that's all her own. She's smart, loving, and brave indeed. And she was born with all she needs!"

"That's right, Butterfly. And don't you forget it."

Mom kissed me on the cheek as I suppressed the tears that wanted to flee from my sad eyes.

"Now fix that cookie face of yours!" she said as we got up and headed toward the kitchen where comfort food awaited me.

CHAPTER 2

When they say sex changes everything, they said a mouthful. After our memorable night Damon discontinued the decent dude promo, and decided to see how well he'd fare as an amateur gigolo. Gone were the days of eating burgers and fries in the Home of the Yankees while cuddling in the nose-bleeding section of the stadium. No longer did he bother with arranging such complimentary hook-ups and freebies via personal connections. Instead we were going to the mall. On my dime.

I, on the other hand, was beginning to develop deeper feelings for Damon, and was hoping for something more for the two of us. He was quite aware of this and opportunistically began thinking of ways to profit from that fact. He began pressuring me to buy him clothes and shoes; expensive jewelry and whatnots. I'd made the grave mistake of loaning him money on a few occasions (if you can call money taken without the sincere intent of repayment *a loan*) and ever since he'd been trying to change my initials from SSS to ATM. And when he saw my new ride, he *really* started seeing dollars signs.

But after calculating my net worth in his greedy little head, Damon should've arrived at a total of zero. Because contrary to what he thought, I was a buck above broke. My brand-new BMW 3 Series Convertible was an early graduation gift from my parents. I'd never see the car note, and wouldn't know what to do with it if I did.

Nonetheless, Damon, at one point, in pursuit of the paper and plastic in my purse, had me pick him up and take him to the mall, feeling it was time for the shopping spree. As we walked through various stores, Damon would casually point out items he "wished" he had. I "wished" he had a better job, because he had pretty expensive taste for a man of his salary.

One item in particular, a pair of sneakers, cost $180. Damon said he loved them, then dropped his eyes, awaiting my response. I didn't say a word. And while I wasn't uncomfortable with the silence, I was very uncomfortable with the scene. I played dumb, but I knew where he was coming from, and didn't like where things were going. He was my first, but I was nobody's fool. I wasn't going to allow anyone to play me that way. So after a few weeks of that nonsense Damon and I abruptly ended our short-lived affair.

Separating from Damon was hard, but thinking about how he tried to use me made it easier. Easi*er*. But not easy. I often became depressed at the thought of my body having been given in vain, and knew that were it not for the fact that I'd had sex with him it was very likely I wouldn't miss Damon at all. But I had. And I did.

The fact that I'd shared my body with Damon—had "given myself" to him, as its described—trapped me in a sense. It was as if my body wanted to claim Damon for its own, even though it clearly wasn't in my heart's best interest. Or maybe it was my ego that wanted to salvage that which should not have been.

Its reasoning said that staying with Damon would keep me in the company of my virginity, or in otherwise close proximity to my vagina's soul, if there was such a thing.

It felt like my virginity was an actual physical object that Damon now had possession of. That he now held inside of *him.* It was as if my virginity was a material thing that I wanted—*needed*—to remain close to. Stand next to. Supervise. That transfer of ownership, that forfeiture of power attached the two of us. It was the umbilical cord that connected Damon and I. Through it flowed pacification that was like oxygen to my ego, trickling to me cc's of self-esteem. Damon now dispensed significant doses of my self-worth. As worthless as he was.

The irony stung.

To add to this, part of me still longed for that fantasy-turned-reality that Mom had. That ever-lasting love story. I wished that I had chosen someone else. That I had quenched my curiosity with a more worthy man. Someone that would've really loved me, or would have grown to love me. Someone I could've locked into for life.

To cope, I tried convincing myself that it was solely Damon's loss. That he was no big prize, and that he needed to drop to his knees and thank the Lord that I even *looked* at him twice. *He was no GQ!* I'd say to friends as I thought of all the ways I'd seen him looking less like the marvelous man I'd envisioned for myself, and more like the seven-minute monster from my momentary bout of weakness. I'd laugh as I thought about it all, trying to giggle away the pain.

But it was no use. I was still hurt. And truth be told, Damon was undeniably handsome. Asshole or not.

But as hurt as I was, I was also resilient. I shook off those depressing thoughts, and decided to get on with my life. That particular relationship had ended, but it was not the end of the world. I told myself that I'd get through this. I was still alive. I was still healthy. And I was still beautiful. I reminded myself that Damon wasn't the only *Joe* in town. Maybe just the luckiest. But his getting-lucky-with-*me* days were over. *We* were over. And through the sting of it all, a part of me felt free. Emancipated. Like I was beginning a new phase of my life. I was going to get over Damon Campbell. I was sure of it. In fact, I was already on my way. I was optimistic and accepting. I was doing just fine.

That is, until that phone call.

RING! RING!

I rolled over onto my stomach and buried my face into my pillow.

Ring!! Ring!!

"Noooooo," I moaned, not wanting to budge. But the caller was persistent.

Ring!!! Ring!!!

"Okay. Okay." I caught glimpse of the clock, which read 11:58 p.m. I really needed to get some rest. Tomorrow was a big day. And Tasha was sure to have me on the go from sunup to sundown.

My cordless was charging on its base in the other room, and my cell phone was in the car.

Ring! Riiiiiiiiiiiiing!

"I'm coming," I said, snatching the covers off of me as cool air attached itself to my body like Velcro.

I slipped my robe over my pj shorts set, and stumbled down the hall, hugging the wall to maintain my balance as sleep threw off my equilibrium, the phone ringing all the while.

"Damn Bam!!!" I shouted as I'd jammed my pinky toe on the corner of the wall, painfully separating it from its pink-polished partners.

I hopped on one foot, massaging my injured phalange, the pain instantly freeing me from the chains of drowsiness that had kept me captive on the way to the phone that had suddenly stopped ringing.

Reaching the counter that separated the living room from the kitchen, toe throbbing at a ten, I picked up the phone—not bothering to hit the light—and heard the double dial tone indicating I had a voice message. As I thumbed in my access code, I leaned over the counter, took a clean glass from the dish rack, and began filling it with filtered tap water as I slid into my slippers that were parked at the barstool.

"You have one message," the computerized voice announced just as I'd looked at the caller ID and learned to whom I'd assign blame for my toe trauma. But then I considered the time the call came in, and, realizing she was probably just an eager beaver with a slightly faster clock, a warm feeling of forgiveness came over me. I took a quick sip of water, and smiled at the thoughtfulness it demonstrated for her to be so on point.

"Message review: 'Sidney, this is Collette. I just found out that'"—she paused as I swallowed my second sip—*"'that Damon got married.'"*

I dropped the glass.

"What?!"

Luckily, my foot was covered in faux fur. I only felt the light pressure of the splash.

I hit the number four button, unsure of what I'd heard.

"Sidney, this is Collette. I just found out that . . . that Damon got married."

Her words hit me like a dump truck.

Jolted, I began to tremble inside like I'd been over-caffeinated on an empty stomach. Like I was about to be sick at any moment.

With unsteady hands, I dialed her back.

She answered on the first ring.

"Hel—"

"Who told you that?" I pounced on her.

"Oh, hey," she said, then cleared her throat. "Um, Carlos. I just got off the phone with him, and he said that Damon got married to some dancer—well, stripper. A stripper named Candy. He said—"

"Wait! Wait! Wait!" This was information overload. I couldn't keep up. A million questions rushed to mind. I didn't know where to begin.

I shook my head in confusion. "Carlos said that Damon got married? *Damon?*" I wanted to clarify.

"Yes. Damon," she insisted.

"Damon?" I said to myself. I processed the information shared with me, and, within the space of six seconds, the betrayal set in.

"That fucking bastard!" I screamed.

Collette didn't say anything. She just listened to the sound of my heart breaking over the phone.

"But . . . he and I were still seeing each other a month ago," I said, wishing I was really as confused as that statement made me sound. But my competent mind showed no mercy. I was crystal clear. "That means . . ."

She knew what it meant. It was the reason she'd called in the first place. It meant that this other woman had been there all along. It meant that I was just a joke. It meant that he had played me.

I placed my hand over my forehead, perspiring suddenly under my arms.

"How . . . How could—"

I couldn't speak. I could barely breathe. *How could he do this to me?* was what I wanted to say. Tried to say. But I was speechless to this news, and was sinking deeper and deeper into the depths of disbelief.

I felt heat rush to the front of my head.

I could handle our not being together, but I couldn't handle that I had been duped. Deceived.

How did this happen? I asked myself, overcome with a huge need to understand just how this was able to take place right under my nose. But instead of answers, what came instead was an unbelievable amount of high intensity heartache.

And a second dose of regret.

I should've asked if he was seeing someone when I met him. How could I have been so stupid? I assumed

Damon and I were exclusive. That he was single like me. But I shouldn't have assumed anything.

I shouldn't have been so dumb! I scolded myself.

But then I redirected my anger back toward Damon, realizing he was the only one to blame.

He lied. He used me!

Damon had taken advantage of me in the worst way by not giving me all the facts. He'd lied from the very beginning. From the gate, he knew that he had zero intentions on being with me permanently. He hadn't any intention on being with me *at all*. He'd already had a long-term partner in mind. On hand. He knew I was a virgin. He knew I was looking at him with stars in my eyes. With hope in my heart. He should have left me alone. Looked elsewhere. But instead I was merely opportunity for him to explore one last time as a bachelor before the big day. I was just another piece of ass.

Oh, my God!! I steamed.

He had no right to use me like that. He had no right to do me that way after the generosity and hospitality I'd shown him and his friends on numerous, frequently unannounced occasions. Carlos. Jay. Cedrick. They'd all swept through my place like a swarm of locust, hollowing my fridge, and using my apartment as a hangout spot when their funds, and blood sugar, were low. Playing cards. Taking over my television. Breaking my toilet and not fessing up. They trampled all over me. Damon would thank me with a kiss for "being so cool". What he was really thanking me for was being such a damn fool. He never cared about me. I knew that for certain now.

It was humiliating. And for the first time in my life I hated someone.

I rubbed my forehead again, enraged, and felt the same heat. Only this time it was sticky. Tacky.

Disoriented, I looked down, and that's when I realized I hadn't dropped the glass after all, but had crushed it in my bare hand. I was bleeding.

Still holding the phone to my ear, I wiped my bloody palm on my pajama shorts, then looked at it. Already another crimson pool was forming right within the very crease of my love line.

"I thought you were calling to wish me Happy Birthday . . ." A tear rolled down my face as I looked at the blurred numbers, 12:00, on the microwave's clock, that now made it official.

Collette's voice softened with finally a hint of shame.

"*Oh . . . that's right . . .*" she whispered, remembering.

Apparently, she'd forgotten all about it in her rush to relay the news.

"Um . . ." she paused awkwardly, ". . . *Happy Birthday.*"

CHAPTER 3

That night **I never did get back to sleep.** The next morning was my birthday, and I looked a hot mess. I resented Collette for being insensitive enough to dish that dirt on what was supposed to be my special day. Though she *tried* to sound somewhat solemn, she couldn't disguise her perverse affinity for misery and pain. I detected enthusiasm in her voice as she gave me the details. Like she wanted to laugh. As far as I was concerned, we weren't friends anymore.

People often said that Collette was jealous of me. That I shouldn't associate with her. But I'd just brush it off. That was a mistake.

Collette was about forty pounds overweight and had horrible teenage acne that left dark scars resembling cigarette burns all over her face and upper body. She'd bookmark *Shape* with a Butterfinger, and never missed a second serving of anything fried. She was hopeless. And heartless. I should've never trusted her. She couldn't wait to see me suffer.

Standing at the sink brushing my teeth with one hand, and looking down at the four stitches I'd received in the other just a few hours earlier in the ER, I was suddenly overcome with nausea and lightheadedness. I knew I wasn't pregnant. Damon and I used condoms. And I had my period since the last time we were together, and was due again any day now. But that didn't stop 98-degree, 12-hour-old food from rushing up my esophagus like hot lava spewing from a volcano, and splattering all over the sink and mirror. I was, literally, sick to my stomach with raw humiliation and absolute disgust. Everything inside of me just wanted out.

Stomach still erupting, I dropped to my knees—never making it to the toilet—and cried as I choked on more than my pride.

When I didn't show up for breakfast Tasha showed up at my door.

"Go away!" I yelled at the knocking knuckles, balled up in a blanket on the couch. I didn't feel like being bothered. Even Mom got sent to voice mail.

"Girl, you better open this door!" Tasha demanded from the outside in her annoyingly-perky pitch.

That was my girl, but the way I was feeling, I could've really let her have it.

I surrendered, answering the door instead.

"Hap—" Tasha, holding balloons and flowers, paused, then frowned. *"Have Mercy!* What in the world is going on with your hair?!"* She eyed my untamed and tangled, sandy-brown mane with her mouth wide open.

I wasn't in the mood for jokes. Especially insults.

"Go to hell!" I snapped.

"Save me a *seat!"* she snapped back.

I folded my arms as the cool morning air that rushed in from behind her sought refuge in the warmer-than-room-temperature apartment.

Tasha looked at me, her face hurt and surprised. I couldn't bear to look at her with my bloodshot eyes. I brushed my tumbleweed hair back with my hand, and showed my eyes to the floor instead.

Tasha brushed past me in her stacked heel boots and entered my living room, immediately noticing the blanket and pillows on the couch. She looked back at me with knitted brows.

"What's your problem?"

I shrugged.

With skeptical eyes surveying me, she pulled off her lightweight jacket, unveiling the coffee bean-colored cashmere sweater I'd bought her for *her* birthday. She looked so good in brown. It was my favorite sweater on her.

"And why did you stand me up today?" Tasha darted her eyes at me.

Her shrill voice was hard to take seriously, even in my somber state. When she got excited you'd swear she breathed helium.

Not wanting to fire my frustrations on an innocent party—especially my best friend—I apologized.

"I'm sorry, Tasha." I shook my head and tried to explain. "It's just—" Before I could tell her what was eating me, I found myself collapsing vulnerably into her arms, shaking with grief.

"*Sidney!*" Tasha let go of the balloons and held me up by my waist. "What's the matter?" Not much bigger than me, she managed to support my hopeless mass as I smashed the pretty flowers against her chest, causing pink petals and baby's breath to litter the sky-blue carpet like confetti.

She probably thought I'd stood her up due to a cold, or cramps. But there I was crying like someone had just died.

When I didn't answer right away that's exactly what she thought.

"Oh My God, Sidney. What happened? Tell me. Did —did someone pass?" She stroked my hair, hoping it wasn't so. *"Sidney, pleeeease.* Tell me!" she begged as my cries grew more intense, my head buried deep in her armpit.

"Sidney!"

"Damon got married . . ." I moaned.

"Damon?" Confusion compelled her to verify.

I shook my head, unable to speak as I dampened her sweater with my tears.

"But you guys just—"

"I know, Tasha. *I know . . .*" I cried, not wanting to hear the painful truth of it all, yet knowing just the same. I *knew* we'd just stopped seeing each other. I *knew* it was too soon for something like this to be happening. I *knew* he'd deceived me.

Tasha was quiet. She was as still as my heart was when I'd heard the news. She didn't say anything, just as Collette hadn't. But *her* silence left me with a feeling of loneliness, as if this was my burden to face alone. Or like it was silly of me to concern myself with a man from my past—no matter how immediate—and that my tears were foolish.

As I nestled my pounding head up to Tasha's warm neck, and muffled my cries that seemed isolated, my pressure-filled head went so limp that I could feel her delicate, perfume-scented pulse. Her main vein pulsated against my forehead until it became somewhat soothing. The predictable rhythm massaged my frontal lobe with a nurturing tempo that could've put me right to sleep like an infant in her mother's arms after a hard cry.

Thump . . . thump . . . Thump . . . thump. The rhythm went, as blood pumped through the life-carrying vessel. No voice. Just the beat.

Thump . . . thump . . . Thump . . . thump.

My head came to expect it. Crave it. I was drifting off to a standing slumber. My tears ceasing. My breath deepening.

Thump . . . thump . . . Thump . . . thump.

Suddenly, the rhythm increased. Heat was born. Its pace, not so regular, thumped as hard as a lambskin drum under a heavy-handed palm.

Thump . . . thump . . . Thump . . . thump!

Thu . . . Thump . . . THU . . . THUMP!—"That fucking bastard!!!" Tasha shattered her silence.

That was my girl.

Tasha felt my pain like she was in my skin. Friends for nine years, we'd met at a fundraiser our mothers co-hosted. Mom was always using her charm for charity. That time it landed me a best friend. Taking me under her wing as the new teen on the block who lived just down the street, it was because of Tasha that I'd settled in so nicely. Both shamelessly conceited, Tasha and I really understood each other, and had always been there for one another throughout the years. Tight like sisters, we were each other's virtual image. We had the same clothes. The same shoes. Same make up. We even had matching cars now. Where you saw one of us, you were almost guaranteed to see the other.

Back in high school Tasha was a triple threat: beauty, brains, and a big mouth. She not only got respect for being class valedictorian, student body president, and voted most popular *and* best dressed two years in a row, but for having the quickest, loudest, most unchallengeable mouths in the entire school, making her captain of the debate team as well. Her quick wit and lovable humor crowned her untouchable. And everybody wanted to be her friend.

Now, as an adult, Tasha was just as phenomenal. A Columbia biotechnology graduate, she'd finished her M.S. in four years, taking full advantage of summer classes, and passing each course on the first try. I, on the other hand, was finishing up my fifth year in pursuit of my bachelor's degree, avoiding any summer classes whatsoever, and changing my major three times before deciding on mass communications.

Moving into her new career, Tasha was moving out of New York. An opportunity presented itself in Atlanta, and in a couple of weeks she would be working for the CDC. I was really going to miss her. But for now, I had other things on my mind.

"Sidney, are you sure? How did you hear about this?" Tasha gripped me by the shoulders trying to get answers as I still struggled to pull myself together. "Who told you?" she asked, attempting to connect with my eyes that were watery and wandering about the room.

I wiped my eyes, her questions finally registering in my head. "Collette," I answered with two sniffs of my runny nose. "Collette told me."

"*Cholesterol?*" Tasha tilted her head, frowning.

I shook my head *yes*.

Tasha's face hardened, just as she believed Collette's arteries one day would. "Figures." She let me go.

When it came to scandal, Tasha knew Collette was the *Oracle*. The ever-notorious bearer of bad news. *Extra! Extra! Grieve all about it!* Tasha was disappointed by my naiveté when it came to Collette. I could see it in her chin. It always wrinkled like a raisin when she was. She'd tried to tell me *Cholesterol* was bad for my health. I should've listened.

"So, what happened?" Tasha asked, already shaking her head before hearing the story.

"Nothing," I replied as I walked back toward the couch. "Except for the fact that my so-called friend found it necessary to wake me up at midnight last night to tell me all about my ex's new marital status." I plopped down on the firm cushions that bounced me twice before settling me.

Tasha followed me.

"I never liked her, Sidney," she grimaced as I crawled back underneath the blanket. "She was never your friend. Even when you let her stay here with you that time after her eviction, there was something sneaky about how she crept around here. Looking shady." Tasha shook her head, remembering. "And why the hell would she want to upset you like this on your birthday?"

"I know, right!? She's a bitch!" I snarled. "She better not call me today either."

Tasha sat down on the edge of the couch beside me. She looked around the warm, pastel-colored apartment and processed this new information as the Mylar balloons that floated themselves into a corner spun around in the line of heat shooting from the dining room vents. She was zoning out in disbelief. And I could tell she was livid.

"Well, who did he marry? Did the Big Bad Birthday Basher tell you *that?*"

"I don't know." A new lump formed in my throat. "Some . . . stripper."

Tasha scrunched up her nose like something stunk. "Stripper?"

I felt the heaviest surge of pain coming, and pulled the blanket up under my chin.

"Stripper?" she repeated in disbelief, maintaining her frown.

I looked up at her just as a verifying tear trickled down my face.

"Ooooooooh . . . " Tasha shook her head. "He needs his *ass* kicked!" she said, growing more and more furious as she witnessed the emotional deterioration of me. She managed to internalize whatever I was feeling, almost in a supernatural, twin-like manner. It was amazing. Or maybe it was just friendship.

"I just can't believe he played me like that, Tasha. I feel so . . . stupid," I cried, blowing my nose into the overly-used tissue that was crumbling in my hands like feta cheese.

"Sidney, you did nothing wrong." Tasha handed me a fresh tissue. I closed my eyes and blew hard.

She said, "Damon's the one who should be feeling like an asshole, that no-good nematode!"

I opened one eye and looked at her out of the corner of it.

She continued. "I mean, what kind of man does something like that? Uh-uh. No," she shook her head, "don't own this. Don't you dare blame yourself for the low-down crap *he* pulled!" she hissed, nostrils flaring. She folded her arms. "*Humph*. He fooled me, too."

Tasha might have felt that way, but I knew I was the only fool in the room. She didn't know *half* of Damon's dirty deeds. I, on the other hand, should've known something was up when he turned my first car into a cannabis-smelling coupe, then lied about it, even as the storytelling-stench of hemp lingered on his very denial. I hated that smell on him. I don't know why I put up with his antics.

Tasha, hands to her face, elbows on her knees, leaned forward and looked out into space. She was hurting for me. She knew how much it had meant to me despite my efforts to pretend as if I didn't care that Damon and I were through. She knew that I'd struggled with the pain of the relationship being so brief. And she also knew that I was just beginning to get over him. I'd have to start the road to recovery all over again. This put me back at the starting line. Square one.

My best friend looked me in my eyes that resembled a child's. Pitifully, my lips quivered in emotional agony as my heart yearned for comfort.

She reached for another tissue. "I thought you were going to tell me you were pregnant or something," she said as she caught the tear that skated down my cheek.

I wiped my nose. "Thank God I'm not."

"Yeah, well . . . that was still some irresponsible shit for him to do." She flung the used tissue onto the table.

"Well, it's not like we didn't use condoms, Tasha."

"Condoms don't always work! There are plenty of failed-condom conceptions in this world. No contraceptive is one hundred percent," she lectured like a health teacher. "Not to mention diseases."

Tasha got up and started pacing the floor. My eyes followed her size-three frame as it made quiet footprints that were a lighter shade of blue back and forth across the puddle of botanical debris. Watching her made me dizzy.

"Well . . . I'm just grateful it didn't get that complicated," I said, trying desperately to see the silver lining in this situation even as I ached. I looked up at Tasha, who was supposed to agree, but she was too deep in thought to hear me. Her virtually-transparent complexion turned "rage red", as if all the blood in her body rushed right to her face, and her usual big brown eyes shrank to a slit-like squint as she ran a finger across her bottom lip. I knew that look. She was up to something.

"What if you *were* pregnant?" She turned to me and asked, confirming my suspicions. "I mean, *what if?* What would he do, then? Look stupid?"

I didn't say anything.

She took a deep breath and ran her hand through her short, wavy hair, still displaying contemplation on her sharp-featured face.

I took a deep breath myself, picking at the velvety tassels roped around the ivory throw pillow, silent enough to hear the mechanical heartbeat of the kitchen wall clock.

Tasha folded her arms in the silence and tapped her foot against the carpet that returned no sound. She looked over at me again, impatiently, as if to see what I was thinking. I offered nothing worth critique. I didn't know what to say. Part of me knew from where her anger originated.

Tasha grew up wanting for nothing except the desire to know who her biological father was. Her mother and stepfather immersed her in a loving and supportive environment, but nothing could pacify her undying urge to know the man who could father her, and then walk away without even knowing whether she was a boy or a girl.

Tasha's mother didn't discuss—or even reveal any information about—the mystery man. His identity, right down to his race, was a secret to my broken-hearted best friend. But by looking at Tasha's ultra-fair skin and satiny hair texture, which were both in stark contrast to that of her mother's, people naturally assumed she was biracial.

Tasha cleared her throat, bringing life back to the room that froze in the upset atmosphere.

"Well . . ." she threw her head back, seemingly surrendered, "that dirty ass Damon sure is lucky circumstances turned out in his favor."

"Mmm hmm . . ." I hummed, still fidgeting with the tassel.

"*Real* lucky," she added.

"Yep . . ."

"Fate was kind," she noted, shaking her head.

"I guess so . . ."

She turned to face me. "But *we* don't have to be," she foreshadowed with a deceptively-raised brow.

My fingers stopped fidgeting.

"What are you talking about, Tasha?" I asked just for the sake of asking. But I knew where she was going with this.

"You being pregnant would ruin everything for him and his new bride."

"Yeah, but I'm not. Remember?"

"*He* doesn't know that."

"Forget it, Tasha." I closed my eyes and rubbed my temples. "I just want to forget about him."

"That's just it, Sidney." She plopped down next to me, the sudden bounce re-opening my eyes. "How *can* you forget about him knowing he's walking around feeling like he got over on you? He's an asshole, Sidney. Pure scum."

"I know he is, but . . ." I shook my head.

"So what the hell are you supposed to do, Sidney? Let them live in holy phony matrimony while you sit here drying out your eyeballs?"

Tasha removed my hand from my face. I looked at her, red-eyed. Her face was just as intense as her words.

"*He* needs to suffer, Sidney. Not you. We can't make him bleed, but we can damn sure make him sweat."

Tasha stood up again and walked back toward the dining room.

She spun around and said, "Yeah, that's right! Let him lose some sleep. Let him lose some weight. Hell, let him lose some *hair!*" she flailed her arms with body language that mirrored her emotions as I clutched my pillow and looked on like an afraid adolescent.

"Sidney, don't let him get off scot-free. Share the stress, why don't you? Show that bastard that he messed with the wrong woman!"

She did have a point. I was the one sitting around looking bad, feeling sad, with no appetite, while he was out playing house with some chick he'd obviously cheated on. He did deserve some of the stress. I owed it to him. And this would be a way to get back some of my power.

My virginity was my power. My control. I was in total control of that. It was one of the main things about me that made me feel special. But Damon took that away. He left me powerless—disarmed—with nothing but the agonizing memory of how he'd swindled me into giving him my power, and then making me feel like an idiot for having done so. Yeah, Tasha was right. I *couldn't* forget about him.

Not until we were even.

CHAPTER 4

Tasha and I spent the afternoon devising a plan. I would tell Damon that I was pregnant, throwing major salt in his game. Then I'd let him sit on that for a while, while I sit back and watch the slug *squirm*!

"You know where you're going, right?"

"Sure. Meka lives just up the block," I told Tasha as I made a left at the intersection.

A few minutes later we pulled up and parked alongside the low curb.

As we got out of the car, I grabbed my purse and put it on my shoulder while Tasha did the same. After we shut our doors, I set the alarm and we began trucking it across the dirt landscaping to Meka's unit.

Tasha looked around nervously.

"Relax," I smiled at her as I knocked on the door.

It was obvious that Tasha was more than uneasy about being in this particular neighborhood. She smiled forcefully, tucking her nervous hands in her back pockets, while I grinned at her paranoia.

Meka finally answered the door, belly protruding.

"Hey, girl. Long time no see," she greeted me.

I knew Meka from the hair salon I used to go to. She worked there for a hot minute, before the salon owner finally realized that the license she kept saying was *"On the way"* never existed. It was a shame because she did the best doobie wrap.

Meka had a rich older half-brother with whom Tasha and I went to high school. At least, Tasha and I went. He'd just show up for homeroom every once in a while, then leave right after attendance. He and Meka were just two of six children conceived by a total of four men, and one very fertile woman. Meka, seeming destined to follow in her mother's footsteps, was barely twenty, and already had two kids by two different guys, and a third on the way whose paternity was to be determined.

"What's up, Meka?" I hugged her as we stepped inside. "This is my girl, Tasha."

Tasha shook her hand and tried not to appear as uncomfortable as I knew she was.

"So, you're Jimmy's sister, huh? Jimmy used to make me laugh so hard, with his ol' wild self," Tasha giggled, trying to warm up. "What's he doing now?"

"Twelve in federal," Meka replied dryly, causing Tasha's grin to instantly disappear.

"Oh . . . I'm sorry," Tasha whispered. Noticeably embarrassed, she looked toward the door.

But Meka was cool enough to brush it off.

"No, it's cool," Meka waved her hand, then turned and began walking that pregnant walk. "So, what's up with this dude ya'll talkin' about?" She plopped herself down into the big, beige recliner, cutting straight to the chase.

I followed her lead and asked, "How many months are you?"—I shook my head—"Actually, that doesn't even matter. Listen . . ." I dug into my bag, pulling out a rectangular-shaped box, "can you take a test for me?"

"As long as I don't have to study for it." Meka laughed.

I laughed with her. "Girl, you're silly. But for real, I need to get this guy for what he did to me."

"You ain't gotta sell it to me, girl. You know I'm down." She leaned back in her chair, examining the ends of her blonde-tipped braids. "It's time we taught these fools a lesson, anyway. Cheatin' asses," she added with a contemptuous lip curl. "On the real, ya'll should get like my girl, Vida. Vida crrrr-azy!" She shook her head, laughing. "'She found out her man was cheatin' . . . *Humph!* She *got* his ass!"

I listened as she explained.

"See, she knew he had a habit of rubbing his eyes first thing in the morning when he woke up. So in the middle of the night she put cayenne pepper on his fingers."

My mouth flung open, imagining what was to come.

"Yep. The hottest!" Meka grinned, getting to the good part. "Check it. Morning came and my girl didn't *need* no alarm clock!"

Meka laughed hard for a full twenty seconds, and then said, "His ass is half blind to this day. *Humph!* He's lucky it wasn't wasabi."

I stared at Meka in shock.

Tasha sat back bug-eyed.

Then, almost on cue, we both laughed a little so that Meka wasn't alone in her sinister chuckles.

"Wow . . ." I cleared my throat, eventually all fake-chuckled out. "Pepper, huh?" I looked at Tasha, who looked convinced that Meka was completely insane.

"Actually, we were thinking of something a little . . . milder."

"Yeah, milder," Tasha shook her head fast in agreement.

"You see, we just want a *little* revenge," I used space between my thumb and index finger to model. "Besides, I'd have to be in an intimate setting with him again in order to pull that one off, and that is *definitely* not going to happen."

"True that. True that. I feel you," Meka nodded, indifferent to whichever method of revenge I chose.

I handed her the pregnancy test, happy that I didn't offend her by rejecting her suggestion.

Meka rubbed her belly and leaned back in her recliner. Studying the pink and white box, she said, "So, how much are ya'll gonna ask for?"

"What do you mean?" I sat back, wondering if we were on the same page.

"The abortion," she said. "That's why ya'll doin' this, right? To get some money out his ass."

Her words smacked me like a giant hand that said '*Wake up, Stupid!*'

It had never occurred to me to consider what I was going to do once I'd actually made Damon believe that I was carrying his child. I mean, I *wasn't* pregnant. How far could this lie possibly go?

I shook my head, not believing we hadn't thought this through.

But Tasha, unfazed by the oversight, quickly came aboard.

"Hell, yeah! Let's get his ass *good*, Sidney." She turned to Meka. "How much do they cost?"

"Usually, depending on where you go, they can run anywhere from three to four hundred."

"Perfect!" Tasha snapped her fingers. "We're going for four hundred."

"Now wait a minute," I interrupted their craziness. "You guys are talking extortion. I'm not trying to get caught up in that. I mean, I just want to make him suffer for a while. That's all."

"And what better way than to hit those pockets?" Tasha reasoned.

Just then, En Vogue's old school rendition of *Giving Him Something He Can Feel* began playing in my mind. I shook my head.

I needed to bring us both back to reality. I was in no way anxious to go join Jimmy in the slammer. "Tasha! How cute would we look in orange onesies? You know that's not our color."

Tasha's look said she wished I'd take this seriously.

"Okay," I said. "All jokes aside, I don't know if I'm down for this."

This wasn't part of the plan. In fact, there *was* no real plan. We'd just thrown this thing together without giving the extended aftermath much thought. I wasn't prepared to make a decision like this on the spot.

Meka looked at Tasha, wondering what the deal was. Wondering why there was even a question. Tasha looked at me the same way. Then two eyes became four. With both of them looking at me it was apparent that I was the only one in the room with even a shred of apprehension.

"I just don't know you guys. This . . . this is—"

"Sidney, *Vic & Tim* are not your role models. Okay? You've gotta fight back," Tasha urged.

"I want to fight back, but—"

"But nothing! It's on."

The next day I took some deep breaths and counted to five. Then I picked up the phone and dialed *67 followed by Damon's cell phone number, unsure of whether it was still the same or not. I hadn't spoken to him since we'd went our separate ways, and now that he was married, I was sure he would've had his number changed, for obvious reasons.

The greater part of me was hoping that he *had* changed his number. I was still apprehensive about going through with this, and a disconnected number would be just the out I needed. But armed with the pregnancy test Meka took for me last night, I was trying to pump myself up just in case.

When the phone rang three long times, I was happy, willing to bet money that I'd get the out of service message at any moment.

I knew he wouldn't have kept the same number. He's not that stupid, I celebrated silently, ready to hang up. But just as I was about to cash in my chips, Damon answered.

"Hello?"

I swallowed fast, then immediately fell into character.

"Congratulations!"

Damon, trying to place the voice, didn't respond right away.

"Hello?" I said, afraid he'd hung up

"Who's this?"

"Awwww. Now that hurts. C'mon, it hasn't been *that* long."

"Sidney?"

"Why *yessss* . . . And congratulations!"

Damon muttered a series of dumbfounded *Ohs*, *Ums*, and even a weak *Thanks*. Then, wondering which one of his big-mouthed friends had spilled the beans about his recent exchange of nuptials, he asked, "Who told *you?* And why are you calling with your number blocked?"

It was hard, but I had to pretend as if I didn't know what the hell he was talking about. Knowledge of his marriage would discredit my claim. I had to play dumb.

"Wait—*What?*" My voice echoed the confusion contained in his. "Who told *me* about it? No, Damon, you misunderstand. Congratulations . . . It's a boy!" I predicted, then added, "*Or* a girl."

Damon, catching my drift, flipped out.

"What the hell are you talking about, Sidney?"

"I'm talking about our baby. We're pregnant!" I announced with artificial enthusiasm.

"*We?*" he scoffed. "I wrapped my man *every time!*"

"Well, you didn't wrap him good enough, dummy!"

"Hold up, don't be calling me with no—"

"To hell with you, Damon! I don't get off on this. I'm just calling you as a courtesy before I hit you with those papers."

Damon was speechless. That last statement fired into his gut like a cannon. And I was jerking the string. His silence, no doubt, was his neat little world busting apart at the seams.

"And how do I know you even *used* a condom?" I saw his *skepticism* and raised him *culpability*. "For all I know, you could've slipped it off, with your sneaky ass . . . Did you?!" I came at him quick.

"No, I didn't!"

"Well, *I* don't know that. You probably put me at risk for all kinds of—"

"Look, I didn't take it off, alright."

"*You* explain it, then!"

Damon got quiet again.

Aaahhh . . . the art of recrimination, I smiled to myself.

I reveled for a moment, but Damon's prolonged silence grew unsettling. I didn't know if I'd pissed him off so bad that he'd hung up on me, or if he was still trying to make sense of it all.

I switched the phone to my other ear. "Hello?"

"I'm here," Damon said with an attitude.

I could already tell that he was drained, and probably losing some of that hair Tasha talked about.

"Sidney, how . . ." he struggled to speak, "how are you gonna call after a month and hit me with something like this?"

"Was I supposed to know immediately afterwards? What am I, an alien? This isn't the movies, Damon. I just found out this morning."

"Well, we're gonna have to discuss this," Damon said with authority.

Who did he think he was? He was in no position to be authoritative. He wasn't in control of this. I was operating this ride.

"Discuss *what?*" I said. "There's nothing else to really discuss right now. We're going to have a baby, and that's that. There's no need for further discussion at this point. Just get your mind right—and your money—and I'll see you around the end of spring."

Sounding as if I was ready to hang up, Damon protested before I could.

"Sidney, wait!"

"What?" I asked, seemingly exasperated.

"I'm not ready for a baby."

"Neither am I. But we better sure as hell *get* ready, because in about seven months, we're going to be parents, ready or not."

I know those words had to knock the wind out of him, because they nearly choked *me.* Just the thought of forever combining my genetic material with Damon's to produce future lineages for countless generations to come made me want to run out in front of the nearest, fastest, heaviest semi!

There was about ten dead seconds of silence where I tortured myself with visions of giving birth to *Damon: The Sequel.* Damon must've been having *daymares* of his own, because I didn't hear a peep out of him. But his silence made me nervous. My legs were beginning to shake. I was beginning to unravel. Silence meant thought. Thought meant analyzing. Analyzing could lead to more skepticism. And more skepticism could ruin this whole thing. I was just one more objection away from cracking.

Panic was fast approaching. Fear was setting in.

Finally, Damon spoke, giving me my legs back.

"Sidney," his voice softened, "can I uh . . . call you back a little later?"

"For what, Damon?"

"Come on. Just let me hit you back."

"Alright," I agreed. "But I can't imagine why."

"Just to talk. I'll call you around 7:00."

Click. I hung up the phone.

I couldn't believe it. Damon was so pathetically-predictable. Just as Tasha said, he was not trying to let me keep this imaginary baby. He would insist on an abortion for sure.

This is so easy it's sad, I thought to myself as I lay back on the couch.

CHAPTER 5

Damon called at nine that evening. Two hours later than he said he would. When my home phone rang PRIVATE, I became nervous all over again. But this time Tasha was there to keep me on track.

"Hello?" I answered impatiently, eyeballing the clock, and wondering why he was now blocking *his* number as if I didn't know it.

"Yeah . . ." Damon said in a dry voice.

That's it? That's what he wanted to call back to say? *'Yeah?'*

"So what did you want to talk about, Damon?" I asked with Tasha's ear pressed against mine as we shared the receiver and a moment of uneasy silence where we waited for Damon's response. I wondered what could've possibly been going on in that pea brain of his. Was he remorseful? Sympathetic? Was the possibility of fatherhood warming his heart?

"Look, Sidney, I'm not trying to raise no baby right now."

"I didn't expect that!" I snapped. "But I do expect your prompt child support payments every month."

Relinquishing her share of the receiver, Tasha dashed off to the other room to muffle her laugh that had spilled out through her nose and onto my cheek. My comeback caught her off guard. And watching her crack up almost made *me* lose it.

I coughed and then sniffed twice to cover in case Damon thought he'd heard suspicious sounds in the background. But shaken by the jolt of my retort, Damon had heard nothing but my sharp words.

His voice got very shaky and serious.

"So. . . how far along are you?" he inquired.

"Probably about two months."

"Probably? You don't know for sure? How did you find out?"

"I took an early pregnancy test," I told him, wondering what difference it made. He was getting too deep into the details. It wasn't so much the *'how far?'* as it was the *'what now?!'* he should've been concerned with. That detail was peripheral to the issue at hand. But then, he wasn't exactly the brightest bulb in the chandelier.

He continued with the questions.

"You mean one of those *home* pregnancy tests?"

I rolled my eyes over the phone. "Yes, Damon. One of those home preg—"

"We want a *real* test," a voice that I didn't recognize suddenly demanded.

Surprised by the apparent party line, I frowned and said, "Who is that?"

Tasha came back into the room with curious eyes and a ready-to-throw-down look on her face.

"This is his *wife!*" the voice emphasized with a haughtiness that made me want to snap. But I knew I had to remain calm if I wanted to stay in character. I had no choice but to play it off.

"W-wife?" I stuttered as if half-believing. I think I was even trying to fool *myself.* But the sound of her voice was painful confirmation of its truth. Its reality.

Part of me was still hoping it was all just an ugly rumor. A bad dream. A long, horrific nightmare. But her voice, her voice made it as realistic as it could get. Real and wrong! I was devastated that he was insensitive enough to put her on the phone. My eyes stung with anger.

"Wife?" I repeated, my breath genuinely weak this time.

"Yeah, his wife," she said. "And we're not entertaining any of this until we see a real pregnancy test. Not some pee on a sti—"

"You don't need to worry about my test. From what I understand, you're the one who needs to be tested, you pole-climbing piece of—"

"Look, Sissy—"

"Sidney!"

"WHATEVER . . . you *thought* ya'll had, it no longer exists."

"What we're *having* is a private conversation." I started getting heated. "What we're *having* is a really hard time communicating with you all up on the line. What we're having—"

Tasha hit the speaker phone button and shouted, "What they're *having* is a baby, so you can just shut the hell up!"

They went back and forth arguing. I couldn't understand most of what they were saying. They sounded like feral felines fighting it out.

After a few low blows were exchanged, Damon finally broke it up.

"Hang up the phone, Candiyah," he instructed his new wife. "I got this."

Tasha frowned. *"Candida?* This chick is named after a yeast infection? NO FREAKING WAYYYYYY!!!" she started laughing. "That's just too fucking appropriate."

I smacked the speaker phone button *Off* and pushed her silly behind out of the way.

"Look, Damon, don't be putting your little *idiot* on the phone with me. She doesn't have anything to do with this."

"She's my wife. So this affects her, too."

"Yeah?"

"Yeah!"

"Well, then tell her to wash out her G-string, because I need ya'll money to be on time and not a dollar short!"

"Hey! Hey!" Damon came to her defense. "Leave her out of this!"

"My point exactly!"

Touché. That'll teach him to put her in my business again. What the heck was he thinking? We didn't have three-way sex. So why were we having a three-way conversation? Tasha didn't count. She was on my side. And together we were one.

Damon sighed in aggravation. I could already hear that our plan was a life-crumbling success.

"Well . . ." he paused as if hesitant to say what he said next. "I think you should have an abortion."

"What?!" I acted as if I was shocked and appalled. "An abortion?"

That was Tasha's cue.

"Sidney, you've got no choice," she pled from the background. "I mean, seriously, what are you going to do with a baby?"

"Raise it!" I shouted.

"Listen to her, Sidney," Damon appealed desperately over the line, suddenly appreciative of Tasha's two cents so long as she was singing his tune. "Listen to your girl."

Do ya mind? I thought to myself. *Stay out of this while my friend and I negotiate the quality of your life for the next few weeks.*

"Look, I didn't say anything about an abortion," I told the both of them.

"But you have to, Sidney," Tasha insisted. "What if it's twins? You know they run in your family?"

She was *gooooood*. I don't know where that came from. Twins did not run in my family. But Damon didn't know me well enough to know that. If he had, he would've also known that there would be no way in hell that I would kill my unborn baby.

Tasha took the phone from me and sat down, ready to drive. I looked at her fearfully, afraid we'd overdo it. Afraid we'd say too much and blow it. Sensing my concern, she winked, not sweating a drop. That's when I knew she had it under control. She was a natural. It was almost scary. She had the ability to convince any*body* of any*thing*. And I had the ink on my back to prove it.

About a year ago, during one of our party-till-we-drop nights, Tasha managed to convince me of the idea of getting twin tattoos. Drunk, she'd created some funky design that looked like an armadillo riding a rainbow, nicknaming it *Sasha* (our names combined), and convinced me that it would look cute on our lower backs.

The tequila told us we'd be soul sisters. Tasha begged, and did a lot of arm-pulling, until I finally caved. She'd always wanted a tattoo, and being her BF, I couldn't just hold her hand while she realized her dream, but had to participate in the skin-engraving procedure that took twenty painful minutes to complete. As I sat there, bleeding like a fool, I realized for the first time just how persuasive she really was. But I didn't see her lining up next to me a few months later to get her belly clamped and skewered, that wuss!

As evident by her and Damon's conversation, Tasha hadn't lost her touch. Hell, she'd convinced *me* to go through with this crazy conspiracy. I was standing right next to her, watching her work her magic, when they started talking figures.

"Well, I've already checked out two places, *despite* what Sidney says," she glanced over at me and rolled her eyes ever so authentically. "The cheapest was $450," she lied.

Naturally, I couldn't hear his response, but based on what she said next, it was evident that Damon thought that was much too high.

"Well . . . I haven't heard of any place less than $350," Tasha reluctantly lowered her bid.

"What the hell?" I objected from the background. "You guys are bargain-hunting with my body?" I snatched the phone back from Tasha. "Hey, you need to be discussing this with me—not her," I told Damon.

"She seems to be more rational than you are right now."

"So you're psychoanalyzing me now? You took a couple psychology courses and you're ready to diagnose me, is that it, Damon? Huh? Huh, college dropout?" I reminded him. "*I'm* who you need to be discussing this with!" My voice shook the room.

Tasha looked at me as I continued to let him have it.

"And did the shrink in you ever stop to consider that perhaps her rationality could have a little something to do with the fact that"—I removed the phone from my ear and screamed into it—"*SHE'S NOT PREGNANT?!!!*"

When I replaced the receiver to my ear, I heard Damon let out a hard breath like my mouth was getting on his nerves.

"No, don't get mad," I told him. "Get used to it," I dangled the threat of a lifetime with me over his surely sweat-beaded head.

Tasha was fuchsia in the face. Her suppressed giggles were killing her. She was tugging on my sleeve, biting her lip to hold her silence.

"All I'm saying, Sidney—"

"All *I'm* saying, Damon, is that I'm not comparison-shopping for an abortion—*if* I decide to get one." I figured now was a good time to throw in that ounce of hope. I'd tenderized him enough.

"Alright, alright," Damon quickly ate the bait like the lowlife bottom feeder I found him to be. It seemed the hope that I would terminate the pregnancy quickly swallowed any doubts or concerns he may have originally owned about the pregnancy itself.

"But like my wife said, I'm going to need a doctor's note before I give you anything," he scratched the victory record that had begun playing in my head.

What was he doing? How *dare* he not trust me? He was the liar. Okay—technically we both were. But he'd started it!

I looked at Tasha, panicked and running out of improvisations. She waved me on with a *'keep your cool'* gesture, not knowing what he'd just insisted upon. I shook my head, trying to tell her. But there was no time to explain.

"Fine!" I said angrily. "But you're going to pay for it," I added, expecting the big *'Never mind'*. But Damon begged to differ.

"No, I'm not. And neither are you," he said. "There are plenty of free clinics you can go to."

I gasped. "Free clinic? I'm not sitting up in any free clinic. You've lost your damn mind." My stomach hurt at just the idea. Then I remembered that I was only faking.

But before I could say another word, Damon said, "Well then, I guess I'll just have to reimburse you. I don't have the money right now. Plain and simple."

Sorry ass! I thought to myself. Thank God I *wasn't* pregnant. His broke ass wouldn't be able to afford baby wipes.

Knowing I wouldn't be sitting anywhere except in class, I gave into Damon's demand.

"Alright, Damon, if that's the way you want it, I'll make an appointment and call you later in the week."

Click. I hung up.

Grinning at each other like the two conspirators we were, Tasha and I collapsed backwards onto the couch like two overturned turtles, kicking our legs up in laughter. We were the perfect tag team, delivering two Oscar-worthy performances.

"Oh my God!! That was craaaazy!" I laughed, kicking the cushions with my bare heels while Tasha rolled around at the other end.

"TDF!" she shrieked.

"Too Damn Funny!!!" I decoded her acronym on the spot.

I tried to sit up, but laughter weighed me down.

"I've gotta ask . . ." Tasha arched her back to look at me, her giggles also acting as gravity.

"What?" I finally propped myself up on my elbows, still spilling chuckles.

"At any point during that conversation did you, by chance, forget that you weren't really pregnant?"

Guilty of getting caught up in the moment, I confessed.

"Yeah. For a minute there, I guess I did."

Tasha looked at me seriously.

I looked back just as serious.

Then we both burst out into laughter again.

Tasha placed a hand over her chest, trying desperately to catch her breath.

"Wow. That's scary," she said.

"Tell me about it," I moaned, helpless to the painful laughter that felt like an abdominal workout. "I think he drove me temporarily insane."

Tasha wiped her eyes that were tearing up in hysteria. "One more question," she said.

"What's that?" I plucked a tissue from its dispenser and handed it to her.

"Is there such a thing as making an appointment at a free clinic?" She raised her brow.

I raised mine, too, as I pondered my blooper, then shrugged. "I don't know. But the only appointment I have is with some ibuprofen. These menstrual cramps are *killing* me." I rubbed my bloated, but baby-free belly with a look of agony.

We both burst out laughing again, roaring in sweet, bare-feet delight, while Damon "The Dirt Bag" Campbell was shaking in his boots.

And deserving every moment of it.

CHAPTER 6

The next morning I called Meka to see if she could help me out with the doctor's note. I figured she could go to a clinic and pose as me in order to get the documentation Damon's dumb ass demanded.

The phone rang once, then a recording came on saying that the number I was trying to reach had been disconnected or was no longer in service.

I slammed the phone down. "Unbelievable!" I shouted, the phone and its base falling to the floor.

There was no cell phone to try. Meka didn't have one. I didn't understand how a person could allow their connection to the outside world to be disconnected this way.

"The phone was just *On* yesterday," I said, returning the phone and its base back onto the counter.

Meka lived almost forty minutes from me. I damn sure didn't feel like driving way back out there. And I never thought I'd have to. Damon had a lot of nerve demanding that I get a doctor's note. Who did he think he was? I was pissed. And I resented the fact that he had the upper hand this round. I didn't have a choice. I *had* to get a doctor's note. I'd already started this big lie. I couldn't fold now.

As if the drive alone wasn't enough, to my extreme dismay, Meka wasn't home when I got there. I guess she had her own, legitimate, doctor's appointment to go to because she rarely left the house before nightfall.

Debating on whether or not to wait around, I slowly walked back to my car, shoulders slumped. My head began throbbing. This wasn't going according to plan at all. I couldn't believe the obstacles I'd already faced. Feeling frustrated, I reached for my driver's side door handle.

"You lookin' for Tameka?" A guy wearing a ladies tank top knotted up in the back and a navel ring approached me by way of an exaggerated twist.

I looked at him, wondering if he'd missed both the weather report *and* the penis between his legs.

"Who?" I frowned. "Oh!" It was that moment that I'd realized 'Meka' was short for Tameka. "Oh, yeah." I shook my head. "Where is she?"

"She went to Philly. Her auntie is sick." He placed a hairy-knuckled hand on his cheek, shaking his head sympathetically.

"When is she getting back?" I asked, worried for my own selfish reasons rather than out of concern for her aunt. The part of me that still had room to care felt pretty bad about it. But the other part, the part that was scared senseless of being made to look like a fool all over again after Damon and his friends discovered what a *'crazy ass liar'* I was, had to stay focused and could not be distracted by misfortune. It took precedence over any usual sympathies I would've otherwise had for the poor woman.

What's happening to me? I asked myself, consciously ashamed, but no less determined.

"I'm not sure when she's coming back," the young man told me. "She took luggage with her, though."

"Aw, man!" I shook my head.

He looked at me strange.

"Alright, well, thanks."

I opened my car door in a complete daze, wondering what the heck I was going to do now.

The man's eyes lingered on me a little longer than necessary before he finally turned away.

As he headed back across the street, I snapped out of my musing.

"Hey!" I called out to him.

He looked back.

"Tell Meka I'm very sorry about her aunt, and that I'll talk to her when she gets back."

He smiled before nodding *Okay*.

As I sat in my car and watched him strut back into his apartment, I realized the plan had completely unraveled. With my hands on the steering wheel, I contemplated confessing it all—coming clean and telling Damon the truth. I thought about just admitting that I'd made up the entire thing. That it all was just a big lie.

But after pondering that option for all of four seconds, I immediately dismissed it, realizing how ridiculous that would make me look. I couldn't give Damon that kind of satisfaction. I knew I had to keep going. There was no turning back now. I *had* to find a way to carry forward. But how?

"Are those your real eyes?"

I nodded *yes*, too zoned out to respond verbally.

"Oh, because my friend Quita has some contacts that looks just like those. They're real cute, too. I was gonna get some but the lady at the meat market said she had to wait for her son to get more boxes in."

What? Meat market?

You'd be surprised what $50 can buy you in the 'hood. After ten minutes of driving around, frantically brainstorming on ways to keep the plan alive, I managed to recruit two girls, one of whom was obviously pregnant (bony with a big belly), and the other, a top-heavy tagalong. After coercing them into helping me, using some on-the-spot lie about how my ex had stolen money from my mom, and, of course, explaining what was in it for them, they quickly hopped in my car and directed me to the nearest clinic.

Having made our deal, I was feeling at ease. But as I drove further and further toward our devious destination, increasingly aware that no one knew of my whereabouts—not even Tasha—I began to realize what a moron I was.

Desperation made me dumb. I didn't know these girls. They could've easily jumped, or robbed me. Paranoid, I wondered how I would explain to police that I'd picked up a couple of strange girls to do some dirt, and then was robbed in the process. I didn't even know their names.

As I continued to drive, I began thinking what if that wasn't a pregnant belly I was looking at after all, but, instead, a crafty disguise. A decoy. Evil masquerading as tenderness and vulnerability—just the image needed to pull off such a caper. Looking in the rearview mirror, I began sizing them up, just in case, convincing myself I could take the little one. The big one, I wasn't so sure. Those shoulders were pretty broad.

Fortunately, I didn't have to find out. Quicker than I'd imagined, we pulled up to the community health clinic. But from that point on, there was nothing else quick about the excursion.

The clinic was jam-packed. We had been waiting for nearly an hour before my butt started itching in the seat from sitting for so long. The sign-in sheet was the length of my arm. And if I hadn't scratched out #16's name and written in mine, we would've been sitting well into the evening. It didn't make any sense to have so many people crammed into one, stuffy little room. I was sure they were breaking some sort of fire code. And if I thought it would get me to the front of the line, I would've called the Fire Marshall myself.

As the pregnant girl and her friend talked casually amongst themselves for the better part of fifty minutes, I was trembling inside. Having tampered with the sign-in sheet, I was afraid somebody was about to call me out, then beat me down. I looked around the crowded room, trying to figure out just who—and how big—Qualanda Kerns (aka #16) was, and hoped she wasn't the six-footer by the water fountain.

"Sidney Shane!"

A sinus-clearing sensation came over me. The kind you get when you know you're doing well over the speed limit, and you catch a glimpse of those police lights in your rearview mirror, just before you realize he's after the other car.

Embarrassed, I peered around the room, hoping no one I knew was in the room. I couldn't believe I'd put my full name on that sheet. It was the dumbest thing I'd done all day, which, at this point, said an awful lot.

As the medical assistant stood there waiting, I waved a hand at the pregnant girl, reminding her that that was me. She looked at me like she forgot why the hell we were there, then, remembering, ejected herself from her seat in a nervous and disorderly fashion.

Once on her feet, the expectant mom grabbed her jacket and tied it around her waist to conceal her obvious pregnant condition. While she held the door open for my recruit, I couldn't help but notice the look of confusion on the assistant's face as she glanced down at her clipboard, then up again at the belly fast approaching.

I looked away.

A good twenty minutes had passed, and my stand-in was still back there. I feared the plan was a bust. She'd blown it. *Preggo* brought cause for scrutiny upon us, and now the police were on their way. All I could think about was that orange onesie.

With sweaty palms I eyed the clock, praying my recruit would walk through the patient's exit at any moment—mission accomplished. My imagination was getting the better of me. Fear consumed me. I mean, she was obviously pregnant. I wondered if *they* wondered why she needed a test to tell her that.

Well, she could need it for insurance purposes, or court—anything, I argued with myself, hoping they wouldn't probe for answers.

Five more torturing minutes had passed before I was finally put out of my misery. When the young mom-to-be finally came through the door, I sprang from my seat like a jack-in-the-box, goofy grin and all. Wearing a grin of her own, she handed me the fifty-dollar slip, her sidekick joining us. With still breath I read its handwritten text. It stated that I, SIDNEY SHANE, was approximately eighteen weeks pregnant. 18 WEEKS GESTATION, to be specific.

I immediately realized that wasn't possible for Damon and me. It hadn't even been eighteen weeks since our *first* time together. Just *nine* weeks ago I was still a virgin.

I tried to think back to what Tasha had explained about the due date calculation method, but couldn't remember for the life of me. Something about the first two weeks, or somebody named Naegele. The bottom line was I had no idea they were going to put the number of weeks on the slip. I figured it would just say *Positive* or *Negative*. *Yes* or *No*. *Pregnant* or *Not Pregnant*.

Alterations were a must. I knew if I could just remove the number *1* it would provide a more realistic approximation for our situation. But it was in ink.

Not giving up, I decided I'd just turn the 1 into an asterisk instead, daring Damon to challenge me. Either way, I wasn't too worried. If he wanted to question the authenticity of the slip, or speculate that

I'd been with someone else, I'd tell him *"fine"*. That we could just wait seven months *"and see"*. I doubted it was a risk he was willing to take. He just wanted this problem to go away. And the important thing was that I got the doctor's note stating that I was, indeed, pregnant.

After dropping off the two girls, paying them an extra twenty for their troubles since I was suddenly in such a good mood, I headed home feeling like I'd just hit the lottery. Nothing could stop me now. With triumph in my veins I continued down the lackluster street lined with buildings that screamed for paint, and a neighborhood that cried for attention, and breathed easy as I decided to take the long way home.

The sun was shining. The skies were clear. Eyes on the road, mind a million miles away, I loosened my grip on the steering wheel and sunk deeper into my leather seat, letting out a relaxing sigh.

But suddenly I lost my comfort. In an instant, it was gone. As if it escaped on the tail of my exhale, floating away on the wings of my respiration, my comfort had left me. Someway, somehow, I was losing my buzz.

Trying to regain that victorious feeling I'd just previously had, I glanced down at the doctor's slip, still not believing that I'd actually pulled it off. The slip, unaware of its deceptive purpose, lay innocently on the seat as if legitimately confirming my pregnancy. It didn't, though. It only confirmed my desperation. It only confirmed my pain and subsequent craftiness to construct such a vendetta against the perpetrator of my excruciating ordeal.

Damon gave me nightmares. The pain was deep. And just when I thought the wounds were healing he'd come along and peeled the scab. I was bleeding. I was bleeding for a resolution. I was bleeding for revenge. I was bleeding for answers. An apology. Any indication of remorse that would aid in regenerating my broken heart and bruised ego. He offered no such thing. He offered only more pain. I thought back to how insensitive he was—how he'd reached a whole new level of *assholetivity*—when he'd put that woman on the phone with me. He'd planned that. I knew he did. Even at a time like this he cared nothing about me. Tasha was right. He was pure scum.

But as I fumed, something inside still begged me to question whether this was the right thing to do. It made me question my decision to go through with such an elaborate scheme to punish Damon for his crimes against my heart. Morally, I knew it was wrong. But if it would provide me with even the slightest bit of satisfaction of knowing that I got back at him for what he did to me, it was worth it, I told myself. Every waking minute, every brain cell it took to comprise this intricate attempt at justice was worth it if I could see him suffer. He deserved this, I kept telling myself. In my mind I knew he did. But in my heart I knew that, no matter how I kept adding and *re*-adding, two wrongs just wouldn't make a right.

As I pulled up behind another car at the red light, I went back and forth over my dilemma. Traffic tried to distract me, but I was too involved in my predicament. This was suddenly not the easy decision

I thought it would be. What I'd hyped myself up for, now, seemed extreme. Insane, even. I wasn't sure if it was worth it after all. I just wasn't sure of anything anymore.

As I teetered on right versus wrong, my concentration was eventually broken by the annoying revving of the engine of the car in front of me. The engine was loud and aggressive. And if the oversized exhaust was any indication, I imagined this guy would take off like a rocket once the light turned green.

I squinted curiously, looking through the light tint of the rear window of the ear-splitting automobile, trying to learn the identity of such an attention-hungry person, already forming an opinion about his character.

When my eyes fell in line with the loud car's rearview mirror I saw long blonde strands and feminine features behind the steering wheel. She wore dark, wide shades that prevented me from getting the full picture of her face, but I imagined she was probably beautiful. An ugly girl wouldn't dare think of drawing so much attention to herself.

I imagined this woman was someone who didn't have the vulnerable heart I had; that no one ever got over on her the way that Damon had gotten over on me. I envied this stranger. I envied her without even knowing her. But I could tell she was strong-willed. I could tell she was tough-hearted. I could tell that she was a fighter. She was different from me. Nothing got the best of her. Nothing made her cry.

I fell off into a short daydream, wondering what kind of life she had. I wondered who she was, and where she was going this afternoon. Probably to meet her professional athlete fiancé, I imagined. Then I thought about *my* life and what *I* was doing right now, wasting my afternoon to scheme on somebody. Somebody who just wanted to go on with his life, and close the chapter on our encounter. Somebody who'd *already* seemed to have moved on. I, obviously, hadn't. Couldn't. *Is my life this small? Am I this lost?* I sat at the light and pondered.

Just as the opposing traffic's light turned yellow I snapped out of my thoughts, ultimately decided that I wouldn't go through with this plan. I'd decided that I would just forget about Damon, and let go of the silly thoughts of revenge and retaliation that only seemed to prolong my pain. I blinked hard, and shook my head. Feeling somewhat of a relief, I let out a long-winded sigh as my grip on the steering wheel relaxed.

It wasn't worth it, I'd decided. It wasn't worth all the trouble. It wasn't worth the energy I'd already wasted. But I wouldn't waste any more, I told myself as I exhaled, finding a small amount of calm buried somewhere in my busy body.

But as my eyes focused I was faced with something. As I bordered on the right- and wrong thing, having finally decided on, what felt like, the *right* thing, there was suddenly something to pull me over the fence again. This sign, so unexpected, jumped out at me like an omen. And it was all the confirmation I needed that I was already doing the right thing.

One last rev of that engine sealed the deal. And as the light turned green, I grinned, realizing I'd regained my justification and found my motivation to carry on.

Just as I thought, the car in front of me zoomed off like a space shuttle. But not before I could get one last glimpse of my sign. As I squeezed the joystick and put my car in gear, proceeding with my journey home, I stayed glued to the license plate of the speedy vehicle that now placed a great amount of distance between us, until the characters NI4NI shrank, and then faded into the heat waves of the day.

CHAPTER 7

It was all set that Tasha and I would corner Damon at his job. He hadn't returned any of my calls, so we felt an ambush was necessary. I didn't like being ignored. And I had gone through too much trouble to obtain that doctor's note that he'd insisted upon to just let things fizzle out because of his, apparent, metacarpal malfunction.

Every part of me was invested in this plan. Particularly, my beauty. The stress had taken its toll on me. My skin was dull and flaky. My eyes had been bloodshot for days. I even lost a few pounds. It had been over a month since I'd seen him, and even though his shenanigans made it so that I no longer found him attractive, I still couldn't let Damon see *me* looking bad.

With that in mind, I stuffed my makeup wedge into the corner of my compact, twisting and turning it in a desperate attempt to conceal the purple hue underneath my eyes, and the trio of stress pimples bullseye on my forehead. But what tiny bit the sponge did manage to sweep up was barely enough to cover an eyelid, let alone my entire face. I had to go shopping. And I had to go bare. Blemishes and all.

"I'm going to make this quick," I said to myself, incognito under my hat and shades, sporting my don't-bother-me jeans, praying I wouldn't run into anyone I knew. But as soon as I swung open the

department store's heavy glass door, there was Collette.

Of course! I frowned.

Realizing there was no possible way to avoid her, I carried on inside.

She appeared to be on her way out, and was joined by some vertically-challenged chick who couldn't have been more than four-ten. But even with the height deficiency, she was cute. Too cute for Collette's company, I thought. I wondered why Collette, being so jealous, would choose to hang around such pretty women. She was torturing herself.

Avoiding eye contact, my face was blank as I didn't wish to engage in any phony conversation with her. I was still pissed with her and didn't intend on playing friends simply because we were face-to-face again.

She had other ideas.

"Hey, Sidney. Haven't heard from you in a while," she said with a guilty smirk.

I could smell her gingerbread body spray from ten feet away.

I tilted my head at her. "You've noticed?"

Her and her new friend looked at each other. I hadn't returned any of her phone calls *or* acknowledged her numerous offers to come over and 'console me'. It was too late for consoling. I didn't trust her anymore. I knew she only wanted to be included in the juicy drama. Up close and personal to it. Not console me. She knew good and well she got high giving me the gut-wrenching gossip. So she should've known we couldn't be friends anymore.

Friends don't take delight in delivering bad news to one another.

Unsure of how to respond, Collette didn't say anything. She *couldn't* say anything. She could only stand there and look dumb. Dumb and guilty. Dumb, guilty, and smelling like gingerbread.

Eventually, her dumb look was too much for my eyes to handle, even behind my shades. Without another word, I brushed between her and her little friend, continuing on with my business.

Nerve! I growled to myself as I walked briskly through the store toward Cosmetics. I couldn't believe she had the audacity speak to me. *What the hell did she expect? Was she messing with me? She* was *messing with me. That rat was messing with me! Oooooh, I should've—*

"May I help you?" the overly-made-up woman behind the makeup counter asked as I stood there brooding over the encounter. She had a huge diamond on her ring finger. The stone was nice, but too large for her petite hands. It made her look greedy.

"Yes," I quickly swapped my snarl for a courteous smile, "I need to replace my foundation."

"Certainly. Which do you use?"

"I wear . . . " Mid-sentence, I was distracted by the sight of Collette and her little leprechaun going up the escalator, looking in my direction. *I thought they were leaving*, I said to myself as I watched their smirking faces, torsos, and, finally, Collette's crusty cankles slowly ascend out of sight. Judging by the mischievous grin on her face I was certain that she was so happy to have been able to introduce to her new friend the heroine of the tragic comedy whose details I'm equally certain shared with everyone she knew. She was probably spreading my life all over town—and the World Wide Web. I told myself that if I found out my business was on her Facebook page she was going to get dealt with. Same with Twitter. She'd get beat for every tweet.

I shook my head as I second-guessed the battery charges. *Lord, please help me keep my hands off that donut-dunkin'—*

"Ma'am?" the woman beckoned my attention.

"Oh, yes. I'm sorry." I snapped out of my loathing. "Studio Fix C4."

"Now *that's* the Sidney we all know and love." I blew a kiss at the mirror.

After a little makeup magic, I was looking like my old self again. Tasha texted that she was on her way. We planned to arrive at Damon's job just after 2 o'clock, allowing him time to stagger in late from lunch since I knew what an unmotivated loser he was, and how he was always running late for *everything*. He egocentrically called it D-Cam Time. I called it being an inconsiderate and disorganized asshole.

I put the last finishing touches on my hair, then sprayed a light mist of Chanel all over my body to give Damon something sweet and pretty to smell while I ruined his day.

Always on time, Tasha was knocking at a quarter till two.

I opened the door. "Hey, girlie,"

"Hey, Sidneywinks." She popped a piece of gum into her mouth and handed me one. "Ready to roll?"

"Yeah. Just let me get my bag."

I grabbed my purse that was sitting on the counter, slipping the doctor's note into the side pocket.

"Bonni Q's going to have to come with us," Tasha announced. "I'm dropping her off at the airport when we're done."

"You know I love Bon Bon." I set the intrusion alarm, then slammed the panel door shut. "Let's go."

It took about twenty minutes to get to Damon's job. He worked as a clerk for a small, local newspaper. Finding his location would be relatively easy since I'd worked there very briefly during my junior year, just before getting the job at the boutique. Familiar with the layout, I remembered that the Mail & Copy room was just beyond the main entrance. I also knew they hadn't developed swipe card access yet since I'd picked Damon up from work a few times.

"You ready for this?" Tasha looked over at me, making sure I still wanted to go through with things. This would bring me face-to-face again with the devil.

I nodded. "Yep, I'm ready."

That's what I *said*, but inside I was scared out of my mind. I focused my vision straight ahead, through the windshield, trying to slow my heart rate. I didn't know what was going to happen, but I'd convinced myself during the drive that I was down for whatever.

"Well, let's go," Tasha said as we got out of the car.

Dressed in our business attire, we strolled through the employee parking lot around to the front of the building past a huddle of smokers who were polluting up the entrance. Casually, we entered the building like we worked there, nodding to the security officer at the front desk who'd looked up briefly from his crossword puzzle. Four doors down, and six suites across, wearing our finest footwear, we click-clacked our way down the right-angled road, cutting the corner leading to the large room where Damon was running off some copies.

I approached him from behind.

"*Hello there,*" I whispered from over his shoulder, my spearmint breath tickling his earlobe.

Damon whipped around.

"What the—" He sprung back, losing his grip on the stack of warm, uncollated papers. The ink-soiled sheets splashed onto the floor.

My high heels doubling as hole punchers, I trampled all over his fresh pile of hard work.

"Surprised?" I grinned.

Damon knelt to gather the loose copies, embarrassed and aware of speculative eyes. "What the hell are you doing here?" he whispered angrily.

"You *know* what I'm doing here!" I darted my eyes down at him. "Now don't play with me, Damon, because it won't be as much fun this time. I can promise you that."

Damon rose to his feet, now looking down on *me,* as I quickly shrank underneath his tall, lanky stature. His face was good and shiny. I knew he was *scamarrassed*: scared, mad, and embarrassed.

"Now, let's go outside. We've got a lot to discuss," I turned, giving him my back to follow.

Damon followed me through the side exit, taking his frustrations out on the door. I knew he probably wanted to really let me have it, but if he had such desires, he'd have to go through Tasha and her cousin, as they followed just a few feet behind us. Knowing they had my back made me less shy about turning it on Damon.

Once outside, I got straight to the point.

"Now let's make this easy." I threw the doctor's slip in his face, as wind as cold as I was slowly cradled it to the ground. "You give me $350, and I'll give you eighteen years of freedom."

I knew he didn't have the cash on him. But I also knew there was an ATM just up the road. We'd passed it on the way. Damon was happily saving up to finally buy a car. His dream car. So I knew he had a little something tucked away. But the car would have to wait. He owed a huge debt to my heart. And with his restitution I'd planned to buy the yellow-and-black suede boots we just got in at the boutique so that I could feel like I was walking all over his hopes and dreams every time I wore them.

Damon looked at me in disbelief as I gave him instructions.

"There's a teller machine just up the road," I motioned with a casual flip of the wrist. "You can go there and be back in less than twenty minutes if you start running now."

Damon stared at me like I was psycho.

"Any questions?" I shook my head and wondered if I'd went too fast for him.

"I'm at work, Sidney. I can't leave *now*," Damon squinted, wondering who this cold person was standing before him. He'd never met her before, but he should've recognized her. She was a product of his design.

"Can't we just get together later?" Damon asked.

I folded my arms. "No."

"Look, Sidney, I'm really going through a lot right now." Damon softened his tone. "I mean, you just don't know."

What I do *know is that you have to be crazy if you think I'm going to fall for your BS again,* I thought to myself as he continued.

"Sidney, look," he addressed me with desperate eyes, "I'll reimburse you, okay? Okay, Sidney? Sidney, I'll pay you back every penny. Every cent. Just give me a couple weeks, Sidney, alright? Give me some time. I'll pay you back. Okay, Sidney?" He kept using my name, probably one of the PSY 101 tactics he'd picked up his first—and *last*—semester at community college. He really should've been up on his financial aid because personalizing his pleas had absolutely no effect on me. Breaking through my brokenhearted-barrier would require much more than what his twelve credit hours could achieve.

But he kept trying.

"Sidney, it's just a really bad time for me," he explained, his front tooth slightly overlapping the other. At one point I found that sexy. But now it just annoyed me having to look at it.

"I'm just dealing with so much stuff right now," Damon said, shaking his head, trying to look pitiful.

Was he serious? I wasn't moved. No amount of pity in his voice was enough to tug at the strings of my four-chambered organ that he'd so cruelly ripped apart. He was wasting *his* breath, and *my* time.

I stood expressionless, neither a look of contempt nor compassion advertised on my face. My thoughts hid themselves, leaving Damon to hope for a moment that maybe his charm and its effect on me had yet to fade.

He nervously ran his hand back and forth across his low, curly-top fade, messing up that morning's mousse job. A few hairs stuck straight up like Daffy Duck.

"I'll get you the money, Sidney. Seriously." Damon kept trying to talk his way out of the three-figure bill. "Just handle things right now, and I'll make sure you get it back. I just need you to work with me. *Please* . . ." He searched my eyes for the smallest hint of mercy before theatrically hanging his head in a pathetic bow.

All was quiet as Damon waited for me to say something. Still in the "head hung" position, he looked at his feet.

I looked at his feet.

There wasn't a whole lot going on down there.

I looked back up at him. He was still looking at his feet.

I looked around for the Hollywood sign. I didn't see it, but Damon was acting like *he* did. I think he was even trying to make his eyes water.

As he stood there, looking like a mallard, I began to look Damon over, wondering what I ever saw in him in the first place besides his usual good looks. But as I tried to see beyond the surface beauty, and see the deceptive, gold-digging gargoyle I knew lied beneath, his looks only tripped me up. I couldn't get past them.

I looked at Damon's face. His skin. His sexy lips. I looked at his eyes. His shoulders. His arms. He had nice arms. Strong arms for such a thin man. I remembered how they used to hold me. Squeeze me till I laughed. Then I looked down at his hands. His large, long-fingered hands.

He was wearing a wedding band.

The very sight of it sickened me. My stomach rumbled in grief. He was married. He was really married. My first was now a married man only two months after taking my virginity.

Damon didn't do social media. And neither did I. That was one of the things we had in common. So I'd asked Tasha to check his friends' Facebook pages for pictures of the alleged wedding, and bride, but she'd came up empty. Therefore, these past few days part of me was still hoping that Collette had lied, or had gotten her information wrong, or that Damon was just playing an in-poor-taste prank on me when he found someone to put on the phone to play the role of his wife. But his finger was wrapped in white gold. He had no idea I'd be coming to his job this afternoon, yet he was wearing a wedding ring. I knew at that point it was no prank. It was real.

Rage boiled within me. But I had to keep it at a simmer.

"Sidney?" Damon looked at me, awaiting my verdict.

I glanced down at my watch. "My appointment is in forty-three minutes." I folded my arms. "It's now, or forever."

Damon just looked at me, his pseudo-sorrowful look erased and replaced with a look of pure despise.

I matched his look.

He pulled his stare off of me and turned his head to look back at Tasha, who waited by the car. Then he looked at Bonni Q, wondering what she had to do with any of this.

Finally, he turned to look at me again, knowing that dealing with me for a lifetime was way more than he'd ever bargained for when he'd used my body under the guise of decency to wiggle out an orgasm.

He sucked his teeth. "I'll be back."

As he stomped off like an angry little boy, I looked over at Tasha. She shook her head and laughed. Bonni Q laughed, too. I cracked a smile, but it was forced. Seeing Damon again did something to me inside.

They say that you can only hate someone to the extent at which you once loved them, but at that moment, I knew that wasn't true. I knew I never loved Damon, though I'd certainly tried to. Yet, at that moment, I hated everything about him. I really, actually hated him.

With unequivocal passion.

I walked over to Tasha and her cousin and leaned against the car. "You think he's coming back?" Knowing Damon, he'd abandon his entire life, and flee to the forests of New Guinea to avoid getting up off some cash.

Tasha's eyes shrank as they watched him walk off.

"He better," she said. Her words formed clouds of warm air. "Otherwise, he'll *really* be sorry," she added, as Damon vanished around the side of the building.

After only five minutes or so, Damon pulled around into the visitor's parking lot in a light-green Kia with June tags. But he was a Virgo. I wondered whose car he'd hot-wired to make the trip.

He got out of the car and began walking toward us. I walked to meet him halfway, while Tasha and Bonni Q stayed behind, giving us privacy to conduct our little transaction.

As we approached one another, Damon reached into his coat pocket. My heart skipped a beat as I hoped his hatred for me hadn't turn homicidal. I hoped this thing wouldn't have an angrier ending than I'd anticipated.

Before my mind could sketch out the deadly scene, Damon pulled out a bulky bank deposit envelope that, apparently, held the cash withdrawal.

I walked within four feet of him and stopped.

"Married, Damon?" I shook my head, squinting my eyes in confusion and disbelief. "You were married?" I knew he'd only just recently gotten married, but I wanted to hear what he had to say for himself while I looked at him one last time.

Damon looked off for a moment, and then looked at me. "You want the truth?"

"Nooooo." I folded my arms. "Waste my damn time."

Damon shook his head and looked away as if he really didn't want to go there. He scratched his head.

"Look, I wasn't married when we—"

"Just give me the money," I held out my hand. I didn't want to hear it after all.

Damon held out the chunky envelope. I snatched it out of his hand like the IRS.

His jaw tightened.

"You know, if you just wanted to sow your wild oats one last time you really should've consulted the back pages of one of your dirty little magazines and left me the hell alone!" My eyes burned as they narrowed on him. I took a controlled breath, and then opened the envelope, getting a whiff of the thick wad of new-smelling bills. They stunk to me. The stench of betrayal coated the pale-green papers that were to serve as the terminator of life. A life that didn't exist, but could have.

"Now I *know* I'm doing the right thing," I shook my head and dropped the money into my purse while Damon looked at me thinking my statement meant that we were on the same page. His eyes were free of remorse, or compassion. I was even sure I saw signs of relief in them when I took the money from him—like it was over. Like at that moment he had fixed everything and could now go back to being carelessly carefree. A happy hubby still in his honeymoon phase. The subtle smirk ticked me off.

I opened my purse, pulled out the envelope, and began counting the money—without discretion—right there in front of a few of his coworkers that weren't quite sure what was going on, but knew they were witnessing something scandalous.

Damon looked around, embarrassed. "Sidney, it's all there. Trust me."

I swiftly looked up at him, staring him right in that lie factory he called *a mouth*. "Trust you?" I shook my head and frowned. "That's cute."

I went back to counting, holding Damon hostage until every single bill bore my thumbprint. It was all there. Three hundred and fifty dollars of blood money intended for the use of killing our imaginary unborn child. I felt sick all over again. And the aforementioned smirk really hurt my feelings.

I looked up at Damon as tears slammed against the back of my eyes, banging to be set free as I still wondered—still struggled to understand—exactly what I could've found so attractive about him. I mean, he was never really good to me. Not really. But something about him, something I couldn't see—something mystifying—drew me in.

As I stood there questioning the quality of my judgment I finally began to realize what it was about Damon, besides his good looks, that had enabled him to sucker me into being with him. It was his aloofness. His cavalier attitude. His failure to fall at my feet that made me feel like *I* was the lucky one.

In every new relationship somebody had to be the "lucky one". And since Damon wasn't acting like it was him, I deduced it had to be me. By default, I perceived myself as the winner in this relationship instead of the other way around. Damon wasn't blown away by me. He acted as if he didn't notice all of the wonderful things about me that other men made clear they had. That made me think that there must've been something special—something extraordinary—about Damon. Something that I just didn't know yet. He'd piqued my curiosity. So I had to have him. I had to find out what was so spectacular, what was so wonderful about this person that he wasn't chasing me. Of course it all turned out to be fool's gold. Total crap. But it had worked. Maybe he didn't need those additional semesters after all.

Damon and I stood face-to-face as I still held the money.

I shook my head. "Thanks, Damon," I told him, still fighting back tears. "Thanks for making my first time so memorable." I stuffed the money into my purse as one warm tear broke free.

Damon just looked at me as I melted right there in front of him. No apology. No explanation. He just watched me cry.

Giving up on all hope of finding goodness in him, I zipped my purse and began to walk away.

My feet had only carried me two yards when he stopped me.

"Wait!"

Finally, I breathed. *An apology*. That was all I ever wanted. Not the money. Not any of this. Just a sincere apology. I turned back around and faced him.

"There's something I don't understand," Damon said.

I stood quietly with wide-open ears.

"If you didn't know about my wife . . . that I was married, then . . ."

I blinked nervously.

"Then why did you call her all those names? How did . . ."

How did I know she was a stripper? was what he wanted to ask, though he never finished his question. Instead he looked at me, awaiting my response anyway, closely watching my body language.

Frozen speechless I just looked at him. And swallowed.

"Dang, Sidney. That revenge must've been so sweet it spoiled your appetite," Tasha referred to my practically-untouched plate as we sat in one of my favorite restaurants just after the lunch rush.

"I'm pacing myself," I explained, sipping my margarita.

Just then her Dooney & Bourke began ringing.

She eyed me curiously from across the table as she dug into her designer bag for her phone.

"Pacing yourself . . ." she said before answering her phone. "—Hello?"

I put my drink down and poked at my baked potato.

We'd ordered almost everything on the menu—but mainly drinks. And I guess all of our eyes were bigger than our stomachs because our booth looked like a buffet station. Crustacean carcasses decked the table. Untouched entrées on standby were getting cold under the wind of our conversation. And empty glasses were crowding our elbowroom. The table was just as packed as my week had been.

Tasha said these were the craziest few days ever, and that she would miss me when she moved to Atlanta. I told her that I'd miss her, too. She was like the sister I'd always wanted, but never had in Chaylene. And now I was losing her to a new job hundreds of miles away.

"Damn Bam!" Tasha hung up her phone, regretting that she'd answered it in the first place.

"Tasha," I looked at her surprised, "I can't believe you just told that man he had the wrong number. You don't think he recognizes your voice?"

"Yeah, well, he needs to recognize a *hint* when he hears one." She took the last sip of her margarita. "He's getting to be a real *pita!*"

"Pain in the ass? Already? I thought you liked him," I frowned, apparently not updated.

"That was before I found out he stays on campus," she said, looking around for the waiter.

"So? What's wrong with that?' Tasha was always finding reasons to drop a guy.

"No, girl. He really, *really* stays on campus," she emphasized.

I still looked confused.

"Girl, he's not registered—he's homeless!"

Bonni Q and I looked at each other, then burst out laughing, as Tasha went on to describe how the poor guy's roommate had kicked him out of his apartment, and he'd drifted his way onto campus where Tasha, unsuspectingly, had made his unhoused acquaintance. She hated that she'd given him her number as he'd been hinting around about a place to crash. Tasha said he was out of luck because if he couldn't afford his beat-up bedroom in the Bronx, he certainly couldn't afford her luxurious loft in the Village.

"Trying to make me feel all guilty," she grumbled. "He's not about to stress me *ugly*."

"Wow!" I shook my head, sipping on my drink. "Kicked out for nonpayment of rent and homeless. You sure it wasn't Collette without her weave?"

Tasha chuckled then shook her head. "Nah. Not pudgy enough." She popped a breaded shrimp into her mouth. "Hey, didn't she gain like twenty pounds in two weeks?" Tasha added.

"Well, what do you expect from The Honey BBQ Wing *Fiend?*" I jabbed. "Political Science my foot. She majored in Gastronomy!"

Tasha and I laughed our heads off while Bonni Q looked at us in confusion. She was always the third wheel when she was with us. I felt compelled to explain.

"Gastronomy. It's the study of food and eating. *Webster's*," I cited before continuing. "I mean, it was like she was always hungry. You couldn't even have a simple conversation without her making some reference to food. Like when it came to colors, for example. It was never just beige, or off-white. It was always *buttercream*, or *cheesecake*. '*Oooh, girl, I just got this new cheesecake suit. I'm gonna hook it up with a chocolate tank, and some raspberry pumps.*'" I imitated, then laughed my eyes closed.

"Wait—or was it pineapple pumps? Heck, I can't remember. I just know it was edible. And when it was all said and done, she showed up to the concert looking like dessert for two."

"Three!" Tasha laughed. "Greedy ass."—She changed her voice and touched an invisible headset —"*Uh, yes, ma'am, and what would you like on your hamburger?*'"

"*A hotdog,*" I answered for an absent Collette.

We leaned over, laughing hard. Even Bonnie Q got a kick out of that one.

"Hey, guys. What's that *Damn Bam* thing you two are always saying?" she decided to ask.

Catching her breath, Tasha wiped the tears from her eyes, then replaced her napkin in her lap while explaining.

"Well, you know how you get mad or frustrated and you say *Damn!*, and then maybe hit the tabletop?" She simulated the fist-pounding gesture while Bonnie Q nodded. "Well, instead of punching the table, or wall, you just say *Damn Bam!* That way you don't hurt your hand."

"That's right," I nodded. "Now, this"—I showed the stitches in my palm—"was just a little mishap."

Tasha shook her head. "Yeah, you thought you were squeezing Damon's balls."

"Exactly."

Bonni Q shook her head and giggled. "You two are so silly."

"*Yeah. We know!!*" Tasha and I said at the same time.

"*See??*" we said again in chorus, then laughed at ourselves.

Tasha sipped her drink and smiled while I finally went to work on my king crab.

First looking around, then over her shoulders, Bonnie Q pushed her daiquiri to the side.

"Sooooooo . . . uh . . . " she leaned over the table wearing a huge grin, "tell me, Sidney. Was it, at least . . . *good?*" Her brows danced up and down on her forehead, while mine instantly formed a straight line.

Eboni Queen Anderson. A queen she was indeed. Her skin was nearly the color of coal, and her hair was long and thick enough for two heads. She kept it in a huge ponytail most times, but on special occasions she let the flat iron do its thing, flaunting her natural mane all the way down her back. I called her Bon Bon because she was so sweet. And even though she was a professional showoff (aka model), unlike her cousin and me, there wasn't a conceited bone in her 18-year-old-virginal body. Just a really curious one.

Tasha and I looked at each other. Then I looked at Bonni Q, who wore the same wide-eyed expression I once wore. Her voice carried the identical tone that once filled my questions about sex and "doing I"'.

I looked down at my glass as I stalled for time, trying to think of just how to answer that question. I picked up one of my crab legs and snapped it. Its juice splattered everywhere. Feeling the effects of my frozen, 40-proof drink, I laughed, triggering Tasha to do the same.

When we finally regained our composure I got back to Bonnie Q's question.

"Okay. Well . . ." I dipped crabmeat into my super-salty butter, "it was like putting on an earring."

Bonni Q glanced over at Tasha. Tasha looked at my glass. Then they both looked at me.

I chewed the last of my bite before explaining. "I mean, I felt it going in, but got absolutely no pleasure from it what-so-EVER!"

Tasha and Bon Bon cracked up laughing so hard that people turned around. Bon Bon's eyes started watering. And Tasha choked on her breadstick.

"No, no, no." Tasha patted her chest, coughing up croutons. "It was like when you got your navel ring,"—she swallowed—"it hurt for a moment, but once it was *in*, you forgot it was even *there!*" We threw our heads back and showed the entire restaurant our molars as we laughed like drunken saloon girls. Merciless, we each took turns taking shots at Damon's disappointing endowment and less-than-stellar performance. The restaurant around us had no idea what all the commotion was about. If they had they would've joined us in the side-splitting, knee-slapping frenzy that was giving us all tummy aches.

Bonni Q, still laughing hysterically, wanted to get hers in.

"No. It was probably like a tampon . . ."

Tasha's laughter tapered off with mine as her cousin and the chattering hum of the restaurant faded into the background. I sat across from her in the booth, Bonni Q at her side. Having dispensed the last bit of chuckle I had inside of me, my focus began to blur. My ears shut off. In my silence, I fell off into a daydream.

When I'd emerged from my semi-conscious state, still deaf to my surroundings, my gaze met up with Tasha's.

In slow motion our eyes caught each other's, locking telepathically, the humor in our faces gone.

She looked at me.

I looked at her.

She offered a smile.

I reciprocated, mine forming in small, twitching increments, clashing with my eyes.

She held hers for about two seconds.

So did I.

Then when our mouths stopped playing games our faces fell flat again.

As my expression worked independent of my will, my eyes began to sting. They grew big and shiny, yet stayed loyal to their task of displaying the happiness that this triumph and celebration was supposed to bring me. But loyal as they may have been they failed their mission. Though cloaked in capriciousness, my contributions to the conversation reeked of unauthentic joy, and soul-betraying laughter, humor that only the outsider could truly appreciate. I was on the inside. The subject. This was *my* life that just happened.

My eyes continued working hard to conceal my thoughts, but catching something in them, Tasha's face began to mirror mine, growing concerned, and soft. It was like, for a moment, she read me. She saw the pain that my bright eyes and top row teeth couldn't blind her to. She saw. So I stopped trying.

Tasha wanted to say something. I could tell.

I wanted to say something. She could tell.

We both wanted to say something, but neither one of us said a thing. We just looked at each other, feeling what we felt, blinking in slow motion as everything appeared miniature around us. However, in our silence we said so much. We said in silence what couldn't be said aloud. We said *this sucked. This whole thing really sucked.*

I snapped out of my trance, shrugging it off and resurrecting my smile in spite of our exchange.

Tasha cleared her throat as she did the same.

Missing out on her punch line, my ears tuned in to Bonni Q, who was just giddy with excitement. I looked at her beautiful face as she giggled, wondering if she'd follow my path. Wondering if she'd guard her virginity with the understanding of its worth, then one day treat it as if it wasn't the gem she'd valued and protected all those years, wasting it on some insensitive jerk. I wondered if she was getting more out of this conversation than just the juicy details her virginal mind so eagerly craved.

As we reunited in the moment, Tasha, her cousin, and I continued jeering over a succulent lobster, shrimp, and crab leg-feast, compliments of Damon. But the moment was beyond bitter sweet. Because even though I had suckered him out of that money, I knew Damon's pain would end that day—or, at worst, on payday. Mine, on the other hand, the pain that was growing within me, would be perennial. Imaginably never-ending. Damon would earn more money. But I'd never get my virginity back.

At that moment I realized that the money and the lying hadn't solved anything. I was still hurt, and he was still married. I had fooled myself into thinking that doing this to Damon would somehow ease the pain I felt, and reset my life back to the wonderful way it was before. But the truth was, it hadn't. The only difference it made was in turning me into a calculating liar and borderline thief.

I wondered what happened to my integrity. That dignity I'd prided myself on. If they, too, had disappeared with my virginity. At least before, I had the opportunity to walk away from the matter retaining my virtues, knowing that one day Damon would realize it was his loss. That could've been the one thing to haunt him in the aftermath of it all: the guilt of knowing he'd mistreated a good woman. But now, "good woman" would be the last thing he'd call me. After today he wouldn't remember anything good about me at all.

As my stomach began the task of digesting the seafood lunch I'd eaten in false triumph I struggled in digesting the shame that was welling up within me once again, and the sadness of the entire episode. I thought about Meka's aunt. The clinic *"recruits"*. How I'd treated them. How I'd looked at those two girls like they were the criminals when it was I who'd solicited them. Even the very issue of abortion was something I'd disrespected. That sensitive topic—that situation—was nothing to play around with. I *had* changed. In more ways than I'd expected. And right now I wasn't so sure anymore if I liked who I was becoming.

That afternoon I may have pretended like I got the last laugh but that night I cried.

CHAPTER 8

Lydia was surprised when I gave her the news. No notice. Just news. As my boss, she said that she was sad to see me go. That made one of us, I thought. Surely she couldn't have been too surprised that I would be moving on after graduation. I had bigger and better things to pursue. And with all the drama that had been going on with my schedule, she had to see it coming. I gave her my email address to forward my final commission statement, shook her hand, and thanked her for the opportunity.

As I made my way out of the boutique, I looked the two backstabbing sales associates right in their eyes, and smiled the sweetest goodbye.

My parents weren't exactly thrilled when I told them of my plans to move. They said that there was plenty of opportunity right where I was, and that I shouldn't be too quick to move clear across the country. I told them I *wasn't* moving clear across the country, just a little South. Florida, to be exact. I'd had my fill of New York and, having graduated, I really didn't see much reason to stay. I wanted a fresh start elsewhere. And Florida seemed perfect. The weather was nice, and it was so beautiful when I'd visited a year ago. After researching it a little, I decided to move to West Palm Beach.

"Sidney, I still think you're being a little too hasty in all of this," Mom tried to talk me out of moving even as dozens of boxes were stacked tall around me. It was 6:30 a.m., and Mom had just arrived in the middle of my packing. "You always were impetuous, you know."

"I know, Mom. But it's what I need: a little spontaneity in my life. Shake things up a little," I told her, as I wrapped my collectibles in last year's *Times*.

"I really think you should've taken that job at Vixion P.R.," she said, unwrapping the crystal daisy I'd just wrapped. "That was a lot of money for a recent grad." I stood up and took the figurine away from her.

"Mom," I looked at her impatiently, "they'll be other jobs. Believe me. Besides," I rewrapped the crystal before placing it back into the box of Styrofoam peanuts, "I want to explore the world a little."

Mom gasped. *"Explore the world?* Honey, you're moving to Florida for heaven's sake. Surely you're not exploring the world."

She began pacing my living room floor. "The country, maybe. But definitely not the world . . ." she murmured.

"Exactly, Mom." I followed her with my eyes. "I'm *not* moving halfway around the world. I'm only moving down south." I was leaving and that was that. I loved Mom, and I was going to miss her, but she could talk until the sun set. I wasn't changing my mind.

"And I thought I didn't see you often enough before." Mom folded her arms and faced her reflection in the curio cabinet.

"Mom-meeeeee . . ." I stepped over the box labeled *Bedroom* and whined, "I'm an adult now."

She looked at me with a raised brow.

I cleared my throat. "Look . . ." my tone deepened. Mom shot me a different look this time. "Ma'am . . ." She rolled her eyes *that* was more like it. "I have to take chances. I need to see what life has to offer me."

"But why do you have to move far away from your family in order to do that?"

"I don't look at it as moving away from my family. I look at it as moving toward my future."

"And why does your future have to be so far away?"

I put my hand on my waist. "Mom, can you at least *pretend* to support me?" I shook my head before hanging it low. Mom was really making this very difficult. She could be downright stubborn when she wanted to be.

"Honey," Mom bumped me lightly with her hip, "I do support you. It's just . . ." I looked up at her when I detected the tremor in her voice. "I'm just really going to miss you."

I hugged her. "I'm going to miss you, too, Mom."

That next weekend I drove to my parents' house to say goodbye. After our conversation I was afraid Mom would lock me up in my room for the next decade. I didn't know what to expect. But when I got there she had a big, Sunday-style dinner as my sendoff. She said she had to make sure she sent me off with delicious memories of home. That way I'd come back.

"You be careful, Butterfly," Mom hugged me tight the next morning. She knew she wouldn't see me for a while, and it was tearing her up.

"I will, Mom." I kissed her on the cheek as the early morning air brushed me on the side of my face.

"And don't forget to call every four or five hours," Dad instructed. "And only drive during the daylight. Make sure you find a hotel before nightfall . . ."

"Okay, Dad. I will," I assured him.

"Now, give me a hug," he held out his arms.

I gave my dad the biggest, tightest hug I'd ever given anyone in my life.

"I love you, Sid." He kissed me on top of my head.

"I love you, too, Dad." I wiped the tears from my eyes, then reached out for Mom, pulling her into our embrace.

I was going to miss them so much. In fact, I was missing them already, even as I held them in my arms.

"I'll see you guys soon." I pulled away, letting go of Mom last. "I'll call you in a few hours."

As I got in my car I wiped away some runaway tears that found homes in the corners of my mouth. I was hurting, but I was also determined to do this. I couldn't let nostalgia prevent me from venturing out like I knew I needed to. This was a move I had to make. I knew that something good awaited me under those beautiful, sunny skies and gorgeous, towering palms.

I felt it in my heart.

✦ ✦ ✦

It was 2:16 a.m. when Chaylene rolled over and glanced at the clock on the nightstand. This had become an all-too familiar scene at their home, and she was torn between confronting him, and keeping her mouth shut to maintain the peace. After all, she had two children to consider. It wasn't like when she was single and free, and could go off on some guy who'd pissed her off without a care in the world as to the repercussions. There were other lives at stake here. She had the boys now. And Dennis wasn't just "some guy". He was her husband.

At 2:57a.m. Chaylene heard the garage door opening. Her heart began to race, though she wasn't exactly sure why. Maybe it was her frustration with Dennis's inconsideration. Maybe it was her suspicions regarding his whereabouts. Maybe it was her adrenaline coaxing her to confront him. She didn't know. All she knew was that she didn't like this feeling one bit.

Eyes open, she lay motionless as she heard Dennis disarming the security system. She wondered where he'd been. Why he saw it necessary to stay out so late. She couldn't believe that Ron and the guys would keep him out until this hour, especially on a work night. She wondered if he was at a strip club, and just how much of the family's hard-earned money he'd blown on some up-for-grabs ass. Then she wondered if he was with a mistress and, if after a steamy night of adulterous sex, the little homewrecker didn't want him to go. Each scenario made her stomach turn. She was driving herself crazy with all of her speculating.

She knew she had to confront him. She knew she wouldn't be able to sleep if she didn't.

Shortly after Dennis entered their home, Chaylene heard the sound of plumbing. She figured he'd used the bathroom downstairs, releasing all that alcohol. Drinks ran through Dennis like water, and he didn't always know when to say when. But the noise, though faint, was unceasing. It persisted much longer than a flushing toilet cycle would have.

What in the world is he doing down there? *she* wondered, anxious to get this over with. What's taking him so long to come upstairs?

As seconds turned to minutes, and the continuous sound of running water replaced the quiet that previously filled the home, Chaylene realized that he was taking a shower. Dennis never took showers downstairs, regardless of whether Chaylene was sleeping. He preferred the shower in the master suite with its custom ceiling showerheads, and the fancy towel warmer she'd bought him for Christmas.

That sneak! He's trying to rinse away the evidence! *Chaylene fumed as she lay there waiting for the sound to stop.*

After getting, presumably, spotlessly-clean, Dennis went into the kitchen and poured himself a glass of orange juice, and finished it at the kitchen table before heading upstairs. Chaylene's ears became satellites as she deciphered every noise that stirred, from the sound of him opening the refrigerator door, to the clink of the empty glass into the sink, to his size-twelves climbing their way to the second floor toward her. At this point, her radar placed Dennis midway up the stairs, probably around the seventh or eighth step, her mind estimated. Her heart seemed to beat with his every footstep. She wondered what she would say to him when he reached the top. She wondered if he would say something first. Surely he needed to explain himself. As she waited for him to appear in the doorway, Chaylene lie quietly. Heart thumping. Breath still.

When he finally entered the bedroom Chaylene watched Dennis through blurred, squinted eyes as he dropped his towel and disappeared into the walk-in closet, putting on a pair of silk pajama bottoms. When he reemerged, Chaylene let loose.

Why didn't you call? Where have you been? Who were you with?! Answer me, dammit! *she demanded.*

Then she realized she hadn't said a word. Only her thoughts were demanding any answers. And when Dennis finally pulled back one corner of the duvet, and slipped his soap-scented body into bed, Chaylene was as quiet as she would've been had she actually been able to sleep that night.

CHAPTER 9

Forty-two hours and twenty-seven minutes later a green sign off I-95 notified me that I was entering Palm Beach County. My eyes gleamed at the sight. *Florida*, I sighed, taking a deep breath, already smelling the ocean. When I thought of Florida I thought of vacations. And a vacation was exactly what I needed. In fact, just being out on the road invigorated me. The New Year had just begun and I was already feeling brand-new.

Tasha was in Atlanta, still getting things situated. I'd stopped through to see her on my way to the Sunshine State. She was doing well. She'd found a cute little condo, and was settling into her new job and city quite nicely. I was so proud of her. She was actually and officially a *working woman*. A single, sophisticated, educated woman on her way up the ladder of professional and personal success. Seeing her set up so nicely inspired me. It made me feel good about my move.

From the directions the leasing agent gave me, I estimated I would be arriving at my new residence anywhere between the next ten to fifteen minutes. The luxury apartment home was relatively expensive, but I wanted someplace nice. Even if I couldn't afford it.

That was another reason my parents weren't too gung-ho about my move: I didn't have a job. I was leaving the life I've always known, and hadn't the slightest idea of how I would make ends meet. Managing to put my shopping compulsion to the side for a few months, I was able to save $7000, but knew that wouldn't last long. There was no question that I needed a job. Fast.

I made a left at the light, then another immediate left toward the entrance of the yellow-and-white, terracotta roof building I'd recognized from the online pictures. I could see the Victorian balconies of the second- and third floor units from over the shrubbery-lined wall that shielded the ground-level view.

My eyes widened as I entered the golden gates that were ajar, showing me one of the three on-property wildlife preservation ponds. There were tall fountains. And circular driveways. Victorian statues. And old-fashioned lanterns. Cloud-kissing palms lined the winding entrance. And colorful landscaping that spared no expense welcomed me toward the cobblestone walkway leading to the leasing office. The ad didn't do this place the justice it deserved. It was an absolute paradise!

I quickly met with the leasing agent to tie up loose ends regarding my pre-approval. After providing her with my signature on the necessary documents to finalize my move-in, I gave her part of my savings, and she gave me the keys to my new apartment.

CHAPTER 10

"Guess who I ran into?" Tasha asked, but seemed too anxious to have me actually guess.

"Who?" I didn't torture her.

"Tara."

"Dactyl?"

"I can't believe you are still calling her that," Tasha said.

"Well, that's how she was looking the night she swooped down on your man."

Tasha laughed. *"Anyway,"* she continued with her story, "guess what she's doing right now—Making an album!" she screamed before I could take a stab at it.

I coughed in shock. "What?"

Tara did sing well. And she always said she wanted to move to Atlanta to get signed. Tasha and I didn't think it was a good idea for her to drop out of school, but by that time we weren't friends with her anymore and couldn't have care less about what she did with her two-faced life.

Tara wasn't our *friend-friend*. But as Tasha's downstairs neighbor she would hang out with us from time to time at the club. She was pretty. Maybe even prettier than us. Which was hard to be.

One night we were all at the club having a really good time, when Tasha, intoxicated and quite possibly horny, was making eyes at some guy she'd recognized from the university. He was cute. And the way he was throwing glances back I knew my friend had it in the bag.

We'd just won the amateur dance contest, Tasha and I, so we were two hundred dollars richer. High off the pocket-padding victory, Tasha was fueled with confidence, and was intent on meeting the cutie. Though completely understanding her enthusiasm, I felt it my duty to advise her to play it cool and let *him* do the approaching. Approaching guys had never been our style. But Tasha, saturated with sex-on-the-beach shots, seemed like she was getting ready to break that rule.

After the club we were all standing outside, moving the party to the parking lot. Tasha's guy still hadn't approached her. He was still looking, but his legs weren't making any steps in her direction to make that desired acquaintance. Meanwhile, during the delay, Tara got it into her head that she was interested in him, too. Figuring she had just as much of a shot—and just as much of a right—she thought she'd beat Tasha to the punch. Before we knew it she was high-tailing her behind over there.

Now that was just a No-No to us. When one of us liked a guy, the other knew it was hands-off. Tara must've skipped that course in friendship etiquette, because she was coming at him hard with neither shame nor regard for the fact that she was riding with us. I looked over at Tasha to read her thoughts. She was pissed. Here we were letting this girl hang out with us, sharing in our spotlight, and she was biting the hands that fed her. It was unbelievable.

As Tara trotted over to the guy and his friends, poking out her butt, and moving like a pterodactyl, Tasha and I watched on in disbelief. She looked like the biggest backstabber to us, skipping off to seize a guy she knew full well Tasha called dibs on. We were furious. And we'd already decided she was walking home.

As Tara approached them, the guy and his friends looked on curiously, probably assuming she was coming over to serve as a kind of catalyst for him and Tasha to hook-up, since they had been too shy to speak on their own behalves. They didn't know that their assumed matchmaker was really a Benedict Arnold without a ride home.

Tasha and I didn't care to stick around to see the finale. We'd seen enough. But just as we shook our heads a final time and prepared to head for the car, Tara fell. Arms out, eyes wide open, she slid face first onto the grass-covered parking lot, eating a mouthful of dirt before finally stopping.

Tasha yelled *Safe!* And the crowd roared.

Tara was so embarrassed that she didn't bother with the fresh blood covering her dirty knees. She limped past the laughing crowd, one shoe shy, until she found a security guard who took pity on her and allowed her back inside the club where she could escape the snickers of eyewitnesses. Even Tasha's cutie was laughing—which totally turned us off. I mean, *we* thought it was funny. But *he* wasn't supposed to laugh. The humor we found in it stemmed only from the standpoint of Tara getting what she deserved for being so disloyal. But the fact that he could laugh at such a thing showed Tasha and me he wasn't anyone she'd want to date after all.

We headed home, leaving Tara behind to clean not only the blood off her knees, but the egg off her face. Ever since, three's just been a crowd.

"Can you believe it? A record deal!" Excitement filled Tasha's voice.

"Wow. How in the world did she pull that off?" I asked.

"I don't know. Just caught a break, I guess."

"I guess . . ."

"I am so happy for her," Tasha confessed. "Aren't you?"

"I guess . . ."

I'd settled into my new apartment over the past six weeks. Already it felt like home. I'd decorated it to perfection, recycling some of the old furniture Mom and Dad had shipped down for me from my old place in New York, and spicing it up with a few new items I'd purchased since I'd been here.

My savings was nearly depleted. And my credit cards were maxed out. Tragically, my Visa privileges had been revoked for carrying an over-the-limit balance. The purchases were under the limit, but the interest put me way over. From this point on it was me and the cash making it happen. At least until I got my new MasterCard in the mail.

I'd completed several applications and submitted countless resumes all over town, but had heard nothing. I was optimistic, though. I knew something would come along soon. When I had spoken with my parents earlier, aware of my job search, they said that if I needed anything at all to just let them know, and even offered to wire me some cash until I found work. I was appreciative, but I didn't want to burden them. They'd already done so much. And to demonstrate my moving toward a more independent lifestyle I even sent back the credit card Dad gave me for my road trip down here. That was a major step for me, considering how broke I was.

Later that afternoon as I browsed the employment ads, I couldn't help thinking about what Tasha had told me earlier about Tara. I guess I was a little happy for her. I mean, she'd followed her dream and, against all odds, had achieved it. Instead of being jealous I decided to use her success as inspiration that perhaps good things were in my future as well. I couldn't sing. But I could dream.

CHAPTER 11

"You be careful, Cookie Face."

"I will, Mom. Talk to you later."

Mom and I usually talked for hours but tonight I had to cut the conversation short. Leann was taking me to the grand opening of this new club. We'd been hanging out every weekend.

I'd met Leann at the DMV. I was getting my new driver's license, and she was replacing her lost one. She'd moved here from Tennessee and had been showing me all the hot spots she'd discovered in her three years of Florida residency. She said I was going to love it here. I agreed.

Mom told me to avoid clubbing as much as I did back home. She said that a young lady shouldn't find herself frequenting such arenas in the name of socializing. I lied, telling her that I'd only gone out once since I'd been here. I knew she wouldn't understand. I mean, I wasn't working and, except for job hunting, I didn't have much reason to leave my apartment. By the time the weekends rolled around I was ready to hit the dance floor with Leann, who'd been working all week and was dying for some Friday Night fun.

I went to my closet and picked out the black sequence top that revealed my dual-diamond navel ring. It tied in the back like laces. One tug of the string wouldn't be enough to disrobe me tonight so I felt sexy *and* safe wearing it. I dared to match it up with skin-tight green pants, and black four-inch stilettos. The pants fit like latex, and seemed to add a little something to my backside. I was loving it. There was a fine line between too much backside and too little and right now, I was proudly working the middle.

It was midnight when Leann called from the gate. I grabbed my purse before racing downstairs to meet her since we were already running late.

As I hurried toward the maroon Honda Civic pumping loud, bass-containing music audible from the outside, I waved at Leann through the windshield. She waved back before reaching over to unlock my door.

"Nice tan!" she said as I slipped in shotgun.

"Cute outfit!" I grinned, then shut my door.

Leann smiled, visibly delighted by the anticipated compliment. She was sporting a sparkly silver, low-cut midriff blouse that doubled her cup size, a hot-pink, low-rise mini skirt a good three inches below her navel that showed off her flat stomach and copper-toned thighs, and black wrap-around-the-calves heels that made me second-guess my outfit for a minute.

Leann continued smiling as she tugged at her top, better revealing the cursive tattoo on her breast that read: *warm*.

She did have a warm heart. I had only known her for a month but felt as if I'd known her much longer. She was as sweet as her southern accent, and was so much fun to be with. Besides energetic, I guess *warm* would be a good word to describe her.

"Oh,"—I leaned down toward Leann's stomach—"I didn't know you had another tattoo." I peeled down her skirt a tad bit with my pinky and moved my face closer to her tummy, squinting to read the small print just below her navel. "What does that say?"

Leann snickered and said, *"Warmer."* I jerked my head back so fast I almost broke my neck.

Leann giggled herself to tears, stomach muscles flexing. I looked at her incredulously, appropriately embarrassed. But eventually I couldn't help joining her in her crazy cackles.

"You are something else, you know that?" I shook my head.

Leann was about 5'3 with the kind of body rappers rapped about. Her eyes were deep and dark—almost spooky, but just making the cut of seductive like she wore eyeliner even those times she didn't. A penny-brown princess who was always dolled-up, even around the house, she managed to express her beauty in such an authentic and nonthreatening way. She truly loved being a woman and wholeheartedly embraced her femininity *and* sexuality.

"Oh, that reminds me," her eyes gleamed as we made a right out of the complex, "there's a single guy who just moved in right above me. It's time you met someone."

"Oh, yeah?" I pulled down the mirrored visor, fussing with my hair. "What does he look like?"

"I don't know."

"Oh, you saw him from a distance?"

Leann got over in the left lane. "I haven't seen him yet," she said.

"What?" I was confused. "So then, how do you know it's even a guy up there?"

"I can tell by the length of his showers. And whoever's up there washes clothes a lot. That means they don't have very many, unlike a woman."

If anyone could sniff out a man it would have to be Leann.

"You hear all that from downstairs?"

She shook her head. "Cheap building. Now, I know that he's *single* because I never hear the creaky-squeaky, bouncy-pouncy, wiggle-diggle," she giggled.

"Then I bet his showers must be *pretty* cold," I laughed.

"Ohhhh, riiiight! Good one!!!" Leann laughed out loud, showing her tongue ring.

By the time we pulled up to the club I already knew I was going to have myself a blast. There was a long line to enter, but nobody looked annoyed having to wait in it. It was like they knew that whatever was on the other side of the door was well worth their wait. They wore their happy faces and patient posture as the bouncers checked ID.

Leann and I got out of the car, still cracking up as we put our purses in the trunk. She said that we didn't need ID, boasting that she "knew people" and how they wouldn't bother us with carding. I wanted to ask if we could leave our money in the car too, as I tucked four twenties into my pocket along with the car key.

Leann stuck her cash in the waist of her skirt, then, nearly forgetting something, leaned over inside the trunk, reaching for her purse.

My eyes widened.

"I see London. I see France . . ." I chuckled, "but I don't see any underpants." Leann popped up so fast she bumped her head on the open hatch.

"Owww!" she wailed.

"Oh my gosh! Are you okay?" I placed a hand on her back, making sure she didn't seriously injure herself.

She rubbed her head. "Yeah, I'm okay," she grimaced, wondering just how much of the European tour she gave me.

"Good," I breathed a sigh of relief while Leann continued rubbing her noggin. "But you could've put on some underwear. We weren't running *that* late."

"For your information, Green Eyes, it's called a G-string," Leann rolled hers at me. "Now, let's go!" she laughed, yanking me by the arm.

We bypassed the line as Leann gestured to security that I was with her. As the bald bouncer unhooked the velvet rope for us I was looking at Leann like she needed her pinky ring kissed. I mean, this place was brand-new. I knew she had it like that at the other clubs, but didn't really believe she would have any clout here already. But while I was surprised, I didn't dare let it show. I just walked right in with her like we were destined for a VIP table.

Once inside, I was glad that Leann knew the bouncer but wished she'd saved her charm for the girl at the register. There was a twenty-five dollar cover charge. That really hurt my unemployed feelings. But as I'd suspected, it turned out to be worth it.

The club was decked out inside. I'd never seen anything like it. There were large, clear pedestals shaped like martini glasses filled with electric-blue liquid where beat-possessed girls danced. White chiffon drapes hung from the high ceiling, illuminated by multi-colored strobe lights. Giant-sized speakers bordered the entire main dance floor. Indoor palms had utility lights glaring up at them like stars on the red carpet. Pink and purple neon strips lined the center stage where the most confident and most wasted dancers showcased their moves. And smoke shot up from hollow ports in the floor creating a hypnotic illusion that just made you want to go wild.

Leann made her way to the main bar where she ordered a round for us, compliments of her association with the bartender.

"Here you go," she handed me my midori sour.

"Thanks," I smiled.

Sipping on my drink, I imagined myself participating in the cluster of motion taking place on the dance floor. Feeling it, I nodded my head, smiling approvingly at the diversity of the crowd.

You had your ballers at the rear of the room, running game on girls who soaked it up like sunshine. You had your wallflowers congesting up the hallways like only wallflowers would. And then you had your party people scuffing up the tile, making it hard on the janitor. Everyone was having a good time playing their respective roles. And the music brought it all to life. Hats off to the DJ because he was making it happen. Bodies were bouncing. Smiles were flashing.

The party was alive. And I couldn't wait to be a part of it.

Before we got started I told Leann I needed to go to the bathroom for a QCC. *Quick Cuteness Check*, I explained. Holding our drinks high in the sky, we squeezed our way through the thick crowd, aware of every eye that watched us. Leann didn't let on, though. She was better than I was at feigning modesty. But I knew she was loving the attention just as much as I was. She didn't put on that sexy outfit for nothing. Guys were breaking their necks to get a glimpse of her baby-oiled body, searching for their reflections in her chest.

Leann and I searched for only a few minutes before spotting the ladies restroom sign, which was pretty good considering the size of the club. As we headed toward it, Leann was stopped by a guy I assumed she knew. My critical eyes instantly labeled him a platonic friend, so I gestured to her that I was going to go ahead. Leann held up a finger and nodded, letting me know she'd be right there. I nodded back before proceeding.

Finding the bathroom was one thing. Getting in was a completely different story. I had to squeeze past pockets of people-watchers, avoid colored toenails, and muscle my way through hordes of coercive conversations. *"Damn, Little Red!"* some guy called out to me as he reached for my hand. Failing the minimum height requirement, I couldn't grant him access into my world. I smiled a *No Thanks,* and kept moving.

Four or five feet away from the door with the sphere-headed triangle, I wiggled my way past a pack of hungry vultures, where one copped a feel. That immediately deducted two points from of my club approval rating. I tried to keep a cool face but inside my defensive pride was boiling. I wanted to turn around and start slapping faces. But I just kept on walking.

A foot away from my destination I came upon two guys who were blocking the bathroom entrance like they had a guest list. I frowned in annoyance, thinking it was so rude for people to just stand right in front of a door, especially when there were so many other crevices into which they could've sunken themselves. One of them—the taller, uglier one—was talking loudly about how he'd slept with some girl, who, apparently was in the club tonight. He was merciless as he degraded her, calling her all sorts of disrespectful names, bragging to his friend, who was a close runner-up in the looks category, about how he'd "hit it on the first night".

"Yeah, man. She's a straight up ho," he said, while I thought to myself that sounded a lot like the fly calling poop *nasty*. I shook my head as I managed to squeeze past them.

Putting my weight against the door, I finally slipped into the bathroom. Miraculously, Leann was right behind me. That outfit of hers must've parted the crowd like the Red Sea.

I made a beeline to the mirror.

"Like it so far?" Leann carved out some space next to me in front of the lipstick-smeared looking glass. It seemed like every pretty girl was in the bathroom glamming it up, and pretending not to notice other pretty girls. Leann and I were the prettiest, though—except for one girl who looked like she could give us some concerning competition tonight, and who looked as if she was thinking the same about us.

I pulled out my cherry wine lipstick. "Yes. I love it!" I told her, dodging pink- and red lip marks, and wondering who actually went around kissing bathroom mirrors at this age. "You weren't lying about your pull either. Pretty impressive."

"Well, you know how I do." Leann put her hand up for me to hi-five it.

"I do *now*." I tapped hands with her.

We laughed before feasting our eyes back on our images. Leann smiled at herself pleasingly. "So, my friend out there said that I look extra hot tonight." She sized up her reflection while I conveniently ignored the part about his friend asking about me. "I guess I *am* having a good night."—She puckered up —"Mmmmm . . . *Smack!*" She kissed the mirror.

"Eah!" I elbowed her. "That's nasty, Leann!" She giggled like a silly girl and continued fawning as I stood there with a look on my face she didn't seem too concerned with. She swished her long ponytail to one side—just millimeters away from my eye—and began raking her fingers through its coarse strands.

"See any cute guys yet?" she asked.

"No," I shrugged, "not yet. Here."—I handed her my drink—"I gotta go pee."

Leann held my drink in one hand, and used the other to reposition herself in her top while I ventured off toward a stall.

I didn't see any cute guys yet, but I was sure they were present. All these girls couldn't have been in the building for each other—at least, I'd hoped not. Not that I was against an estrogen-exclusive club. But I was looking for a man. Besides, this place was too nice to exclude anyone or limit itself to just one particular crowd. Between the three floors with six dedicated rooms for various genres of music there was a little something for everyone.

"Much better," I breathed as I made my way to the sink opposite Leann, who was still fussing with herself.

I turned on the faucet and held my hands under the flow of warm water, looking at myself in the mirror. I was having a good night, too.

I turned to Leann. "Ready?"

"Always."

Leann and I stepped back out into the hall, passing the same faces we'd passed on our way in. The music was still pumping loud. I bumped her with my hip, getting into the groove, anticipating my footprints on every dance floor. Leann smiled, snapping her fingers and nodding to the beat while we headed for the crowd that threw their hands up in the air and waved them like they just didn't care.

Just before we got to the dance floor we were stopped by her platonic friend, who I'd noticed slipped something into her hand.

We stopped.

"What's this?" Leann looked down at the tiny white pill, then smiled at him gullibly as people behind us impatiently bumped us out of their way.

He rubbed his chin, grinning like a wolf. "It's—"

"It's what guys give girls so that they can do every disgusting thing imaginable to them," I answered for him.

He and his sneaky-looking sidekick were clearly bothered by my interjection.

"Come on, Leann." I tugged on her arm as I evil-eyed them. "Let's go."

As Leann reluctantly waved bye to him, the guy and his friend looked pissed. The feeling mutual, I stared them down until we rounded the corner.

I turned to Leann.

"I thought you said that was your friend?"

Leann just looked at me, not knowing what to say.

"Humph!" I rolled my eyes. "Some friend."

Shaking off that drama, it seemed the moment Leann and I hit the very first dance floor we were bum-rushed. Already working on our third dance partners for the night, I was grooving with one guy, while she was shaking her derriere with another.

"So, what's your name?" my dance partner asked. He wasn't that cute. And I think I smelled Black & Mild on his breath just then when he spoke. "I'm . . ." I closed my eyes, trying to think of a fake name. still dancing as I stalled for time. I hated giving guys my real name. I opened my eyes and looked around the room and said, "I'm Gladys Friday!"

Dancing for a good twenty minutes already, Leann and I were sweating like we were guilty. Looking at her and her partner it seemed their moves weren't so innocent after all.

Bump. Grind. Wiggle. Bump. Grind. Wiggle.

It looked more like simulated sex than dancing. Her guy was way too hands-on for me. And I wondered if she'd forgotten that she'd barely put a mitten on her kitten. She certainly was acting like it. But I let her do her thing. She'd worked hard all week and was, no doubt, dancing off some stress.

Leann sold real estate. She was once top in her office. But despite her nonstop efforts and constant hustling, the sales just weren't coming in lately. To supplement her income she was working part time in the office of a handsome optometrist she used to date. Between the two gigs she was easily pulling sixty hours a week. Considering the circumstances, I was willing to let her have her moment tonight. But eventually it seemed that her dance therapy was producing one very uncomfortable side effect for *me*.

It seemed that my partner, watching Leann and her guy bust their moves, grew bold, and began grinding on me. Hard. And whatever he had in his pocket—keys, pen, ice pick!—was killing me.

I tried backing away, putting my hand on *The Grind Reaper's* chest to govern our space, but that only seemed to fuel his aggression. Realizing that might have been *'his spot'*, I quickly removed my hand from his chest and replaced it with an elbow. I looked around the room, embarrassed, wondering who was witnessing this mugging in motion. In the event my knee had to acquaint itself with his groin, I'd need some witnesses. But as the music worked against me this time, I saw that everyone—including Leann—were all too busy enjoying themselves to notice what was happening to me.

As I still attempted to push my dance partner off of me, soft breath whispered in my ear.

"You're dancing with the wrong person."

I turned around to see who'd felt my plight. Who'd heard my silent cries. Who'd testify at my battery trial where I'd be the defendant. And, there, walking by, was a man with light brown eyes and cinnamon skin grinning at me like he recognized me from my very own dreams.

I smiled bashfully, wondering who he was. Whoever he was, I wanted to be rescued by him. I wanted to be saved by this man who'd found me in distress. He was gorgeous—so gorgeous he seemed to carry a glow around him. A golden aura that I wanted to penetrate with my kiss.

In a daze, I watched him walk by giving me *that look*, until he finally disappeared.

In old school fashion, Freak Nasty's *Da' Dip* was playing for my dance partner and me, instructing me to put my hands up on his hip. When I'd dip, he'd dip, we'd dip. But I paid no attention to the song, *or* my dance partner. Hypnotized in the aftershocks of this gorgeous guy's presence, I ignored the music, and had even forgotten all about my touchy-feely attacker for the moment, giving him free rein of my body. His hands were on my *butt*—not hips!—at this point.

"Get off of me!" I found my muscles, pushing him into the dancing couple behind him. They frowned, pushing his worm-like body back into its previous spot where I'd just vanished from.

By the time I found the gorgeous guy again he was in the Reggae Room already dancing with someone else. But she didn't look like much competition.

I walked over and whispered in *his* ear this time. *"Who's dancing now?"*

When he turned around and saw it was me, he smiled. I smiled back, waiting for him to give his partner the boot. But to my extreme dismay, he shrugged his shoulders—as if to say I was too late—and kept dancing with her.

Surprised, I just looked at him. He looked at me for a while, too, as I waited for the comic in him to say, *'Just kidding. C'mon, let's go!'* But as I studied his handsome face that didn't crack a smile, I soon realized he wasn't joking.

Blinking slowly in awe, I kept standing there like a doofus, absorbing the unprecedented moment, not believing what he'd just done—and *didn't* do. Then, taking with me the teaspoon of pride I had left, I walked away.

Lowering my eyes to conceal the embarrassment they advertised, I squeezed past the large crowd of paired-up partiers, who bumped me around like a giant-sized pinball. Getting tossed around, and stumbling most of the way, I told the Reggae Room to go to hell as I exited and eventually found myself at the foot of the steps leading to the next level.

I hesitated for a moment as I looked around for Leann in the midst of the madness, seeing if she'd remained where I'd left her. Indeed, my eyes found her dancing with the same guy, and looking like she was having a superb time. Everyone looked like they were having a good time.

Everyone except me.

Maybe I should just wait in the car, I thought to myself as I made my way up the slippery steps that were coated with someone's ten-dollar drink.

Just as I reached the top I felt a pair of hands around my waist. Thinking it better not be the guy who was grinding on me a while ago, I turned around, ready to fire.

"Wanna dance now?" Gorgeous Guy smiled at me as I un-cocked my cherry wine-coated weapon and, instead, used it to smile back a *Yes*.

Gorgeous Guy and I danced for six songs straight. We were having so much fun. I almost felt sorry for the poor girl who he'd ditched right in the middle of their dance. But then I saw her bent over, dancing with two replacements—one in front, one in back. She looked at me from across the floor as our glistening-with-sweat bodies moved in sync. My guy's back was to her as he was facing me. It felt awkward having her look at me the way she did while the less desirables tended to their business of using her body like a beige blow-up doll. She looked kind of miserable, dancing with them like it was work, rather than the pleasure it should've been. Rather than the pleasure it was when she was dancing with the guy that, now, danced with me.

My moves slowed as I watched her watch me. Her eyes affixed on my body with a wistful stare as the dancing duo encapsulating her concentrated on

133

further exploiting her body. She watched me, almost resentfully, as if I'd ruined her night. As if I'd come along and intercepted destiny, and had sentenced her to spend the rest of the night with these two poor excuses for consolation prize—dregs of the gender—by direct result of my actions. Her eyes focused on me while the twins, *Lewd* and *Lascivious*, focused solely on her breasts and backside.

I began feeling guilty. I began to feel that maybe I *had* sentenced her to this unpleasant fate, having stolen the only prince in the room right from under her nose. Maybe I *was* responsible. Maybe I was even wrong. I felt I had to say something to her. She was looking at me so pitifully, I felt I owed her. But what could I say? How could I set things straight between us? How could I make it right?

As we continued looking at each other from across the room I made the only gesture I could.

"*Sorry,*" I mouthed silently from over my guy's shoulder, not knowing what else to say. She looked at me as I offered my guilty apologies. I watched her, waiting, not necessarily for a nod, but for any conscience-clearing indication that it was cool between us. That she held no grudge. That she wouldn't be waiting for me outside with a crowbar. But she just danced, still looking at me. Then, after a few seconds, she turned around, bent over, and shook her practically in my face as if telling me to kiss it. The guy in back of her—now up to bat—spanked her on it as she swung it his way.

I turned my head and frowned.

Humph! It looks like she's right where she's comfortable, I thought to myself as I resumed my pace with guilt-free grace and continued to move with this gorgeous guy that was, now, legitimately mine.

After about an hour, my guy and I called it quits. The drink he'd bought me was knocking on my bladder walls and was getting ready to show itself out. I was standing on the outskirts of the dance floor, squeezing my legs together, looking for Leann.

"There she goes again," I heard the ugly guy from the hallway earlier telling his friend. "Biggest freak in the club."

"Damn! She's fine, though!" his friend said, looking like he wanted a turn. "Titties wrapped in silver like Hershey's kisses. I'll take a sip of that hot chocolate *any* day!"

I turned around to see who they were talking about —to see who was desperate enough to have sex with Ugmo's ridiculous ass. And that's when I saw Leann dancing down the aisle, drink in hand, shirt shimmering.

"Hey, *girrrrrrrlllll*," she sang out to me, drunk and giggling.

I looked at her, my thoughts momentarily on pause, then smiled. "There you are." I hugged her, then looked back at the two assholes and shot them a cold stare.

"I was looking for *youuuuu*," Leann said as she wrapped her arms around me, sharing her cranberry and vodka breath. It was obvious she was smashed. Her hair was all wet around the edges, and her walk, shaky like a newborn calf.

135

She finished the last of her drink. "You ready to go?"

"I sure am."

Just then my gorgeous guy walked by.

"Bye, Sidney," he smiled. "I'll call you."

"Bye," I waved as he and his friends headed toward the exit.

Drunk and louder than she realized, Leann said, "Oh, my God! Who is *that?!*"

Watching him leave, I smiled and said, "That, Leann, is my new boyfriend."

CHAPTER 12

Rico lived in one of the poorest pockets outside West Palm Beach. When I arrived at his place I was taken aback by the run-down area and overall condition of the apartment complex. The building should've been condemned. But there it stood, providing substandard housing to low-income tenants. I was thirty days away from being a resident myself. If my job situation didn't improve, I'd likely be Rico's new neighbor.

I managed to find a parking space right in front of his building. The lot was packed full of broken-down cars on bricks, and other in-progress *do-it-yourselves*. I armed my Beemer and took a quick peek inside, making sure no valuables were visible. Then I stepped onto the cracked concrete curb, and trailed the weed-sprouting walkway toward Rico's apartment.

Glancing back once more at my car, I reluctantly hiked up the creaky stairs, beginning to second-guess this whole Rico thing. Looking around, maybe he wasn't such a catch after all. But before I could even talk myself out of the visit, I was already knocking on the door.

I nervously straightened my clothes and tossed my hair around with my hand as my heart started thumping.

How is it possible that someone so gorgeous could live here? I thought to myself.

I didn't imagine him living in anything less than a place of luxury. Refinement. This didn't fit my winning image of him. It didn't fit into the visual equation I saw last night. His good looks didn't go with any of this. Even the number *1* on the door hung upside down, swinging by its nail, leaving only the *zero*.

As I stood there pondering it all I began to hear footsteps coming from the inside. The latch turned. I inhaled, putting on my 'I've got it all together' face, hoping I looked as cute as I thought I did in my outfit. But when Rico finally opened the door, my eyes shrank at what *he* was wearing: faded shorts and a promotional T-shirt he probably got for free for filling out a credit card application at some outdoor flea market booth. Even his expression was unmotivated and lazy. Right then and there I knew we weren't going anywhere.

I sighed, disappointed. Seeing him dressed this way, naturally, made me lose my motivation. However, by contrast, when Rico's eyes finally focused on me he immediately came to life.

"Wow!" he gasped. "You're beautiful!"

"Thanks," I managed a smile.

He invited me in, then shut the door behind me.

"I mean, I knew you were pretty last night, but . . ." he paused. "Wow! I don't know what to say . . ."

Hearing him sound so surprised I didn't know whether to be flattered, or offended. I mean, what was he trying to say? I didn't look good last night?

Why did he even call me, then? I wondered to myself as I debated on whether or not to ask him.

"Here"—Rico removed a CD case from the sofa —"have a seat." He tossed it onto the table. The place was disappointingly untidy. I found it strange that he didn't bother to straighten up a bit before I came over. It's not like he wasn't expecting me. I wondered what type of women he was used to dealing with that would make him think it was okay to invite someone over to his place when it was in such a state of disarray.

Rico quickly made his way to the kitchen.

"Would you like something to drink, Sidney?"

That depends on whether you've got clean glassware.

"Do you have bottled water?" I asked.

"No. But I have orange juice, sweet tea, and . . ." he searched the fridge, "milk."

"I'll have sweet tea," I decided easily.

I sat back and tried to make myself comfortable, as I looked around the living room. Like the refrigerator, it, too, was practically empty. Aside from the entertainment center, the awkwardly-shaped coffee table, and the sofa I sat on, there wasn't anything else in the room. There were no plants. No pillows. There weren't even any pictures on the walls.

Rico brought over a purple cup filled with sweet tea, stealing glances as he handed it to me.

"Thanks," I smiled, then took a sip of what had to be the sweetest, nastiest, most-syrupy-tasting tea I'd ever had in my life. My lips puckered as I reluctantly swallowed the unpalatable beverage.

I sat the cup down on the table and folded my hands in my lap, thinking this wasn't going so well.

Rico went back into the kitchen, shuffling things around with no specific purpose. I imagined he was embarrassed as he now regretted not running a vacuum across the floor. He hung around in there for a few minutes before rejoining me in the living room.

"So," he clasped his hands together, sitting on the edge of the couch, "did you find the place alright?"

"Yeah. Yeah, I did," I nodded, wondering how I could ever miss such an eyesore.

"This place is only temporary," he explained as if reading my mind. "Just until I get my own place."

"Oh, you have a roommate?"

"My cousin. But he's hardly ever home so it feels like it's my own place."

I kept nodding as I looked at the weight bench sitting in the middle of the dining room where a table should've been. I'd missed that during my original inventory. I turned to Rico.

"So, where are you from? And how long have you been here?" I wondered just how "temporary" it had been.

"Well, I was born in South America."

"Oh," I perked up. "You speak Spanish?"

He shook his head. "Nah. I was just born there. Actually, I've spent my whole life in . . ."

My interest faded along with the sound of Rico's voice as I calculated the time *I'd* already spent *here*. I was looking around the apartment and shaking my head inside. This just didn't make sense.

". . . And I've been here for about three months now," he concluded.

"Oh. Okay," I nodded, pretending as if I were actually mentally present for his little autobiography.

Rico smiled.

"That's real nice," I added, hoping there wasn't a question somewhere in his story that I'd missed my cue on. He nodded with a funny grin that made me think there was. I smiled with happy brows in the awkward silence. Then my stomach growled.

"Is that your stomach?" Rico asked.

Embarrassed, I put my hand over it, trying to muffle the sound. Skipping meals to come see some guy was nothing to be proud of. His knowing was even worse.

It growled again.

"Whoa! Let me fix you something to eat," Rico offered.

I shook my head. "No. That's okay," I said almost frantically.

I hoped that now I could use my hunger as an excuse to depart early. "Really. You don't have to—"

"It's no trouble at all," Rico insisted. "Besides, I can't just let you sit here with your stomach crying the way it is. You like pasta?"

"I do, but—"

"Coming right up!" Rico sprang up from the sofa, and headed toward the kitchen before I could say another word.

He flipped on the light, then bent down and reached into the bottom cabinet. It struck me as odd that he would store his Cup O' Noodles down there instead of in the pantry. I was further confused when he emerged with an actual pot. But when he went to the faucet to fill it with water, I suddenly got top ramen flashbacks and found my bearings once again.

Though his approach was slightly pushy, he was right. I knew if I sat there any longer with my stomach sounding off the way it was, I was bound to get sick, at which point I'd *really* have to stick around until my stomach settled back to normal. I definitely didn't want that.

I sat back against the sofa's extra-soft cushions and decided to make myself comfortable for, at most, another fifteen to twenty minutes.

Sitting solo, I figured I could at least make small talk while he made me lunch. That way we could get all of our conversation out of the way, and after slurping down those salty noodles, I could leave.

"So how do you like it so far?" I asked, referring to his new Florida residency.

Rico shrugged. "Oh, you know, so far so good. I'm loving the beach—Oh, you can turn the channel if you want," he gestured toward the remote control sitting on top of the entertainment center.

"Uh, okay." Indifferent to what was on television, I took the hint no less. He wanted to concentrate on heating up those noodles.

I got up and walked around the awkwardly-shaped coffee table, bumping my shin in the process. Stumbling, I crashed into the entertainment center, my hand landing smack dab on the remote.

Rico, apparently, didn't have the premium package, because when my palm pressed multiple buttons simultaneously, a gray snowstorm erupted.

"You okay?" Rico, concerned, inquired from behind the kitchen counter, catching the tail end of my tumble as I fumbled frantically with the remote. I punched in channel 8, trying to quiet the thunderous roar pouring from the television's speakers. A hair color commercial appeared across the screen.

I spun around.

"Yeah, I'm o—" Catching me by complete surprise was a package of uncooked pasta, four tomatoes, an onion, parsley, cloves of garlic, oregano, basil leaves, foil-wrapped French bread, ground meat, and a block of parmesan cheese alongside a grater. *Oh my God,* I thought to myself. He was about to cook!

"I'm okay . . ." I felt my way back to the sofa with my eyes pinned on Rico as he reached into one of the drawers for a cooking utensil.

"I've really need to get a new coffee table. I can't tell you how many bruises I've gotten from that thing." He shook his head. "Or maybe just get those corners filed down. My cousin keeps saying he's going to . . ."

Rico's mouth may have formed words, but they did not reach my ears. I was still hung up on the harvest around him. Steam was already beginning to pump from the pot. And it was really starting to smell good, even as things appeared to be in the early preparation stages.

Seeming to be in his element, Rico was focused. So was I. I forgot about the apartment's disarray, and focused my full attention on the man in it. My eyes took him in while he spoke. His complexion had a healthy glow; his teeth were pretty and straight; his lips were a natural pink shade, giving them a soft, sweet-tasting appearance. And his smile was male-model grade. He was just as I remembered him from the club—absolutely gorgeous.

As he continued preparing lunch from me, telling me all about his time here so far, I didn't take my eyes off of him. Smiling, I picked up the purple cup and took a sip.

My shoulders sprouted chill bumps in the evening air, but I resisted the urge to rub them, afraid that Rico would think I was trying to throw hints. As much as I wanted his arms around me, I dared not appear to be asking for it.

In the silence of the moonlit sky, I looked at Rico and smiled. "Where on earth did you learn to cook like that?"

Rico smirked and said, "Lots of practice."

My smile disappeared at the thought of him "practicing" on a different girl every weekend.

He explained when he noticed my expression.

"My mom worked nights, so, being the oldest, I had to cook for my little brothers and sisters a lot."

Dinner was delicious. His pasta contended with Leann's, who could cook better than anyone I could think of. I was having such a wonderful evening that I didn't want to leave. But it was already eleven o'clock. I was sleepy. And I didn't want to be too tired for my drive home.

Walking on my left, Rico finally wrapped his arm around me and rubbed my right shoulder, closing the two-foot gap between us just as we'd approached my car.

I pressed my key remote.

"This is your car?" Rico asked, surprised when I nodded yes. "Nice," he said.

I leaned against the driver's door, face-to-face with him.

"So, Sidney," he smiled, "I had a really good time tonight."

I picked a stray thread from his shirt and patted his chest. "Me too."

"Let me ask you question." He leaned into me.

I moved back slightly, stiffening. "Why in the world don't you have a boyfriend?—I mean, don't get me wrong. I'm *glad*. But look at you. I'm sure you have guys falling all over you."

"Not the *right* ones," I blushed, looking into his chestnuts eyes. "I guess I just haven't found the man that's really good for me," I whispered before looking away.

Rico turned my face back toward his with a gentle touch of his hand. My eyes followed. He tilted my chin up. I looked at him.

"Sidney . . ." Rico said.

"Yes?"

"You just found him."

I readied my mouth to respond, but before I could he kissed me.

CHAPTER 13

"How many guys have you been with?" Rico asked from the shower as I stood in the steam-filled room, keeping him company.

"Two," I answered, immediately thinking back to my Damon rebound.

I'd been so torn up over the whole episode involving Damon that the only way I could think of to numb the pain was to erase him as the last person I'd been with. It was silly. But it was somewhat effective. Sleeping with someone else stripped Damon of his "Last One" status. I couldn't change the fact that he was my first, but I'd be damned if he carried *both* titles. Being with someone else revoked Damon's secondary status, removing his territorial scent from my mind, body, and soul. At least, that was my emotional logic at the time.

I handed Rico a towel as he stepped out of the shower and onto the bath rug with beads of water chasing each other down his clay-colored chest. I swallowed as I watched him rub the porous cotton over his Black- and Brazilian body, starting from the neck I loved to nibble on so much, down to the feet that moved with such grace when we danced together 'center carpet' in his living room.

We'd began sleeping together about a week ago, and last night he told me he loved me. I can't even describe how wonderful it made me feel to hear that again. I hadn't heard those words from a guy since I was eighteen years old. I couldn't believe it. I was in love again.

Rico and I had been dating for two months, and we were learning a lot about each other. As I discovered during my first visit, contrary to what his name would suggest, Rico was anything but rich. In fact, he'd been out of work for quite some time, and had been collecting an unemployment check from North Carolina, using it to pay his half of the rent.

I, on the other hand, had recently taken a job as a customer service rep with an insurance company. Answering phones wasn't exactly my idea of public relations, but it was good to have a check coming in while I waited to land my coveted position. In my spare time I was volunteering at the recreation center near my job. It gave me something to do after work besides running to Rico's every day like I had been doing.

While Rico got dressed I sat in the living room and wrote in my journal.

"What do you write in there?" Rico, finally emerging from the bedroom, smiled curiously.

I closed it and stood up. "I don't know," I shrugged. "Just . . . stuff."

Rico walked over to me, linking his fingers through my belt loops, pulling me close to him. "Just stuff, huh? Anything about me in there?" He nuzzled up to my face, grinning playfully.

"Maybe." I put my arms around him. *"Mmmm"*—I closed my eyes, burying my face into his shoulder —"You smell good."

"That's my deodorant." He let me go and walked over to the foyer.

I followed him.

"So," he bent down and grabbed his shoes, "I'll call you later on when we take a break, okay?"

"Do you know how long you're going to be? I mean, is everything packed already, or do you have to help with that too?"

"Knowing Lee, *dishes* are probably still in the sink," he laughed.

"What?!"

"Just playing," Rico shook his head, laughing as I frowned. "Look, everything should be ready to go. I'm just moving some furniture and a couple boxes. That's it."

He tightened his shoelaces then stood up, putting his hands around my waist, wearing a smirk. "Why?" he asked. "You wanna come with me?" He began planting kisses all over my neck.

"No," I squirmed. "I want you to come with *me*."

"Next time, baby. Okay?" Rico assured me as I poked out my bottom lip. "It'd just I promised I'd help out today," he said, still seducing my neck in appeasement. "But we'll go next weekend." He puckered up.

I gave him a quick kiss on the lips.

I hadn't met him yet, but I wasn't liking this *Lee* person very much. I mean, hadn't he heard of professional moving services? So busy trying to save a hundred bucks he was pulling my man away from me on a beautiful Saturday afternoon.

But Rico didn't seem to mind moving heavy loads in this early-summer heat. He seemed happy to be of help.

I walked over to the counter and grabbed my keys.

"Well, just call me when you're done."

Rico yanked me by my pants loop and kissed me on the lips. It was like kissing a ripe peach. I think he had the softest lips I'd ever felt. I closed my eyes to enjoy it.

Rico was what some would call a *pretty boy*. He had dark, wavy hair, a smooth reddish-brown complexion, and with those perfect little teeth of his, he had a smile that made dead daisies bloom. He possessed this intoxicating sort of sex appeal that drove me absolutely crazy. Less than three months into the relationship and I was already head over heels for him.

Rico kissed me on the forehead. "Have fun, okay?" he told me.

"I'll try."

Just as I was leaving my apartment the phone rang. The caller ID read TASHA.

"Hey, I'm going to call you from my cell when I get downstairs, okay?"

"Okay" was all she could get out before I'd hung up the phone.

I grabbed my sweater, purse, and keys, then set the alarm before skirting out the door.

I fastened my seatbelt and dialed Tasha back.

"Hey, girlie." I adjusted my earpiece. "What are you doing?"

"Hey, Winks. Just taking a break from this mound of paperwork and thought I'd give you a ring."

Tasha had been doing really well in her new position, but said that she'd never anticipated there being so much paperwork involved. But she complained only for the sake of complaining. I knew she loved the feeling of being busy. She always did.

"So, what are you up to on this fine Saturday afternoon?" she asked.

"I'm on my way to the movies." I took a right out of my complex and onto the main road. The movie theater was just up the block, at the next light. I could've walked there if there if I wanted to.

"Oh. Well, let me say hi to Rico."

"He's not with me."

"Oh, you're meeting him up there?"

Distracted by the conversation, I slammed on my brakes the moment the light turned yellow, while the guy behind me emphatically expressed that he wished I hadn't.

"Uh . . . no," I told her, reading obscene gestures in my rearview mirror. "I'm going by myself."

"What?!" Tasha smacked her lips. "That's what *boyfriends* are for, you know!"

"And you should know these days, shouldn't you? How *are* things with you and Glen, by the way?"

Tasha was dating an ex-football-player-turned-sports anchor. I tuned in to one of those sports channels to catch a glimpse of him, and *Sweet Jesus* was he fine! Repeated knee injuries forced him into early retirement from the field, but he looked just as talented to me sitting behind that desk wearing that tailored Armani suit.

I was happy for Tasha. It was refreshing to even hear her use the word *boyfriend*. For a while there she had me worried. She'd seemed to have given up on finding love. But now that she and Glen were an item, she was back to being a believer.

"Well, enjoy your movie, Sidney. Next time get Rico's ass in the seat next to you. He's losing points with me right now. Just saying."

"And I love you, too, Tasha."

I didn't even wanna go there with her.

✦ ✦ ✦

It was 8:00 p.m. and I still hadn't heard from Rico since I'd left his apartment earlier that afternoon. I figured he and his friend probably went out for beers and a bite. I knew how guys were when they got a little exercise.

"What's wrong, Butterfly?" Mom detected something in my tone when I'd answered the phone twelve past the hour. I had hoped it was Rico calling, and was disappointed that it wasn't.

"Oh, nothing. How are you and Dad?" I asked, trying to sound more cheerful.

"We're fine—"

"Hey, Sid!" Dad spoke from the background.

"Your father said *hi*."

"Tell him I said hello. I miss you guys."

"We miss you, too, honey. How are things going down there?"

I really didn't feel like discussing anything too deep such as my job situation, so I just told Mom that things were really good, and that I was happy. If she knew how disappointed I was with my current employment she'd worry that I wasn't eating right and not getting enough rest. Under normal circumstances she would've been right to assume so, but Rico helped to alleviate a lot of those negative feelings. I was okay for the time being. He was the best distraction.

In the meantime I wanted to convey an attitude of contentment to Mom.

"Everything's just fine, Mom," I said as if I had a huge smile on my face.

"I hope you're taking care of yourself, Sidney," she said in spite of my attempt. "You haven't been night-clubbing too much, have you?"

"No, Mom."

"Well, good. You know how I feel about that."

"Yes, I do, Mom," I replied dryly. Sometimes Mom was a bit too old-fashioned.

"So, have you met anyone new?"

"And just how am I supposed to do that if I don't go out, Mom?" I hadn't told her about Rico yet. I didn't want to get her hopes up too high right away. Besides, after striking out with Damon I implemented a four-month rule. I figured a hundred and twenty days was a good period of time to begin predicting the course of a relationship. Rico and I were barely halfway there.

"Sidney," Mom began her rebuttal, "the club isn't the only place in the world where you can meet a man. There are plenty of other things to do, and places that you could go—museums, workshops, community events—to find someone to share your time and interests with."

Maybe there was. But I didn't know of any. Besides, the main reason I went to the club was to dance. Being in a building full of men who were all dressed up and smelling good was just a bonus. How could that be wrong? And if it was the *quality* of a man that Mom was referring to I'd quickly argue that if I was in the club (and I certainly considered myself to be a woman of quality), then why would be crazy to suspect that a quality man would be there too? Quality people liked to dance and party as much as the next person. And besides, I hadn't met Damon in a nightclub. I met that devil perched right up in church.

Mom probably thought I was hopeless trying to find that needle in a haystack, as she saw it. Perhaps I should've told her about Rico after all. But I just didn't feel the time was right. I wanted to make sure Rico was for keeps before Mom called the caterer. *Maybe next time we talk I'll tell her*, I thought to myself as I began feeling guilty about concealing this from Mom, and sort of anxious to spill the beans anyway.

"So, Mom," I quickly changed the subject, "how are you and Dad?"

"We're hanging in there, sweetie. You know your Dad," she laughed. "There's never a dull moment."

"Yeah, I bet," I laughed with her. "And Chaylene and the kids? Have you talked to them lately?"

Mom stopped laughing and said what she always said when I asked that.

"Have *you?*"

CHAPTER 14

Everything was blurry *as Chaylene lie the lone occupant of the cold, king-sized bed. She'd been up for as long as he'd been out. He'd promised to return before ten, but it was after five a.m. and Dennis had yet to return, or call.*

Chaylene was frantic. She pictured him on the side of the road in a horrible accident, in need of help. She pictured him lying in an emergency room hospital bed, wondering if she'd get word of his condition. Then, she pictured him frolicking in the company of some tramp, smiling and admiring her intellectual simplicity. She didn't know whether to feel panicked or pissed. This wasn't the first time Dennis had stayed out late, but lately his hours of arrival seemed to be getting more and more ridiculous. How could drinks with the guys turn into such an all-night, early-morning affair? The clock told her it was bull.

She decided on pissed as her pounding head searched for a dry spot on the pillow.

When Dennis finally arrived at a shameful 6:46 a.m., slowly and ever-so-precisely inserting his key into the lock, Chaylene was waiting at the door.

"I won't bother asking where you've been," she said, her foot against the door. "Judging by the stupid look on your face it's more than obvious. I guess the real question is, where will you be staying?"

Dennis hadn't fully recovered from the shock of seeing her there.

"Chaylene, sweetheart," he chuckled nervously, "time got away from me."

"So has your mind. Do you know what time it is?" she hissed in a fiery whisper, mindful of the kids sleeping upstairs.

"Look, just let me come in and I'll explain." Dennis put pressure on the door. But Chaylene wasn't budging.

"You're not getting in here."

Dennis looked at her like she had lost her mind.

"Chaylene, it's late. Now quit playing." He finally forced his way through the door, nearly knocking her to the floor. Chaylene was pretty strong for her slim build, but she was no match for Dennis, who outweighed her by almost eighty pounds.

She caught her balance and shot Dennis a piercing stare. "You're right. It is late. But you're the only one playing around here. Now get out before you wake the kids." She pushed him toward the door

"*Get out?*" Dennis chuckled again. "Don't you think you're overreacting?"

"Dennis," Chaylene spoke in a slow, calm voice, "if I were overreacting, I would twist your balls off like grapes, and then try to make wine—Now get out!" she stomped her foot as a sample of what he could expect if he didn't do as she asked.

"*Chaylene!*" Dennis's eyes enlarged with shock. Just the very mention of his testicles being handled in such a fashion made him light-headed. "Baby, why are you talking like this?"

"The *moon* called it a night before you did," she snapped, catching glimpse of the golden hue over his left shoulder. "And that *'hanging out with the fellas'* excuse is as tired as I am of your lies, so don't insult my intelligence," she warned with hands firmly planted on her hips. "Now," she took a deep breath, calming herself again, "I want you to leave my house."

Seeing the pain behind the anger, Dennis's eyes softened. He reached for Chaylene's arm, but she snatched away.

"Don't touch me! You come home looking like *guilt*, and reeking of twenty-dollar-perfume and you want me to let you inside?" She clutched the collar of her robe like he was a dirty stranger. "You think I want you next to me? Touching me? Breathing on me? You stink!" she spat.

Dennis tried to explain himself.

"Chaylene, baby, I was out with Mitch . . . a—and Ron," he stuttered his words, ". . . and we ended up at this spot downtown—"

"I can't believe you're going to stand here and lie to me. Looking the way you do, you're gonna still stand here and fucking—"

"Chaylene—"

"Get out!" she shouted, her chest rising in preparation for a fight. Blood rushed to her neck. Her nostrils flared. Her eyes turned red.

Dennis searched those eyes but found no signs of ambivalence. In fact, he saw just how serious she truly was.

He wanted to apologize. He wanted to make one last plea. He wanted to grab Chaylene, pull her close, and promise her he'd never do it again. But he knew his promises didn't carry much weight these days. And he knew he really didn't want to explain what "it" was. There was nothing he could say. Chaylene's eyes dared him to try.

Chaylene twisted the doorknob, forcing open the heavy oak. The faint sound of a barking dog rang out from somewhere in the distance.

Dennis looked at Chaylene. She looked away. He kept looking at her for close to a minute, hoping she'd change her mind about him leaving. But eventually he found himself back in his car, just as unaware of his destination as he was of his place in Chaylene's heart.

As her husband backed out of the driveway, behind the sturdy, sound-proof door Chaylene wept. Sitting at the bottom of the staircase, her face in her hands, she felt her world crumbling around her. Dennis was all she'd known since she was nineteen. She wondered what was happening. How he could betray her this way. She'd never cheated on him, though it certainly wasn't due to lack of opportunity. Finding opportunity to cheat on Dennis would've been as easy for Chaylene as walking out the front door. But she never went there. She never threatened him with her beauty. The thought of being unfaithful to Dennis had never even crossed her mind in all the years they'd been together. It hurt her to send him away. But it hurt even more that he would disrespect her this way.

As she struggled over her next decision, Chaylene's senses began overwhelming her, underscoring the facts her heart so desperately tried to dismiss. And if the smell of his jacket, the sound of his lies, or the bad taste in her mouth weren't valid enough reasons to send Dennis away, then surely the lipstick on his lapel was.

✦ ✦ ✦

When my flight arrived at Chicago O' Hare it was all I could do to get off the plane. The little girl sitting behind me kicked my seat practically the entire flight, like she was practicing for her black belt. When the fasten your seatbelt light went off I jumped up, quickly grabbed my bag from the overhead compartment, and was one of the first people off the plane despite my rear cabin assignment.

Chaylene was picking me up from the airport. The thought of seeing her again made me nervous. There was no question, I had mixed feelings about it. I was surprised when she'd called me last week. We rarely spoke. In the past, Dennis and I spoke more than Chaylene and I did, so when she invited me up for the weekend I knew things had to be pretty severe.

Past issues aside, I had to be there for her. I always knew that the worst thing someone could be is *absent* when someone else really needed them.

On the phone, Chaylene revealed to me that she and Dennis were getting a divorce—or rather, she was divorcing him. She'd kicked him out of the house, and they'd been separated for a week since he'd come home late one night. She told me how she'd threatened to play hacky sack with his nuts—or was it pool? Whatever it was, it sounded pretty painful. And if I were a man, it certainly would've gotten me out of the house for sure.

As I walked through the airport my heart did that funny dance. Immediately, I began feeling insecure. I always felt that way when I was around Chaylene. She was so beautiful. A real perfect ten. You thought you were beautiful until she walked into the room. I knew firsthand.

Growing up she had Victoria's Secret legs with a Frederick's of Hollywood chest, while *I* was built like the Pink Panther. Luckily I improved in high school. But then, so did she. No matter how much I improved I could never catch up with her.

When I reached the gate I saw my sister standing in the crowd of other passenger-greeters. Chaylene was tall like Mom, so it was easy to spot her, but as I got closer, I almost didn't recognize her.

My paced slowed as I immediately took notice of her effortless appearance. This was not the Chaylene I knew. Her hair was pulled back in a fuzzy bun. She wore baggy sweats that swallowed her. And those dingy-laced sneakers she'd put on her feet were unsuitable for public appearances. I suppose it would've been a contradiction to put on makeup, so she wore none—not even mascara, which she wore faithfully. She said it brightened up her face. I never knew just how much until now.

Unsure of how to greet her, I gave Chaylene a one-handed hug that left a good four inches between us.

"Hi, Chaylene." I added two quick pats on her back.

"Hey, Sidney." She did the same.

Before we parted, my nose caught whiff of her thick, papaya-scented hair. Her face smelled like moisturizer, and her clothes of fabric softener. She was clean. But judging by the way she looked one wouldn't have assumed so.

Chaylene and I had the same hair color, hair texture, high cheekbones, and identical complexions. We also shared a widow's peak front and center where they're found. But that was where our physical similarities ended. Physically, she was what every man wanted: perfect height, perfect size, and perfect breasts. I think childbirth bumped her up from an already-impressive C-cup to a testosterone-enticing D. Her hair was several inches longer than mine, extending toward her tailbone. And, although I never saw it much, she had an award-winning smile. The best smile four grand and three years of braces could buy.

As if God hadn't thrown enough beauty her way, Chaylene had eyes that seemed to sparkle. I'd swear her pupils were set in multi-carat diamonds. She had deep, double dimples, heart-shaped lips, and her flawless skin was as supple as a newborn baby's. No wonder she was able to snag a guy like Dennis. What she lacked in personality she definitely made up for in looks. But *this* Chaylene was far from the perfectly-put-together, beauty-conscious queen I was used to.

Careful not to look her over, I asked about the boys.

"They're with Dennis," she told me, then glanced down at the lonely bag by my side. "You have more stuff?"

"Nope. Just this."

I figured, given the circumstances, we wouldn't be doing a whole lot of outdoor recreation. Therefore, I packed light for the weekend.

When we made it down to short-term parking, Chaylene pointed her key at the shiny new Bentley and made it whistle.

"Nice car."

"Thanks." She popped the trunk.

I tossed my bag inside.

Chaylene and Dennis sure don't seem to be hurting for anything, I thought to myself, envious. But then I realized that even with all their financial wealth and success, it couldn't buy happiness for the two of them right now. Chaylene's face was evident of that.

I got inside the car and fastened my seatbelt, sinking into the soft leather.

By the time we finally arrived at the six-bed-four bath home in the richest part of town I was certain that I'd seen Oprah, at least, three times since we'd entered the posh, gated community. I went upstairs to put my things away while Chaylene went to the kitchen to fix herself a drink. After emptying my suitcase I freshened up in the bathroom, then headed off to go join her downstairs. On my way I passed by her and Dennis's bedroom.

Curious, I peeked, then walked inside, the huge, wood-floored room, spacious and tidy, and looked around at all the little knick-knacks that served a decorative purpose. Everything painted a picture of perfection: the crisp white walls were clean and border-free; the exercise ball was in the corner near the flat screen, silver and plump; the pictures of Ty and Alex on the nightstand by the bed that captured precious moments of childhood; the African art Dennis loved to collect, with faces that smiled and frowned at me as if worn by actual people. Everything gave the room character. And the burgundy rug, fluffy and round, invited any pet to have an enjoyable lay.

Even with all the home furnishings that attempted to warm the room, it still felt cold. The flimsy white drapes that floated like sails on a summertime vessel were reminiscent of frost from hot mouths of human beings bundled in heavy clothing. Even the walls resembled large sheets of ice, solid and burning-cold to the touch. I hated being cold. That ranked second on my list of micro-dislikes (cheap shoes and long lines ranking first and third, respectively).

Feeling the draft, I backed out of the room and continued downstairs.

Chaylene was still in the kitchen having some scotch. I didn't think she drank that hard stuff, but when I walked into the living room she was tossing back the last few drops of the chest hair-sprouting elixir.

I could appreciate that she wanted to unwind, but hoped she wouldn't have too much. Chaylene joined the Navy every time she got drunk. The language that came out of her mouth when she had been guzzling booze all night was enough to scare off any awestruck admirers she may have had at the top of the evening. It just didn't match her look. It was a classic case of cognitive dissonance, as Tasha would label it.

My sister licked her lips, then sat the empty glass down on the marble counter top, leaving behind but a memory of what once filled the 4-ounce crystal.

"Would you like one?" she offered.

"Uh . . . sure. Thanks," I took a seat in the plush, leather chair that swallowed me whole. Uneasy, I looked around the beautiful living space, trying to find comfort in being in my sister's home again. I'd only visited a couple times—when Mom and Dad were with me. Never by myself.

Chaylene uncapped the expensive-looking capsule, and as she poured us both a glass, I noticed the tan line on her finger.

I turned my head.

"So you said the kids are with Dennis?"

"Yeah. He's got them this weekend." She picked up the glasses and walked into the living room, handing me one before plopping down on the loveseat adjacent to me.

She took a smooth, heavy sip.

"So . . ." she cupped her glass, "how was the flight?"

I took a tiny sip of the pee-colored poison and licked my lips. "Not bad. A little bumpy. But not bad."

I figured she had bigger problems. The last thing she cared about was a preschooler kicking my seat.

I took another careful sip of my scotch, which tasted how isopropyl smelled, and kept my eyes affixed inside my glass, allowing her to set the tone and pace. After a few moments she told me that Dennis had confessed to having an affair.

"How long?" I asked.

Chaylene shook her head, gazing into space. "Three months," she muttered, then took the last sip of her drink. "That man has been fucking around on me for three months. Three . . . fucking . . . months!"

The rage in her voice startled me. My eyes widened and my body stiffened.

"Anyway," she looked down into her empty glass, "I don't want to talk about it. I called you up here to keep me company, not watch me sit around being depressed."

In spite of that conviction Chaylene drifted off again in her thoughts. While she was gone, I noticed the olive-tinted stress bags that had settled themselves underneath her eyes. I cleared my throat.

"Okay, well . . ." I sat my drink down and moved to the edge of my chair, clasping my hands together in an unnatural way, "I'm just glad to be here," I declared with words that flowed effortlessly off my tongue, yet felt very strange leaving my mouth.

Chaylene pulled her eyes from space and put them on me. I looked back, careful not to wear a look of sympathy, but lending a supportive smile designed to shield the awkwardness we shared. It felt like she was looking right through me. Chaylene had interrogative eyes that made you feel like the unwilling recipient of a mental X-ray. She could sniff out inauthenticity like no one else I knew.

Dark and penetrating, her eyes made mine lose their confidence. Growing nervous, my top lip was on the verge of trembling. My smile was waning. The room was warming. I pulled my hair back, twisting it up in a knot, fleeing her uncomfortable stare.

As my hands were busy behind my head, Chaylene's eyes moved from mine, to my left arm and its scar that ran just above my elbow, curling eight inches inward toward my wrist. Frozen for a moment, she quickly blinked herself out of her disturbed gaze.

She sat her drink down and got up. "Let's sit out by the pool."

"Sure." I tucked the ends of my hair under the large knot, and tried to sound peppy. "I could use some fresh air."

After Chaylene drew the blinds I followed her out onto the deck that fashioned an Olympic-style pool that resurrected my envy. I looked around the yard and patio and saw so many lovely things: colorful shrubs, a pond, a fountain—all the soft touches that comprised a beautiful home—and found it hard to imagine it as any place but a happy one. The volleyball net loosely draped across the pool, and the built-in barbecue pit still housing pale charcoals were sure to inspire many social gatherings. This was a house built for fun. But Dennis and Chaylene didn't entertain too often. In fact they were typically homebodies who preferred the company of only each other, which made it neon-sign suspicious for Dennis to keep such late hours socializing *"with the guys"* all of a sudden. It didn't take intuition for my sister to know that something was wrong. Just common sense.

As Chaylene and I sat by the pool and said absolutely nothing to each other, I soon forgot all about the home's comforts and amenities. They didn't matter anymore. Fun was a far place from here. I thought about my nephews, and wondered what impact this was having on them. I had only been there twenty minutes and already the misery had seeped into my skeleton. I knew this would be no vacation.

It was weird being with my sister, just sitting there in the sunset, looking at the sky. I didn't know what to say, so I played it safe and let the evening air do the talking. But I'd hoped that just my being there would somehow comfort Chaylene. Though it was awkward, I had to admit that I liked that she'd called me. It made me feel like, for once, she needed me. And even better, that she wanted me around.

CHAPTER 15

Saturday morning shined down on me as Chaylene did what the sun on my face couldn't.

"Wake up!" she shook me as I buried myself further into a deep couch cushion. "It's eleven thirty. Time to get up."

I turned over onto my back, squinting up at her.

"Get up, Sidney!" she groaned.

I opened my eyes all the way and blinked twice as things slowly came into focus. Chaylene was standing over me showing a drastic improvement in her appearance. Her long, curly hair was blow-dried straight. Her brows had been freshly-arched. She'd paired a form-fitting, yellow blouse with dark denim, and wore peekaboo pumps that revealed matching yellow polish. Her makeup was flawless with her lipstick coated thick. She was even wearing her wedding band again. Chaylene was back!

She put her hand on her hip and gave me a threatening stare when I didn't move.

"Okay, okay," I said, patting down my scarecrow hair with one hand, and scratching my side with the other. That scotch was like a damn tranquilizer. I'm glad Chaylene was my sister and not some psycho I'd just met at a bar.

"We're going out today," my sister announced.

"Where?" I yawned.

"Anywhere." She straightened the creased cushions as I slid my way off the couch onto the floor.

Six bedrooms and I couldn't find my way to one last night.

I gave myself a good stretch. "Okay. Well, just give me forty-five minutes."

Chaylene suggested we go shopping. She said that using Dennis's credit cards always made her feel better. Armed with some platinum, she drove toward The Magnificent Mile as I rode shotgun.

On the way to the upscale section of Chicago's Michigan Avenue we listened to Gloria Gaynor's *I Will Survive*. We were so funny, driving down the highway, singing at the top of our lungs like we were in a karaoke contest. I saw that Chaylene could be fun when she wanted to. I enjoyed this side of her, *and* the song. But after its sixth consecutive play I wondered if my ears would survive the trip.

When we finally arrived it was *game on*. Chaylene hit up every overly-expensive boutique she could find. As I shadowed her from shop to shop, appointed her official box-and-bag carrier, it was obvious that moderation was not on her mind. Every shop from A to Z gave her approval numbers to bury Dennis alive financially. She was on some serious retail revenge, and even tried to get me to pick out some items for myself, saying it was Dennis's treat. I declined the ominous offer, reluctant to get in the middle of their domestic dispute. The last thing I needed was Dennis coming at me with his hand out after he and Chaylene reconciled. Playing it safe, I limited the extent of my participation to helping her accessorize the outfits she'd picked out for herself.

But watching Chaylene try on all those things she didn't even need made me realize even more just how sad the whole thing was. She was kidding herself if she thought clothes would console her. It was only a temporary diversion, at best. After the clothes were all hung up and put away the pain would resurface. I had a closet full of experience.

"Where did you get that?" I asked a half-naked Chaylene, who'd pulled off her blouse to try on one that looked just like it. We occupied a giant-sized dressing room that was bigger than my bedroom.

Chaylene looked down at her necklace.

"Oh, Mom gave it to me after Grannah died. Remember?"

I shook my head *No,* while fascinated by the blue benitoite crystal pendant that had always captured the slightest bit of light—even in the darkest of settings—and scattered it across the room like a disco ball.

Chaylene rolled my late grandmother's gem between her fingers. "She said Grannah would've wanted me to have it. Mom used to wear it—"

"All the time. I know . . ." my voice trailed off, still hypnotized by the rare gem that belonged to my grandmother before she'd given it to Mom.

"Yes," Chaylene sighed, zoning out herself. Her eyes told me she was with me on Memory Lane. That was a rough year for our family. I felt my emotions conjuring up.

"Well, anyway," Chaylene shook herself out of the spell. "Let me try this on. It looks a little small, but

170

you never know." She pulled the yellow blouse over her head.

Six thousand four hundred and twenty-six dollars later, Chaylene and I had shopped up an appetite. We ducked into a little Italian bistro on the way home, and began winding down over Chianti. As the opera music and burning candles relaxed us, I asked Chaylene how often she came here.

"Dennis and I would come every week when we first moved here. We were really too poor to eat out as often as we did, but we were even lazier when it came to unpacking all those dishes." She laughed.

I laughed, too.

"If it wasn't cereal or sandwiches, it was this place." She looked around and smiled. "But it gave us a chance to break in the city, you know? We were so excited to be here. We had a fresh start. A brand-new life to build. We were so in love."

Her eyes glistened as she reminisced of better days. I never saw two people more in love. Even the love Mom and Dad shared with each other seemed almost to pale next to Chaylene and Dennis's mutual adoration. And even though it was her idea, it was plain to see that this divorce was tearing my sister apart.

Seeing my sister in such pain, I wanted to get up from my side of the table, throw my arms around her, and tell her it would be alright. But our relationship was too estranged. I didn't know *how* to be affectionate toward her. It would've gone down as the most awkward moment in history. So instead, I remained on my side of the booth and just listened as my sister described things illustrated only in my dreams, and moments that, for her, were to become merely memories.

After our meals were served Chaylene ate every morsel on her plate. She could really put it away. Where it went was always a mystery. High metabolism was an understatement. Chaylene burned calories *eating*.

I pushed my half-finished gelato to the side, not as metabolically-blessed as her, and took a deep breath of happy air while Chaylene enjoyed her biscotti and wine.

Full, and finding myself getting caught up in the rare moment of hanging out with my big sis, I couldn't resist telling her so.

"I'm really glad I came, Chaylene." I smiled blissfully. "It's so good to see you again and to spend this time with you."

"Oh, don't get all *Sidneymental* on me," Chaylene erased the smile from my face, then took a sip of the attitude-relaxer that seemed to stop working.

Would it have killed her to return the gesture? Would it have burdened her that much to say something nice to me?

I ran my finger across the rim of my glass, hurt and wondering why I even bothered.

"It's good to see you, too," she finally reciprocated. It was forced. But I didn't care. It still felt good to hear.

Chaylene set her glass down on the table and wiped her already-clean hands on a napkin in order to flee from the sappy moment.

My smiled reappeared. Chaylene looked at me as it did, unable to draw a sincere one across her own face. Stuck in a confused and conflicted state, her eyelashes did the dirty work of concealing her own sentiment. She blinked stubbornly—tensely—as I looked at her. I'd never seen someone try so hard to suppress their softer emotions.

"So," she picked up her glass and brought it to her mouth, "how are things in Florida?"

After another half hour of wine-sipping Chaylene whipped out the gold card this time and signaled for the waiter.

"So," she picked up the pen to authorize the triple-digit transaction after our waiter had returned with the check, "you ready to go somewhere else?"

"What do you have in mind?" I queried.

"Well, there's this little tiki-like bar just up the road. I figured we could drop by for minute," she said while adding in the gratuity.

"Oh, wait, let me get that." I pulled some cash from my purse.

Chaylene stopped me.

"No. Put that away. It's the *least* Dennis can do."

I didn't want to appear too needy in front of her, as if I couldn't even cover the tip. I'm sure she was aware of my lousy job situation and I certainly didn't want her to feel as if she had to throw money my way like I was some charity case.

"Well, actually, I think our waiter deserves a double tip today." I tossed my twenty-percent contribution onto the table as we stood up.

"Fine with me." Chaylene tucked her purse under her arm. "Better for him. Let's go."

✦ ✦ ✦

As we idled in the valet line I took note of this place Chaylene had brought us to.

"So *this* is where the beautiful ones mingle?" I asked as I looked around, pleased.

Chaylene threw the car into park and we got out.

"Yep," she replied, exchanging the key for a ticket from the valet. "And the two of us fit right in," she added confidently as she strolled those long legs of hers inside like she was on the catwalk, sounding the most conceited I'd ever heard her sound.

Chaylene's confidence was completely justified, of course. Two seconds through the entrance and every guy's eye was on her. Even the women were checking her out. But certainly not with the same approval. I was pulling my share, but nowhere near the volume Chaylene was. I'd wished she would've told me we'd end up at a bar. I could've spruced up my look a little more. I was wearing more of a hanging-out-with-my-big-sister outfit. But then I guess it didn't really matter what I had on. I would be in my sister's shadow regardless.

As Chaylene and I sat at the bar men lined up against the bamboo fence like paper dolls, all waiting their turn to solicit my sister. She kept them all at bay with commanding eyes that dared any one of them to approach her a moment too soon. After a drink she began to loosen up, and one bold guy's timing was perfect.

"Ladies, you both are looking very lovely this evening," he spoke—*after* his cologne.

"Thanks," Chaylene smiled like it was the first time she'd ever heard that while I looked him up and down wondering what was wrong with his olfaction. How the hell could he not know he'd spilled the entire bottle of *Axe* on himself? I blinked hard as the overwhelming fumes made my eyes water.

Chaylene, on the other hand, must've been holding her breath. She didn't even flinch. She sat there smiling, seemingly interested in his lame conversation. Everything out his mouth was about his small construction business and his financial worth. His construction business was *this*. His construction business was *that*. He had *this*. He had *that*. Little did he know he was bragging to a woman whose husband earned way more than he could imagine. Surely she wasn't as impressed as she'd led him to believe. This guy was small potatoes compared to Dennis. And I was bored with him.

Not a complete case of inutility, however, Chaylene's admirer did order us some drinks. I stood back and sipped on that free drink elbow-to-elbow with my sister as his look begged for privacy. He wasn't getting any. Unfortunately for every guy in the spot I was Chaylene's Siamese twin for the night and didn't plan on making room for anyone. If they wanted to talk to her it would cost them two drinks for the attention of one.

To my delight, Chaylene *poof!-be-gone'd* him as soon as her drink disappeared. "Enjoy your night!"

She waved him on his way politely. "And thanks for the drinks."

"Yeah. Thanks," I raised my glass, smirking as I slurped the last few drops hiding between ice cubes.

When he was gone I turned to Chaylene.

"So, how are you feeling?"

"Sidney, didn't I tell you I don't want to talk about it?!" she blew my ears back.

I looked at her like she was crazy.

"I was talking about the drinks." I blinked my wide-opened eyes in shock. She was such a hot head. I never knew when that blowtorch tongue of hers was going to scorch me.

"Oh," Chaylene looked down at her empty glass, pausing where an apology should've been. "I'm feeling . . . like another. Bartender!" She held her empty glass in the air and flagged him down with twenty-dollar bait.

"This round is on me." I placed a crisp bill of my own on the bar.

Chaylene looked at me with tipsy eyes. "I pay. You pay. They pay."—She pointed to all the guys watching her—"*Who cares?* As long as I get drunk. *Kheeee - Heeee!*" she laughed, spraying me with mango margarita mist from her mouth.

There had to be no less than twenty guys that had approached my sister within the two-hour period we were there compared to my eye-fanning four. Each had their own little gimmick, trying to outdo one another. Chaylene sat back like the queen bee and soaked up all the attention as I saw that *Ms. Popularity* still reigned.

After dismissing, yet, another hopeful wooer, Chaylene looked across the bar. "Look. There's Dennis's friend, Ron," she said.

I swung my neck around. "Where?"

"Dang! Don't make it so obvious, Sidney!" she scolded me.

"*Where?*" I whispered, looking less conspicuous this time.

"There," she nodded. "In the white shirt."

I didn't say anything but it had to be written all over my face.

"And don't even think about it. He's married," Chaylene burst my quickly-forming bubble.

I relaxed my posture.

"Besides," she gave him the evil eye from across the bar, "he's probably an adultering asshole just like Dennis." She raised her glass to her mouth, pausing before taking a sip. Then with a premeditated look in her eyes, said, "Watch this."

"Chaylene, what are you doing?" I questioned as I watched her give another contender the OK. She was clearly using him. Hadn't he seen the others come and go having only fulfilled the purpose of buying us drinks? He had to know he'd suffer the same fate.

Chaylene tossed her drink back then sat her empty glass on the bar. "Let's give Ronnie Boy something to talk about."

"Chaylene, I don't think it's such a good idea to flirt with other men in front of your husband's friends." She was taking this ego-boosting exercise too far. Now she was playing with fire.

"Screw him! Dennis has done a lot worse. Besides," she pulled down her blouse for that added effect, "a girl can talk."

I didn't understand her bizarre behavior.

"So why did you even bother putting your ring back on, then? If you were going to act this way, why did you even bother?"

Chaylene chuckled. "Sidney, haven't you paid attention to anything? This thing is a magnet." She waved her wedding band in the air. "Do you know for the past several years I've had to beat the men off like a pack of hungry dogs?"

I looked around the bamboo fence at all the men who did seem to have their tongues hanging out.

"You'd think it would be a deterrent," she looked at the plain, shiny gold band and shook her head, "but by the absolute contrary. Just ask *Dennis!*" she grimaced.

"Chaylene—"

Before I could finish my objection the guy came walking up with that hungry dog grin on his face she'd just educated me on.

I sneered as he approached.

"Well, *hello* . . ." he said, looking Chaylene up and down, flashing a row of ultra-white teeth at us that were too ivory to be real. His purple polo was wrinkled and had those little balls of its own fabric dangling from it, like it had been worn a billion times before tonight.

Chaylene smiled back at *Gritty Grape*. "Would you like to join us?" she asked.

"More than I should probably say," he replied, pulling up a barstool.

I rolled my eyes.

"Can I get you a drink, Beautiful?"

"Sure," Chaylene said. "We'd like two mango margaritas, please."

"No thanks," I flipped my wrist, having my fill for the evening and, quite frankly, tired of this whole charade. Chaylene, on the other hand, was on drink number four and looked as if she was just getting started.

The guy got the bartender's attention while I looked over at Dennis's friend to make sure he wasn't seeing any of this. For the time being he was preoccupied with his own little fan club, as swarms of pretty women competed for his attention. From what I could tell he was shooting them all down. I guess he wasn't anything like Chaylene had said after all. One by one, I witnessed each woman walk away with that perplexed look that begged the question of why Ron had even come. Just as I had begun to wonder.

"I'm going to the bathroom," I announced with an attitude.

Neither Chaylene nor her company acknowledged me as I got up and walked off.

I couldn't believe this. I was in a bar full of mostly good-looking men, and they all wanted my sister. My married-ass sister!

In my frustration I walked past Ron, looking at him secretly, or so I'd planned. He looked right at me, his face saying that he'd seen something familiar in mine.

I hurried into the restroom.

By the time I came out, fifteen minutes later, I was surprised to see the guy in the purple shirt back on his pigeon stoop. *Maybe his card got declined*, I thought to myself, knowing he was most likely too broke to try to play Paymaster.

Chaylene was standing at the bar alone. I watched her for a moment, taking advantage of the opportunity to do so without reprimand. She looked so vulnerable. Lonely, even. In all her arrogance and brashness I caught glimpses of sadness and disappointment behind the deceptively-cool hair toss she so habitually executed for as long as I had known her. From across the way her true beauty shined through in spite of herself.

But as I approached that all changed.

"Oh, there you are," she said. "I thought you fell in."

I stood there, embarrassed to find a handsome man holding two drinks turn around, handing one of them to Chaylene.

"This is Roderick Lane," Chaylene told me. "He's a sports agent. He reps two Chicago Bears and one Cub."

He proudly extended his hand toward me, smirking at Chaylene's cheerleading style of introduction. "Hi. And *you* are?"

"Karen Less!" I folded my arms, passing on the palm shake.

He looked at Chaylene like what was my problem. She laughed and batted her hand at me. "Sidney, quit being silly. This is my sister, Sidney. She's visiting from Florida," she explained while I looked over my shoulder to place Ron again. I found him enjoying his drink—directly across from us.

I had to do something.

"Um, did my phone *RING* while I was gone?"

"Sidney," Chaylene's brows collapsed, "you took your phone with you."

"Ohhh, yeah. That's right," I pretended to remember while Chaylene looked at me like I was high.

Chaylene and the guy continued their conversation. He was laughing. She was laughing. They were having such a slap-happy good time.

"Whew!" I shook my head. "You know, that bathroom line was so long we practically formed a *RING* around the building." I chuckled. "You'd think they were giving out *diamonds* or something." Two more phony chuckles spilled out of my mouth.

Paying me no mind Chaylene and her sports agent went back to their nighttime negotiations, but it wasn't long before I interrupted again.

"You know, I think we're too close to this speaker!" I shouted, plugging my ears with my fingers. "My ears are starting to RING*!*"

The two of them looked at each other.

"So, Sidney," he finally turned to me, "you're from Florida, huh? I was just down in Bradenton last month. Are you familiar?"

"Hmmm . . ." I rubbed my chin, shaking my head. It doesn't *RING* a b—"

"I'm going to *WRING* your neck if you don't quit acting silly!" Chaylene put an end to my antics. "And get that toilet paper off your shoe!"

I looked down, realizing why I'd received such an increase in attention in the last few minutes, but more interested in knowing why it took Chaylene five minutes to tell me.

"You know, speaking of toilet paper," I used one shoe to free the single-ply sheet from the other," I'm feeling pretty crappy. We should go."

"Sidney, we just got here."

"Just got here? Chaylene, we've been here for more than two hours."

"Sidney," she looked at me impatiently, "would you relax? Look"—she pointed to the other bar—"why don't you go over there and mingle."

"Chaylene, I'm tired. I really just wanna go," I insisted.

I liked Dennis. I figured any man who could put up with Chaylene's attitude was worth giving a second chance. I didn't want to see her jeopardize any hopes of their getting back together, especially over something as phony as all of this was.

I tugged on her arm. "Come on, Chaylene." I was trying to remove her from Ron's radar before he saw her with this other man and went back and gave Dennis a hyperbolic play-by-play.

"Sidney!" She pushed me away, loud and visibly under the influence.

That got Ron's attention.

I panicked as Dennis's friend sized up the scene, wondering what his buddy's wife was doing out at a bar cozying up to some other fella.

"Look," I whispered to Chaylene, hoping she'd do the same, "I know what you're trying to do. But what happened between you and Dennis had nothing to do with him thinking no one else would want you. You can stop trying to prove yourself. Yes. Yes. We all know that *evvvvveryone* wants you," I said with an extra-long eye roll.

Chaylene looked at me.

I shook my head, realizing I'd said that last part out loud.

"Look, Chaylene, all you're doing is giving Dennis's friend good reason to run back and tell him everything you're doing. Don't play these games. It's stupid. Now let's go." I tugged on her arm again. "I'm ready to leave."

"Uh—if you want to go ahead, I can take her home," Chaylene's hungry dog told me, then smiled at her.

I whipped my head around like The Exorcist. "I'm sorry. Was I talking to you, Mr. Rogerick? Was anybody talking to you right now?"

He looked at me surprised.

"Just shut up and mind your own stinkin' business!" I told him.

I didn't respect this man. Chaylene was right. Whether in spite of, or *because of*, men were gravitating toward her as she wore the wedding ring she'd made no attempts to hide.

"And don't you hear what we're talking about? Can't you take a hint?" I snapped at him again. "If your eyes don't work surely your ears do. *She's married!* So why don't *you* divorce this situation?" I turned my head away from him and loud-whispered, *"Asshole!"*

"What?" He moved in closer and stood over me. "Now wait just a damn minute—"

"Get away from her!" Chaylene sprang to her feet, getting between the two of us.

We might not have been the closest but I was still her little sister.

As if holding back some form of rage, he sucked on his bottom lip. "Alright." He shook his head. "Alright then, I'm out!"

"Good!" I stuck out my chest, bolder than I should've been, then quickly cowered when it looked as if I had pushed my luck. Securing my safety, though, Chaylene stood between the two of us until he took himself, and that threatening look of his, to the other side of the bar.

Following him with my contemptuous eyes they led me straight to Ron. His eyes were glued steadily on my sister and me.

"Let's get out of here." I reached for Chaylene's hand.

"Dammit, Sidney!" she snatched away, racing toward the exit.

When I got to the front entrance of the tiki bar, Chaylene, standing there with her arms folded and looking like an angry version of Mom, had already given the valet our ticket.

"*I'm* driving," I told her, aware that she was in no condition to be toting us around town.

She ignored me.

When the valet pulled the car around I handed him a ten dollar bill, quickly claimed the keys, and walked around to the driver's side of the car.

Chaylene grabbed the passenger side door handle, fuming. "Why did you do that?" she asked me from across the Bentley's roof.

"Because you're not in any condition to drive."

"No. Back there!" She gestured back toward the bar. "Why did you do that?"

"Do what? Embarrass you in front of some idiot you'll never see again?"

"Intercept my action."

"Action? Please. You didn't want any of those guys."

"That's not the point. I'm a grown woman. I know what I'm doing."

"Really?"

"Really!"

"And what were you doing, Chaylene?"

"For the first time in a week I was feeling happy. I was having fun. But you ruined that."

"Chaylene, the only thing I ruined was your chances at ruining the possibility of you and Dennis reconciling."

"*Reconciling?* Are you out of your green-eyed mind?" She looked at me as if I were. "My husband put his penis in another woman's vagina and you're standing here talking to me about reconciling?!"

Other people turned around at Chaylene's remark. I cut my eyes at them, wishing they'd mind their own business despite how hard Chaylene made it for them to do so.

"There's no reconciliation, Sidney!" She opened the passenger door. "You know, you really need to grow up!" She got in and slammed the car door shut.

I opened my door and got in as well.

"Chaylene—"

"No, leave me alone, Sidney. You don't know anything." She fastened her seatbelt.

"Dennis loves you. I know *that*."

"Loves me?" she frowned. "*Loves* me? Sidney, the L is for *Loyalty*."

I looked at her, momentarily at a loss for words. I knew what she was saying, but everybody made mistakes. I felt Dennis was worth, at least, the consideration of working things out. He had been with her through their miscarriage, cared for her when she had the nastiest strain of influenza I'd ever seen, and kept her glamorous in all things Gucci. He wasn't some bad boyfriend. He was her husband. Someone who really loved her.

"Chaylene, I just—"

"Look, I don't even believe I'm having this conversation with you. You're as single as the day you were born. Please don't think just because you've had a few fly-by-night flings that you know something about relationships now because I can assure you you don't."

"I'm just trying to help you. Dennis is—"

"*Dennis. Dennis. Dennis.* You know, Sidney, you're something else," she shook her head.

"How's that?" I frowned.

"You think I'm blind? You think I don't see the way you look at me? My life? Like I don't deserve it. Like I don't deserve it and *you do?*"

"That's not the way I—"

"Bullshit!"

Her anger forced me stiff against my seat.

"Here"—she proceeded to twist her wedding ring around her finger—"You want my life so bad? You think Dennis is such a good man?" She yanked off the ring. "Then here!"—She snatched my hand open, smashing the ring deep into my palm—"*You* wear it!"

I snatched my hand away from her and glared.

She shot me a cold stare.

As I opened up my hand and looked down at the sparkling ring that sat in the middle of my pink palm, Chaylene said, "Yeah. Take it. It may be the only one you'll ever get!" She turned away, her angry reflection cast on her passenger side window. I looked at that wicked reflection, not believing this was what the Universe had given me in a sister. Not understanding how this was supposed to be someone for me to love, and who was supposed to love me back. As I sat there thinking about it a huge lump formed in my throat. So I didn't say anything.

It would've hurt too much to try.

CHAPTER 16

I pulled into Leann's complex, parking right next to her car, then peeled off my pantyhose that had been cutting off my circulation all day. I couldn't believe company policy insisted I wear nylons. Aside from the fact that we were mere miles from a muggy Miami we were in the twenty-first century. Hosiery was history. Bare legs were in. It was just another annoyance I had to deal with in addition to the agony of the job itself.

It was six o'clock and I just wanted to go straight home and crawl into bed. But I'd promised Leann I'd stop by. She was excited about her newly-remodeled kitchen and was anxious to show it off. Usually on Tuesdays and Thursdays after work it was straight to Rico's for me. But he hadn't made it back from visiting relatives in Clearwater. I hadn't seen him since I'd helped him pack for his trip on Sunday upon returning from mine.

Since Rico had been working we saw less and less of each other. He worked crazy hours down at the warehouse, and by the time he got home he barely had enough energy to hang *in* much less *out*. I mean, I was glad that he was working and all. Unemployment seemed to be weighing on his self-esteem. I just hated that our five days a week together dwindled down to two.

As for his job, Rico constantly complained that he didn't make enough money. I wasn't exactly an authority on premium pay since I, too, was getting pimped at the insurance company. But I assured Rico that everybody had to start somewhere. And when it came to paying bills, *something* was definitely better than *nothing*.

Rico would look at me strange when I'd tell him that the amount of money he made wasn't important to me. He'd say that most girls would frown upon a guy who came home every night with dirt under his fingernails and very little money to show for it. And for the hundredth time I reminded him that I wasn't *'most girls'*.

I got out of the car and headed for Leann's apartment. Like me, she also lived on the third floor of her building. Trucking it up those stairs this evening was murder on my unconditioned calves. I felt like I was climbing Mt. Everest. When I finally made it to the top I heard light sounds of R&B thumping through the pewter-painted wood.

I knocked on the door.

Leann swung the door open, smiling.

"Hey, Sidney."

"Hey, girlie." Leann may have said come in, but it was the irresistible smell of homemade chocolate chip cookies baking in the oven that actually welcomed me inside. They were prepared from scratch—I'm talking flour and yeast!—as made evident by the messy mixing bowl Leann cradled against her powdered apron as she whipped up another batch.

Leann loved to cook. She'd taken some classes a while back. And though she enjoyed making those fancy foreign dishes and gourmet entrées her passion was baking. It seemed every time I went over her place she had something sweet and delicious in the oven.

Giving me a tour of the new kitchen Leann beamed with excitement when I told her what a wonderful job she had done. The wallpaper actually matched the rug. I don't know how in the world she pulled that off. Right down to the smallest details, she'd done her thing. The drapes were pretty and stylish. And the crystal chandelier she had installed totally lit up the adjacent dining room. She had also redone the tile.

"Ooooooh," I sang the tune of trouble to come. "You know you're not supposed to be messing with the tile. They're going to penalize your pockets for that."

"As long as I pay rent I'll decorate as I please." She looked down, admiring her forbidden work with a smile. "Besides, they ought to owe *me* money. This is an upgrade."

"Dangerous," I shook my head, knowing she could kiss her deposit goodbye. "You're right, though," I admitted. "They definitely owe you some money. This looks amazing."

"Want some tea?" Leann took two teacups from the cabinet then lifted the teapot from the stove, filling the dainty little cups with the brown, steaming-hot liquid. "It's this new blend I found at the Farmer's Market."

She handed me the warm cup as we walked into the living room where she pushed the patchwork quilt she was working on to the side, making room for us on the multi-colored sofa.

"So how's your sister?" She sat down, careful as she leaned back.

I sat beside her. "Not so good." I sipped my tea. "She's really taking this hard."

"Is she really going through with the divorce?"

I nodded, sure that she would. Chaylene was very headstrong. And it looked as if she had her mind made up.

"But anyway . . ." I sat my cup down, wanting to pick a new topic. I'd already decided before I left Chicago that I would never speak to my sister again, so I definitely didn't want to talk about her.

"What about you, Leann? Did you go out this weekend?"

Leann shook her head. "No. I just stayed home and cooked for Reggie."

"Reggie?" I tilted my head. "That skinny guy from the club?"

Her top lip melted into a grin.

"You didn't tell me the two of you were talking." I remembered their dirty dancing but didn't know she had exchanged numbers with him.

Leann just kept grinning.

"You little sneak!" I nudged her.

"Uh-oh," she said, steadying her teacup.

"Oops. Sorry." I made sure none had spilled on her while inside feeling left out and disappointed that she'd sat on something like this when I was telling her *everything*.

"Well, at first I wasn't going to call him," Leann explained. "But then I figured since you were spending so much time with Rico I wanted someone to do, too."

I laughed. "You mean some*thing,* don't you?"

Leann hid her mouth behind her cup. Two guilty eyes peered over its rim.

"Leann!"

She burst into a laughing confession. "Well, I can't say that I regret it, Sidney." She sat her cup down. "It was great. I mean really, really great—like rip-the-sheets-off-the-bed, climb-up-the-walls, pull-my-hair-out-my-head grea—"

"Okayyyy. I get it." I laughed with her. "Man, I can't turn my back for one weekend," I said, shaking my head. "So are you guys together now, or what?"

Leann began to fidget.

"Well, I guess so. I mean, we haven't really defined anything yet," she brushed imaginary lint from her pants.

I looked down at her lint-free lap then frowned.

"Well, why not? What's up with that?" I connected with her eyes.

"I don't know. I guess we just wanna take things slow."

"How is humping him taking things slow?"

"Well, you know," Leann sat up, reaching nervously for her tea again, "I don't want to rush him into a relationship if that's not what he wants right now. I'm going with the flow." She took a sip just for the sake of taking one.

I could tell my prying made her uneasy. I backed off.

"Well," I tapped her on the leg, "I'm glad you have some*one* to do."

"I'm *gladder*," Leann smiled, taking an honest sip this time.

As evening fell Leann and I ate some of the leftover pot roast and potatoes she'd made the night before and snacked on those cookies for dessert. After lollygagging for the longest I told her I had to be going. Earlier in the evening I'd left a message for Rico to call me when he took his lunch break. I wanted to close my night with his voice in my ear.

CHAPTER 17

When the sun came in and tapped me on the shoulder it was 7:02 a.m. I opened my eyes to greet the day and, at that moment, realized I hadn't heard from Rico last night. I was sure he'd gotten back yesterday, and wondered why he hadn't called. A worried feeling came over me as I reached for the phone.

By the time the phone got to my ear I got Rico's voice mail. I grabbed my silk robe from the foot of the bed and went to the bathroom. Today was my pre-scheduled personal day off, so after getting dressed, I'd decided to just go over to Rico's apartment.

By the time I got to Rico's apartment it was a quarter after eight. I didn't see his car in the lot but knocked on the door anyway. I figured his roommate, Sam, could at least tell me where he was. And since I had all day I could just wait for him.

I banged my knuckles against the rock-hard wood until they got sore. I couldn't believe Sam wasn't opening the door. *Lazy bum!* I said to myself as I surrendered my way back down the steps, figuring Rico and I would just have to hook up later.

Just as I reached the bottom of the steps I heard the door creak open. I looked over my shoulder and saw Sam standing there.

"Hey, where's Rico?" I hiked back up the stairs.

"I don't know," Sam shrugged, looking like an angry, twenty-three-year-old baby, rubbing his eye hard in the corner. It must've felt really good because he was twisting his mouth to the side, disappointingly oblivious as to how ridiculously-awful he was looking. I thought he was going to rub his eyeball right out of the socket.

"Well, did he make it back from Clearwater?" I asked, hoping he'd stop the rubbing, and desperately avoiding any eye and/or nose contact with his morning mouth.

I raised my brows when he didn't answer. "Well? *Did he?*"

He squinted like the question was painful. *"What?"*

Just then I'd caught whiff of his hamster breath, which nearly knocked me back down the stairs.

I shuddered, then sucked my teeth. "Never mind."

It was obvious his drowsy-ass was incoherent.

"Just tell him I came by, okay?" I searched his face for the slightest bit of cognizance. He just stood there with half-shut eyes, swaying back and forth slightly, ready to tip over and knock himself back unconscious at any moment.

"Okay??" I widened my eyes.

He snapped out of his standing stupor. "Yeah. Yeah," he frowned, preparing to shut the door in my face. "I'll tell him you came by."

I would've asked to wait inside but judging by Sam's personal presentation I was sure the apartment wouldn't exactly smell like potpourri.

"Thanks," I muttered, seeing his hand on the knob.

I turned around and headed back home where I knew the air was fresh.

I did a couple loads of laundry and cleaned the bathroom to busy myself while I waited for Rico to call. I thought he would've called by now, but it was a quarter to twelve and I still hadn't heard from him.

I put the scrub brush down and reached for the phone that sat on the toilet's lid, deciding it was probably a good time to reach him.

After three rings, Rico finally answered.

"Hello?"

"Hey, you!" I said, happy to finally hear his voice in three days.

"What's up?" Rico said coolly like he was Snoop Dogg and I was Dr. Dre.

I ignored the passionless greeting, chalking it up to tiredness.

"I missed you last night," I told him.

"Oh yeah?" He offered no explanation or apology.

"So what happened?" I asked, disappointed that he hadn't.

"Nothing. I was just chillin'."

"Did you get my message?"

"I got it."

"So . . . ?"

"So . . . What?"

"So how come you didn't call me back?" My voice was still perky.

"Because obviously I was busy, Sidney."

"What's that?" I switched the phone to my other ear, not hearing him clearly.

Rico breathed hard into the phone. "Just forget it."

"What's wrong with *you?*" I felt the nerves buzzing inside my body like a hand-held fan's tiny little motor.

His tone was starting to get to me. He had never spoken to me this way before. "Why are you getting so snippy with me?" My feelings were hurt.

"Look, Sidney—"

"No, *you* look!" My hurt feelings quickly morphed into anger. "If you didn't want to do anything that would have been fine. No big deal. But to not even *call* me . . ."

I didn't know what else to say. I was totally caught off guard by his attitude. I couldn't believe he was coming off so cavalier and disrespectful.

Rico breathed hard into the phone again.

"Look, Sam told me you came by."

"And?!" I said, giving him my own little attitude now.

"And I feel like you were checking up on me."

"Checking up on you? When did it become *that?*"

"I just felt like that's what it was."

"I was coming over to see you. I thought maybe you didn't call me last night because something was wrong."

"Well, quit worrying so much, Sidney."

I took a deep breath. "Yeah. Okay." I mustered up the softest tone I could to camouflage what I was really feeling inside. My voice was calm, but on the other end, my foot was tapping against the tub in agitation. I couldn't believe he'd turned this around on me.

Rico must've sensed my emotions because he softened his tone as well.

"Look, everything's okay, Sidney," he said reassuringly. *"We're* okay."

"Okay, Rico. This is stupid. Let's not fight about it anymore."

I didn't want to blow it any further out of proportion than we'd already had. I figured he'd just woke up on the wrong side of the bed this morning and I didn't want his crankiness to cost us our relationship.

"I'm cool," Rico said like all was forgotten.

I closed my eyes and rubbed my temple, feeling a major headache coming on.

"Anyway," he said, "let me get going. I gotta get ready for work. I'm going in early today."

I looked up at the clock wishing we hadn't spent our two-minute conversation arguing.

"I'll call you later," he said, "Okay?"

"Okay, Rico," I stoop up, opening the medicine cabinet for some aspirin. "I love you."

"Me too." He hung up.

I blow-dried my hair, using a brush to turn the ends under so that I didn't have to follow up with the curling iron. After I was practically salon-fresh I put on my makeup—heavy on the mascara—then went to my closet and pulled out my black capris and white off-the-shoulder blouse that clung to my body, accentuating my twenty-four-inch waist. I looked myself over in the mirror, loving the match-up. Then I slipped into my suede, zebra-printed sandals with the three-inch heel to bring it all together. I wanted to look nice even though it was just lunch with Leann.

The Cracked Crab was a popular eatery, probably because of the generous portions they gave. I could never finish the entire meal in one sitting so I was always guaranteed lunch for the next day. Best of all, the prices were right within my budget.

"Ditto!!!! . . . WDTO! Playing the same damn songs every damn dayyyyy!" I said in my DJ voice as I switched stations on the radio. It was such a beautiful day. I was feeling so good.

Ten minutes later I pulled into the restaurant's parking lot, which was full, as usual. As I backed into a space I saw Leann pulling in as well. *Perfect timing*, I thought to myself as I grabbed my purse and got out of the car.

Leann double-parked opposite my row, then stepped out of the licorice, reflection-casting Mercedes looking sassy! Her money wasn't right, but her credit definitely was. She'd always talked about getting a fancy new car and a couple of weeks ago finally went down to the dealership and signed her name on the dotted line. She was officially the Benz's bitch, having to work even more hours at the optometrist's shop just to make the payments. But she was riding nicely. Several steps up from the old '99 sedan she was previously pushing.

"Hey, High Roller!" I greeted her with a check-to-cheek air-kiss.

She giggled, turning back to arm her new toy.

"Yeah, you *better* separate it from the masses." I referred to her intentionally taking up two spaces so that no one could park next to her. Her economy-car-carelessness had definitely dinged a door or two in its day. So game recognized game.

Leann dropped her keys into her purse. "I'm starving. Did you get us a table?"

"No. I just pulled up myself."

"Oh. Perfect timing.

"That's what *I* said," I laughed.

When we approached the entrance of the restaurant the door swung open as the host greeted us. He was nice-looking. I saw Leann checking him out from the corner of my eye. But what caught my eye even more was the hand-holding couple coming out from behind him.

"What the—" Mouth wide open, I couldn't believe what I was seeing.

Rico turned gray when he saw me. He looked like he'd just seen a ghost.

I stepped back, giving them room to come out, resisting the urge to jump to conclusions even if it did walk and talk like a duck.

"Rico," I looked at him, surprised and confused, "who's this?" My eyes bounced back and forth between him and his companion.

He didn't say a word.

I looked at him, awaiting an answer.

She looked at him then abruptly stuck her hand out at me.

"I'm Felecia."

I didn't say a word.

She smirked as she withdrew her hand, running it instead through her Kool-Aid-shade, flaming-red hair that clashed with her sallow complexion yet perfectly matched the embers of acne on her face quite well.

"What's going on, Rico. Who is she?" My once-calm lips twitched as I assigned them an impossible task, finding it more and more difficult to suppress my natural reaction.

I could feel her eyes burning a hole through me, studying me. But I wouldn't look at her. *He* was my focus. I pretended I didn't notice her frowning at me in hostility, wishing looks could kill. I knew that if I'd looked at her I'd snap. Lose it. I stayed affixed on his eyes instead. His eyes that played hide and seek with mine.

"Rico?" I still waited.

Leann excused herself, walking back toward the car.

"Look, we're running late for our movie," the young woman told me. "So if you'll excuse us."

Rico resisted the tug of her hand as I stood there looking at him in awe.

Battling the stillness of his weight, she looked at the both of us with impatience. Then giving in to her second tug, Rico's feet took their first steps away from me.

I was stunned.

"So what? You and *Fellatio* are just going to walk off like that?"

"Felicia," she turned only to correct me.

"Rico." I walked toward them. "Rico, wait!"—I jumped in front of him, putting my hand on his chest. His companion shifted her weight onto her other foot and huffed. I could still feel her eyes on me but I refused to look at her—not in the face. There was no need to. I'd already permanently stored her image in my mind from the moment I saw her coming out of the restaurant. She looked better tonight than she did the night I saw her bent over in the club, sandwiched between those two guys, dancing like a skank—though, not too much better. Why was he with her? Why was he listening to her? And why was he still holding her hand?!

Rico backed up from my hand in his chest.

"What do you want me to say, Sidney? You want me to lie? I mean, what *can* I say?" he shrugged.

"I want you to say she's your cousin. Your sister. Your brother in drag! Anything except that you're out here cheating on me," I moaned.

"Look, honey . . ." she began to address me in a condescending tone but Rico put his finger to his mouth, urging her silence when he saw the quick, crazy look I finally threw on her. He was trying to save her life. She was running out of freebies. And she was about to catch a zebra up her ass.

I peeled my fiery stare off her and put it back on Rico. He had a fresh haircut and was sporting new threads. He even had the nerve to be out smelling like my money, wearing the one-hundred-and-thirty-dollar cologne I bought him for his birthday.

"We're okay?" I threw his morning words back at him.

Rico didn't say anything but seemed to look at me with some remorse.

Seeing his expression, his companion finally let go of his hand, growing increasingly impatient as if I were endangering their movie plans.

"I thought you loved me, Rico," I said in a weak voice. "Isn't that what you said?"

Rico exercised his right to remain silent. But even though his lips were still, I knew I'd moved his heart. His eyes locked with mine—which were on the verge of losing their battle with tears. His date folded her arms as she saw the effect I seemed to be having on him.

"Are you coming?" she asked with angry lips.

I looked at her and knew she'd just sealed her fate with that question. Yes, I'd caught him cheating but he was still my man and, no doubt, would be leaving with me. He'd spend the entire night explaining and apologizing, pleading for my forgiveness, though I hadn't decided if I would easily extend it or not. But she was dumb to make him choose. It was no contest. Rico cared about me. I knew he did. He was *my* man.

So imagine my surprise when he walked away with her.

Passing on the gamble and going with the sure thing, Rico left me standing there by myself while the host, who still held the door ajar, watched the unbelievable conclusion of the intense showdown. I'd forgotten about him until now. He tried but couldn't avoid looking me in my eyes to see the pain they displayed. I saw an awkward blend of sympathy and intrigue in his.

I turned away.

Rico's back was to me. I watched on devastated as his date tried to walk off all sexy in her clear-bottom stilettos with a champion's gait. She was walking off with my man. He was letting her. I couldn't believe it.

Didn't he love me like he said he did? In fact, he'd said it *first*. And since we'd already been intimate at that point I figured there was no reason for him to lie, not when he was already receiving the special rewards.

What's more, didn't Rico understand the sacrifices I'd made for him all in the name of love? I was loyal to him. Good to him. I accepted him—Broke and all. When he'd sit around all day in his boxers and sip Big Gulps one behind the other, playing video games like they were going out of style, I'd go put on a pair of his boxers and get into lounge mode right along with him. Anything to make him feel comfortable. When he'd come home at midnight sometimes, tired and filthy, I'd clean him up. I'd give him facials for the fun of it, helping to preserve that handsome complexion that working in a dirty warehouse stood to threaten. I didn't know I was polishing him up for someone else. I never imagined I was grooming him for her!

I continued to watch as Rico and his redhead walked away, still not fully coming to grips with what was happening. I had to do something. I couldn't just let him leave.

"Wait!" I ran up, grabbing Rico's shoulder, swinging him around to face me. "What are you doing? How cou—" I swallowed, suppressing my tears that wanted to flow free. "How could you do this to me, Rico?"

My eyes stung. I couldn't believe this was happening. My mind thought back to those Redbox and Netflix nights. The all-night checkers tournaments. Our silly WWF Superstars simulations. The times he'd cooked for me. My mind recalled the good times—the great relationship I thought we were having—while my eyes saw the truth. I stood there shaking, feeling like someone had just pulled the rug from under me.

As Rico held his tongue I continued swallowing cotton, blinking hard to keep down the wave of emotions that was brewing within me. But something had to come out.

"You're a fool. You know that?" My voice cracked, wanting to do what it did best. But no way was I going to let this ketchup-headed homewrecker see me cry.

"You're choosing this"—I looked her up and down —"raggedy mess over *me??!* She looks like *shit on fire!*" I dared her to open her mouth again. I was ready to punch those teeth straight.

Normally I wouldn't blame the woman caught in the crossfire. But this girl was acting like she couldn't see the tears in my eyes. That told me she knew about me. I was the only victim here.

Rico, unmoved by my ranting, gave me that *'Are you finished yet?'* look. I was shocked. How could he fix his eyes and distort his face to look at me in such a way? Didn't he recognize me? I was his girlfriend. The one he said he loved.

My lips quivered. So much was going on in my mind. "I loved you," I told him, using the past tense, but still hoping he'd realize the err of his ways, snatch away from her, and fall apologetically into my arms. But he didn't. He didn't even say anything. Instead he looked right past me. Like I wasn't even there. Like I never even mattered.

I squinted my eyes and shook my head. "You're a disaster, Rico," I told him, looking him up and down. "A fucking disaster!"

He still didn't say anything. He maintained his silence like the grip on her hand. I looked down at that blatant message of disrespect and insensitivity and felt my stomach rumble with grief. And when his date saw me look down at their hands she gave his a deliberate squeeze.

SMACK!!!

I slapped Rico's face so hard his skin should have come off on my hand.

"I hate you!" I spat, then braced myself, ready and willing to take the imminent butt-whipping I feared was coming. I looked into those foreign eyes set in that familiar face and was fearless. A fist in my face couldn't possibly match what he'd just done to my heart. Nothing could've hurt more.

To some relief Rico chose not to strike me. Not that he ever had before, but I didn't know what to expect from this *new* Rico. Instead he rubbed his face and looked at me with cold eyes. Eyes I'd never seen before. Certainly not the same eyes he'd once looked at me with. These eyes belonged to a different man. A man I didn't know. A man I would've never fallen for. This man looked evil. Callous. This man was not the Rico I had fallen in love with. The person in front of me was someone I'd never met. Someone he'd never introduced me to. Someone he'd kept secret from me all this time. I despised this person. I looked at this new person in disgust until I couldn't look at him anymore. Until it hurt to have him look at me. Then with a devastated heart and broken spirit I walked away.

As our opposing directions placed meters between us I felt my world crashing down on me. Pitifully, I looked back, perhaps in a telepathic plea, still unconvinced. Still not believing that he'd made such a decision. But my eyes confirmed it. He was walking away from me. He was walking away with her.

Just as I was about to turn my head back around *she* turned around—I guess to see what I looked like from behind being dumped. To see if my shirt bore slash marks from Rico's dagger of deceit, and if I was bleeding through my blouse. Her curiosity turned her head just as my curiosity had turned mine. I wanted to see what *she* looked like walking off with another woman's boyfriend. How she was able to keep her balance with the weight of scandal heavy on her shoulders. She seemed to have no difficulty. I looked at her, our steps still placing distance between us, wondering how it was that she could be walking away with him and I could be walking away alone. It didn't seem real. She looked back at me, almost as if she couldn't believe it herself. As if her victory was a mystery even to her. Yet she was basking in it just the same.

As she continued clutching the arm of my boyfriend, connecting her eyes with mine, I felt sick. I felt so sick to have her look at me that way. What the hell was she looking at, anyway? She'd already won. She'd already successfully stolen my man right out in broad daylight. Wasn't that enough? Wasn't the prize on her arm satisfaction enough?

She kept her eyes on me, taunting me, almost as if she wanted to say something. I wanted desperately to turn away, feeling the unbearable tension, but somehow couldn't. Like a spider paralyzing her prey she held my attention. Hypnotized me. It was like I *couldn't* turn away though I desperately wanted to.

Still determined, I fought her spell, coming closer to freeing myself from her stare that worked hard to break me. I was nearly free. But just as I prepared to turn around her eyes locked on mine. Like the arachnid moving in for the kill, her walk slowed. Her eyes glistened. Her face glowed. And with a mocking smirk—one that caught my eye just before I turned my head—she mouthed, *"Sorry."*

CHAPTER 18

*"Thank God!" *I whispered** a sigh of relief as I hovered over the public toilet and smiled at the bright-red droplets freshly staining my underwear.

The last time Rico and I were intimate, when it was over, the condom didn't get the memo. You'd think I would've been embarrassed having him probe inside my body like he was giving me an ultrasound. But I was too scared to be modest. In my mind I kept thinking back to Tasha's *condom kids* lecture back in New York, wondering if this was how they came to be.

After a few frightening seconds—and a lot of silent prayers—Rico eventually retrieved the runaway rubber. But it was no consolation to me that its contents appeared to remain inside the prophylactic. I knew that was no guarantee that droves of *RJs* and Little *Ricolas* weren't Michael Phelpsing their way to my Fallopian tubes. That little mishap cost me a trip to the drugstore to buy the best behind-the-counter emergency contraceptive my $30 perscription copay could afford, and the last two weeks of sleep wondering if it had worked.

I was a wreck. A terrifying situation in itself things got even scarier when Rico and I broke up just days after the ordeal. Praying for my period to arrive, I couldn't sleep. I couldn't eat. I'd put food in my mouth with the inability to chew, much less swallow. And to top it all off I had diarrhea for days that left me weak —drained, like there wasn't a trace of nourishment to be found in my body. The scale nose-dived from a head-turning one hundred and twenty-two pounds to a wind-blown one-ten in just five days. I couldn't concentrate on work or domestic duties. My apartment looked like it had been ransacked. I couldn't do anything but feel the pain I felt. Perhaps it was just the stress of it all that was responsible for my delayed cycle—I'm not sure. But whatever it was I was just glad that my period was finally here.

The immediate days following the restaurant incident Rico tried calling me. But there was nothing to talk about. He'd not only lied and cheated on me but had humiliated me. To have that woman thinking she was better than me—even for a day—was unforgivable. My ego wouldn't allow it, and my heart would hear nothing of it. Besides, I didn't catch it at the time, given how mad and caught off guard I was, but it had later dawned on me that she was the *"Lee"* who he'd, supposedly, helped move out that day. What a sneaky bastard. We were through!

A broken windshield wouldn't have *begun* to serve as payback for the damages sustained to my broken heart. So at Tasha's recommendation I passed on the brick-tossing mission suggested to me by a coworker. Tasha said he wasn't worth the time, or the record. She was right. I could find better things to do with my time these days than to waste any more of it on Rico. And besides, I couldn't do to him what karma could.

"I should've never trusted him," I voiced my regret. "That was so stupid of me."

There was a moment of silence where Tasha was gracious enough not to say 'I told you so'. But she had.

Tasha always said that to "trust" a man who was acting suspiciously was "*T*o *R*ationalize *U*ntil *S*tupidity *T*riumphed". And that's exactly what I had done. I knew something was wrong with our relationship, but I ignored it, making all sorts of excuses for his behavior, afraid to be right.

"Why does this keep happening to me?" I whined.

"Sidney, you have to demand respect. Otherwise, men are going to walk all over you."

"That's just it, Tasha. I don't want someone from whom I need to *demand* respect. I want someone who respects me because he wants to. Because he knows I deserve it. Because it's decent. Not someone who would dog me lest I *'demand'* he didn't."

"But ask and you shall receive. Decency doesn't come standard with everyone. You're dealing with a lot of monsters out there."

"Well, I don't want to convert the monster, Tasha. I want a man who's *naturally* decent. Not a defeated opportunist who couldn't take me down."

"No one respects a pushover, Sidney. That's all I'm saying. If you let a man walk all over you, he will."

"I didn't exactly know I was 'letting' him do *anything*. I thought I was loving him."

"You were. But if you don't establish your boundaries you give a man too much control over the relationship. And some men will abuse that power. Sidney, I'm just saying—"

"I know what you're saying, Tasha." I took a deep breath. "I do. It's just all so hurtful, that's all."

Tasha's voice softened hearing mine trail off the way it did. "I know it is, Sidney. I know."

I drifted off, thinking about everything. Wondering why it had to turn out this way.

"He's just such a liar." I wiped my tears as heat seeped from my nose. "He said he deserved me. He said he deserved me when he didn't!"

"What do you mean?" Tasha sounded confused. "Like, what, you *asked* him?"

"Well . . . yeah, I asked him. I asked him if he deserved me, and he said *yes*. He lied. Just like Damon. He lied!" I found myself getting upset again.

Tasha was quiet as I tried to pull myself together.

I turned on the AC, positioning the vents toward me. I had to get back inside soon. My lunch break was almost over, so I couldn't get myself too riled up.

"Well, you can't give up, Sidney," Tasha encouraged me, sensing defeat in my tone. She placed excitement in hers when she said, "We've just gotta dust you off and get you back out there. It's like you once told me: *you gotta get back out there and get your feet wet.*"

"Get wet? Tasha, I've got *pneumonia!* And the only thing that needs to get wet is this foolish flame I keep carrying around for these lying-ass losers."

"Come on now. You know there are still good guys out there."

"Oh—I know. *I'm* just not bumping into any," I grumbled.

"Well, what about Stan? He sounded like a nice guy."

"You mean *Stain?* That dirty dude from Leann's complex? I'm so mad she gave him my number. Talking about how much we have in common. I'm trying to be nice about it but he really needs to stop calling me. He's not even cute."

"Well, maybe she figured since you both are originally from Arizona—"

"Not even if he was the *last* fool in the desert."

"But he tap-dances on Broadway."

"I don't give a damn if he tap-dances from Tempe to Tampa, Tasha. He's not my type!"

"Wow!" Tasha laughed. "Say that three times fast."

I laughed, too. "I'll say *No* three times fast. How about that?"

I mean, I wanted a boyfriend. But not *that* bad.

Tasha huffed. "Sidney, you're just too picky for your own good. You are always focusing on looks. You need to give average-looking guys a try. You might be surprised."

"Tasha, I know you are not talking about me right now," I said, shocked at her sudden transformation from ONLY THE HANDSOME NEED APPLY, to ADVOCATE FOR THE UGLY. "Give average-looking guys a try? Need I remind you of that six-foot-three, two-hundred-and-twenty-pound *Adonis* you climb into bed with every night who, by the way, happens to be loaded? I know you're not telling me anything about the average man. He's the least average man I know. And besides," I told her, "average-looking is not the cure-all. You can turn on any one of those rowdy talk shows any day of the week and see some *marsh mutant* cheating on his woman. Now tell me that isn't true."

Tasha got quiet on me like she always did when she knew I was right. I mean, who was she kidding? Between Remedial Romell who, in the eleventh grade, stuck a note inside her locker saying he thought she was *'real qute'*, to Crazy Curtis who, freshman year, after she'd broken up with him for Craig, called her from outside her dorm room saying she *'bet not* 'come outside, Tasha had certainly had her moments where she'd sacrificed substance for superficiality. In short, she'd dated some really good-looking losers—or "icing", as she'd later refer to them. Given her past and, most importantly, her present bedmate, I wondered how Tasha could even fix her mouth to say such a thing.

Her argument completely blown apart, Tasha laughed that embarrassed laugh. "You got me," she chuckled admittedly. She couldn't deny the facts. Not when she was waking up next to them.

But though I felt I argued a good point, in actuality, I was confused inside. I didn't know what was right anymore. Was it wrong of me to reject a guy just because I wasn't physically attracted to him? Or was it downright dishonest for me to date a man, allowing him to invest time and money courting me, knowing all the while I wasn't the least bit attracted to him? Was *that* fair? I honestly didn't know, so I just did what felt right.

All this talk about men and dating was only making me more depressed.

"Anyway, Tasha, when are you coming down to see me?" I changed the subject.

"I'm not sure. Soon, I hope. I've just been so tied up with work. But who knows? Maybe I'll surprise you."

"Alright. Well, speaking of work, my lunch break is over. And since I'm going to the center tonight, I'll probably just give you a call tomorrow."

"That's nice," Tasha said, happy to hear that I was making steps toward a healthier routine that didn't revolve around Rico. "I'll talk to you later. Luv'ya, Sidney."

"Luv'ya, too."

When I pulled into the parking lot of the rec center a guilty feeling came over me. It had been going on three weeks since I'd last shown up. Usually I'd come right after work and hang out until about seven-thirty, then I'd go home and get ready to go over Rico's when he got off work. But since he and I had broken up it had been a different story. I had been MIA.

The kids were out in the yard playing softball when I walked up behind the bleachers. I sat down, trying to inconspicuously blend in with the other spectators.

"Hi, Sidney! Welcome back." Gail instantly blew my cover.

"Thanks, Gail," I spoke with an ambiguous tone. "Who's winning?" I got into the game.

"Red team. Manny's coaching. He's over there," she pointed. "Look at him pacing around like a junkyard dog."

215

"That's a shame." I shook my head. I looked around. "Where's Earl?"

"Inside."

"I'll be back." I got up, brushing off my backside.

"Okay—*Awww! That was safe!*" Gail argued with the umpire from behind the fence. "Sidney, tell him to bring out the other cooler! We're out of ice!" she yelled to me as I made my way to the office.

I waved my hand over my head to let her know I'd heard her.

As I walked upstairs I could hear Earl on the phone. He was yelling at the person on the other end. It sounded really heated so I didn't want to interrupt. I hung around in the hall waiting for him to finish.

"I just gave you $400 last Friday!" he shouted.

There was a pause.

"Well, then you need to budget better."

From the sounds of it he was speaking to his kids' mom. They shared four kids together—ages thirteen, eleven, nine, and five. I wondered why they never got married. They seemed to get along pretty fine for at least *eight* years, the gap between the oldest and the youngest.

Earl said his ex was always hitting him up for money. He was an alright guy but he really needed to tighten up on his domestic situation. He'd complain about what a money-grabbing witch his ex was, and how his check was picked to pieces by the time he got it, but I didn't feel the least bit sorry for him. I figured while he was doing all that multiplying he should've known some division would come into play. It was time for him to divvy up those dollars. And while I admired his philanthropic ways when it came to the kids at center, I felt he needed to focus on his own children a little more. She couldn't have been complaining for nothing.

I shook my head as I continued listening.

"I'm not a money machine!"

I covered my mouth and snickered.

"Sidney!"—Startled, my gum slipped right down my throat.

I heard Earl tell his ex he'd call her back, realizing his conversation had been eavesdropped on.

I turned around to find Kiana standing behind me.

"Hi, Kiana. How are you, sweetheart?"

She dove into my waist. "I missed you, Sidney."

Kiana was eight years old, and small for her age. Her mother was drug-addicted, and she had a deadbeat, now-you-see'em-now-you-don't daddy too dumb to know what a great person he was missing out on. She didn't have anyone at home to look up to, so the center was where she found her role models. I hoped I wasn't one of them because my life was in shambles.

"I missed you, too." I hugged her.

"Where were you?" She looked up at me for answers. Answers I couldn't really provide.

I stroked her hair. "Sweetie, I had some things I had to sort out. But I'm really glad to be back." I smiled.

She smiled back.

"Why aren't you watching the game?" I asked her.

"The red team is cheating. Manny's coaching *and* making calls."

"Well, we'll just have to do something about that."

"Hey, ladies," Earl said as he stepped out into the hall.

"Hi, Earl," I spoke nervously while trying to read his face to see if he knew that I was listening in on his conversation.

"Uh . . . Gail said we needed the other cooler. We're out of ice," I quickly justified my presence. I was also going to apologize for my absence, which was the reason I'd gone to see him in the first place.

He scratched his head, still looking preoccupied with his call. "Okay, well . . . I'll go get the cooler and bring it outside." He walked toward the steps, then stopped and looked over his shoulder. "You two coming?"

"Yeah, in a minute," I told him, wanting to speak to Kiana privately.

He nodded then continued down the stairs. After I heard enough footsteps I turned to Kiana

"How are things at home?"

She dropped her head and mumbled, "Fine," too young to have mastered the art of lying.

I respected her adolescent pride. It showed strong character.

I knelt in my heels, looking up at her. "Well, remember what I told you. If you need anything—anything at all—you call me, okay? You still have my number?"

Kiana nodded humbly. She had about an ounce of innocence left and I wanted to preserve that for as long as I could.

She looked up at me and smiled. I smiled back. Then she lunged into me with a great big hug.

I giggled, squeezing her tight while, from over her shoulder, my smile faded at the thought of just how unfair things were for her.

I straightened my face before letting her go.

"Okay," I stood up, "let's go downstairs and tell Manny to quit cheating. You ready?"

We went downstairs to find Manny jumping around like a mad man. Like he had money on the game or something. "Relax!" I shouted from the stands. "It's just a game!"

He batted his hand at me like I didn't know what I was talking about.

After the game the kids and us volunteers went inside for a snack—before the mosquitos came out for *theirs*.

I helped Kiana with her homework while we waited for her mother to pick her up.

"I hate math!" Kiana ran her eraser across her lead-smudged paper, tearing a hole in it this time from repeated friction.

"It's not so bad. You just have to keep practicing." I brushed the pink bits away, encouraging her to give it another try.

"But it's hard," she grumbled, her elbow on the table, fist to her cheek.

"So is *everything* before you learn how to do it. Tying your shoes. Braiding your hair. Reading. Even walking."

Kiana looked at me like I was silly. "Sidney, all that stuff is easy. *Walking?*" she laughed.

219

I laughed with her. "Well, it is *now*. But I bet when you were a baby it wasn't so simple."

She looked at me as I explained.

"See, it's called repetition."

"I've heard of that before."

"Yeah, it's when you do something over and over again—you practice something so much—until it becomes second nature."

"Second nature?"

"Yeah. That's when you don't even have to think about something anymore in order to do it. You just do it automatically—without even trying. Sometimes without even realizing you're doing it at all. Like calculating two plus two. That's easy, right?"

Kiana shook her head and said, "No."

I looked at her, worried.

She smiled and said, "That's repetition."

Our bodies shook with laughter as we took a giggle break.

CHAPTER 19

You *had* **heterosexual.** Homosexual. Even bisexual.

And then there was me. Asexual.

Translation: I wasn't getting any love and affection.

My life had become one big solo act, full of dry spells and mood swings. And there wasn't a weekend that rolled by where Leann didn't remind me that you couldn't even pronounce the word *happiness* without inadvertently saying 'penis' in the process. If she had it her way she'd change the spelling altogether.

Though I couldn't fully support her language arts ambitions I had to admit that Leann was right. I needed some male contact. Even the red-eyed bugs splattered on my bumper had been getting more action than I was these days. Rest their souls.

But my nonexistent love life was just one problem. Before I knew it was September, and it had been six months that I had been working at the insurance company. They gave me a raise but it was nothing big. Just gas money, really. Gas money to get my butt right back there to hop on those phones all over again the next day.

But all was well in *Not-Me Land*. Tasha was still with Glen. And Leann was still with Reggie. He'd even moved in with her. I hadn't dated anyone since Rico. For months I hadn't heard from him. It was great. But then all of a sudden, out of the blue, he began calling again. It started out with a call or two here and there then later snowballed into a call a week. He was blowing up my phone like a grenade. But I was letting it ring like freedom. In fact, I had wonderful plans for a drama-free remainder of the year. So Rico was simply wasting his prepaid wireless minutes on my voice mail.

For the most part I'd stayed pretty close to home, moping around, letting myself go. But tonight Leann managed to convince me that a night out was just what I needed in order to get out of my funk and kick-start my life again.

Initially I'd told her I'd have to give her a raincheck. But knowing how they always bounced, Leann insisted on tonight. She said that nobody ever met anybody sitting at home watching depressing movies. I told her that meeting somebody was exactly what had me depressed in the first place. But the more she talked, the more tempting it became. Before I knew it she had me up, showered, and ready to step out again.

I entered my walk-in closet and took a long look around at all the neglected clubwear that was almost unrecognizable to me. Shiny pants. Glittery blouses. Rhinestone belts. Slinky dresses. Each garment seemed to scream: *"Pick me, Sidney!" "No—wear me!" "Hey—Remember us?"* It had been a while since I'd squeezed into a mini skirt. And stilettos were just a memory. As I made a move toward the red mini Mom's voice suddenly rang in my head. I pictured her, shaking her head, hands on her hips, pleading, *"Sidneeeey . . . wrap your presents, sweetheart!"*

I put the mini down and grabbed the more modest knee-length number instead.

When we finally got to the club, as usual, Leann managed to get herself lost within the first five minutes. I told myself that I was glad I'd elected to drive my own car. Her previous behavior and spur-of-the-moment departures had made me wise up to taking separate vehicles, especially since her and Reggie were each other's sexual equal and couldn't get enough of each other. There had been, at least, two occurrences where she'd left me to party stag in order to go home and hanky-panky with him.

Left to forage for my own fun I tried to remind myself of how it was that I'd ended up here in the first place. It was all so hazy. I just remembered it going something like:

"Hmmm . . . I don't know, Leann. This movie is due back tomorrow."

"Aww, come on, Sidney. We'll have fun."

Well, she was *half* right, I thought to myself as I made my way to the bar.

Flying solo I was standing at the bar, nodding my head to Ne-Yo, when I was approached by a man in a crisp, white tailored suit. Clean he may have been, but cute he was not. However, thinking back to my conversation with Tasha I suppressed my urge to tell him to get lost, and decided to 'give an average guy a try'.

That turned out to be a mistake.

"Cindy?"

"No. *Sid*-ney," I enunciated, already annoyed.

Perhaps if he was looking at my mouth rather than my breasts he would've heard me right the first time. Fooled by my fifty-dollar push-up-bra he never even looked at my face.

I lowered my head to meet his eyes, leading them upward to a more appropriate level.

"And *you* are?"

"Oh!" He got the hint. "I'm sorry, baby," he shook his head, "but you look like a million bucks tonight. Are those your real eyes?" he asked, finally getting familiar with my facial features.

"Uhh . . . yes." I looked the other way, showing obvious signs of disinterest that he just wasn't picking up on. "That's right," I added, scratching my neck, wondering *why me?*

As I eventually found my way to the other bar I spotted Leann. She was sipping on a drink, laughing her head off with some man. I thought she was living a little dangerously seeing as how Reggie had that stalker kind of love. But she didn't seem too worried about a possible bust. As for the company she was keeping he looked a little long in the tooth. Semi-gray and balding I estimated him to be in his late forties or early fifties. I couldn't tell whether he was drinking a White Russian, or Ensure. I knew tonight's musical band attracted a classier, yet slightly older crowd, but this was unexpected.

"So, this is where you vanished off to?" I walked up on the two of them, looking for the *S* for *Sugardaddy* on his chest.

"Hey, Sidney. This is Alawicious."

Ala-Who?

"Nice to meet you," he extended his hand, smiling.

I smiled back in spite of my thoughts.

"He stays on *your* side of town," Leann gave me the 'nudge and wink', while I looked at her wondering if she needed some rewetting drops for her trial pair of whisper gray color contact lenses.

I shook Ala-Whatever's hand and hoped this wasn't supposed to be a hook-up. He was, at least, twice my age. I knew Leann wouldn't be trying me like that. But I didn't want to stick around to find out.

"Alright, well, I told Christopher I'd be right back."

Leann looked at me, rightly confused since there was no Christopher.

"Nice meeting you, Alopecia," I waved over my head as I walked away. Leann was tripping. If she wanted to spend her time senior-sitting she'd have to do it *sans Sidney*.

I walked myself to the next room, thinking about how I would let her have it later.

By now I'm sure the bartender was probably tired of seeing me, especially since I didn't order any drinks, but I posted up anyway. The club wasn't all that big so it wasn't like I had much choice. I was positive there wasn't a patch of carpet left in the building that my pumps hadn't already tracked across.

I was getting pretty bored. But from the looks of it I was the only one. People were talking and dancing and mingling all around me. I even saw *Crispy White* on the dance floor breaking it down like it was his birthday. He'd met a girl who, apparently, didn't mind him staring at her breasts all night.

I sighed.

"*Damn*. You look like you need to take your little mad self home!" a complete stranger told me, apparently noticing the frown on my face as I leaned against the bar.

"If it's one thing I can't stand it's a mean-looking pretty woman. Don't make no damn sense. *Ugghh!*" he shrugged like I gave him the jitters then strolled on by like that was the end of his public service announcement for the night.

I couldn't even argue with him.

In light of his critique I decided to remove myself from the high-traffic, high-visibility bar area and go walk around until I found a more inconspicuous space that I could occupy. One that didn't offend the senses of those more committed to the goal of having a good time tonight. And since he'd made me feel like a party-pooping buzz kill, I began pretending as if I was enjoying myself as much as everyone else by dancing in place. But it was a struggle. The DJ must've been drinking on the job because he was experimenting with some crazy mixes and talking all over the music. The only amusement I found was in watching the people on the dance floor lose, and then find again, the beat, as they tried to keep up with his madness. I imagined they all, like me, must've wanted to tell him to shut the hell up and let the record play.

Thinking about it I let a laugh slip out.

"Someone seems to be having a good time," I heard someone say. I looked behind me to find a handsome man wearing the sexiest grin.

I couldn't believe I hadn't noticed him standing there. *What else did he see?* I wondered, thinking back to whether I had pulled my thong out of my behind for the thirtieth time that night, believing I was all alone in this corner of the room.

Damn! I thought to myself.

To make matters worse, as my special kind of luck would have it, he wasn't just an everyday kind of handsome, or novelty pretty boy cute. He was Mr. January through December Handsome. *Happy New Year through Happy Holidays Hot!*—Tall, nicely-built, clean-cut, but satisfactorily rugged. He had great skin. A nice smile. And he was expensively-dressed.

I swallowed nervously.

"You okay?" He asked, noticing my instant change of facial expression.

"Yes," I said with a nauseous look and flat tone. "I was just trying to remember if I'd pulled out my wedgie in front of you before I knew you were standing there."

Shocked that I said such a thing he laughed harder than I predicted he would.

My memory confirming that I *had* actually dug into backside since I'd been standing in that spot I figured after what he'd *seen* I didn't care what he heard.

Putting a hand to his chest as if I'd taken his breath away, he shook his head. "Wow. Are you real?"

"Real crazy, I suppose." I looked toward the exit. I figured I hadn't a chance in hell with this man at this point, and was already picturing myself back in my car.

"Please tell me your name," he said, pulling himself together from that unexpected laugh I gave him.

"Sidney."

"Nice to meet you, Sidney. I'm Jared." He stuck out his hand, smiling.

I looked down at mine and said, "You sure you wanna shake this?"

Jared laughed again as I reluctantly gave him the hand that had been so busy.

"Oh, my. That's refreshing," he said.

"What?" I asked, withdrawing my hand then sweeping my hair to the side as it suddenly got warmer in the spot where we stood.

Jared explained. "Well, sometimes very attractive women take themselves so seriously—I mean, it's okay, I suppose. But, wow . . . to meet a woman who can laugh at herself—especially when she's so intimidatingly-beautiful—is quite refreshing."

I looked at him, trying to see if he was sincere, or pulling my leg.

"And, for the record," he added, "I didn't notice a thing."

"Aww, you did." I sucked my teeth and nudged him with my elbow.

"Honestly. I didn't," he laughed. "But thanks for sharing."

"Well, if you stick around for another few minutes you may catch a replay," I squirmed, wishing I hadn't worn last year's thongs. Now that my weight was back up this week they were much too small and kept slicing into my most tender regions. I made a mental note to clear out my panty drawer as soon as I got home.

Jared watched me wiggle in search of comfort.

"I'm . . . sorry," he said, watching me shimmy. "I wish I could help."

We both looked away for a silent moment before bursting out laughing.

"Ohhhhh . . . I bet you do!" I rolled my eyes and shook my head, still laughing with him.

Jared and I looked at each other as we eventually brought out laughter to a close. Just then a slow song came on.

He stared into my eyes.

I stared into his.

"You know, *Sidney* is a very pretty name," he said.

"Thanks," I smiled.

"Can I take you out to dinner?"

CHAPTER 20

"Right this way, ma'am."

I straightened my dress nervously as the hostess led me inside the dimly-lit restaurant that had soft sounds of the violin emanating out of the walls. Jared and I had spoken on the phone a few times over the past couple of weeks but this would be our first time seeing each other since that night at the club. A gentleman, he'd offered to pick me up, but I declined, preferring to have my car in my possession for our first date.

Jared told me that he hadn't been on a date in almost two years, and to pardon his manners if he seemed a little "out of touch". I couldn't believe that. Someone as handsome and seemingly-refined as him being dateless was just too hard to imagine. But he explained how busy he'd been with his work, and how that left very little time for romancing and companionship. I told him that my date book was nothing to write home about either, so not to worry. We'd be the blind leading the blind tonight.

As I walked through the restaurant it was like I was living out a scene from one of the most romantic movies. I'd never been to such a fine, five-star place since I'd been living here. The only man I'd dated since I'd been in West Palm was Rico, and he was too broke to even *think* of taking me to a place like this.

With my beaded clutch pressed firmly against my thigh the hostess and I approached the center of the room where I saw Jared seated at a table sipping water from a goblet. The way the candle chandelier shined down on him made my heart flutter. The butterflies started buzzing up in my body but I told them to hush. Now was no time to be all sweaty and nervous. I wanted Jared to see me at my best. He put the *h* in handsome. The *s* in sexy. And a great big smile on my face.

Jared stood up when he saw me, his face mirroring mine as I approached.

"Hi, Sidney."

I hadn't seen him in weeks. And now he was standing right in front of me. I was an iceberg in the desert.

"Hi, Jared."

Jared came around to my side of the table and pulled out my chair. "Thank you." I sat down and smiled as he pushed it back in with me in it. I could smell his cologne. My heart started beating fast. And those defiant little butterflies were back.

Jared walked back around to his side of the table, staring at me all the while. "You look amazing."

"Thanks," I blushed.

The hostess smiled. "Your server will be with you momentarily," she said before leaving us to ourselves.

I sat my purse on the table, trying to calm myself. My hands were shaking. I was angry with them for trying to humiliate me. I placed them in my lap before Jared could notice, and nervously looked around the restaurant in a wide-eyed sweep. When I brought them back to our table they found Jared staring at me.

A look of insecurity washed across my face.

"I'm sorry for staring," Jared smiled, "but . . ."—he leaned in closer to me as my breathing paused, feeling the warmth of his face grazing mine—"how many beauty marks do you *have?*" he asked with a captivated gaze.

"Seven," I smiled.

God got a little carried away when he decorated my face. All the beauty marks I had were sprinkled above the neck—every last one of them. Mom, who had several as well, called them *cosmic kisses*.

An observant Jared continued staring at the crazy phenomenon that formed a slightly crooked question mark-shaped constellation that I hoped he wouldn't notice.

He leaned back in his chair. "Wow. Seven, huh?"

I nodded.

Jared shook his head. "Then I must be a lucky man."

My face lit up like a rainbow.

We shared appetizers and champagne over pleasant conversation as Jared and I waited for our entrées. When they finally arrived my steak was much rarer than I preferred. I could still see blood. Hit with a sudden loss of appetite I just stared at it.

"Are you okay?" Jared, noticing the repulsed look on my face, asked with concern.

Yeah, I'm *okay. But I think my dinner needs a doctor.*

"Didn't you order your steak well done?" he followed up when I didn't say anything.

I blinked hard at the meat. "Yes. But . . . it's okay," I said, yet frowning at the practically-raw flesh that made me want to turn vegetarian on the spot.

I didn't want to seem difficult, but I knew full well I wasn't eating anything that was still bleeding. I should've just ordered the seafood linguini like I had wanted, but reluctant to slurp noodles in front of my date, I opted for a prissier, fork-and-knife approach. But I imagined having Jared watch me tear into some dripping-raw meat wouldn't do much for my daintiness factor either.

The gentleman in Jared wanted to see me satisfied.

"No. You should have what you ordered," he insisted, trying to get our waiter's attention, who was already on his way back to the kitchen and didn't notice.

But the petite, young waitress across the room sure did. She ditched her table and scurried over to ours.

"Can I help you, Sir?"

"I'm sorry. I was trying to get the gentleman's attention," Jared explained.

"Oh, that's okay. I can help you," she smiled flirtatiously.

I looked down at my plate to hide my thoughts.

"Well, my beautiful date here"—Jared started, causing a huge smile to flash across my face —"ordered her steak well done. But, as you can see, it's quite rare. "

"Oh, I'm sorry." The waitress picked up my plate. "I'll have the chef cook it a little more for you." She smiled at Jared.

For me. *You'll have the chef cook it a little more for* me!

She finally turned to me as if hearing my thoughts.

"Oh, um, would you like something else while you wait?"

Just you out of my date's face, please.

"No, thank you." I smiled and sipped my water.

As she walked off to pull the plug on the cow, a million thoughts about Jared ran through my head. I was quite impressed with him. In his concern for my satisfaction he'd blended a classy combination of heroic assertiveness and common courtesy. Some men would've either been too preoccupied with their own dinner, leaving me to eat bleeding bovine, while others would've come on way too strong in a rude and overdone effort to come to my rescue. Jared showed class *and* patience. I loved it.

Midway into our meal I was talking his ear off, but Jared didn't seem to mind.

"So, there it is, in a nutshell," I closed, having finished the conversation I'd started last week on the phone about my crummy job. "I know it's not a glamorous gig," I shrugged, "but it's only until I find work in my field.

"There's no shame in honest work." Jared moved his glass toward his mouth.

"I know, but—"

"*Do* you?" He hesitated on the sip to second-guess me.

"Yes . . . I do. But . . . I mean . . ." I shook my head. "Well, I didn't go to school to be a customer service rep."

"I can appreciate that," Jared nodded. "It's great that you continue to set professional goals for yourself. But don't knock yourself for where you are right now."

I looked at him.

"And who says you have to do exactly what you studied in school? It's not exactly written in stone anywhere," Jared said.

"Well, that *was* the plan," I answered, inserting a chuckle, careful not to come across as defensive.

Jared wiped his hands with his napkin and said, "Well, take me, for example. I graduated pre-law. And here I am today in investment banking."

Jared, five years my senior, in addition to having a pre-law degree, had his MBA from NYU by the time he 23. He worked for one of the nation's largest investment firms. But his real dream was to establish his own retail brokerage firm. That's why he'd moved to the area a few months ago. He felt the market had major growth potential. But even though that was still just a dream for him right now I knew he couldn't be comparing his six-figure-salary to my barely-making-ends-meet pay stubs.

"Maybe customer service will help you to become a better P.R. Rep, just as law has helped me in my industry. I don't know. But what I'm saying, Sidney"—he leaned in closer to me again—"is that fate takes us through unexpected turns, and you just have to ride them out until you find the path that leads you to your desired destination. Meanwhile, don't be so hard on yourself. I think you're an amazing woman."

I sat quietly and listened, believing that maybe I could learn something from this man who himself had found such professional success.

"Thank you," I told Jared. "I guess I never really thought about it like that before."

Jared smiled at me.

"And thanks again," I said, "for not asking me what I did for a living, rather letting *me* be the one to bring it up. I can't stand it when people I've known for all of five seconds do that. It's so rude and invasive. And I know they're only asking because they either have an awesome job themselves that they can't wait to brag about, or they're asking simply to size me up. Either way it's just plain bad manners." I shook my head. "I mean, no towel man—no guy with a chamois cloth hanging from his back pocket—at the carwash will ever ask me in his first few minutes of meeting me what I do for a living. Right?"

Jared laughed. "I can't say. But thank you for sharing a bit of your story with me, Sidney. I hope to hear much more—when, of course, you're ready," he added.

He raised his glass. "Here's to . . . good manners," he laughed.

You mean, good man.

I followed and raised my glass. "To good manners," I joined Jared in his toast. But secretly I was toasting to our future together. This felt like something special.

✦ ✦ ✦

When we pulled up to the waterfront property in the affluent Palm Beach Gardens I was speechless.

"Welcome to my home," Jared opened the door for me as I stepped inside, already knowing what to expect as evident from the outside.

As I entered I found myself surrounded by beautiful replicas of classic artwork. *Starry Night. Le Château Noir*—pieces I'd only recognized from Art and Humanities classes. Beyond the tall archway, separating the living- and family room, flanked on either side of two columns, were huge vases, large enough for me to fit into. Golden and bronze they stood six feet, erect like pillars from ancient times.

Overwhelmed by the home's décor, I tilted my head back, looking up through the sky window, only to find the moon, full and glowing, spying on Jared and me. It swept across the violet-magenta sky, catching its breath behind cirrus clouds, like a sea urchin drifting through blue waters. Like me, it seemed to be smiling.

I took my eyes off the moon to look at Jared who I found smiling at me, too.

Jared's home felt so warm and inviting. Feeling that vibration, and probably more by force of habit, I unfastened my shoes, kicking my heels off right there in the foyer.

As my feet touched the cold marble, Jared looked at me peculiarly.

I looked down at my feet, toes wiggling happily over their newfound freedom, and instantly felt my face redden with embarrassment.

"Oh, I'm sorry," I said, rushing to slip my foot back into my shoe. I couldn't believe I'd made the mistake of making myself way too comfortable much too fast. Seeing the look on Jared's face, I feared I'd shown an inadvertent sign of disrespect.

"I'm sorry. I wasn't thinking. I—"

"No," Jared said as I struggled with the strap. "I love that you feel comfortable in my home." Helping me with my balance as I impersonated a flamingo, he added, "It's a compliment. And I'm deeply flattered."

Jared gave me a tour of his home. Everything was as perfect as he seemed to be. Even his plants seemed greener and healthier than any I'd ever seen indoors. I didn't know how he managed that, being out of town as often as he said he was. I wondered if he had a maid, or—*gasp!*—girlfriend come in when he was away.

"Would you like some champagne?" he asked as we made our way back to the living room.

"Yes, I would. Thank you."

Jared went to the wet bar to pour us both a glass. As he bent down to grab the champagne bottle from the mini fridge I made a move toward the mantelpiece.

"Who's this?" I picked up a crystal frame that held a photo of him and a beautiful young woman.

Jared looked up from his task. "Uh . . ." he closed the fridge and stood up, "that's an old girlfriend."

I don't think either one of us knew that I'd end up at his place tonight. I imagined Jared wished he'd foreseen my visit so that he could've removed her picture from display.

I cleared my throat and, as innocently as I could, asked, *"Recent,* old girlfriend?" I was sure the jealousy I tried to mask had shone through in my tone. She had a smile like Janet Jackson, and the longest eyelashes I'd ever seen. Jared said he hadn't been out on a date in two years. I was trying to make sense of the math.

Preoccupied with the bottle's cork, Jared's response came slow. "College, actually." He filled the first flute with soft and sparkling bubbles.

I flipped the frame over and it read: *Jared and Janeyse, 2005.*

"She's pretty." I set the frame down and walked back toward the couch just as Jared came over with the champagne.

An hour slipped away as we kicked back, laughing and talking like we'd known each other for more than just the two weeks we had. I was really feeling like Jared was someone special. Someone I could really let in. In my head I'd already had him approved by my parents. Mom would be doing backflips if I made him her son-in-law.

"You did really well tonight," Jared told me. "Are you sure that was your first time?"

Earlier, after dinner, Jared said he had a surprise for me. Remembering one of our phone conversations where I'd shared with him that I wanted to take Salsa dance lessons, he'd arranged for the two of us to do so this evening. After our hour-long session was over I felt this man had danced his way into my heart.

"Yes," I smiled. "It was my first time. But it won't be my last, I can assure you," I said, sipping on my second glass of champagne.

"Well, I am glad you enjoyed it."

"I did. Thank you again."

"And, um, sorry about your toe," Jared said, regretfully.

"Oh," I batted my hand, "don't worry. That nail will grow back in one, two years tops."

Jared looked horrified.

"I'm kidding," I laughed as he breathed a sigh of relief. "Every nail is intact. You did pretty OK yourself," I told him.

"Nah," Jared shook his head. "I have two left feet."

"No you *dooonnn't* . . ." I love-tapped him on the shoulder, finding any excuse to touch him again.

He smiled at my not-so-sly attempt. We looked at each other, falling into that dinner gaze again.

"So," Jared changed subjects, "you never told me why you switched your major from dance to mass communications. My mother was a dancer in her younger days."

"Oh, really? Wow. That's awesome. What a coincidence." I took a quick sip of my champagne. "Well, my dad said that dancing was for recreation, not education. He was afraid I'd end up broke and heartbroken after graduation—go *figure* that happened anyway." I threw in a joke to lighten the topic that was kind of a sore one for me. "He thought that I should stick with something more practical." I ran my finger around the rim of my glass, thinking back to that discussion.

"It's okay, though." I shook my head. "He was probably right."

I looked at Jared who seemed genuinely interested in what I was saying.

"But, don't get me wrong."— I stood up—"Dance is still very much in my veins." I did a newly-learned Salsa sway.

"Yes, it is." Jared watched me. "It certainly is."

I carried on, feeling the effects of the champagne. I moved my hips, then threw my arms high above my head and twirled around, losing my balance.

"*Whoa*." Jared caught me.

I laughed as I stumbled into his arms, feeling good n' goofy, and just plain glad to be in such wonderful company.

"You know," Jared looked at me as my limbs went limp in his arms, "you're one of a kind, Sidney."

I smiled.

Jared helped ease me back onto the couch. A half glass past tipsy, I glutinously reached for my champagne flute again, raising it from the coffee table to my mouth, humming a happy tune.

"What's that?" Jared asked.

"*It's a Small World.*"

"No," Jared laughed. "That." He pointed to my arm.

"Oh—" I swallowed, then set my glass down —"This?" I ran my thumb down my scar. "Well, the *one* time my parents asked my sister to pick me up from school she wrapped the car around a pole."

Jared looked at me, surprise rushing to his face.

"Yeah . . ." I nodded. "She walked away unscathed while I won a 3-week, all-expense-paid-trip to the hospital. After two surgeries, *unbelievable* doses of morphine, and twenty-three days of post-op, they sent me home with this little parting gift."

I looked up at Jared and said, "Quite the souvenir, huh?"

Jared shook his head, trying not to frown at the unsightly scar that looked like a snake had burrowed then died underneath my skin.

"Wow," he sighed, first gazing at it, then at me. "I imagine that must've been extremely scary for you and your sister." His look showed genuine compassion. "And *painful*," he added.

"Naaah." I shook my head and looked at my scar, stroking it with my hand. "What hurt more in those three weeks was that she never came to visit me." I zoned off, thinking back to that night and how things were before my sister and I had our brush with death. I was so fascinated with her yellow sports car that went from zero to sixty in 3.5 seconds—until it went from sixty to zero in 1. Not only did I walk away with a scar but I'd lost partial hearing in my right ear.

Lost in my flashback it must have been Jared's eyes that shook me out of my daze.

"But, hey," I shrugged, perkily, "I'm just glad the scars on my *face* healed nicely."

Jared moved closer to me on the Italian leather sofa then leaned forward and brushed my cheek.

"So am I," he said.

I blushed shyly at his gentle touch before bailing out of our stare.

"But not everyone left me to rot in my hospital room. My mom came to visit me *twice* a day. She and Dad would come together during the day, then she'd come back later by herself at night. I guess it was really hard on her, especially since my Grandma Hannah—*Grannah*, we called her—had passed away unexpectedly in that very same hospital just two years earlier while visiting us. I guess seeing me there Mom just . . ." I shook my head and took a deep breath, swallowing back the tears brought on by the memory of seeing my Mom so sad.

I smiled to maintain my composure before continuing. "I can remember a few nights I'd open my eyes—just barely from all the medication—and in my squinting I'd find Mom sitting there in the darkness, holding my hand. Most nights I didn't even know she was there. But every morning—every *single* morning —I'd wake to a room full of fresh gerbera daisies. Sweet-scented evidence that she had been there."

I smiled reminiscently as Jared looked at me.

"It's been my favorite flower ever since."

Sade was pumping through the surround sound speakers. Dying candles flickered in the air, sending wisps of dark smoke to float above orange heat like ghosts in black tie. Two hours and half a bottle of champagne later, kissing led Jared and me into the bedroom.

"You are so beautiful," Jared whispered as he placed me onto the sand-colored silk whose coolness excited my back into a surprised arch. Traces of my lipstick stained both his upper and bottom lips.

Trembling, my legs were possessed with a combination of desire and nervousness.

But along with my desire was a disappointment in myself. This was not how I wanted our evening to turn out. I wanted Jared to like me. To respect me. It was pretty safe to assume that a man was not likely to respect a woman who served it up on the first night, and with the repressed energy running through me, I was ready to lose *all* of Jared's respect right there in his room.

I couldn't believe we were about to do this. I couldn't believe *I* was about to do this. My mind said *"Too soon"*. But my body screamed *"Too late!"* As the two duked it out the whole evening flashed before my eyes chronologically as I remembered how we'd ended up here. As I recalled it was *my* overzealous and intoxicated voice that had whispered: *'Jared, your house is beautiful. But you haven't shown me your bedroom.'*

As my ownership of that moment taunted me, Jared, hovering above, looked at me intensely, searching my eyes for any signs of doubt. Though my mind was doubtfully active no such signs existed in my eyes. Only the obvious green for *Go!* was displayed around my pupils.

He obeyed.

Slowly, seductively, Jared unhooked my dress from behind my neck. The tiny, usually-uncooperative clasp gave him no trouble. He paused, looking at me. Making sure I was just as comfortable as he was to take such a leap. My irides, forever unchanged, continued speaking for me.

As heart-pounding, heavy-breathing, eye-watering anticipation built within me my senses began to overload. Invisible steam rose from my body. And sweat began to form above my lip. Looking in Jared's eyes only intensified the moment. They were so filled with the same desire that neither my body nor mind could refuse at that point.

My chest rising with every hot and heavy breath, Jared took a moment to look at me as I lay there. Slowly, he ran his hand from my sternum down to my stomach, stopping to circle my navel. I shivered, my back still allergic to the sheets, as he looked at me penetratingly. My eyelids fluttered. My legs trembled. My heart was the loudest thing in the room.

Jared reached down and grabbed my hands, bringing them to his mouth. First planting soft kisses on them, he wrapped them around his neck then leaned into me, covering my mouth with his. Gently, I cradled his head in my hands as I tasted his sweet and moist mouth that fed warm breath down the inner shaft of my body. I inhaled to pull him deeper into me, sucking his energy right into my soul, savoring the seconds that swiftly passed in the magical moment that was my reality.

Then, he stopped.

"Are you sure you want to do this?" Jared asked in a heated whispered.

That was it. My opportunity. My get-outta-jail-free card with a potential built-in bonus *forgiveness* feature for having worked him up in vain. His tone said it was okay. It was patient as his body awaited further instructions. Even as mixed signals tried to sneak their way into my eyes Jared's were careful to convey compliance. Though desire wasn't far behind.

I looked into those hybrid eyes of his, seeing mine in them, and falling out the other end of a deep breath were the words *"Yes . . . I am."*

Jared and I began kissing again, our bodies further warming. Still untouched below the waist, tension mounted within me as we both prepared to slip into a new dimension of our freshly-budding relationship.

But just as we were reaching scorching-hot temperatures, I asked it.

"Do you deserve me?"

Jared froze at the whisper in his ear. I could hear his breathing change.

He pulled himself from my body. I looked up at him. He looked down at me. Then, after a long pause, he replied.

"No."

Shock rocked through me.

"Probably not," he added as he began backing off.

In sheer disbelief my eyes widened. My lips parted.

"What?" I sat up.

"I don't," Jared said. "Not tonight, anyway. Not yet." He stroked my hair. "But you're definitely worth waiting for. I'm not as anxious about this moment, Sidney, as I am about spending time getting to know you."

Having felt his *'anxiousness'* against my pelvis a moment ago I realized that said a lot.

I leaned back, elbows into the mattress, feeling the beating inside my chest and suddenly realizing it was on rhythm with another, more southern, pulse flowing through my body. A pulse that had, amazingly, began to intensify in those few moments he'd spoke the unexpected.

Jared let out a controlled exhale that I recognized as the first step of the cooling down process. I'd heard that sound before during my virginal years after I'd thrown up a red flag right in the middle of second base. Only this time it didn't carry the tone of anger or disappointment that I was used to hearing. It was much more disciplined and understanding.

Jared motioned for his shirt that lay at the foot of the bed. As his body separated from mine coolness rushed in between us. Feeling the draft—and seemingly by reflex—I quickly pulled him back on top of me.

Jared looked surprised. He looked into my eyes and, through them, I spoke.

"Are you sure?" he whispered.

I kissed him deeply, ambiguity absent. Yet, sensing he wanted verbal confirmation this time, I affirmatively whispered, *"Yes."*

And as the candlelight casts our shadows onto the walls, and the stereo made our moves instrumental, my body completely surrendered to Jared as we made love.

CHAPTER 21

Jared held me as we looked out at the tangerine sun.

"Sidney," he said, "can I ask you something?"

"Yes."

"How many guys have you been with?"

Why do guys always ask that? I thought to myself, wondering what difference it made. Just what did they plan on doing with this information? Of what use was it to them? Did they think they could use it to decide whether wearing protection was a good idea? Did they believe they could determine the type of person I was based on my answer? And most of all, did they actually expect that I would tell them the *truth?*

Considering that I'd slept with him on the first date I didn't expect Jared to believe any answer I provided. He was my fourth sexual partner and, a month from turning twenty-three, I didn't think that was so bad. But then maybe it was considering the fact that I had only been sexually active for just over a year.

I looked up at the slow-rotating ceiling fan.

"Three," I finally answered, regardless of how plausible—or promiscuous—it sounded.

I turned my gaze back toward the window, finding Jared's reflection behind mine. "Why do you ask?" I lay my head back on his arm.

Jared rested his chin atop my shoulder and shrugged. "I don't know. I just . . ." he gently pushed away strands of my hair that obstructed his view of the side my face, "I just feel like I got something really special."

I watched Jared's reflection for a moment as he lay unaware, his eyes closed once again in morning content.

I smiled at him from over my shoulder and said, "You did."

✦ ✦ ✦

Jared invited me to hang with him and his friends this afternoon. He said that one of his buddies had just bought a house and was having a little cookout to celebrate. I was flattered that he would take me around his friends so soon.

Telling Jared I'd be ready by two o'clock gave me enough time to reinvent myself and make a good impression on those close to him. I left his house looking a makeup-smeared mess. And to the public, my evening dress at 11:00 a.m. was a blatant advertisement of my Saturday night sleepover. I hated to risk any sightings but was riding on fumes. I had to stop at the gas station on my way home.

As I stood at the slowpoke pump, daydreaming about last night, I heard my cell phone ringing from inside the car. I opened the rear passenger door and reached down into my bag. When I pulled out my phone the caller ID read: *Rico.*

I sucked my teeth and threw the phone down onto the seat. "Nerve!" I shook the nozzle to hurry the gas, irritated, and snarling inside at the thought of him suddenly sniffing around again. After dogging me the way he did you'd think he had a harem of women—a *clan* of *Felecias*—rendering him much too busy to bother with the likes of me. I was convinced he was crazy. Looking at me with those dead eyes one day, then begging me back not long after. It just didn't make any sense.

To be clear, Rico's resurrected interest didn't flatter me the least bit. I suspected the real reason he was calling had very little to do with me, and much to do with his own selfish, insatiable ego. I'm sure he couldn't stand the fact that I had moved on with my life and appeared to have forgotten all about him. The truth was I hadn't forgotten about him. But I had moved on.

When I got home I had two messages on my land line's voice mail. One was a hang-up from Rico. The other was from Leann. After listening to both messages I deleted them and headed for the bathroom.

I took a long, hot, steamy bath, then coated myself in rich cream as I sat on the tub's edge with lemon-scented candles filling the room with a fragrance that made me feel relaxed and free. For the first time in a long time I didn't have that anxious feeling going on in my chest. I felt totally at peace. Finding it rare, I took a brief moment out of life to enjoy that weightless feeling.

I smiled to myself, feeling excited as I thought about Jared. Last night was so special. Never in my life had I experienced a more perfect evening. I meant it when I told Jared that he'd received something special from me. When I woke up with him this morning I knew that what I had shared with anyone else before him didn't matter. I was his. I was completely Jared's.

When the phone rang at 12:30 p.m. my heart skipped a beat. I was hoping it wasn't Jared. I was nowhere near being ready.

Luckily, it was Tasha.

"Hey, girlie," I answered.

"Hey, Winks! What are you doing?"

"My nails." I fanned my wet toenails with my free hand.

"Right. So, I didn't hear from you last night? How was your date?" Tasha wondered why I hadn't called her afterwards like I'd promised.

"It was good," I replied vaguely, making her work for her answers. Tasha had just as much patience as I did. I loved to torture her.

"Sidney, don't even play with me. You've been talking my ear off about this man for weeks. Now tell me!" she demanded, unable to withstand the suspense.

"Okay. Well, first we—"

"Wait"—she interrupted before I could even begin —"Shoot! That's my boss on the other end. Dang-it! Well, quickly. Tell me this," she said, suddenly pressed for time. "Do you like him?"

"*Like* him? Tasha, I think I love him."

✦ ✦ ✦

Jared called at around 1 o'clock to make sure there wasn't any change in plans. No way had I changed my mind. Maybe *he* had since I'd left his house looking like the Tasmanian devil. But as for me, I was booked solid with plans of hanging out with him all day. Still a gentleman, he said he'd like to pick me up this afternoon, and after insisting on meeting him last night, I couldn't refuse. I didn't want him to think I was hiding something. Or *someone*. Like a male roommate or live-in boyfriend.

When I heard the doorbell I hurriedly put the last finishing touches on my hair, strategically arranging a few ringlets to frame my face. I tossed the hairspray bottle under the sink and zipped into the bedroom. Scanning my vanity, I grabbed my most expensive perfume, letting my neck, wrists, and shoulders have it. I even kissed the back of my legs with the love potion like I'd seen on T.V. Finally, I straightened my dress as I power-walked to the door.

When I looked through the peephole I couldn't see anything.

The doorbell rang again.

"Jared? Is that you?" I said, still stretching myself vertically to see through the blurred lens that needed a good polishing.

"Hi, Sidney," Jared's voice said in the darkness that was my view.

I opened the door and, to my surprise, Jared peeked from behind the biggest bouquet of assorted gerbera daisies I'd ever seen.

"Oh, my gosh! I can't believe you . . ." I was touched beyond words. Jared handed me the enormous bouquet that looked like a painting.

My eyes shimmered at them. "They're so pretty."

"Here." He plucked one from the bunch, tucking it behind my ear. *"Now* they're pretty."

I looked up at him, my eyes aglow. "Thank you so much, Jared." I hugged him.

He hugged me back. "You're welcome, baby."

My ears perked up.

Baby? Did he call me 'Baby'? I smiled as I buried my face into his chest. His arms felt so nice around me. Pressing his sexy-scented body against mine reminded me of last night.

I reluctantly released my hold.

"Wow," I said, still grinning at the enormous bouquet.

Jared held out his arm for me to latch onto. "Are you ready?"

"Yes," I smiled, *more* than ready to go anywhere with Jared 'The Godsend' Graham.

CHAPTER 22

The party was underway. Smells of charcoal briquettes and flame-cooked meat traveled throughout the house, while toe-tapping beats poured from the outdoor speakers, encouraging a few attendees to dance with their drinks poolside. There were about twelve guys and twenty or more girls who'd passed on the spacious living- and dining room for the kitchen and outside deck. I assumed the disproportion of the sexes to be a result of so many successful bachelors in attendance, the majority working with Jared in some capacity.

Jared and I floated onto the patio where most of the guests gathered around the bean-shaped pool. We walked over to the refreshment table hand-in-hand.

"Do you want something to drink?" Jared bent down and opened the ice-filled chest. "Soda? Beer? Wine coolers?" he gave me a few choices.

"Uh ..." I leaned over his shoulder, looking at the selection, "Beer stinks. Soda burns. Ummm . . . wine cooler, please," I decided as I looked inside the bottomless cooler filled with every beverage you could imagine right down to V8.

Jared twisted the cap off my peach cooler before handing it to me. "Yeah, you don't look like the beer type."

"Really?" I laughed. "And just what 'type' do I look like?"

"You look like the type that . . ." Jared bent down, moving his face closer to mine. My eyes widened. "The type that could steal my heart." He planted a soft one on me.

I wasn't used to this. Public displays of affection were something neither Rico nor Damon spoiled me with. Sometimes Damon wouldn't even hold my hand in public, as if to give the illusion of being alone. Jared was showing me a different world.

As the gathering grew, more guests flooded the house and trickled out onto the patio where Jared and I were still behaving like two lovebirds. We were eating off the same plate, laughing and fooling around. I was feeding him a hamburger, trying to be silly and sexy at the same time, when a big blob of ketchup squeezed out from the backside of its bun and landed right between the straps of my new sandals.

"Uggghh!" I froze stiff, looking down at the mess I made like a kid whose top scoop had just toppled off her three-tiered cone.

Jared sprang into action.

"Oh, let me get that, baby." He set the plate down and went to get some napkins, while I stood on one foot, cringing at the unpleasant feeling. When he returned, he knelt before me, wrapped his arm around my leg, offering his shoulder as support as I slipped my foot out of its sandal and into his hand like I was Cinderella.

"Pretty toes," Jared noted, giving the little one some extra attention. "If we were back at my house I would *really* clean these off for you." He grinned sinfully.

Blushing, I wiggled my foot free of his hold and slipped it back into its shoe, looking around the patio to see if anyone heard him. But they were all too busy grubbing on wings and ribs to hear anything over their own smacking and finger-licking.

Jared stood up.

"Look at you turning red," he noticed the maroon mask I was suddenly wearing.

I bumped him with my shoulder. "You are so bad."

"And you are so beautiful."

"Hey, there he is!" a guy in a red shirt waved a hand and stepped out onto the patio. "Larry told me I could find you out here." He approached Jared and me wearing a huge grin.

"Hey, what's up, Mark." Jared slapped hands with him. "Sidney, this is Mark. Mark, this is Sidney. Mark and I work together," he filled me in.

I shook his hand and smiled. "Nice to meet you."

"Likewise," he nodded, not letting go of my hand.

There was a moment of silence. Mark looked like he was trying to hypnotize me.

"So, you guys work together, huh?" I asked what I had just been told just to create a conversational diversion while I reclaimed possession of my hand.

"Yeah," Jared reaffirmed. "Mark was actually the one who assisted me with my relocation. He checked out a couple places for me. Sent some information . . ."

"Yeah, I set him up real nice," Mark added, while his attention was still uncomfortably focused on me.

"Found'em a great place. Beautiful area. I don't live too far myself."

"Six doors down," Jared said as they chuckled together.

I laughed too.

"So," Mark looked me up and down, "*you* put those frowns on those faces back there, huh?" he gestured with his cup toward the huddle of women who, suddenly, didn't look too happy to be here.

"What do you mean?" I asked, confused about my role in that.

"Aw, don't worry about it," Mark batted a backwards hand at them. He looked at Jared and grinned, then put his eyes back on me.

"So, you must be pretty special to tear this guy away from work. It's been a minute since I've seen him with a woman. I was beginning to wonder about my man, if you know what I mean." He nudged Jared, teasingly.

"Hey, watch out now," Jared turned on the bass.

"Naw, I'm just playing," Mark chuckled a final time. "Shoot"—he took a quick sip of his drink —"women would be rioting in the streets if this one traded teams." He slapped Jared on the back, squeezing him between the shoulder blades.

"Aw man, get outta here," Jared's modesty brushed it off.

I nodded fast, siding with Mark.

"So, have you two been knowing each other long?" Mark inquired, tracing his eyes up and down my body.

"Feels like it," I grinned, looking up at Jared again, who seemed not to notice his friend's overly-friendly demeanor.

"Well, that's nice . . ." Mark nodded, forgetting the fact that my eyes could see *his*. "So, um, do you have some friends that look like you, Sidney?"

"Heyyyy," Jared put his arm around me, "give her a break," he told a hungry-looking Mark.

"Aright, alright," Mark laughed, easing up on me.

But the truth was, I didn't mind that question as much as I did the burning stares he was subjecting me to. He was looking at me like Jared wasn't even standing there. Guys that bold gave me the creeps. His good looks were his only salvation. Rating him as high as a nine, it was only the fact that he was handsome that made his behavior *bearably* bothersome. Even still, I didn't how much longer I could hold my fake smile.

"So, Sidney," Mark took another sip from his cup, "what do you do?"

That wiped it right off.

Jared looked at me as my bottom lip dropped.

I took a deep breath and said, "Now, why in the world—"

"Baby," Jared interrupted, rubbing my arm, "can I get you a beer?"

"Beer?" I said, confused, having just told Jared I didn't drink beer, and simultaneously thinking about Mark's question and wondering why my occupation was so important to him.

"Yeah, baby, you ready for another one?" Jared squeezed my hand and gave me a look.

I finally caught on.

"Oh!—Yeah, I'm ready for *another one*," I played along.

Jared draped his arm back around my shoulder. "We'll be back, Mark."

"Oh, alright, then," Mark nodded, wondering if it was something he said.

Once we were in the clear, Jared and I looked at each other. We both burst into laughter.

"Sorry about that," Jared apologized for his friend.

I shook my head. "It's okay."

It wasn't Jared's fault that his friend was nosy and tactless.

"And sorry about that other thing, too. You'll have to excuse Mark. Ever since he and his girlfriend broke up, he's been drooling over every beautiful woman he sees. He doesn't mean any harm."

So he *had* noticed his friend's not-so-subtle flirting.

I nodded. "I understand. Breakups have a way of mutating people's minds. I'm sure Mark's a good guy."

"Yeah . . ." Jared looked back at his friend, who stood where we left him. "He's one of my best buddies. Trust him with my life," he said as we walked back into the house.

We stayed at the cookout until about 8 o'clock. When we got back to his house Jared said that he wanted to make sure he got all the ketchup off my foot, so we took a shower together. It was so sensual. It made me feel so close to him. Like we were married or something. I loved Jared already. I wouldn't dare tell him. But I knew I did. I loved this man.

As Jared dried himself off with the same towel he'd just dried me off with I stood there smiling. Then I caught glimpse of myself in the small, steam-repellant mirror.

I looked like Chaylene.

Ugh! I blinked, shaking my head free from that vision. That damn widow's peak we shared haunted me through my own reflection. I hated it. It made me look mean. Though I believed it fit Chaylene quite well.

I quickly pulled some strands of hair forward to cover it.

"No, don't hide it," Jared said when he saw what I was trying to do. "I think it's beautiful."

He brushed my wet hair back with his hands, then cupped my face. "You don't have to hide anything from me, Sidney."

I looked up into his eyes and smiled.

He smiled too.

Then he leaned down and kissed me.

When Jared and I went to the bedroom I quickly slipped under the covers, already turning into jelly. I couldn't wait for him to touch me. I couldn't wait to touch *him*. With giant hearts in my eyes I watched him ditch the towel before sliding into bed himself.

As Jared reached over me and turned off the light I squirmed with delight, letting out a playful giggle. I was ready for a repeat session of last night's lovemaking.

But then, confusing me, Jared told me goodnight.

"Oh . . ." I looked at Jared, his head on his pillow. "Okay . . . Goodnight."

I leaned over and kissed him on his cheek.

Jared put his arm around me and smiled as I nestled into his chest. Being with him was the best feeling I'd had in a long time. I couldn't help but shut my eyes and Thank God as I listened to his heartbeat. At that moment I believed he was the man I'd been waiting for my whole life.

But as we lay there, comfy and cozy, something inside me couldn't help but spoil the moment. Stealing the joy that should've otherwise engulfed me was a painful reminder. A messenger I wanted to shoot. It warned me not to get too attached. It advised me to simply enjoy the moment for what it was: a moment. It cautioned me that I was getting ahead of myself. After all, I'd slept with Jared on our first date and, now, here we were in bed again for the second time. He was probably still high off the previous night's postcoital endorphins. But after they wore off so would the newness of me.

I pulled the covers up to my chin and snuck a look at Jared. He caught me looking and smiled at me, unaware of the agonizing thoughts that whirled around in my head. Looking up at him I smiled back, but inside I wanted to cry. I wanted to cry my heart out inside because I knew that, most likely, in a matter of weeks it would all be over.

CHAPTER 23

I reached into the bag of taffy as if my fingers could determine the wrapper's color simply by touch. Pulling out a yellow one I resorted to peeking inside the bag, searching for the last red wrapper I saw just moments ago.

"Did you eat my last cherry?" I looked at Jared, whose jaws were in serious motion.

His eyes got big and guilty.

He shook his head. "No—*Gulp!*" He swallowed the wad he'd been working on for a while.

The golden nimbus he tried willing over his head with those wide eyes of his wasn't materializing. What I saw, instead, were two cherry-red horns.

"You did!" I accused him. "You ate my last cherry."

"No, baby, I didn't."

I put my hand on my hip. "Open your mouth."

"Baby—"

"Open your mouth!" I insisted, tempted to pry his jaws open with my bare fingers.

Jared said *Ahhhh,* as I got up from my side of the table.

Standing over him I squinted suspiciously, then bent down and looked around inside his mouth, adjusting my head's tilt, wishing I had a flashlight. Then my eyes landed on his tongue.

Cherry red.

"You did!" I said, appalled that he'd lied even with the irrefutable evidence saturating his palate. He knew cherry was my favorite. Everyone knew. Tasha was grape, and I was cherry. Did he dare deny me the last cherry? What I'd anticipated for the past ten minutes? Had I known, I would've been sure to enjoy the previous one much more than I had.

Jared laughed as I looked at him like he was a criminal. "I didn't. I promise. It was strawberry," he swore while the truth lie mashed in his molars.

"*Strawberry . . .*" I narrowed my eyes at him. "Stick out your tongue!"

Jared sputtered out two disbelieving chuckles. "What?"

"I said, stick out your tongue!" I was dead serious.

Amusing me, Jared stuck out his tongue that couldn't sit still outside his mouth. He laughed, still saying *Ahhhh*, but he laughed alone.

I placed my hands on the back of his chair, one by each shoulder, to balance myself as I slowly leaned into him, drawing in a long whiff of his fruity-smelling breath.

I couldn't tell. I couldn't say for sure. I was unable to precisely ID the scent. It was definitely some kind of '*erry*', but which one, I didn't know.

Face-to-face with Jared, whose wiggly red tongue was inches outside its tunnel, I brought my eyes up to his, our lashes practically touching, my perfume filling his nostrils.

I looked at him with focused intensity.

He looked back.

Then, with one slow and long stroke of my tongue, I licked Jared's tongue from its tip all the way to where our lips met.

"Mmmm . . . " he moaned as my tongue pressed hard against his.

When he tried to turn it into a kiss I pulled back. This was no time for affection. I ignored the surprised flames I saw rising in his eyes and looked at him with piercing ones as I deliberated on the sample.

Suspenseful, Jared looked at me as I smacked my tongue twice to confirm the taste, sending the signal straight to my brain, requesting flavor-specific data.

It returned a match.

As Jared anxiously awaited the verdict, I narrowed my eyes, this time unmistakably defining the taste.

I looked at him grimly.

"Strawberry."

"See!" Jared pulled me into him and began tickling me.

I squirmed, stubbornly holding in my laugh.

"I would never lie to you," he said, finally squeezing a giggle out of me.

"I was wrong," I sighed, feeling bad for making him go through the inspection. "Sorry . . ."

"It's okay, baby," Jared said, grabbing for my hand. "In fact," he smiled, "it was my pleasure." He pulled me back down and shared his strawberry mouth with me.

I couldn't dream up a better man. Jared was everything I ever wanted, and more than I thought I could have. He made me feel like such a beautiful and complete woman. Like I could stimulate him in multiple ways. I wasn't just the physical for him, I was everything. And he was *my* everything. He was not only my lover, he was my friend. My dear friend. He was like Tasha with testosterone. Our connection was so amazing that it scared me at times. I'd find myself getting scared that none of it was real. That I'd been dreaming. That for eight hours, I'd only *dreamed* the past thirteen months and would soon wake—heartbroken and lost—in love with a character from a realistically-cruel dream.

But every night that I spoke to Jared, every night that I was with him, I realized more and more that I didn't have to worry because he *was* real. Our love was real. Finally. It was real.

I pulled myself away from Jared's lips and walked back to my side of the table.

"*Whew*. That was good," I said, fanning myself.

Jared nodded in agreement, looking at me like he wanted seconds.

"So do you forgive me?" I asked sweetly, batting my lashes as I sat down.

Jared put his finger to his chin as though he needed to think about it, then grinned playfully. "Of course I forgive you, baby."

"Thank you," I grinned back, glad to be back in his good graces.

"Now"—Jared cleared his throat and stretched his arms over his head, cracking his knuckles—"will you forgive *me?*"

I looked at him, confused. "For what?"

"For this" —he picked up his queen, then hollered —"Checkmate!"

CHAPTER 24

The theater resembled a circus as anxious moviegoers swarmed the lobby and concession stands in a scurry to get their popcorn and candy before their respective movies started. Jared and I were practically regulars. The ushers should've known us by name.

"I can't *wait* to see this movie," I squeezed Jared's hand, smiling as the pimple-faced boy tore our tickets in half and directed us to theater thirteen to our left.

"You want your usual, right?" Jared asked as we made our way to the snack line.

"Yep." I swung his hand in mine.

"Sure, but *I* better not get too much," Jared said. "I don't wanna spoil my appetite for my victory dinner."

Jared couldn't resist rubbing his win in my face. He'd previously confessed that I was the best chess player he'd ever battled, so whenever he beat me he always relished the moment. Plus, it meant that I had to cook homemade blue crab chowder, which was a pain.

"Yeah, yeah." I rolled my eyes at his gloating. "I'll go grab us some seats."

I stood on my tiptoes to kiss him, feeling four eyes burning a hole in the left side of my head as the two young women in line in front of us were constantly looking back at Jared and me, playing it off like they were looking for someone. I smiled at Jared, who pretended not to notice, before I headed off toward our theater.

Jared and I liked to sit in the far rear corner of the theater. That way we didn't have to worry about people excusing themselves and stepping all on our toes as they squeezed past us to go to the restroom, or to restock on refreshments. We also enjoyed the privacy that the back corner offered us in case my mischievous hand found its way into Jared's lap. He'd always spank my hand, telling me to behave. But I rarely did.

I'd been trying to see this movie ever since Leann told me it was a tear-jerker. But since he'd started his investment firm last fall Jared was doing way more traveling than he had in the past—if *that* was even possible. His trips to New York, amazingly, doubled. But I never complained. He did the best he could to balance his work with our relationship. He was actually doing a good job of it. I just made it a point to savor every moment we spent together.

As I walked into the dark theater, they were already showing previews of *Coming Soons*. We never could get there before the lights went off. And, as usual, it was my fault. Jared never had a problem getting ready on time. It was always me who was responsible for our just-in-time arrivals.

Looking around the theater I put my 20/20 vision to work. I couldn't believe how many other women had dragged their husbands and boyfriends along. I looked around at the faces of all those men, and they looked just as they did when they sat in soft-backed department store chairs waiting for their fashion-hungry women to decide on the perfect pair of pumps. I laughed to myself, knowing that I was just as guilty of preparing to hold my man hostage for the next hour and a half, when he'd rather be home watching sports highlights.

As I scanned our favorite corner I was disappointed to see that some other couple was already cuddled up in it. In fact, I didn't see any available paired seats at all. I kicked myself, fearful that my primping would cause Jared and me to sit separately and, for that, we'd just as soon forfeit the cost of the tickets and leave. But unwilling to wait another week to see the highly-recommended film I continued my search.

Finally, my big eyes and determination found an available pair of seats. Like Michael Jackson in Billie Jean, I hot-stepped my way up the lighted steps to claim them.

As I was approaching the row of my desire, I saw the young lady sitting next to my prize pair quickly toss her jacket into one of them.

"Excuse me . . . Excuse me," I had to say twice since she acted like she didn't see me standing there, much less hear me. Besides the neck-cramping, eye-straining front row they were the only paired seats left in the theater, sandwiched between her and another couple who looked to be mother and daughter.

I leaned over and spoke. "Hi."

She finally looked up at me.

"Is this seat taken?" I pointed to the seat with the jacket in it. Unless it had its own ticket in one of its cotton-blended pockets it was about to end up on the floor.

She glanced over at her partner, who wore an embarrassed-to-be-with-her look on his face. Then, without saying anything to me, she reluctantly removed her jacket from the seat.

"Thank you." I sat down next to her. She declined telling me whether or not I was welcome. She just looked straight ahead, shunning me with an attitude I didn't earn.

What's her *problem?!* I thought to myself, moving over to the second seat, leaving one seat between us.

Surprisingly, she seemed somewhat put at ease by my new seating arrangement. I realized why when I saw her grab her man's hand with seemingly-renewed comfort.

Really? I thought to myself. It was absolutely ridiculous how insecure some women were. *Get a grip, girl!* I thought to myself, rolling my eyes inside.

Just then I saw Jared coming up the carpeted stairs with boxed refreshments cradled against his chest and drinks in his hands.

"Over here, honey!" I waved.

The screen had just announced our feature presentation as he reached our row.

"Here you go, baby," I removed my sweater for Jared to sit down. He squeezed past me after handing me my nachos and strawberry lemonade. "Did you get some napkins?"

"Yeah, one sec." He placed his drink into the built-in cup-holder, then pulled some napkins from his pants pocket along with his cell phone. "Here you go." He handed me a few.

"Thank y—" As Jared was settling in, I noticed *Jacket Girl* checking him out. She ran her eyes up and down his fabulous frame, assessing his stock.

With a slight forward lean, I took inventory of *her*. Her shiny, tan legs poking out of her short jean skirt. Her French pedicure complete with rhinestones across both big toes. Her C-cup bosoms in her B-cup bra spilling over the white halter that barely restrained them.

Her ugly boyfriend, whose hand she was no longer so concerned with holding, didn't notice her salivating over my man. But I sure did. She was looking like she wanted to upgrade.

"Jared." I tapped him on the leg.

"Yeah, baby?" He put his cell phone on silent before putting it back in his pocket.

"Let's switch seats."

He looked at me incredulously, having just gone through the trouble of finally settling in.

"Pleeeeeeease . . ." I batted my lashes.

Jared shrugged, ultimately indifferent. "Sure."

He gathered up his popcorn and drink then stood up as we crossed each other, trading positions in the narrow aisle.

Having squeezed by without incident, I plopped back down into my original seat and turned to *Jacket Girl,* with whom I, now, competed for an armrest.

"I hear we're going to *love* this movie," I told her, claiming the cushioned divider, and looping my other arm through Jared's.

✦ ✦ ✦

I was flipping through a magazine on the couch when Jared finally hung up with his mother. He had been on the phone with her since we got out of the movie over two hours ago when he saw that she'd left him a message on his cell. I'd showered, cooked dinner, and had already eaten by the time they finished talking.

"How's she doing?" I moved my legs, making room for him on the sofa.

He sat down. "She says she's doing alright," he sounded unconvinced, "but I think she's just being stubborn."

Jared's mom hadn't been feeling well lately, but she was so willful she'd never go to the doctor despite how many times Jared begged her to, or how awful she felt. She'd joke her way out of visits, saying doctors were around too many sick people for her. But this was no joking matter for Jared.

When Jared couldn't persuade her he tried shaming her into going, telling his mom that it was silly and irresponsible for her not to. But she didn't listen. When I met her last winter, on our trip to Indiana, she looked as healthy as anyone else. But the last few times I'd spoken with her on the phone she didn't sound like herself.

"You think she'll be okay?" I snuggled up to Jared's arm as he looked out the large bay window.

"Yeah, I'm sure she will." His voice tried to sell optimism. But his face couldn't close the deal. His soft, reassuring words couldn't veil the sounds of his concerned heart.

Jared also looked worried. Even more worried than he'd been looking for the past few months. I hated seeing him so troubled. Even a selfless, charming smile couldn't disguise the agony occupying his mind. But he didn't have to be brave for me. He could've been free with his emotions. That's what love was. But I understood. He was trying to be strong. He was trying to be strong even as his hope was growing weak.

I looked up at him, wishing I could extinguish all his worries. Wishing I could bring authenticity to the optimism in his voice. Wishing there was real power in what I said next.

"Me too."

Jared rested his head on mine as he gazed out into the damp darkness. The only light was that of the moon's glistening off water beads that slept on leaves, accompanied by its own reflection rippling through the water.

I was quiet. I didn't know what else to say. What *could* I say? How do you console the inconsolable at an inconsolable time?

"The chowder came out good." I hoped his favorite food would cheer him up, if only temporarily. Besides, he'd still won the chess match.

"Thanks, baby," Jared whispered, still staring out the window.

We were both quiet. I was the biggest chatterbox in the world around Jared, but I didn't know what to say right now. I didn't know how I could've helped. I wished there was a way I could've changed everything and made it better.

I exhaled as I rested my head against his shoulder. Jared looked down and noticed my sad face.

"So," he sat up, "did you enjoy the movie?" He shook my leg and smiled, trying to mask his real concern for the benefit of me. He was always thinking of me. Even when there was so much more to think about.

"I did," I grinned as I played along. "It was sweet. Did *you?*" I wanted his take on it. It was such a romantic movie. The guy and girl got married at the end.

Jared gave the typical male answer to my question.

"It was alright." He nudged me and said, "But I heard *you* over there sniffling, though." He laughed.

"I was not!" I smacked him on the arm with a throw pillow.

"Mmm . . . hmm . . . I saw you." Jared took the pillow from me, letting it fall to the floor. His playful grin slowly faded as he looked me in my eyes. He lifted my chin and kissed me, soft and slow at first, then hard and deep. Matching his rising intensity I kissed back just as hard, barely able to breathe, gasping between kisses. My body was warming. My heart began racing. Passion filled me. Then disappointment quickly replaced all of that when he pulled away.

"What's wrong?" I whispered, wondering why he'd stopped.

Jared looked at me with serious eyes. "You know I love you, right?"

"Yes ." I blinked in slow motion. "I do. And I love *you.*" I leaned in with parted lips, wanting to pick up where we'd just left off. But Jared pulled back.

"You mean a lot to me, Sidney." He caressed my face. "I just want you to know that."

I started to get scared, wondering where he was going with all this. I knew he loved me, but it made me uneasy to hear him say so in such a way. It felt like he was leaving me or something. Like he was going somewhere.

"And I'm *not* going anywhere. So get that look off your face," Jared read my panicked expression and replaced it with a relieved smile.

"I just want you to know that you're the best thing that's ever happened to me." He ran his thumb across my cheek, his words matching his touch. "And I appreciate the love you show me. I never want to lose you, Sidney." He finally kissed me again.

Maybe the movie had an effect on him after all, I thought to myself.

"*Why* do you love me?" I boldly asked, wanting to know exactly what it was about me that had been able to secure his love.

Jared looked at me and said, "Telling you why I love you would be like you telling me why you like to dance, or asking Mother Nature why the sky is blue. It just is. I just do."

"Try, Jared. Tell me why it is that you love me and no one else," I pushed.

"Sidney, whatever my heart feels. Whatever my soul feels when I'm with you tells me that I do. I love you. Sure, my eyes may like the way you look. My ears may enjoy the way you sound. My hands may love the way you feel. But none of them control my heart. None of them control my soul. To tell you why—to tell you how much I love you—would be a ridiculous attempt to describe the indescribable. It would be ridiculous for me to even attempt to describe the extent of my love for you, and an even more ridiculous attempt to describe the rationale behind it. And that's because there is no *one* thing that is responsible for how I feel about you, Sidney. I won't minimize the magnitude of my feelings for you with one or two single adjectives that may describe you. It's you. It's simply you. Your *everything*. Your *Sidney*. Your essence, and how it interacts with mine. It's us. Just *us*. We match. We complement each other. We figure it out on a soul level—Not just a mental or physical one. It is beyond us to know why. When I sit with you. When I talk to you. When I hold you. Think of you. Love is what I feel. I *feel* it. And I will never *unfeel* it."

Jared held my hands as he still tried to make me understand.

"To describe how much I love you," he continued, "would be like trying to describe how hot the sun is."

I paused, then said, "*Very???*"

Jared laughed. "Yes, Sidney. *Very*." He brushed his nose softly against my ear and whispered, "*Sidney, I never . . . wanna . . . lose you,*" he repeated in between soft kisses. "*Do you understand? . . . I never . . . wanna . . . lose you.*"

I breathed heavily under the meltdown of his moist pecks. "*You won't,*" I whispered, but more focused on kissing him than assuring him. To me, that was a given. Though I couldn't put it into philosophical words, I knew that I loved Jared with all my heart. I sure as hell wasn't going anywhere.

As we kissed Jared slowly moved his hand from my face and reached through the leg opening of my pink boxers as I squirmed with excitement, still fused to his lips. His fingers found their way to my panties, pulling them to the side while his tongue made friends with mine.

"I want to be with you forever, Sidney," he whispered warm breath into my ear, kissing my neck that twisted and turned to facilitate his oral massage. *"I want . . . to be . . . with you . . . forever."*

I sucked in cool air and, on the brink of ecstasy, whispered, *"You will."*

CHAPTER 25

"I better go grocery shopping," I said to myself as I looked into the practically-empty refrigerator after eating the last bagel with my morning tea. Evidently, Jared had been too busy to go. A near-empty carton of eggs, cheese, a container of chopped vegetables, a shriveled orange, condiments, and a sip of apple juice were the only contents of the otherwise hollow fridge. After whipping up a semi-respectable meal, I carried the breakfast tray into the bedroom.

Jared was still sleeping. He was usually the early bird, but it was 8:35 a.m. and he hadn't moved a muscle. I guess his flight really wore him out. Good thing he wasn't working today. I figured he could use the rest. Jealous of his day off, I called in this morning, telling my boss's voice mail that I had a migraine. Jared didn't like me playing hooky. But I missed him. And he had to fly back out on Wednesday, so I wanted to spend as much time with him as possible before he left. In the beginning Jared's business trips and busy schedule were a turn-on. Now they were torture.

"Good morning, sweetheart." I leaned over and kissed Jared on his forehead.

Jared's eyes opened to look at me but they weren't red. "Good morning, baby." He cracked a smile. "You made me breakfast?"

"I sure did."

I set the tray in his lap as he sat up and propped a pillow behind his back.

"You didn't have any turkey bacon, though. You're out of *a lot* of things."

Jared picked up the fork to taste the omelet. "Yeah, I've gotta get to the store."

"I'll go," I volunteered, accustomed to doing Jared's shopping from time to time, and loving to play house. Six and a half more months had gone by that Jared and I had been together, totaling nearly twenty. I had broken my record. I finally had relationship success! And playing *wifey* to Jared was simply practice for what I'd hoped would soon be made official.

"Oh, thanks, baby. I'll give you the card."

He took a sip of the half-glass of juice, then a bite of toast.

"You're not going to eat?" he asked me.

"I had half of a bagel earlier."

"You know, Beautiful, I love your sexy little body, but uh . . . " he palmed my backside, "you don't need to lose any weight." He squeezed my left butt cheek like a bicycle horn.

"Heyyyy," I swatted at his hand. "I'm perfect just the way I am."

Jared pulled me back by the hand as I tried to wiggle away. "Yes, you are," he agreed, planting a gentle kiss on my hand.

"Okay, then." I rolled my eyes and snatched my hand back, stepping just out of his reach.

Jared went back to eating, enjoying the cheese eggs.

"Well . . . I tugged at the belt of my satin robe, "I'm going to go take a shower now." My robe flew wide open, widening Jared's eyes as I gave him a not-so-innocent peek.

He put his fork down and reached out for me.

"Ah-Ah!" I dodged his touch. "I wouldn't want to burn any calories." I made a teasing face at Jared and headed for the guest bathroom, leaving the master bath for him.

Twirling my robe's belt and whistling, I stopped at the thermostat . Checking over my shoulder first to see if the coast was clear, I inched it up to seventy-two.

"*Sidney!*" Jared called out, making me jump.

"Huh?"

"Are you going to work today?" he asked, realizing the hour.

I inched the thermostat up one more degree then hurried down the hall into the bathroom.

The water felt so good cascading on me like a warm spring. Wet strands of hair stuck to my face and neck, transforming my bed hair into stringy, wet locks. I closed my eyes to enjoy the feeling of the full body massage.

Jared's shower was heavenly. It had multiple jet streams that caressed me from every angle. And his water seemed a lot softer than mine, too. It was like a stand-up-style Jacuzzi.

I opened my eyes and looked around the large shower, tickled by all of my belongings. My razor, body wash, back brush, loofah sponge were all scattered along the ledges. Without even realizing it I guess I was kind of marking my territory. The only thing that belonged to Jared was a shrunken and cracked bar of dehydrated soap that needed to be tossed out.

I smiled as I picked up my loofah sponge and squirted raspberry-pear shower gel on it, squeezing it until fluffy suds were born. Starting with my neck, I ran the sponge all over my body, slowly, until I reached my stomach. In a slow, circular motion, I ran it across my navel ring, watching how the tiny soap bubbles shrank, then vanished from the curved sterling silver. Burrowing my finger behind the jewel, I played with the tiny barbell that held the precious stones, flicking it with my finger, when suddenly the shower door opened.

Jared, who'd abandoned his breakfast, stepped inside with an ardent stare.

"Breakfast was good," he smiled. "But I'm still hungry." He closed the glass door behind him.

Still holding the sudsy puff, I ran it across his chest, noticing how the suds clung to the fine chest hair that sparingly decorated his pecks. His hands hungrily enveloped my breasts as his mouth pressed hard against mine and sucked the air right from my body. I traded the sponge for his firm buttocks and reciprocated the force with which he kissed me. The steam grew thicker around us as our bodies produced a warmth of its own.

With the leverage his hands found behind my knees, Jared lifted me slightly, backing me up against the tile. Our passion, for the moment, turned the cold, wet wall into warm satin sheets.

Jared entered me as I gasped for air through the spraying mist. I latched onto his neck and rolled my tongue around his, moaning in yummy delight. We found our rhythm and rode the waves of passion as the water rained down on us just as the waterfall had in Fiji last summer, and Tahiti the spring before. But in this moment, we were in our own private paradise.

Jared covered my neck with his mouth. Our bodies swayed in a rolling, rhythmic interpretation of love as a tidal wave of satisfaction engulfed us, sweeping us toward the shores of ecstasy. Taking a firm bite of the vein that pumped so rapidly at the feel of his teeth, Jared sent sensuous pain through my body that excited me, and I let go, causing him to release as well. In an instant, my warm, wet center squeezed and then released, again and again around him, until all that once filled him, filled me.

"I love you so much, Sidney." Jared opened his climactic eyes. "I love you so much," he breathed, his legs giving way at the pinnacle of pleasure.

"I . . . love you, too," I gasped before we collapsed in a sea of satisfaction, clinging to each other on the shower floor like two castaways unconcerned with rescue.

"Your water bill is going to be obscene." I dried off, having finally actually showered.

"I'll gladly pay that water bill." Jared winked at me through the mirror's reflection as he brushed his teeth.

My face grew a giant smile.

"You're glowing," he said through words that were barely audible.

"What?"

He stopped brushing. "I said you're glowing."

I looked at myself in the mirror, realizing he was right.

He went back to brushing.

"So," he said, "since you're obviously not going to work, what do you want to do today?"

"Huh?" I over-dramatically brought my brows up, pretending I didn't hear him.

He stopped brushing and looked at me.

I laughed playfully and then said, "Wanna go to the beach?"

"Sure, we can do that," Jared agreed, then rinsed. "If," he stipulated, "you promise not to do this again." He looked over his shoulder and pointed to the sunbaked *S* on his back.

"Don't fall asleep then!" I threatened, knowing there was more sunblock where that came from. "Oooh, and if we get back early enough maybe we can go to the movies."

"Sure. What's playing this week?"

"I'm not sure." I reached over him into the medicine cabinet for my deodorant. "But I'll find something good after I get back from the grocery store."

Jared wiped his mouth with a towel. "Oh, you're going to do that now?"

"I can go later." I held one arm in the air, applying a clear stroke.

"No, that's fine." Jared slathered shaving cream on the bottom half of his face. "How long are you gonna be?"

"Well, that all depends on how much money is in your account," I joked, knowing he knew how reckless I was with finances.

I thought it was pretty funny, but Jared didn't laugh. I looked at his reflection and saw it was off somewhere in a world of its own.

"Jared?"

He emerged from his daydream, looking at me through the mirror. "Oh. *When?*" He picked up his razor and proceeded to shave.

"I should be back within the hour." I watched him carve out a clean path of cocoa-brown smoothness across his face, wondering what had him zoning out so early in the morning. "You okay?"

Jared put the razor down and turned to me. He grabbed me by the waist. "When I'm with you, Sidney,"—My eyes widened as they saw *his* looking at me so seriously—"I'm better than okay."

Before I could say anything, he kissed me. I could taste the toothpaste in his cool, fresh mouth as he played in mine like he was fishing out a piece of candy or something else sweet that he was determined to retrieve. My legs were ribbons all over again. Just before I passed out from the heatstroke of the passion, he let me go.

"Wow," I exhaled heavily, blinking and feeling light-headed. "What was that for?"

Jared backed his face away from mine, showing me with his eyes that he meant what he was about to say.

"For making my life so full and happy."

My eyes danced back and forth between his, feeling the depth and sincerity of his profession.

Then, inexplicably, he burst into moment-killing laughter.

"What?" I looked at him, dumbfounded. "Do I—do I have something on my . . . " I caught a glimpse of myself in the mirror. Shaving cream covered the rim of my mouth like a rabid animal. Jared was laughing hysterically.

"Alright, alright." I picked up the hand towel, wiping the white fluff from my mouth. Jared was standing there chuckling like it was the funniest thing he'd ever seen.

"Is it really *that* funny?" I raised my brow, while he tried covering his mouth with his hand as if it also concealed his bouncing shoulders.

"Mr. Funny Man today, are we?" I shook my head at his silliness.

He still kept laughing.

"Okay, then. You give me no choice." I picked up the can of shaving cream.

Jared threw his hands up. "No, baby. No," he pleaded, backing away.

"No, no, no," I insisted, moving toward him. "You're full of laughs this morning. So, this'll be funny, too. " I held the can over his head as I slowly approached.

Jared backed up further, shaking his head and trying to reason with me. But before he could say another word, I squirted shaving cream all over his face and chest, turning him into a human sundae. Then, laughing myself, I snatched the towel from around his waist and took off running as he chased after me naked.

✦ ✦ ✦

The lines were longer than I'd expected. Even the express checkout was moving at a snail's pace. Some lady with obviously more than ten items tried stacking them on top of each other like she was the slyest person in the world, while the man behind her was giving her dirty looks like she was a criminal. Finally, he bailed out to the customer service line for his speedy checkout.

Appearing to have even more coupons than items, the woman slowly fished out another penny-saver from her coin purse when I saw a familiar face enter the store. I quickly turned my head toward the magazine rack, wishing I was invisible.

A few moments later I turned around and my ghost was gone. The cost-conscious woman took her time putting her change and receipt into her purse. I was sure she was doing so deliberately, sensing that I had grown a bit impatient, and punishing me for it.

When she finally moved out of the way, I began putting my items on the conveyor belt. Just as my groceries slowly made their way toward the cashier, Rico walked up behind me.

"Hey, Sidney," he poked me in my side like he still had privileges, even two years later.

I didn't speak.

"Hey, I've been trying to call you," he told me as if I didn't know.

"Why are you talking to me, Rico?" I watched the clerk as she scanned the apple butter, wishing she would move faster.

"Look, Sidney," Rico's voice softened into a discreet whisper, "I uh . . . I met her a month before I met you."

"Spare me," I said, fumbling through my purse, looking for Jared's debit card, hoping Rico couldn't tell that my hands were trembling. I didn't give a damn if he'd met her in the neonatal ward on the day he was born. He still lied. *And* cheated.

"Look, it wasn't you, Sidney. It was—"

I whipped my head around and looked at Rico, knowing he wasn't going to give me *that* line.

He shook his head. "No, what I'm saying is I just wasn't ready for what you were trying to give me at that time. That's all. It really was as simple as that."

The clerk's pace slowed as Rico tried to explain.

"When we met, I didn't . . . " He struggled with his words. "I didn't know we'd—"

"Do more than just have sex?" I put the *'Die now!!'* stare on him.

Sensing he'd hit a brick wall, Rico stuttered his way toward another explanation.

I held up my hand. "Save it, Rico."

I knew what he was trying to say. He was trying to say that, though he'd played along for a while, he didn't really plan on actually dating me when we'd first met. That I just looked like someone to play around with for a little while. Maybe it was my outfit. My clothes. Perhaps my skin-tight pants and sequin top made me look disposable to him. Like a single-use camera. He'd use me to make some fun memories, then discard me for a fresh replacement.

He was a jackass. I made no apologies for my club clothes. I liked my party outfits. Besides, it was like Leann said, '*Conservative clothes can camouflage . . . something that rhymes with 'toes' but starts with an h'*. Any woman could throw on a headband and a cardigan and declare herself demure. Rico was a dumbass for prejudging me.

After getting an earful—and running out of items to scan—the clerk finally confirmed my total. I swiped Jared's card and entered his PIN number as Rico breathed something into my ear about a second chance. My hands shook as I pushed the keypad. I hadn't been that close to him since that day at the restaurant. In that parking lot. I was upset at myself for feeling the way I felt. Our love affair was brief but the passion left a permanent mark on my heart. After all, he was the first guy since high school to tell me he loved me.

But he *didn't* love me, I remembered. *He lied!* I reminded myself as I mashed the green button harder than necessary.

As my transaction was quickly approved, the clerk seemed reluctant to hand me my receipt. I held my hand out and looked at her as Rico continued to ramble. And when she finally gave it to me, I stuffed the receipt into my purse and flew out of the store so fast that I accidentally left the groceries behind.

CHAPTER 26

*W*HAM!!* **I assaulted** the alarm clock, knocking it to the floor.

Still beeping out of control, I pulled it back up by its cord and smacked it silent. "Nice. I wake me *and* the entire complex up," I mumbled as I threw off the covers and stomped my way to the bathroom.

At 5:00 in the morning I looked pretty rough. It was apparent that my face wasn't ready for a new day. It wasn't finished doing whatever it does while I sleep. It was as if my cells weren't fully replenished or something. My eyes looked awful, like they'd seen hell and back in my dreams. They were bloodshot and had dark circles under them, and that was just some stuff I wasn't used to. Even my hair was a stranger pre-dawn.

They had a lot of nerve declaring mandatory overtime this week. They needed to hire some more damn people! Then they'd have adequate coverage to handle those calls. Making me come in an hour and a half early and taking only half my lunch just wasn't right. I didn't like being there my normal eight hours. Ten was just going to kill me.

Some people were psyched about the additional dollars in their paycheck, especially post-Christmas. But the time and a half didn't tempt me. I didn't really need the overtime. Jared paid off all of my credit card bills a few months ago. One day, I'd opened the statements to find that they all had zero balances.

Discovering the elimination of debt, I told Jared that it was a federal offense to open other people's mail, but added that since he was the best man on the planet, I wouldn't press charges.

I splashed water onto my face, hoping for an instant improvement in my ghastly appearance. It didn't work. Just thinking about walking into that office today made my stomach hurt. I didn't know how I was going to get through it. I knew it was going to be a busy week, too. That's why I didn't feel the least bit guilty for calling in yesterday. They'd sent out notices over the weekend basically telling people that their premiums were increasing, while their benefits were decreasing. That was sure to send our already-busy call center into a whirlwind of chaos.

I turned the bathroom light off and went back to bed. "The hell with them. I'll just say I forgot," I muttered as I snuggled up to my pillow and wiggled my body in search of that warm spot I'd just abandoned. But it wasn't so much the guilt of being dishonest as it was the threat of unemployment that wouldn't allow me to regain that comfort. I couldn't delay my fate any longer. I got up again and prepared to face my doom.

After fighting traffic for forty-five minutes I finally made it to the boiler room I called *work*.

"Hold the elevator, please!" I yelled out to Sarah and Margaret as they stepped onto the steel deathtrap just after glancing over at me. I knew those sea hags weren't going to hold it for me unless I acknowledged I saw them. Elevators ran slow around this place. Waiting on another one would make me late.

I speed-walked as not to delay them, but certainly minus the kiss-ass quality they would've preferred.

"Thanks," I smiled as I stepped onto the elevator.

Instantly, I could feel the daggers on me. They scanned every part of my fabulous sixty-four-inch-body with their jealous, crow's-feet-covered eyes. Sarah was our team lead. She got what I called a 'promotion without pay'. But even something as simple as that was enough to go to her head. When they gave her that title she started giving everybody the cold shoulder. Except for Margaret, that is.

Margaret was a 'kiss-up on her way up', or so she'd hoped. She *stayed* in Sarah's butt. It was ridiculous. She was one of those coffee- and cigarette addicts that reeked of that burnt smell all day. She'd smoke right at her desk if she could. And she had a dry, raspy voice that matched her leathery, pore-printed skin, and a matching hack that just made the hair on the back of my neck stand up.

Between the two of them they made working at the insurance company a bigger drag for me than it already was. Determined to backstab their way to the top they were ruthless. It was even rumored that they were the ones who spilled the beans that I was logging off the phone a couple minutes early in order to beat the parking lot rush. They didn't know that I knew. But secrets were hard to keep around this place.

"Good morning," I finally spoke to the two of them.

Margaret hacked.

Sarah cleared her throat and said, "I like your shoes," rather than *Good morning*.

"Thanks," I said, then intentionally glanced down at Margaret's flammable-looking pumps that nervously shifted positions, aware of the scrutiny.

When the elevator door opened to the eighth floor I immediately stepped off while Margaret and Sarah stayed back a bit so that they could gossip about me. As I approached the brown double doors I held my badge up to the small black box until the red dot turned green. Hearing the click, I took a deep breath, then swung the doors open to the hustle and bustle that was to be my life for the next ten hours.

"Hi, Sidney," I was greeted when I walked into the break room where most of the early birds were just wrapping up their morning hearsay session. "Aren't *you* brown?" Pat spoke of my tan.

" Good Morning, Pat. How's it going?" I smiled.

"Only Tuesday," she yawned. "I missed you yesterday."

"Yeah, well, I didn't miss this place." I fed quarters into the vending machine. "I can't *wait* for the weekend to come back around. I can't believe this overtime crap." I bent down to retrieve my bottled water.

Pat rolled her eyes, shaking her head in agreement. "Well, at least you have *Tom Bomb*," she laughed.

Tom Bomb was what Jared and I nicknamed the stress ball he gave me to squeeze out my frustrations on when angry callers made me want to explode. Instead of me exploding, *Tom* would. When I squeezed the orange, black-eyed ball, the eyeballs and tongue popped out in a simulated scream. It was Jared's second attempt at relieving my job stress since I'd declined his primary offer which enabled me to quit and move in with him until I found something better. I hated my job with a passion. But I disliked total dependence even more.

"Well, like I told you, one of these days you're going to open your desk drawer and there's going to be an IOU where *Tom* used to be," Pat threatened, fed up with the department herself.

"No way, Pat. He's like my mute button: I can't do my job without him."

We laughed for a moment at how much we hated our jobs.

"So, how are those little muffins coming along?"

Pat rubbed her pumpkin-sized belly. "Oh, they're fine. But I feel like I've gained a hundred pounds." She looked down, praying her shoes matched. I couldn't believe she was even here. She was due any day now.

"Well, even if you have, you still look great," I assured her.

"Yeah, not everyone can look this good carrying twins," she agreed.

"See, now that's what I'm talking about." I turned my water bottle up.

Ruth entered as Pat and I were laughing like school girls.

"So, this is where the party is," she said, wondering what all the fun was about.

"Hey, Ruth," we said in unison.

Ruth was nice. But she smelled like pickles. I think it was because she perspired so much. Pat and I didn't want to tell her that we were talking about the babies because we knew she'd been trying to get pregnant for the past two years. We didn't want to make her feel bad, so we avoided the subject whenever she was around.

"You girls ready for a long, busy day?" Ruth shattered our temporary moment of joy.

Pat and I grunted, dreading the very thought of putting those headsets on.

Ruth smiled in spite of our grunts and said, "Well, Kyle and I didn't get any sleep last night."

"Why's that?" Pat inquired on cue, while I took another sip of my water.

"We were up all night discussing our next plan of action. You're not going to be the only one carrying peas in the pod," she touched Pat's belly and grinned.

"Oh my God!" I got so excited that my water went down the wrong tube. I coughed, trying to clear my trachea.

"No, no, no," Ruth threw her hands up as I choked. "It's not what you think. Well—not yet, anyway," she said.

"*Oh*," I managed to squeeze out, apparently drowning right where I stood all for nothing.

I continued coughing.

Pat took the lead while I recovered.

"So, what's going on?" she asked.

"Well, Kyle and I are seeing a fertility specialist," Ruth explained. "But it's so expensive. Our insurance only covers a portion of it, so we're trying to look into other options to finance the treatments."

My face wore wide, concerned eyes and an interested smile, accompanied by the occasional *'I'm with you'* nod, while my mind flashed forward ten years from now where she tells a misbehaving child: *Watch yourself! I'm still making payments on you!* Threatening to default on the loan and have the child repo'ed.

The thought crumpled me. Pearly whites weren't even a prelude to my hysterical outburst as my imagination got the best of me. Before I knew it, I found myself erupted in full, mouth-open, eyes-closed laughter.

Mortified that I'd let it slip, I quickly covered my mouth, afraid Ruth would think I was being insensitive to her situation as if I thought what she was going through was funny. I certainly didn't. But I also didn't know how I was going to explain myself.

Apparently (and luckily) one of them must've said something funny at the precise moment I'd lost control of my thoughts, because they were both laughing, too.

Whew! That was close, I thought to myself, falsely joining them in their laughter.

After a couple chuckles, I called it quits.

"Alright, you guys. Let me get going." I played it safe, figuring now would be a good time to make my exit before my luck ran out. Besides, it was almost time to log in. "Pat, I'll see you at lunch."

"Yeah, I better get going, too," Pat moaned as we all scattered toward our respective cubicles.

"Oh, Sidney!" she called out to me just as I'd disappeared around the corner.

"Yeah?" I swung my head back around.

"Yesterday morning I came in and found someone had left a big yellow pillow, and a pair of fluffy slippers at my desk. And when I went to slip my foot into the slippers, I found a $300 gift card. Any idea who?" she smiled.

I shrugged my shoulders. "No."

Pat wrinkled her forehead and put her hand on her hip, looking puzzled. I looked back just as puzzled, then cracked a telling smile before vanishing around the corner again.

"Thanks, Sidney!" I heard her call out as I walked off.

Pat was sweet. We were the same age but she was already married. Her husband drove trucks for a furniture company, and she had been with the insurance company for five years. Five years and the dirty rats didn't have the decency to throw her a shower. They had money in the budget for Sarah's 40th birthday bash. But nothing for Pat and her upcoming event. I didn't think that was fair at all.

As I made my way to my 4' x 4' cubbyhole, I heard someone call out, "Hey, Sid."

I kept walking. I hated when people called me Sid. Only my dad called me that. I'd never authorized anyone else to shorten my name that way and hated when they took it upon themselves to do so.

"Sidney," she called out more appropriately this time.

"Oh, hi," I turned and spoke to Vanessa. "How was your weekend?"

"Good."

"Mine too," I smiled and kept walking. "Have a good day."

Vanessa had to be the most negative person in the office. First to complain behind the scenes, she was also the first to smile in the faces of management. And when it *was* a good time to air her gripes during meetings, you heard nothing but crickets. She couldn't be trusted. When it came to her I learned to speak fast and keep it moving.

"Oops!" I dodged Ernestine *and* her cup of coffee. Neither one of them were looking where they were going.

"Whoops!" She turned around in a swooping motion. "Sorry, Sidney."

I smiled it was okay.

"Hey, actually, I was just going to come see you," she said, following fast behind me as I hadn't broken my stride. Ernestine worked as our written correspondence clerk and was responsible for sending out all of the responses to member inquiry letters every Tuesday, yet she was prancing and zig-zagging around the office as if she'd finished already.

"Can you cover me this afternoon, Sidney? I have a doctor's appointment."

Your 'doctor' does the best nails in town.

"Sure, no problem," I smiled.

Coincidentally, she had a doctor's appointment every two weeks, just when her French manicure was looking less French and more fried. But I didn't mind helping her out today. That gave me an hour off the phones.

"Thanks," Ernestine smiled, finally dropping out of the race.

"Don't mention it," I waved to her, still making strides toward my workspace.

Upbeat only in body, not in mind, I was already wishing it were 5:30 p.m. I still didn't know how I was going to pull off the ten-hour miracle. Everyone else was buzzing around like busy little worker bees.

"Morning," I spoke back to my coworker who was all signed in, head-geared up, and ready to go. She had the best attitude in the office. Her name was Jenny, but they called her *Androjenny* behind her back. It wasn't so much her excessive facial hair they despised as it was the fact that they thought she made them look bad, from a work standpoint. They saw her dedicated performance as a threat to their lax work ethic. Her hard work exposed their laziness. I thought she was nice. But they were ruthless.

Last Christmas some employees put a disposable razor and a bottle of aftershave in the stocking hanging outside her cubicle. It was nothing short of a miracle that I arrived early that day and was able to intercept the cruel prank before she discovered it and got her feelings hurt for the holidays. Some people were just plain evil.

"Hi, Sidney," a crooked mouth under a long nose and two devious eyes spoke to me.

Speak of the devil.

"Morning, Richard," I returned the greeting without a stutter in my step. I got to my workstation and sighed defeatedly as I realized I'd left my desk in total disarray last Friday.

I sat down and immediately started sorting through the mess, gathering up documents that needed to be filed and shoving them into a manila folder. Just as I was making progress, a shadow hovered over me, blocking my light. I looked up with wide eyes at the unexpected eclipse.

"Sidney, why do you call me Richard?" Dan had gotten up from his seat, bringing his balls with him, to confront me.

I knew what his damn name was. But *Richard* seemed more appropriate. He was the unofficial office snitch, and almost got Pat fired. Too many backs had slashes in them to his credit. I learned that watching *mine* meant watching *him*.

I smiled inside at his newfound nerve. I'd been calling him that for months. It must've taken a lot for him to conjure up the courage to confront me. I looked into his eyes that were evident of his deteriorating nerve as he second-guessed his actions, and could see in them that he was already one nut down. I took a sip of my water, thinking here goes nothing.

"I call you Richard because you're such a di—"

"Sidney, you signed in yet?" Margaret interrupted, saving my job before my mouth set itself up for starvation.

I looked at her with impatience, rather than the gratitude I owed her as I watched Dan turn around and lurch back to his desk. "No. I'm not signed in yet." I looked at the clock on my desk phone. It read 6:28. "Why?" I wrinkled my brow.

"I was wondering if you'd received an email from Donald Miller regarding his prescription reimbursement."

"Why would Donald Miller be sending me an email? I never give out my internal email address."

Margaret wore a guilty look.

"Oh, I gave him your email address on Friday," she reluctantly confessed before explaining. "You were on the phone, and he said he needed to follow up on his inquiry."

"That's what the 800 number is for."

"Right. But he said he was working with you last time."

"Yes. On *that* particular day he was. I answered his call in the order in which it was received, explained to him that he'd reached his cap, and recommended that he file an appeal if he felt so inclined. I handled the call to completion."

The nerve of her giving out my email address. She knew it didn't work that way. We were not dedicated reps, by far.

"Anyway, he needs to contact Appeals, at this point, Margaret. I don't have a say in the matter. You know that." I looked at the hundreds of freckles that covered her otherwise fair face, fascinated, and thinking if they were any closer together she could pass for an entirely different race. "They only cover up to five. After that, it's out of pocket."

This man and his Viagra! I thought to myself as I explained, adamant that he wasn't about to drive me crazy over his out-of-order pecker.

"Well, I just figured . . ." Margaret continued explaining herself. I didn't hear another word after that. Whatever she was saying, I was sure it was just a long, elaborate way of saying '*Sidney, I'm a* lazy *ass. Don't you get it?*'

Finally, I stopped her.

"Fine. I'll check my email."

Margaret was just plain ridiculous. Rather than owning the call and assisting Mr. Miller herself, even if it meant starting from the beginning, she'd referred him back to me. I didn't like my job *either*, but I *did it* when I was here. I didn't look up the last rep who'd noted a member's account and dump the call off on them.

"In the meantime, Margaret," I caught her just before she skirted off, "I'd ask that you refrain from giving out my internal email address in the future. If there's an issue you feel you absolutely cannot handle, then please see your team lead for assistance." *You know, the one whose* ass *you live in!* "Thanks." I smiled.

As she walked away I cringed. *Ugh!* She was such a pain. And she'd already wasted the first three minutes of my day. Because of her, I was now late logging onto the phone.

After punching in my employee ID number twice, I signed onto my phone and computer, going straight to my email. Lo and behold, there was Mr. Miller's 5-page appeal letter with my name all in it, as if it would give him leverage. I clicked the *Print* icon, and then pulled up the rest of my work sessions, still mindful of my log-in time, knowing the tattletale report would rat me out. Just before pressing the *In-Calls* button, I looked at the picture of Mom and Dad. It always helped me to look at something pleasant while I was deathly miserable. Staring at the photo, I took a deep breath, wishing they were here, and missing them terribly. I swept my eyes over to the 5x7 of Jared and me that we'd taken on Valentine's Day. I kissed my hand then touched the image that reminded me that life *was* good. Then, after that mini vacation, at 6:32 a.m. I reluctantly reached forward and, with just the touch of my index finger, opened the floodgates.

CHAPTER 27

"*Are you **sure*** you're right-handed?" I squinted as I tried to decipher the chicken scratch Leann called directions. "This is some of the poorest penmanship I've ever seen."

"Been all my life." Leann looked in the visor's lighted mirror, putting on what had to be the reddest lipstick she could find.

"Well, give your left a try." I turned the paper 45-degree angles and back. "You might be in for a 20-year-old revelation." I started laughing.

"Give me that!" Leann snatched the paper clean out of my hand as I drove uncertain as to whether I was even going the right way. Her last-minute attempt to jot down directions had been just as unreliable as my GPS had been lately.

"We're gonna be late," Leann's friend, Isabelle, moaned from the backseat.

I wanted to like her. I really did. But she'd been getting on my nerves ever since we'd picked her up. Maybe it was the way she got in my car and didn't speak to me even though I'd greeted her with an enthusiastic *Hello*. Or maybe it was just the way she looked in those horrible acid wash jeans. Whatever it was, I was beginning to resent having to pick her up in the first place.

"We're okay," Leann told her, looking at the clock, then looking at me as if I had any real control in the matter.

Club *Waxx* wasn't going anywhere. But the option of our getting in free was quickly closing in on us. Leann had never been to this place, so she didn't have anyone to hook us up with free- or front-of-the-line privileges. Bouncers, *Skull* and *Crossbones*, usually had our backs in situations like this, especially since Leann had dated *Crossbones* for a quick minute. But this was a different story. It was looking like we would have to fend for ourselves tonight.

"Ooooh. That's my song. Turn that up!" Isabelle scooted up closer towards us. Leann reached over and turned up the radio as her friend made herself way too comfortable in my ride. "You mind if I smoke?"

I shot Leann the meanest look ever.

"Um . . . Sidney's allergic to smoke," Leann explained, trying desperately to maintain the peace as I squirmed in my seat in aggravation. Quite frankly, if it wasn't Leann's birthday, I would've turned the car around and taken them *both* home.

I pulled up to a red light and whipped out my mascara, trying to make the best of tonight, despite our company. But, honestly, I just felt weird being out without Jared. These days, nightclubs seemed pointless without him. That *sand to the beach* stuff didn't apply to us. Whenever I got the urge to go out dancing, I'd sooner drag Jared out than call Leann. It wasn't that I was acting funny. It just seemed more logical to bring my man along. The benefits were clear. For one, admission and drinks were taken care of, and came without the burden of being stalked all night by some guy intent on cashing in on his ten-dollar investment. Secondly, I had an all-night dance partner—someone I *wanted* to dance with, and wouldn't mind if they got a little touchy-feely. Finally, and probably the most attractive perk, was being able to go home with him after we'd left the club tipsy and feeling frisky because he was all mine. A night out just didn't get any better than that.

But tonight, well, I was slumming it.

Leann put her lipstick away and pulled out her eyeliner while I proceeded to plump my lashes. "Oh, can I use that?" Leann corner-eyed my mascara while simultaneously tugging an eyelid and running a charcoal pencil across it.

"I love you, Leann. But pink eyes just aren't as cute as they sound." I applied a final stroke, hoping she wouldn't be too offended.

Leann just giggled.

"I've got some," Isabelle volunteered, reaching for her bag on the floor.

"Never mind." I quickly handed Leann the pink-and-green tube. "Here. Keep it. I have another one at home," I said while making a mental note to stop at the drug store tomorrow morning to replace it.

"Thanks." Leann smiled as she proceeded to coat her lashes.

"Speaking of eyes, are those really yours?" Isabelle asked what she'd been dying to since she'd laid *hers* on me.

I answered that question for probably the hundredth time in my life. "Yep."

She sucked her teeth and sought a second opinion.

"Are they, Leann? Those aren't some samples from your job, are they?"

"Nope." Leann applied the mascara without blinking. "Sidney's all natural."

Isabelle took her word for it, turning back to me.

"So, Sidney, where are you from?"

"New York by way of Arizona."

She twisted her face. "What does that mean?"

Leann peeked out the corner of her eye at me.

"It means I'm originally from Arizona but lived up North for nine years."

"What brought you down here?"

Nosy! She was asking too many questions. I didn't understand why she just couldn't sit back and be quiet while Leann and I talked up front. I had speakers back there.

I pretended like I thought my turn was coming up and ignored her.

By the time we got to the club it was eleven-eleven. Twenty dollars poorer, we made our way inside as I looked around to see if it was a bargain or a rip-off. I couldn't tell yet.

I ordered Leann and myself some drinks after reserving a pair of barstools for us right in front of the dance floor where the male revue was about to take place. Normally, I didn't get into the show. Seeing a man dance around in their own version of panties just didn't do it for me. But tonight I'd planned to wave each dancer in Leann's direction for some special birthday attention that I knew would make her night.

Meanwhile, Isabelle had wandered off to the bathroom to check herself out, and somewhere along the way bumped into some guy who must've liked the way she looked in those jeans. As I watched her trying to smile as if she was all sweet and lovely, I was thinking to myself that he just didn't know who he was talking to.

"How'd you meet *her?*" I asked Leann, wondering where on Earth she'd found her. "She's *beyond* annoying." I frowned.

"She works at Torch. She was one of our hook-ups."

"Oh." My frown relaxed.

I cleared my throat and quickly changed the subject.

"So, um, how does it feel to be twenty-four, huh? *Feel like an o-o-old la-aaady yet?*" I put a tremor in my voice, nudging her with an imaginary cane.

Leann smiled and said, *"You'll* know before the year is out," wiping the grin right off my face.

"Happy Birthday to Leann and all the other Tauruses in the spot toniiiiiight!!!!" The DJ, a special friend of Leann's, with whom she'd been intimate in the past, gave a shout out over Luke's booty-shaking birthday classic. Leann had 'special friends' stashed away everywhere. Not only did she love to have sex more than any woman I knew, but she was also the ultimate mooch magnet.

Though she didn't have very much of it, Leann didn't mind spending the little money she did have on her men. The opposite sensation for me, it must've been a turn-on for her keeping her men the way she did—Or a power trip. Either way, Reggie was the latest recipient of her financial generosity.

"Why don't you just go over there and talk to him already so we can go dance," I encouraged Leann, who, after the show was over, dragged me all around the club to stalk some stripper named *Crush*. She was practically drooling over the slicked-down dude whose shirt was so tight that I was able to determine that his left nipple was the smaller of the two.

I wasn't too keen on the hunt, and was mildly embarrassed, but Leann was absolutely obsessed with this guy. Knowing this I had to be there to curb her impulse to make a complete fool of herself. We were standing off to the side, looking like paparazzi, when she caught a sudden case of the jitters.

"He sees her!" Isabelle was tactless enough to say what I was thinking. "He's just feeling himself with all those girls around crowding him."

"Yeah, Leann. He *is* acting like he doesn't know you." I hated to agree with Isabelle, and hoped I didn't hurt Leann's feelings too bad, but it was true. I felt bad because she had invested several dollars in this man's career, following him around to various venues. There had been many nights when he'd walk off the stage wearing what looked like a grass skirt, as his thong was garnished with Leann's livelihood. And now he was acting like he didn't even know her.

"Maybe he just doesn't recognize you without a dollar in your hand," I joked, attempting to lighten the mood.

"Very funny," Leann sneered, letting me know I'd failed. I tucked away my grin as she went on to complain.

"I mean, why does he have to talk to *her*?"

Isabelle, who knew the girl Leann was referring to, shook her head. "I don't know. But she did just get that new boob job."

"So, what?!" Leann frowned. "I'm supposed to be jealous because she went out and bought three thousand dollar's worth of self-esteem?"

"Two thousand," I appraised, trying to make up for that dollar remark.

Leann laughed. "Yeah. They do look lopsided."

"Sure do!!" We slapped hands in agreement, laughing at those topsy-turvy titties.

"And she doesn't even have a butt," Leann added. Oh—no offense, Sidney."

"Uhhhhh . . . None taken???" I made a crazy face at Leann with my straw hanging from my mouth.

"I mean, everyone knows *you're* gorgeous," Leann offered, tapping my wrist in consolation. "But *her* . . ." she narrowed her eyes at the young woman and shook her head, "She's flat as a pancake in that skirt."

I wasn't *too* offended. But that was the third time Leann had made reference to my 'less is more' rear end. I was beginning to grow paranoid around her. Not everyone could have curves as perfect as hers.

"She probably just wants his money. That was his Range Rover outside."

"Yeah. I don't know why so many guys mess with these money-grabbing girls," Isabelle huffed, looking at me while she while she was saying it.

"Because they're dumb!" Leann said.

"First of all," I interjected, "it's him who wants *her* money. Remember? Stripper?" I sipped my margarita

308

and shook my head. "And besides, everyone's confused. Real love isn't about money or material things."

Isabelle gasped.

"The girl wearing someone's mortgage in her ears and another person's *rent* on her wrist isn't into material things? Now, that's funny." She swung her head toward Leann. "What did you just tell me her boyfriend did again? Invent *money* or something?"

Leann had yellow feathers hanging out of her mouth and eyes like saucers as I realized my solo trip to the bathroom was an informative one for Isabelle.

She strategically brought our attention back to the guy with the groupies, while I made faces at Isabelle who was too dumb to notice.

"I can't believe him!"

"I can't believe *you*, Leann. He is not even all that. And aren't you forgetting about Reggie?"

I was becoming frustrated. When I told her I'd take her out for her birthday gawking at some greasy guy all night wasn't exactly what I had in mind.

"I would never forget my man. But, yeah . . . you're right," she conceded. "He's not all that."

"Mmm . . . But *he is!*" Isabelle shook her head as her eyes followed a really cute guy headed in our direction.

"Heyyy . . ." she tapped him on his shoulder as he passed by.

He barely looked at her.

I laughed.

"Homo!" Isabelle scoffed, feeling quite dissed. "Excuse the hell out of me for having a vagina!"

Leann burst out laughing.

I let a crackle slip out myself but not for reasons assumed. I was laughing *at* Isabelle, not *with* her.

"Anyway," I tapped Leann on the shoulder, getting bored, "let's go get another drink." I turned to walk off.

"No, wait!" She nervously tucked her new short hair behind her ears. "Here he comes."

I looked and saw *Crush* coming our way, having the nerve to be looking at me as he approached.

Leann pressed her color-coated lips together.

I curled mine up.

"Alright, well, I'll just meet you downstairs," I told her before slipping away.

I squeezed through the crowd that seemed to quadruple just in the hour that we'd been there. Playing solitaire, I walked back downstairs where I found Isabelle's *"homo"* all pressed up against some much-prettier-than-Isabelle *female*, whispering in her ear and grinning suggestively.

I laughed to myself, wishing Isabelle could see this. She was perpetually bitchy. And I had been ignoring her slick comments all night. I'd love to see her feel rejection twice in five minutes.

I walked around the frolicking couple and found an empty booth occupied only by half-finished drinks and water-ringed napkins that doubled as coasters. Claiming the spot, I slid in and leaned back against a wall that turned out to be a speaker. But decidedly settled, I slipped off my shoes, propped my feet up on the seat across from me, and sat back and watched so many others hunt to find what I already had with Jared.

CHAPTER 28

Where are you? *What are you doing? And why can't I get a hold of you?!* I wanted to ask the voice mail when the fifth ring connected me to Jared's pre-recorded voice.

Beep.

"Hey, honey. It's me again. Call me when you get this. I love you. Bye."

I hung up the phone even more aggravated than the first two times I'd called. Frustrated, and not knowing what else to do, I went to my bedroom for the sole purpose of moping.

Just as I plopped down on the mattress, the phone rang. I reached over and answered. "Hello?"

"Hey, girl!"

It was Leann.

I tried to hide my disappointment that it wasn't Jared. "Hey, you. . ."

It was already 9:30 p.m. and I hadn't heard from Jared all day. When I'd dropped him off at the airport yesterday, it didn't really bother me that he didn't call when he got to the hotel. I knew he probably had a ton of things to go over before his early morning meeting.

He was meeting with a major potential client, and the fate of his new firm could ride on this one investor. Two, actually. They were brothers who had a combined wealth of over three-quarter billion dollars, who were interested in some personal investments. Jared was very antsy about the meeting all week, so I could understand his wanting to prepare last night. But today was a different day, and I expected him to call me hours ago, if nothing else but to tell me how things went. It wasn't like him not to call, even if it was just for a quick minute to say hi. I was beginning to worry. Since 5 o'clock I'd left two messages for him at the hotel. And for some strange reason I couldn't reach him on his cell.

Leann, unaware of the drama playing out in my head, sounded as if she had a huge smile on her face when she said, "Reggie and I just got back from *Dos Velas.*"

"Oh yeah?" That was Jared's favorite restaurant. "Did you enjoy yourself?" I asked, trying to drum up some enthusiasm, but finding it difficult.

"It was great," she slurred, sounding as if her grin interfered with her speech. "The food was so delicious. The atmosphere was way romantic. It was so expensive."

I wondered who'd paid. Reggie was a cheapskate if I ever knew one. Leann was always picking up the tab for them. And right now, he was between jobs— whatever *that* meant.

"That's really nice, Leann," I told her after she'd finished describing her meal in full detail. "I'm glad you enjoyed yourself," I added dryly, no longer able to disguise my gloom.

She sensed my surly mood.

"What's wrong, Sidney?"

I exhaled. "Nothing really. It's just . . ."

I felt silly that I was about to complain, but I had to get it out, and was glad she'd asked.

"I haven't heard from Jared all day. And I can't even reach him on his cell. I've left two messages already, and he still hasn't called me back. I don't know what's going on," I whined.

"Well, Sidney, maybe he's busy working on that proposal you told me about. You said he was trying to acquire more investors." Her tone suggested I was being unreasonable.

"Well, business is over at five!" I flipped over onto my back, staring at the ceiling fan that failed at cooling me down.

"Sidneeey," she drew out my name like I was a bad girl, "don't you think you're being a little less than understanding? Selfish, even?" she added.

I sat up. "No. I don't. There are one thousand four hundred and forty minutes in a day and I can't get *one?* —Not even to say *hi?* You think that's asking too much, Leann?" I snapped at her.

Easy for her to say. She had Reggie's worthless ass lying next to her every night, even if he *was* a bum. All I was asking for was a simple phone call to let me know he still had a pulse. I mean, he always carried his cell phone on him, yet I felt disconnected from him. Intentionally shut out.

"Well . . . I guess you're right," Leann agreed, catching whiff of my wrath. "He'll call. Don't worry," she assured me.

I simmered down. "Yeah. I know . . ."

There was a long, slow pause that told me that Leann had called to tell me more than just how much she enjoyed her entrée. And she certainly didn't call simply for me to take my frustrations out on her. I could tell there was something else she wanted to say. But too preoccupied with my own troubles, I figured if she wanted to say something, she'd better had just say it.

Finally, she broke her silence.

"Well, I feel weird now, telling you the good news and all," she admitted, timidly.

"What good news?"

"Reggie proposed! We're getting married!"

I needed to run right back to my audiologist, because I knew she couldn't have said *married* and *Reggie* in the same sentence.

"What did you say?"

"We're getting married, Sidney."

"Oh my God. Are you serious?"

"Yes!"

"Oh my God!" I screamed. "Congratulations, Leann!" Surprisingly, I was struck by sudden excitement. "That is so wonderful! I am so happy for you!"

"YAY, Me!" Leann shrieked.

She was ecstatic. I don't think I ever heard her so loud and happy.

"Oh, my God, Leann! Ok. So, how did he propose?" I wanted all the romantic details, apparently forgetting it was Reggie we were talking about. I mean, how romantic could it have been when she had to whip out her own money when it was time to wrap up dinner?

Leann explained. "Well, after dinner, he got up from the table, got down on his knee, took my hand and said, *'Leann, I love you. I've always loved you.*

And I want to love you for the rest of my life. Will you marry me?'—Sidney, the whole restaurant was applauding. It was so sweet!"

"Oh, Leann. That's great. When is the wedding?"

"Well," she hesitated, "we haven't really set a date. But we're thinking late 2016, early '17. He wants to get his job situation straight first, and finish up school." The hesitation in her explanation told me she knew how ridiculous it was going to sound before she said it. This was May 2013. That killed all of my enthusiasm.

"Well, did he at least give you a ring?" I asked, trying to salvage some hope of its validity.

"Not yet. But he will," she said naively.

I just wanted to hang up the phone. Getting me all worked up for something that may never happen was just wrong. Reggie was a con man. That job/school excuse was just that: an excuse. How and why would a job, school, or any plans, for that matter, delay serious plans of getting married? It was reasonably possible to attend to all of those things *and* get married at the same time. And if Reggie, for some bizarre reason, didn't think so, then he should've delayed his proposal. I wasn't buying it. But, apparently, Leann was.

I did the best I could to hide my sudden drop from excited to irritated, as I simply lent my ear as Leann went on for several more minutes about these so-called marriage plans.

"Okay. So you gotta go with me to shop for a gown —and bridesmaid dresses," Leann said excitedly.

"Like, when?" I wondered why the rush.

"I don't know. Next weekend maybe."

"Well, Leann, don't you think it's just a little too early?"

She didn't respond, but she answered me with silence.

"I mean, you might find something you like even better when it comes closer to that time," I quickly backpedaled, careful not to appear jealous or unsupportive. But I knew that the damage was already done.

"Yeah . . . maybe. I'm just so excited, Sidney. That's all . . ." Leann's voice trailed off.

"I know. I would be, too. It's just . . ." I caught myself, realizing I still stood the risk of hurting her feelings. "On second thought, you know what? Let's go look at those dresses. I just won't let you buy one yet. Deal?"

"Deal!" Leann bounced back. "Ohhhh, I have so much to do to get ready. Invitations. Arrangements . . ." Leann's mind traveled a mile a minute. "I haven't even called my parents yet."

"Now you know you can't keep a secret to save your life."

"No, I plan on telling them. It's just they're still visiting my grandmother in Charleston right now, and I am *not* about to call while they're staying at her house, with her mean self. And she's not invited to my wedding either!"

"You still haven't made up with your grandmother yet?"

"She's evil. And I'm not talking to her no effin' more," she didn't curse. It was always funny to listen to Leann try to express her frustrations with cleaner variations of the words she really meant. Still, she was very angry with her grandmother, who'd previously criticized her and Reggie's cohabitation, saying that they were immoral for shacking up. Leann hadn't spoken to her in weeks as she felt her grandmother owed her an apology, specifically for calling her a *little poochie mama*. Though the seventy-something senior had mispronounced the old school derogatory term, Leann knew what she'd meant.

"She needs to apologize for what she said, Sidney. And until she does, she won't hear from me," Leann pledged with conviction.

I didn't argue. I was not about to get in the middle of that, and wished we hadn't chosen to take that terrible stroll down memory lane. I remembered how much it had hurt Leann when it first happened.

"Alright, girlie, well let me get off this phone."

Sensing Leann's altered mood, I felt that was my cue. "I promised Kiana I'd take her to the movies tomorrow, so I gotta get up early to get my car detailed."

"I thought you still had Jared's car."

"I do. I'm alternating."

Leann laughed. "Alright. Well, I'll talk to you later."

"Okay— Hey," I caught her before she hung up. "Congratulations, again. I needed some good news tonight, and yours really cheered me up."

"Anytime," she giggled. "Bye."

"Bye."

As I hung up the phone my mind went right back to Jared. I thought about everything I could've possibly said or had done wrong. It was a quarter to ten and he still hadn't called. I thought back to our last conversation. Nothing unusual jumped out at me. We always ended our conversations the same way: saying *I love you.* And we never argued, so I couldn't understand why he wasn't reaching out to me. I began thinking that maybe things didn't go so well with his meeting. Maybe he just needed some time to clear his head.

I rolled over onto my side and looked out the huge water-specked window, through raindrops that magnified images of trees, and thought of how much I loved Jared. How lonely I was when he wasn't around. I thought about all the ways he made me feel so special, the ways he showed me that I was important to him, and wondered why, all of a sudden, he didn't feel I was even worth a phone call to let me know he was alright and how things were going. My heart started feeling all funny as I grabbed for my pillow and hugged it.

Moments later, the phone rang.

I leaned over and looked at the caller ID.

"Hello?"

"Hey, baby," the semi-deep voice on the other line said, instantly taking away that uncomfortable feeling.

"Hi, Jared."

CHAPTER 29

Kiana was excited all week about our plans today. She even knew exactly what she wanted to wear. I decided I would wear my cream blouse to match the shorts set I got her for Christmas. Leann said $140 was too much to spend on any article of children's clothing, but Kiana was worth it. And besides, it wasn't like I had to pay for it all at once. The designer set would only cost me roughly $15 a month at 8% APR.

I told Kiana I'd pick her up at ten. It was a quarter after nine when I left my apartment. I tried calling before I left, but Lorraine had allowed the phone to get disconnected again. I played it safe and assumed, like me, that Kiana hadn't eaten yet, and stopped to pick up breakfast for us.

When I arrived at her house it was exactly ten o'clock.

"Right on time," I said, switching my playlist. Jared downloaded all of our favorite love songs for me, and I listened to them whenever he was away. Plenty pleasure-filled nights were kicked off to the sensuous tunes I knew were inappropriate for a child's ears.

Last night, when Jared and I spoke, he sounded a little funny. Stressed, even. He didn't complain but I could tell there was something bothering him. I didn't push because I knew our relationship was strong enough to where if he wanted to talk about something he would. I just told myself that when he got back in town tomorrow I would make him feel like the winner he was.

As I walked up to the gate I looked around to make sure that mean dog wasn't in the yard. They had a pit bull. And had the nerve to call it *Buddy*. I was thinking something more along the lines of *Negligence,* or *Lawsuit,* was more appropriate. Kiana said they got rid of it but I wasn't about to take any chances.

I rattled the gate and waited a few seconds listening for any ferocious footsteps charging. After about ten seconds I assumed the coast was clear and made my way inside the unkempt yard, stepping over aluminum cans and makeshift ashtrays along the way. As I walked up the steps onto the porch and knocked on the paint-chipped door a sense of sadness came over me.

"Oh, hey, Sidney," Lorraine answered the door, cigarette in hand. "Kiana's in the back. KIANA!!" she yelled over her shoulder. "Come on in," she told me.

"Hi, Lorraine," I spoke, hoping she'd wait until after I left to light up.

As I followed her inside, I noticed how pitifully-skinny and sunken-in she was. "How are you?"

"Not too bad," she said as she led me inside.

I watched her as she walked through the living room into the kitchen. She looked horrible. She thought her drug-use was a secret. But the real secret was that it wasn't a secret at all. She was only kidding herself.

I sat the breakfast down on the cluttered kitchen table and pretended not to notice the roach scurrying away from under the takeout menu as the bag made impact with the obscured oak. That roach ran away with my appetite. It concerned me that Lorraine's addiction had gotten so bad that the upkeep of her house was no longer a priority. I could only imagine the effect it must've had on Kiana.

I pulled my purse from my arm, reluctant to set it down in light of the infestation. "You said Kiana's in the back?"

"Yeah, she's back there fooling around with her things. I told her you were probably on your way. KIANA!!!" she yelled again.

"Oh, that's okay. I'll go see what's keeping her." I hung my purse on the chair, and went to go see if my little friend was ready yet.

As I walked toward the back of the house, just approaching Kiana's bedroom, I saw that her door was cracked. I peeked inside and saw her sitting on the edge of her bed, staring into space.

I tapped lightly on the door before pushing it open.

"I thought you were wearing your jumpsuit," I said, entering the room.

"I can't find it," Kiana replied with her head hung.

I sat down on the bed beside her as she fidgeted with the sleeve of her sweater.

"Did you ask your Mom?"

Kiana looked up at me. "She said she doesn't know where it is." She dropped her head again.

"Okaaaay . . ." I rubbed my denim legs and looked around the room, trying not to jump to any conclusions in my mind. But I couldn't help thinking about my purse hanging on the back of that chair.

"Well, are you ready to go?" I stood up and placed a gentle hand on her back.

"Yeah," she muttered.

"I got breakfast for us."

Kiana grabbed her jacket from the foot of the bed and stood up. "I'm ready."

"Did you want to eat here, or on the way?"

"On the way."

I shut the door behind us as we started back down the hall.

"Alright, mama," Kiana said, heading straight for the door.

I gathered up the food, examining it on the sly, making sure it wasn't taxi to a pregnant pest. I shook my purse when no one was looking. Then I grabbed my keys, telling Lorraine we'd be back by six.

"Alright. I'll see ya'll later." Lorraine blew smoke into the air like she was howling at the moon.

"Have fun," she added, sounding as if she couldn't wait to be alone.

"Okay." I coughed, fanning the air in front of me as I headed for the door. "Can I bring you anything back?"

"Oh— can you bring me back a pack of Newport 100s?"

I lowered my lids as I reluctantly responded, "Yes."

"Thank you," she said, patting her chest for her lighter then tossing it onto the table before sitting far back on the couch.

"Alright, well, we'll see you later." I closed the door.

Kiana was awfully quiet when we got in the car. I began to wonder what else besides the outfit was eating at her.

I fastened my seatbelt. "Everything okay?"

She followed my lead and fastened hers but didn't say anything.

I figured she was upset with her mother about one thing or another, and needed time to warm up.

I didn't press. I knew she'd snap out of it once we got going. But as we backed out of the driveway I glanced over and noticed two quiet tears streaming down her face.

I stopped the car in the middle of the street.

"Sweetie, what's wrong?" My heart pounded.

Kiana's cries found volume as she began openly weeping.

I didn't know what was wrong. She couldn't be this upset over some clothes.

"Kiana, tell me, sweetheart. What's the matter?" I placed one hand on her back as I waved the car behind me to go around us with the other.

Kiana cried, "She's sending me away, Sidney. She's making me go away!"

"What? Who? Who's sending you away?"

"Mama. She's sending me to Missouri. She's sending me to live with my uncle." She continued spilling tears all over her face.

I didn't know what to say. I couldn't ask *why*. I already knew why. Lorraine couldn't care for her anymore. I'd been giving Kiana lunch money here and there for the past three weeks since Lorraine, more frequently, 'forgot'. Declining any form of welfare, she refused to sign Kiana up for free or reduced lunch. While I respected her pride I questioned her wisdom and judgement. Pride aside, Kiana needed to eat. Lorraine needed to swallow that foolish pride that was starving her daughter. Maybe she was going to seek help. Perhaps she knew that she wasn't in any condition to take care of Kiana, or herself.

But I wondered if sending Kiana away was the right decision. I always felt Kiana gave Lorraine's life purpose, and some degree of stability. Without her around, I worried that Lorraine would totally succumb to her addiction. Spiral completely out of control. It really was no mystery what happened to the expensive jumpsuit.

I hugged Kiana tight as the next car behind us went around. She was shivering. She said she didn't want to go. She barely knew her uncle and cousins. But I assumed they offered her more of the stability that *she*, as a child, deserved.

I ran my hand over her hair as she continued to cry, telling her that maybe it was just for a few months. It wasn't really my place, and I knew I shouldn't have offered anything I had no control over, but I just didn't know what else to say.

"When are you leaving?" I asked, wiping the tears from her eyes.

She wiped her nose. "Friday."

I looked out the windshield, tallying up the time we had left together. That only gave us a week.

My lip tightened.

Kiana looked at me and started crying again.

"Sweetheart," I hugged her tight, "Listen. It's probably just for a little while," I told her again. "It's okay."

"You think so?" She looked up at me again, her face shiny with tears, but hope now in her eyes.

I stroked her hair. "I *know* so."

She rested her head on my chest. "I love you, Sidney."

"I love you, too, Kiana."

CHAPTER 30

I rolled up in the champagne-colored cat-on-wheels and parked Jared's jag in the first visitor's spot of the multi-unit complex. Since he was bogged down with work all week, Leann and I made plans. She was doing fondue tonight, which I found irresistibly exciting. What's more, she said that Reggie was going to his cousin's house so it would just be the two of us. I did a silent dance, glad that I wouldn't have to see his freeloading face tonight. I still thought he was leeching off of Leann and cringed every time she spoke of the alleged wedding plans.

She still didn't have a ring.

As I walked toward Leann's building, my night vision spotted Reggie's truck parked near the fire hydrant. I quickly scanned the lot for Leann's car, hoping he'd just chosen to burn up her gas, but the Benz was double-parked a few spaces down.

Dang! I stomped my foot and frowned.

Midway through my work week I dragged up the stairs, tired and feeling the effort of every step. And the sight of Reggie's truck added the feel of ten-pound weights to each ankle. As I climbed each concrete block, my mind was talking my body back down the stairs. I didn't have the energy to sit around and act phony with that penniless parasite. I'd used it all up at work, absorbing every caller's emotions. Just thinking about it all, made me want to get back in the car and go home, using the 15-minute drive to think of the perfect lie as to why I didn't show.

But as tempted as I was, I couldn't do Leann that way. After all, she was doing this for me. She knew I had been down about Kiana, and this was her selfless attempt to cheer me up.

I tapped on the door, then looked over my shoulder back toward the parking lot, still slightly tempted by the thought of going AWOL. But before I could change my mind, I was suddenly face-to-face with Chabaka.

"What's going on, Sidney?" A shirtless Reggie stood in the doorway, brushing his waves. My stomach did a somersault at just the money-siphoning sight of him, the inked image of the canine co-star etched across his naked chest growling at me.

"Hey," I spoke plainly.

"Sid-neeeeey," Leann sang from the kitchen.

I came to life.

"Heyyyy, Leann!" I brushed passed Reggie, kicking off my shoes. "Mmmm . . . " I put my nose to the wind, "something smells good."

Reggie headed off to the bedroom.

"Girl, I tried calling to tell you not to worry about bringing anything," Leann referred to the bottle of champagne in my hand.

"Oh, it's no trouble." I walked over to the counter that divided the living room from the kitchen to find bacon-wrapped pineapples sizzling on the Foreman. "Yum!"

"You still eat pork, right?"

"Yes, that's right. I've got no beef with swine. That's Jared," I clarified.

Leann laughed. *"Beef with swine."*

"You like that?" I grinned as we giggled together.

Just then Reggie emerged from the bedroom.

"Alright. See ya later, my sweet truffle." Wearing a fresh white tee and jeans, he jiggled keys in his hands.

"Don't wait up," he said.

Don't wait up?

I looked at the keys in his hand, seeing if I could spot the usual Benz logo dangling from them.

"Alright, babe." Leann smiled. "When will you be back?"

My ears perked up, wanting to know what time I needed to vacate the premises.

Reggie blew a kiss. "Late, boo. Late."

He shut the door behind him.

I stared at the door for a while, then looked at Leann. She wore a serene smile on her face as she ran the large knife through the gorgeous green apples.

I frowned. "I can't believe you don't mind sleeping with that *beast* every night?"

Leann laughed. "Oh, girl, he's had that tattoo for so long I don't even notice it anymore."

Who's talking about the tattoo?

Reggie simply annoyed me. He was so shady. I couldn't see how Leann couldn't see it. *Late, boo. Late???* If I were her I would be checking his phone messages every chance I got. With his weird Star Wars obsession I'm sure the 4-digit PIN wouldn't be too hard to crack. *R2D2 . . . C3PO . . .JEDI*— one was bound to work if the movie's title words alone didn't.

"Besides," Leann added, "it's way better than that squiggly, bubbly brand my last boyfriend had. Eah!" She squirmed. "Just thinking about it makes my flesh crawl." "Eah!!" I squirmed, too. "That expression makes *mine*."

Leann evil-eyed me for being overly dramatic.

"Anyway," she rolled her eyes playfully and went back to slicing, "I like my men nice and smooth. Tattoos don't bother me at all."

"Smooth, huh?

"Yep."

"Smooth like a *sweet truffle*?" I snickered.

"That's right," she shook her head, not the least bit embarrassed by the pet name Reggie used in my presence. "I'm 80% milk chocolate"—she rubbed her mahogany shoulder, "and 10% dark chocolate"—she swung around in that short skirt of hers and patted her behind.

"Crazy is what you are." I shook my head, laughing. "Wait a minute"—I did the math—"That's only 90 percent."

Leann put her hands on her hips. "Do you *really* wanna hear about my cherry center?"

My eyes left hers, taking my smile with them. "No, Leann," I said regretfully. "I suppose I don't."

She laughed. "Okay, then, Ms. Mathematician."

I shook myself out of my shock-induced daze. "So," I leaned over the counter, eyeing the food again, "what else do we have here?"

"Well," Leann waved her hand over the serving bowls and platters, "we have basil and lemon dip, Thai prawn salad with garlic dressing and frizzled shallots, mozzarella and tomato skewers, cherry tomatoes with pesto, tuna rolled in red peppers, charred artichokes with lemon oil dip . . ." I licked my lips. ". . . Crisp-fried crab claws, chicken satay with peanut sauce, hot crab soufflé, vegetable tempura, and, for dinner, beef carbonnade with roasted potatoes."

"Wow," I gasped, losing count of it all in my head.

Leann shook her head, having really outdone herself. "And I want you to try *everything*."

"If you insist." I grinned hungrily, dipping my finger in the dip.

"Ah-Ah!" She smacked my hand.

"Ow!" I snatched back.

"Not yet," Leann scolded. "Wait for it to thicken some."

Everything looked so delicious. There were strawberries, kiwi, cherries, various cheeses, apple slices, and melted chocolate. My mouth watered as I got an eyeful of all that *'set the mood'* food. I told Leann she better not start looking at me all crazy after she had a few strawberries.

"Isabelle asked about you," Leann told me as she reached into the cabinet and took out two champagne glasses.

I turned up my lip. "For what?"

"She said she had so much fun the other night. She thought you were really cool."

"What??! Leann, Isabelle is a bi—"

"Sidney!" she hushed me before I could sin.

I shook my head. "Well . . . she ain't no '*belle*'. That's for damn sure."

Leann pulled the chilled bottle of champagne from the freezer and placed the bottle I'd brought with me inside.

"Izzy's cool." She prepared to pop the champagne's top as I took cover. "She just takes some getting used to."

"Well, I don't have that kind of time." I knelt beside the barstool.

Leann applied some pressure, and the cork shot across the room like a bullet, ricocheting off the wall and hitting the bookcase before losing life.

When all fire had seized, I rose.

"Am I hit?" I touched my blouse, checking for any entry or exit wounds.

Leann laughed, but then got right back to Dizzy Izzy.

"Yeah, but she's good people, though, Sidney." She poured me a glass of champagne, handing it to me.

I rolled my eyes, unconvinced. "That girl—"

"Anyway," Leann cut me off again, "you've *gotta* try this." She stuffed a pâté-topped cracker into my mouth to shut me up.

We sipped on champagne and laughed as Leann told me about how she looked when Reggie got down on his knee to propose. She said she'd thought he'd dropped something, and wondered why he was looking up at *her* instead of the floor. She even thought about getting down on her knees to help him find whatever it was he'd lost. I was thinking her confusion probably came from the fact that he didn't have a ring in his hand. But I kept that to myself.

Despite the missing stone, the reenactment was pretty hilarious. Leann described the same, stupid expression I imagined I'd have if Jared dropped to his knee and asked me to be his wife.

"Girl, what is that on your leg?" Leann pointed to the sunbaked J on my thigh.

"Jared's revenge," I said, looking down at the lighter-colored letter.

Leann laughed. "You guys are perfect for each other. You know that?"

I nodded and smiled.

"So when are you two gonna get engaged?" she asked.

That's what I wanna know.

"I don't know, Leann. Soon, hopefully." I knew I wanted to be with Jared forever. My life would be a success if I could have his ring on my finger.

"We'd get married in New York. Our wedding colors would be pearl and periwinkle. We'd honeymoon in the Bahamas. And then we'd—" I stopped.

Leann looked at me. "What's wrong?"

"But," I looked away, "he's been so busy lately. I mean, he's been back for three days already and I haven't seen him at all."

"Well, that's what happens when you date a super-successful man," Leann charmed a half smile out of me. "You know, you guys would make a pretty baby."

"You think?" I began to imagine what our children would look like. "Maybe if we have a daughter she'll look like Kiana," I gleamed, then grew sad at the memory of her leaving.

Seeing the change in my expression, Leann placed a hand on my knee. "Are you still going to see her off tomorrow?"

"Right after work." Just then my phone rang. "Oh—hang on a sec."

I dug in my purse and pulled out my cell.

"Girl, I just love that phone," Leann admired the metallic toy, pink and personalized, with J *loves* S engraved on the back.

"Yeah, isn't it cute?—Oh, it's my honey. Hang on—Hey, honey," I answered.

Leann helped herself to some more champagne, while I talked to Jared.

"Oh—okay . . . Uh-huh. Of course. Ummm . . ." I looked at my watch ". . . I can meet you at my place in an hour . . . Leann's . . . Uh-huh . . . Okay . . . Alright . . . Okay. Bye."

I snapped the phone closed and bit my bottom lip.

"What's up?" Leann asked as I sat there blinking.

"Jared says he wants to talk to me. He sounded, well, anxious."

Leann grinned. "You don't think he . . ."

I looked at her excited face and instantly read her mind. "Oh, noooo." I batted my hand, dismissing her assumption before she could even say it. "I'm sure he just wants to tell me about the deal. You know, the two brothers delayed their answer. They've been keeping him waiting while they make their decision. Jared's been really low-key with me about it lately."

"C'mon. You gonna ignore that coincidence?"

"What coincidence, Leann? It's a phone call."

"Sidney!" she chirped. "You haven't seen him all week. And you said he's been acting suspiciously lately, didn't you?"

I started grinning too.

"Sidney, that's exactly how Reggie was acting before *he* popped the question."

I dropped my phone back into my purse and shook my head. "Don't be silly. He probably just wants to go out and celebrate or something. Do you know how much this deal is worth?"

"Sidney, I'm telling you—"

"I gotta get home and freshen up before he gets there. You don't mind if I skip out early, do you, Leann?"

I felt guilty about wasting her efforts. We hadn't even touched the actual dinner yet. "I mean, if you want me to stay, I can call him back and—"

"Are you crazy?!" Leann looked at me like I was. "Girl, you better get out of here! We can do this anytime—Here—take this!" she shoved the unopened bottle of champagne at me that we'd just taken out of the freezer.

"But I brought this for you."

"Take it!" She stood me up by my arm and led me toward the door.

She was practically throwing me out.

"Uh"—I raised my brow—"can I get my keys, please?"

"Yes. Yes. Hurry." She let me go long enough for me to do so.

As I walked over to the kitchen counter I continued to reason with her.

"I mean, I told you. It's just dinner. He just wants to celebrate the deal probably. Trust me. I've been through this a zillion times."

"Go! Go! Go!" Leann shooed me out, not listening to a word I said.

"Okay. Okay. I'm going." I rushed toward the door at her urging.

I turned around and hugged her. "Thanks for everything, Leann."

"You're welcome." She hugged me back as we stood in the foyer. "Now get outta here!" She spun me back around.

"I'll talk to you later," I said as I walked slowly down the stairs, shaking my head and laughing at her silly assumptions. Sometimes that girl really let her imagination run away with her, I thought to myself, careful of the third step from the bottom that always gave my heels trouble.

"Call me tomorrow!" Leann yelled from the balcony, catching me in a full sprint with the bottle of champagne tucked under my arm tight like a football, one stride away from losing a shoe.

She shook her head, laughing as she went back inside.

✦ ✦ ✦

I stepped out of the shower and reached for the oversized towel, wrapping it around my body tight like a tortilla. I stood in front of the mirror and wiped myself into view.

As much as I argued with her I couldn't help but indulge in Leann's optimism. If she was right, my life was about to change forever.

I lit the trio of candles sitting on the bath counter, and tossed the flame stick back into the drawer.

"Come in, honey!" I yelled when I heard the knock at the door.

Another few seconds had passed when I heard a second knock.

I went to the front door and looked through the peephole. I saw Jared.

"Hi, honey," I said as I opened the door. "How come you didn't use your key?" I reached out to hug him.

"Oh," Jared shook his head, "I wasn't thinking. Um . . ."

"How are you?" I asked, closing the door behind him. "I've missed you so much." I stood on my tiptoes and began planting kisses all over his face. When he grabbed hold of my waist I started kissing faster.

"Uh . . . Hang on, Sidney . . ." Jared pulled me off of him, gently pushing me back a step.

"What's wrong?" I asked, not used to that.

Jared looked at me. "Sidney, we . . ."

"Jared, what's going on?" My eyes chased his as they avoided mine.

He took a breath. "Sidney, I'm afraid . . . that it's over between us."

"*What?*" My heart began to race. "What are you talking about?"

In an instant, I began feeling jittery and sick.

Jared shook his head. "I can't be with you anymore, Sidney."

"What? Why?" My lip trembled.

"I just can't."

"But I don't understand, Jared. What did I do?"

"You didn't do anything."

That took away hope. If I didn't do anything wrong that meant I couldn't do anything to make it right again.

Jared said, "I really don't want to hurt you. I really don't. But things must end between us."

"Jared, I don't understand." My eyes warmed with tears. "Why would you say that? What's wrong? You don't even look like yourself." I reached for his hand.

"Sidney, please," Jared said, backing away, still not making eye contact with me. "You're making this harder than I already knew it would be. I'm sorry. It's just . . ."

"Just *what*? What, Jared?" I finally made hand-to-hand contact with him. "Tell me. I mean,"—I shook my head, confused—"is . . . is there someone else?" Jared was quiet. "Well, *is* there?"

Jared still didn't look at me when he finally replied, "Yes."

I let go of his hand. "What? What did you say?"

Jared finally brought himself to look at me for a moment.

"Yes, Sidney. There *is* someone else." His eyes said he was sorry. But that didn't help with what his mouth was saying.

"But . . ." A lump worked its way up my throat. I couldn't speak.

"Sidney," Jared's face looked sympathetic as I still found myself unable to speak. "I'm sorry," he said. "I really am."

He turned around to leave.

"Jared!" I called out.

He stopped, his hand on the door knob, and his back to me.

My chest rose and fell as I struggled for the right words. "You said . . . you said that you wanted to be with me forever . . ." My voice weakend as I fought to bring forth breath. "Is this it? The end of forever?"

Jared turned and looked at me with creases near his eyes.

"I'm sorry, Sidney." He shook his head. "I really am." He opened the door. "Goodbye," he said, then walked out of my apartment.

Even as I heard his footsteps going down the stairs I couldn't believe he was leaving me. I just couldn't believe it. So I stood there, counting the steps. Waiting for him to come back and say it wasn't true. That he'd meant none of it. That he still loved me. I stood there hoping that my ears that conspired with his lips were nothing more than vicious liars.

I stood there for an hour.

Then I lied down for three days.

CHAPTER 31

People thought I was doing well because I didn't cry. Mom even called me strong. But I don't know if it was so much strength as it was complete emotional fatigue. I compare it to getting hit in the gut with a 30-mile-an-hour football. It hurt so bad—the blow was so forceful—that I *couldn't* cry. There wasn't sufficient breath left in my body in order to do so.

Since he never gave me an explanation, it was my assumption that Jared had gone back to his ex. I remembered he was pretty vague that first night at his home when I'd asked about her picture. The picture that suddenly disappeared from the mantelpiece when we began dating, and later turned up in a photo album in his closet. I had a feeling there were unresolved feelings between the two of them. It seems I was right.

In fact, it would be reasonable to say that finality wasn't exactly Jared's forte. He'd left so many loose ends between the two of us. His car even sat in my parking lot for three whole weeks until I eventually drove it back to his house. As I sat in his half circle driveway, awaiting my cab, I wanted so badly to knock on his door or, even boldly, use my key in order to try to talk to Jared. To find out just what was going on. But I was too scared. I was afraid of what I might've found, or *who* I might have encountered. I also didn't want any painful or embarrassing confrontation, or trouble with law enforcement. So I stayed put, soaking up the last traces of Jared's scent that lingered in his car.

When my taxi came I left my key to Jared's house in his glove box, along with everything small he ever gave me. Every greeting card, every piece of jewelry, even the rare bottle of my favorite perfume found its place next to the car's owner's manual. As for the clothes, shoes, and big ticket handbags he'd purchased for me over the course of our relationship, I donated those. Someone else could feel good wearing those things. I couldn't. I wanted to rid myself of Jared's memory. I wanted to forget he ever existed.

◆ ◆ ◆

"Hey, Winks. I was going to leave a message. What are you doing home?" Tasha asked, surprised that I'd answered at two in the afternoon. She'd called last week, but I was too depressed to return the call. Now she was on the other line, and I didn't have an acceptable reason as to why I'd ignored her previous messages.

Thankfully, she didn't ask for one.

I rubbed my left temple as I walked into the living room. "I took the day off."

"Burnout?" she asked, as I sat down on the sofa and sighed.

"Meltdown."

"I feel you. I'm playing hooky myself. But they owe me this one. I've been working my tail off for the past few months. Weekends too."

I didn't say anything. I just curled up, drawing my knees up to my chest, tucking the phone between the sofa cushion and my face as I lay there.

"Anyway," Tasha said, filling in the gap, "what's going on with you? Did you get my message last week?"

"Yeah. I was going to call you this weekend," I said, embarrassed that she'd decided to ask me after all, and feeling terrible that she'd beat me to the punch. But coming home and getting on the phone just wasn't high on my *can't-wait-to-get-home-to-do-this* list.

"So . . ." she asked again, sensors activated, "what's going on?"

"Nothing much. Just working," I delivered a high-pitched response designed to throw her off my scent. Tasha usually smelled deception. And that happy-go-lucky delivery of mine took all the strength I had. But if she asked me again I was sure to crack.

Tasha sighed. "Well, I was calling to tell you the news."

"What news?"

This sounded almost like another engagement story. But Tasha's prelude sigh told me it wouldn't be.

"Glen and I broke up," she revealed, confirming my worst suspicions.

"What?! Why?"

"A lot of reasons. I can't even say for sure. It's just we haven't been seeing eye-to-eye lately. We disagree about everything these days. The truth is we're just not a good match for each other. And I'm not willing to waste any more time on an obvious no-go. For example, he told me that he doesn't ever want children."

"Awful."

"You're telling *me*. I heard a few of my eggs crack when he told me that."

I laughed.

"I'm serious," Tasha insisted. "I found them sunny-side up in my underwear last week."

We giggled together that time. This was the first time in a long time that I'd laughed.

"Well, are you okay?" I asked Tasha, hoping she wasn't too broken up about it.

"Yeah, I'm fine," she said. "It's really not a big deal. I mean, he never looked me in the eyes when he told me he loved me, so it was just a matter of time."

That was surprising to hear. Tasha never told me that. If she had, I would've told her to give him the ax a long time ago.

"And you know what else, Sidney?"

"What's that?"

"I'm kind of glad."

"What do you mean?"

"I mean, it might sound bad, but I feel like I've been given a new journal. You can relate to that, right? Like, now I can start writing something new, and *better.*"

"I guess . . ." I shook my head, not really sold.

I was disappointed for Tasha. I wanted relationship happiness for her. I thought that Glen was going to turn out to be her soulmate. But he turned out to be just another asshole wasting somebody's time.

"Men!" I sneered.

"Yeah. Men!" Tasha seconded.

"Who needs'em?"

"We do!" she quickly jumped ship.

"Humph! Speak for yourself. All I need is my hand and my imagination."

"Sidney!"

Tasha and I laughed as we spent a few minutes reflecting on the challenges of finding the right guy. It seemed to me these days that there might not even be such a thing.

"So, are you sure you can't make it to the wedding?" Tasha asked, changing the subject.

"Unfortunately not. I can't get that Friday off," I lied, having never put in the request. "But tell Bonni Q I'll send her a really nice gift, along with my sincerest congratulations."

I felt guilty for lying. But I just couldn't bear to witness Tasha's little cousin living out my dreams.

Tasha sighed knowingly. "Okay. I understand. But she's going to be so disappointed."

"Yeah . . . I know. Sorry."

Tasha didn't press.

She took in an audible breath. "Alright, Sidneywinks. Well, I'll talk to you later, okay?

"Okay."

"I love you."

"I love you, too, Tasha."

CHAPTER 32

Melvin wasn't exactly my type. For starters, his name was Melvin. What's more, he was married. I'd never gone there before, but these days life had made me more flexible. And Tasha was right. I did need a man.

Even if it was someone else's.

I'd concentrated on getting over the stigma of being the other woman. Everything that had gone wrong in my relationships for the past few years had, in one way or another, something to do with another woman. I'd realized I had been living in a bubble of my own beliefs.

Relationships weren't at all how I'd envisioned them to be when I was growing up. They were less real, and more of a game. And the rules of the game were that there were no rules. Other women had stepped on my toes in the past, so Melvin was my equalizer. And besides, I didn't want to steal him. I just wanted to borrow him for a while.

Though I believed I'd sufficiently worked it all out in my mind, walking up the restaurant stairs, a funny feeling shot through my heart nonetheless. I knew what it was. But I quickly dismissed it. I refused to let it ruin my night. It had been seven months, three weeks, and one day since Jared left me standing in my living room, and I wasn't going to allow a little thing like guilt send me running back to those cold lonely walls of my apartment. Besides, Melvin was fine. I didn't particularly care for his huge muscles. But aside from that, with his sky-scraping stature and Herculean build, he was the perfect mood booster. And at least he was honest, I figured. He did tell me he was married. So this time I knew exactly what I was getting into. And to leave my heart—and 'forever after' expectations—at home.

The evening's forecast predicted a breezy night, which proved to be accurate as Melvin and I sat outside by the water. I wore a gold halter dress; Melvin a stretchy acrylic shirt and rather form-fitting slacks. From speedos to muscle shirts I couldn't appreciate clingy clothes on men. But I returned Melvin's compliment and told him he looked nice, as we looked over our menus.

I ordered the main lobster, having a huge craving. Melvin ordered the steak. He'd also ordered oysters on the half-shell, joking that they were aphrodisiacs. I didn't know whether that was true or not, but three slithery swallows later, I *was* actually feeling a bit frisky.

"How's your lobster?" Melvin asked with a full mouth.

I nodded, not wanting to follow his lead.

"Steak's a little tough." He sawed off another piece. "It's flavorful, though." He popped the tiny piece of seasoned leather into his mouth.

I swallowed then took a sip of my wine. "Good," I finally answered his question, and acknowledged his comment all at the same time, then took another sip.

Melvin grinned as the bitter red potion kissed my lips.

"What?" I sat my drink down on the table.

He shook his head and resumed his chewing.

The live band filled the gaps in our conversation as Melvin and I flirted with our eyes. The music's clandestine melody and soft strings created an alluring sound that seemed especially selected for us. It was like the song was telling on us. That we were forbidden to be together.

By band's intermission Melvin's plate was absent its baked potato and string beans. My plate was still full, but my wine glass needed refreshing. The wind had really picked up, so I needed the liquid fire to warm me from the inside out. My teeth were nearly chattering in the mild blizzard. Melvin tried his hand at chivalry and gave me his jacket to drape over my shoulders in the meantime, but the thin windbreaker cloaked me like fishnet stockings in below-zero weather, breaking nothing but my ability to sit still, as its itchy lining tortured me more than the actual wind itself.

I sat there, slowly turning into a creamsicle, as Melvin was still rambling on about his rocky marriage.

"It's just my wife and I don't see eye-to-eye sometimes," he explained after swallowing down a huge bite. "That's all."

Oh how I wish, I rolled my eyes inside, bothered by the topic, and the length of it. I sipped my wine, savoring it, wishing he'd shut up about his wife already. He'd been going on and on for what felt like forever about how they met; how she was a graphic designer, successful, blah . . . blah . . . blah. If he missed her so much he should've invited her too.

"She's a good person," he added. I rolled my eyes, this time in plain view, prompting Melvin to quickly change directions. "But she's not as pretty as you are, Sidney." He leaned forward, rubbing his thumb over my hand.

I smiled for his benefit.

"So," he picked up his fork again, "what do you think about this place?"

"It's beautiful," I smiled, reaching for my glass. "I just love the setting. It's like casual upscale." I glanced around admiringly, taking a sip from my virtually-empty glass.

"Yeah, I love it, too," Melvin looked around himself. "My wife and I come here all the time."

—I choked on my sip.

"You okay?" Melvin leaned forward as I cleared wine from my windpipe.

"Yeah, I'm okay," I patted my chest, thinking he had to be insane for bringing me here.

Melvin went back to his steak. "Yeah, she loves this place a little *too* much, though. That's how she gained all that weight. And I can't get her in the gym to save my life. Hell, I can't get her in the gym to save *her* life."

Melvin and I actually met at the gym. He'd strut around shirtless, spending the majority of his time on the bench press, checking out women only to see if they were checking him out. Tonight was the first time I'd seen him in regular clothes.

I looked at him as he continued.

"She's really let herself go." He shook his head like it was a shame. "She used to be so fine."

Figuring if I went along and participated a little that he'd drop the subject, I sat my empty glass down and said, "That's odd."

"What?"

"Well, that you're so fit, and she's . . ."

"So fat?"

I broke eye contact with Melvin and faded out of the conversation. I was going to say 'not motivated by that', but he didn't let me finish. I felt weird talking about the woman. I mean, it was bad enough I was out with her husband. I didn't want to stomp on her *too* much.

As the night continued Melvin chewed his food savagely. I, on the other hand, had barely touched mine. While he enjoyed his meal like it was his last, I looked around the restaurant, remotely invading the lives of the other patrons.

Giving the patio a curious scan, I noticed the fair number of couples that were out tonight. My eyes quickly acquired the information my curiosity craved:

Table #1: Four hands. Two rings.

Table #2: Eight hands. Three rings.

Table #3: Four hands. No rings.

Table #4: Rings all around.

Table #5: Four big hands. Two little hands. Two rings. One Ring Pop.

Table #6: see Table #1.

There was relationship diversity throughout the crowded patio but the couples clearly outnumbered the single-status diners. Almost everyone looked happily attached. No one seemed out of place. Then, my eyes got to Table #7. Our table.

Four hands. One ring. One huge mistake.

"It's hard sometimes to be with someone who doesn't take pride in their appearance." Melvin was still babbling on as my stomach flipped with embarrassment over the fact that we were the only scandalous-looking table. Melvin didn't attempt hide his marital status tonight, but I was beginning to wish he had. I wish I could've asked him to take his ring off for the night as I imagined the scrutiny I was probably receiving from observant patrons like myself.

I watched Melvin as his jaws processed the meat that looked tender on his plate yet, in his mouth, seemed to require a lot of work, and studied the sweat bead that was ready to ski its way down his forehead. *How is he sweating?* I wondered, shivering cold.

"She just doesn't give a damn," Melvin said. "Not like you. It's obvious that you know what a man likes. You keep yourself real nice." He looked me over approvingly. "And you smell good, too. That's important," he punctuated with his fork, wearing Dizzy Gillespie cheeks, chewing and talking simultaneously.

In spite of it all, my hormones had me surveying his physique. Looking Melvin in his eyes as he spoke, I was on a mental vacation. I was imagining what he might look like naked. Completely naked. I wondered if he had been 'blessed'. I wondered if I could make some predictions based on his hand- or shoe size. I leaned back in my chair, slipping my eyes under the table to look at his feet.

"See, my wife, she's a professional woman. An artist. So she's got all the brains and creativity." *Chew. Chew.* "The money." *Chew. Chew.* "Oh—and she can cook." He licked the steak sauce off his finger, then put the second-to-last bite in his mouth.

By now I had worked my way up his calves, remembering that they were nice and developed, not scrawny like those top-heavy iron-pumpers who had the biceps of the Brawny Man, but the calves of a kid.

"Yeah, she's downright brilliant. But you," he swallowed, "you got *alllll* the beauty."

Melvin grinned at me seductively as if believing his last statement was a compliment.

I couldn't resist saying something.

"I'm sorry. Did you say she was curing cancer?"

Melvin seemed caught off guard by my sarcasm. He immediately tried to do some damage control.

"Well, no, don't get me wrong. You have something special too. It takes a lot of patience to be a customer service rep. And I *love* a patient woman." His eyes glimmered with lust. "More women need to be that way." He finally popped the last bite of meat into his mouth.

"Well, thanks. And you're right. It does take patience. But I have a communications degree. I'm actually pursuing a career in public relations," I told him, rubbing my Achilles.

Melvin's chewing slowed, as I wondered how he found room in his mouth for food *and* his foot.

"Oh," he said, surprised. "I didn't know that."

He wiped his greasy lips with a napkin and pushed his empty plate to the side, reaching for my hands across the table. Reluctantly, I gave them to him.

"Wow," he said, caressing my palms, "you have the softest hands."

I could only feel his rough, callused ones that felt like the earth's crust scraping against mine. I wondered if he'd heard of weight-lifting gloves. Or lotion!

While I tried simmering down, Melvin continued to look at me seductively, eventually melting my icy demeanor.

Realizing that maybe he didn't mean to be insulting, I surrendered to a smile.

"These hands probably really know how to make a man feel good. I bet you give great massages," he grinned.

While Melvin caressed my hands I found myself thinking about Jared, and how I used to give him massages after a long flight. I'd have him moaning with pleasure, begging for me to never stop. Jared's back was like silk-covered steel. The pleasure was more mine to knead and squeeze on his beautiful brown body.

As Melvin flirted with my fingers, I thought back to *his* physique, and, by now, had worked my way up to his chest. As I recalled from the gym, he shaved his chest. Spiked keratin sprouted through his brick-hard torso, giving him that human cheese grater look. Nonetheless, my mind continued its virtual tour around Melvin's protruding pecks and rock-like arms.

Melvin smiled at me as he continued rubbing my hand raw.

"How's that feel?" he asked.

"Nice."

By the evening's end, the band had regrouped for their last session. As the music began to play some of the couples got up to dance.

"So," Melvin tried seducing me again with his eyes, "are you still enjoying yourself?"

"Yes," I replied, feeling the effects of a full glass of wine on a practically-empty stomach.

"You hardly touched your food." Melvin looked at my plate that looked like it had just been set in front of me. "You didn't like it?"

"I did," I nodded otherwise. "I guess I just wasn't as hungry as I thought."

I looked at Melvin as my morals melted in dissolving discretion. Red hot thoughts displayed themselves in the windows of my eyes. And Melvin was enjoying the view.

"I could get lost in your eyes," he climbed inside of them, basking in my stare that held desire for him. I smiled, allowing him access, knowing how much he loved looking into my eyes.

He leaned back and grabbed his beer. "So, am I the first married guy you've dated?"

"What?" I blinked, kicking him out.

Taken by surprise, and embarrassed, I couldn't believe how he'd shattered the moment with such a question. Dirty details and filthy facts were not to be discussed. They had no place here. Melvin had absolutely no finesse.

He repeated himself, believing I really hadn't heard him.

"Am I the first married man you've gone out with? Or do you normally prefer to date men who are unavailable?"

I didn't know what to say. Melvin had dragged the scandal out by the hair, kicking and screaming, and put it right here on the table in front of us.

"Well, I . . ." I couldn't believe I was trying to answer this question. "I haven't . . . I . . ."

"Aw, it's alright." He chuckled. "It's nothing to be ashamed of. Women always want what they can't have. Matter fact—I get more women *because* I'm married," he added, laughing harder. "That's why I never take my ring off." He took a huge gulp of his beer, while I couldn't help but recall Chaylene's comment back in Chicago.

Melvin didn't mention any degree of his own, but he must've had his master's in Making-Me-Feel-Like-Shit-ology. I had never been so embarrassed.

He released the suction the bottle had on his lips and popped them free, the sound echoing in my ears.

"Yeah. There's no need to feel bad about it. In fact, women like you actually save marriages." He signaled to the waitress. "You done?" he asked me before she reached us.

I nodded as he proceeded to dig into his scrotum-squeezing pants for his wallet, pulling out his credit card.

"I mean, ya'll remind us of what's important. What a man *really* needs." He sat the card at the table's edge.

"I don't understand."

"Well, take my wife for example. Yeah, she's a little heavy in the hips. And yeah, she could be a real nag sometimes. But I knew the moment I saw her that she was the marrying type." He reminisced with a stupid gleam in his eyes, then snapped out of it, and continued explaining.

"You see, your type reminds us of what we have at home. And that's a big help to men like me who often forget."

I narrowed my brow. "My type?"

The waitress came over and refilled my glass. "Dessert tonight?" she asked, wearing a perky, tight-lipped smile.

"You want dessert, baby?" Melvin asked me.

"No." By the way this conversation was going, I wasn't sure I wanted anything else from Melvin.

The waitress took the credit card and left.

I shook my head and squinted. "You were saying?"

"What? Oh yeah," Melvin recaptured his thoughts. "So, I'm saying, we men need women like you to remind us of what's really important, but at the same time to take care of our more uh . . . what word am I looking for?" He looked up toward to sky. "*Carnal needs ,*" he declared with a dirty grin that made me feel exactly that. "You know we can be real animals sometimes," he chucked, grabbing his bottomless beer.

As I watched his Adam's apple bob up and down like a boa constrictor swallowing a field rat, Melvin chugged his brew, neglecting to notice that he was the only one laughing.

My eyes felt hot. My hands grew nervous. I erupted.

"*Animals?* So, who am I? The fucking zookeeper?!"

Melvin's mouth froze dead in its tracks. The bottle was still at his lips when his surprised eyes found mine. He moved it away, looking at me as if those offensive words hadn't originated from his mouth in the first place.

He chuckled while trying to explain, as the eyes he'd once admired narrowed on him. "No, I'm not saying—"

"What *are* you saying?" I locked a stare on him, sick of his underhanded insults.

Melvin's silly grin faded when he saw I was serious.

"Well, what are you getting so defensive for?" He said, changing tone. "I wouldn't have figured you for the sensitive or self-righteous type."

"Is that right?"

"That offends you? Come on, Sidney. I mean, why are you pretending like you don't know the ending to this story?"

"What?!" I frowned. "You think I'm going to *sleep* with you tonight?" I was. But I'd changed my mind. Degrading comments like his had a way of strangling my desire. "Who said I was sleeping with you?!"

I followed Melvin's eyes that intentionally landed on my forty-dollar plate. I gasped.

"This lobster didn't say *shit!*" I shoved my seafood platter across the table right into his lap.

Melvin rushed to his feet as the contents of my barely-eaten meal fell from the seat of his pants onto the ground.

I stood up, glowering, my body steaming-mad, blood pumping fast. Melvin's mouth was begging for a slap, and my right hand was about to be his genie.

Completely covered from the waist down in my dinner, Melvin wiped only his hands, then tossed the soiled napkin onto the table and looked at me.

"Then why are you here?"

"What?"

"If it's not to fuck me later, then why are you here, Sidney?" he asked in a tone that was colder than the evening air he had me standing in.

I just stood there, not really knowing what to say.

Why *was* I here? That was the question of the day—of my life. And it would take me all night to answer it.

So I just walked away.

My head spun the entire way home. My stomach was in my lap. And my eyes were sweltering hot. Midway through my trip I'd called Melvin and told his voice mail what an asshole he was, and that he looked like he had a vagina in those tight-ass pants of his. When I finally got home I headed straight for the shower to cool off.

When the cool water turned *too* cold, I turned it off and reached for a towel. My hand swept the air back and forth, clawing for what, apparently, wasn't there. I drew the curtain to find an empty towel rack just above a full hamper whose lid was barely balanced atop an overflowing hill of laundry.

I planted one wet foot on the bath rug, followed by another, my reflection and I looking at each other. I'm not sure what it saw in me, but in it I saw a pitiful sight. Black paint dripped from its eyes, smeared and smudged across its face. Red tinted eyes shot from its sockets like lasers. And wavy-when-wet hair met slumped shoulders.

"What were you thinking?" I asked my reflection. What in the *world* were you thinking tonight?"

It didn't say anything. It just looked back at me.

I took in a deep breath.

"He thinks you're a tramp, you know?" I leaned over the sink, my head bowed in disappointed. "He'll spend his whole life remembering you that way."

I looked up at the silent reflection again. "How could you let that happen?" Tears started rolling down its face. Its nose turned red and began to run.

As the spinning in my head slowed, my perception sharpened. Things started coming together. With the buzz of the bathroom's fan in my ear, and the feel of my feet on the damp rug, my own image began materializing before me.

Emotions developed in the sacks of my eyes. My hands began to tremble at the sight of myself. Faced with my own shame, my fist balled.

"Dammit!!!" I struck my reflection in the face, slicing open my hand in the process.

As glass came crashing down geometrically-shaped shards filled the sink. And as I bowed my head to hide from shame, a hundred eyes watched me.

Blood where pupils should be.

CHAPTER 33

The mattress hadn't completely contoured to my body before my ears opened my eyes. Exhausted, my arm debated on whether to reach across and answer the phone that denied me five more hours to put with my three, or to snatch the cord right out of the wall.

"Hello?"

"Rise and shine, Sidneywinks!"

I squinted at the clock wondering if Tasha had lost her mind *and* her concept of time.

I breathed hard into the phone. "I'll call you back," I told her, my thumb rounding toward the *End* button.

"No—Wait!" she yelled in the nick of time.

I put the phone back to my ear.

"I'm on my way," she said.

"Where?" I yawned, convinced she wasn't going to let me get back to sleep any time soon.

"West Palm. I'm on the plane right now."

I sat up and brushed my hair back. "No way."

"Yes way!" she said. "I'm in the company of the clouds as we speak."

"Are you serious, Tasha?" I asked, hoping she wasn't just pulling my leg.

Tasha laughed.

"You're serious, aren't you?!"

"Yes, I'm serious. Look, I know you haven't been yourself lately. I could hear it in your voice," she said, hers taking a more serious tone. "And I heard that Tori Amos playing in the background the other day."

359

"Heyyyy, Tori's my girl," I defended us, laughing.

"I know. She's mine too. But let's get you on some other stuff. Some happy tunes. Something you can dance to. Get your blood flowing. Sound good? Whadayasay?" She had contagious spunk in her voice. "You ready for some fun?"

I grinned wide on the other end of the phone.

"Yes."

I knew Tasha would be looking for my car to circle around. But I wanted to give her a surprise of my own. As I walked past baggage claim, through the automatic doors, I saw several people waiting curbside for their rides. I gave the crowd a slow scan, in search of my BFF, but didn't see her. I wondered if I'd just fallen victim to the biggest hoax ever. I pulled out my cell phone.

Having dialed Tasha's number, I continued to put my eyes to work while my phone searched for a signal. I began wondering if I had gotten the flight information mixed up. As the phone's tone rang twice in my ear people climbed in cars and limos; a little boy hugged his grandparents; the two Morehouse guys were looking like they wanted a taste of Columbia, salivating over the two Latinas in floral dresses while the wavy-haired blonde in Baby Phat denim fumbled with her shoulder bag. I huffed impatiently, the phone still ringing in my ear, as she knelt in her skinny jeans to unzip the side pocket of her carry-on.

As the blonde's back bent I caught a quick glimpse of her tattoo just before it ducked back into its denim horizon upon her standing up. I touched the red button on my phone.

I crept up behind Goldilocks as she checked her missed call.

"Gotcha!" I double-poked her in the side.

Startled, Tasha swung around.

"Heyyyyyy!" she screamed, falling into me.

"Hey, youuuuu!" I hugged her, smelling her familiar fragrance. I was so glad to see her. Her timing was perfect. I really needed her right now.

I squeezed her tight then let go to take a look at her.

"Look at you. You look so good!" I said, not pinching an inch on her trim waist.

"A lot of sex will do that for you."

"Then I should be morbidly obese," I rolled my eyes.

"On second thought, me too. Lately, anyway," Tasha laughed, then froze. Her mouth formed a perfect O.

"Sidney! Oh my God! You cut your hair!"

I stroked the back of my inch-long cut self-consciously. "Yeah . . ."

"At first I thought you just had it all pulled back, but . . ." she shook her head, speechless to my new look.

"You like it?"

I really shouldn't have asked. It looked awful and I knew it. I don't know what possessed me to cut it so short. I'd just woke up one day and decided to do just that.

I looked at Tasha, awaiting her critique.

She smiled. "With a face that pretty you can rock *any* style," she conjured up a creative *No.*

I smiled back knowingly, yet appreciative.

"My Gosh . . . it makes your eyes look like *jewels*," she giggled then yanked me into another hug.

"I'm so happy to see you," I whispered in her ear then looked at her with watery eyes.

"I'm happy to see you, too."

Tasha's eyes looked like mine. She squeezed my hand and smiled. People probably thought we were lovers, the way we carried on. But we were just best friends who hadn't seen each other in what felt like forever.

Tasha swung my hand in hers, her eyes still trying to adjust to my new look as mine adjusted to hers. It was like we'd switched hairstyles.

"You look so nice," she told me again, her smile warm and wide. She was so pretty.

"Look at *you*." I tugged on one of her soft locks, then let it spring back into its ringlet shape.

She shook her big hair. "Surprised?"

"Big time. I haven't seen your hair this long since high school. You couldn't send me a selfie?!"

"Well, maybe if you ever get your butt on Facebook."

"Yeah, I know . . ." I looked away, owning my social media aversion.

"And why didn't you send *me* a picture?" she countered.

"I don't knowwww . . ."

We laughed, embracing once again, as we slowly rocked from side to side, just giddy with joy.

Other passengers still scurried around us.

"You don't know how glad I am to see you, Tasha."

She pressed her face firmly against mine.

"I'm glad to see you, too."

Tasha insisted on renting a car. She broke the news to me that her return flight would leave at six the next morning, and said she didn't want to inconvenience me by getting me up too early to take her to the airport. I was disappointed to hear I'd only have her for a day. But I tried not to dwell on that. I was just glad to have her here.

After getting Tasha's rental, we caught up over breakfast. As we enjoyed our special-requested floppy bacon, I told her about Melvin, and what had happened last night. She was stunned.

Tasha knew married men weren't our style. Disappointment shot from her eyes. I beseeched her to save the lecture. My conscience had already sufficiently scolded me, as did Melvin's barbarian style of behavior. I'd definitely learned my lesson.

Since I was taking Tasha out tonight, she wanted to go shopping. She was really excited to check out South Florida's nightlife.

"You like this?" Tasha held up the almost-see-through dress that could've doubled as lingerie. We were at the mall.

"Yeah, right," I chucked, amused by her endless sense of humor. Then I noticed that she wasn't laughing.

I sat my item down. "Are—Are you serious?"

"Yeah!" Tasha held it up to her body admiringly. "It's funky."

"Well, that *is* the word that comes to mind," I wrinkled my nose, wondering what Glen had done to my friend's fashion sense. We pushed the envelope sometimes, but we were far from tacky.

Tasha, still looking toward me for approval, turned her head from side-to-side as if its angle would change my opinion. "You really don't like it?"

"How can I put this?" I wanted to choose my words carefully. "You won't like the kind of man who likes that dress. And the kind of man you *do* like won't like that dress at all."

Tasha nodded. "Yeah, I guess you're right."

She put the dress back on the rack where it belonged.

I nodded too, relieved.

"But who's looking for a man?!" she snatched it back up.

"Give me that!" I wrestled the forbidden fabric away from her, and pulled her by the arm.

After spending two hours finding the perfect dress for Tasha she suggested that we both get manis and pedis. We also got our eyebrows—and upper lips—waxed, and even got facials. I was feeling better already. I was so glad she'd came.

Following a two-hour matinee, our appetites led us to an old-fashioned burger joint where the servers zipped around on skates. After showing no mercy to our chicken fingers and fries we answered to our undying sweet tooth and wrapped ourselves in conversation until reminiscing melted our ice cream. We asked for straws and glasses, and, shamelessly, made milkshakes of the soupy dessert.

Time was slipping away like sifted sand through an hourglass. And we were trying to stretch out every moment.

"So, is Leann coming with us tonight?" Tasha asked, as her elbow dodged the vanilla puddle next to her glass.

I wiped my milk mustache. "We're not exactly talking right now."

"What? Why not?"

"Well, a few weeks ago, I kind of . . . sort of . . . accidentally . . . told her that her fiancé was a bum," I admitted, embarrassed.

"What?"

"Well, I didn't *mean* to say it," I explained. "She was going on and on about him and her so-called engagement. And then she said that one day I'd find someone just like she had found Reggie. And then I said, *'Yeah, but I don't want to settle'.*"

Tasha's jaw dropped.

"Yeah. That's how *she* looked." I dropped my eyes in my lap, opposite of proud.

I continued explaining.

"You know, I didn't mean to say it, Tasha. It just sort of slipped out, at which point I was forced to elaborate."

"Elaborate?"

I shook my head with a regretful look. I truly did feel bad about the whole thing. But then part of me thought back to Leann and how she could be insensitive at times herself, always talking that 'flat butt' stuff. She wasn't exactly flawless in her ideology either as she'd said of me during that unfortunate exchange.

"Well, what did she say?" Tasha asked as I played with my straw.

"She said something about me having pearls at the opera."

"What??"

"I don't know. Something about hyper optics . . . high purple something—I really don't know, Tasha," I shook my head, sure I was mispronouncing it. "Wait— Hyperopia. That's it."

"Farsightedness?"

"Is *that* what that is?" I batted my hand at that nonsense.

Tasha looked confused. "Well, why did she say that? There's nothing wrong with your eyes."

I shrugged. "I don't know. Just mad I guess . . . saying crazy stuff that doesn't make sense." I picked up my milkshake. "Hanging out with that eye doctor of hers too much."

Tasha looked at me as I began to slurp loudly.

"Hmm . . . Well, that's too bad." She sounded disappointed. "I was really looking forward to meeting her."

I stopped slurping.

"You were?"

"Well, yeah. I mean, I've heard so much about her. Why not?"

I shook my head. "Yeah, well, *three's a crowd.* Right?" I slurped my shake until it was gone.

CHAPTER 34

By the time we got to my apartment it was just after eight o'clock. I threw the latest stack of mail onto the table with the rest then pitched the corned beef sandwich that I'd ordered to-go into the trashcan in the kitchen.

"I knew you weren't going to eat that," Tasha said.

"You did?"

"I sure did. I knew it when it was sitting on the table in that banged-up Styrofoam container. I knew it when it was parked lonely at your feet in the movie theater. And I knew it when it was in the back seat, stinking up the car on the way here." Tasha shook her head. "Thanks for finally putting me—and *it*—out of our misery."

I laughed at her silliness. "You're welcome."

"Wow! Sidney, I love your place." Tasha ignored the mountain of junk mail and bills piled high on my table, as well as the dirty dishes dumped in the sink.

"You've always had such great use of space." She walked over to the window. "How are your neighbors?"

"What neighbors? I have neighbors?"

We both laughed.

Tasha walked over to me. "You know, I've really missed you, Winks."

"I've missed you, too, girlie."

We took our time, dancing around in our towels before finally deciding to finish getting ready. When

Tasha asked me what happened to the bathroom mirror I told her I'd opened the medicine cabinet too fast and shattered it by mistake. She called me clumsy and got ready in front of the cheval mirror in my bedroom instead while I sat at the vanity. It felt just like old times, when she'd come over my house and we'd get ready together before a party or game.

"Don't forget mascara." I tossed the tube from across the room, then turned around and began sweeping bronzer on my cheeks.

"Thanks." Tasha caught it midair. "You know, I sure wish you'd change your mind about Jamaica. I'd hate to see Glen's ticket go to waste. Tara's been hinting around. Especially since her deal hasn't been going as well as she'd expected."

I smiled *Thanks*, but I didn't want to go. That was the last place Jared and I had been. The memories alone would kill me.

"Drinking appletinis and piña coladas just isn't going to be the same without you, Sidney." Tasha walked over to me, her reflection joining mine in the mirror.

"Well, we'll just have to make up for that tonight. Won't we?" I said as I put my arm around her hip.

She poked out her bottom lip.

"Alright?" I smiled up at her.

"Alright." She put her hand on my shoulder. "Tonight's the night."

We finally headed out at 11:30 p.m., looking and smelling delicious. We'd decided that we wanted to check out a couple of places before deciding on a final spot. Spring-breakers shared the roads with us as we cruised down the street, enjoying throwback mixes on the radio.

I was tapping my thumbs on the steering wheel, when Tasha decided she needed some fresh air.

"*Whew!* It's hot in here." She rolled down her window halfway as we made progress toward our first destination. She'd styled her hair bone-straight, showing off her sunny highlights. She was definitely going to grab up all the attention tonight. I felt proud to have her with me and couldn't wait to show her off.

"My Goodness! I can't breathe. Feels like the Devil's in here," she said, with wind blowing into the car like a hurricane.

"Look, *Summer!*"—I rolled it back up, child-locking it—"lay off the sauce until we get there. Wouldja?"

Tasha fanned herself, laughing with sweat beaded on her nose. We'd made a pit stop at the liquor store so that she could 'get the party crackin', as she'd put it. And now she was reaping the intoxicating benefits at the cost of an inferno raging inside of her. But she'd just have to let it burn like our man Usher was singing on the radio, because it had just finished raining and the lurking humidity was stalking my haircut. I was not about to show up to the club with a miniature fro.

"Want some?" Tasha held her cup under my nose.

I frowned, getting a sharp whiff. "My gosh! What in the world did you put in there?"

Tasha scratched her head. "Uhh . . . Tequila Rose, Goldschläger, Sunny D," she peeked inside the pale orange concoction, trying to remember the rest, "a splash of chocolate liqueur, aaaaannnd . . . Absolut."

"Absolutely not!" I pushed the cup from under my nose, blinking hard. "And could you keep that cup of *tear gas* low, please? You know my tint is light."

Tasha lowered her cup, then burped.

"Okay. Now, you're gonna melt my glass." I fanned the hot fumes of resurrected alcohol from my windshield, letting the window down for my little dragon after all as I laughed and shook my head at her.

As the desired breeze hit her face, Tasha let out a feel-good groan. "Oh my God! I can't wait to get up in the club tonight!"—she snuck another quick sip—"I am going to party like I have absolutely no sense!" She clapped her hands one time loud, then began doing her signature move.

"Awww. Work it out! Work it out!" I cheered her on, while she fed off the encouragement. "Do the Tasha! Do the Tasha!"

Hands on her waist, she rolled her shoulders around in circles, lips puckered out, butt vibrating in the seat. I laughed until my jaws hurt.

I downshifted as we came upon a red light, as the DJ's seamless club mix got Tasha in the mood. As she moved to the techno beat, I stared at the light until my mind started drifting. Shielded by the music I slipped off into a daydream, thinking back to last night.

As headlights and traffic signals projected off my eyes behind them I remembered how badly things had been last night. How I'd let a clown like Melvin make a fool out of me. How I'd even *allowed* him to. How it was my fault for being there in the first place.

I tightened my grip on the leather-covered shift and took a deep breath, trying to put those prickly thoughts away, at least for tonight.

Tasha took another sip from her custom cocktail, finishing it. As she leaned forward to set the empty cup into the holder beneath the stereo she paused.

She hadn't noticed my knuckles earlier. I'd done a masterful job of concealing them throughout the day. Only my manicurist saw the hellish bruise that was bluish-purple in color. But as night fell I grew careless.

Aware of her scrutiny, I fumbled around with the stick shift, shaking it fast to limit her view of the fresh, raw cuts that glistened with the virgin sheath preceding the scab. I tossed the stick around unnecessarily, until the green light justified my movement.

Tasha looked at me as we accelerated.

"You alright?" she asked, eyes half-squinted, lips parted.

"Yeah," I smiled, shifting to third gear before burying my injured hand into my lap. "I only got three hours of sleep last night"—I yawned for effect—"I'm just a little tired, that's all." I blinked my eyes, then swallowed. "But hey,"—I nudged her—"I'm ready to par-*tay!*"

Tasha looked at me, forcing a smile under her doubtful eyes.

"Okay," she nodded, but was still looking at me as if attempting to read my thoughts.

I kept my eyes on the road.

"You know, we don't have to go out, Sidney. I'll have just as much fun hanging out with you back at your apartment."

"No way." I shook my head. "Not after I took the tag off this dress," I protested. But what I really wanted to say was *Oh, bless you!,* then make U-turn at the next light.

I didn't, though. Instead, I followed up with, "Besides, I'm ready to show off my best friend."

By the time we got to *Torch* it was 12:15. Just in time for us to make our grand entrance.

"Ohhh yeah! The roof *is* on fire!" Tasha bounced in her seat, approving of the 21-and-up-crowd. "We're going to have fun."

Tasha and I weren't going first class tonight, since Leann wasn't with us to ensure such VIP status. But first class, or coach, when we stepped inside, Tasha and I walked in like they were waiting for us. And the way all eyes fell upon us, you would've thought they were. Getting energized off the attention, I smiled to myself knowing how good we looked. I felt amazing in my dress. Head-to-toe knockout. And Tasha took everybody's breath away with what she was wearing, and how beautiful she was. Some of the women in the club immediately

started acting up. We had them confused. They didn't know whether they wanted to hate us, or hang with us. I decided for them. Hate it was. Because Tasha and I were a duo. Period.

I turned to Tasha. "QCC?"

"Yeah, you know *me*," she laughed.

After giving the room a quick scan, we ventured to the bathroom. As I led the way Tasha followed close behind, looking around, absorbing the atmosphere, appearing to already be having a good time.

"Wow!" some guy touched my hand as I walked. "You look just like that black girl from Clueless. Can I have your number?"

"*As if*!" I frowned, snatching back my hand and wiping it on my dress.

Tasha laughed.

"Hey, cutie," another guy jumped directly in my path and spoke. "What's your name?"

"Kenya Move?!!" I narrowed my eyes at him.

Once he got out of my face I pushed open the bathroom door.

Tasha laughed as we made our way inside.

"*Kenya Move*. Girl, you are still crazy."

I walked over to the mirror while Tasha laughed her way into a stall to break the seal. I guess that witches' brew from the car must've been working on her.

I stood in front of the looking glass and readjusted the rhinestone clip in my hair. I was actually quite pleased with how my hair had turned out tonight. I was rocking the 'Betty Boop', spending more time on it tonight than I had since I'd gotten it cut.

Tasha came out of the stall. "Girl, did you see that cutie in all black?" She asked me as she walked over to the sink.

"I thought *I* was the only cutie in all black tonight," I smiled.

Tasha rolled her eyes and laughed. "*Besides* you."

"Oh. No. I must've missed that. Was he scrumptious?" I played in my hair to pass time while she washed and dried her hands.

"Super-scrumptious. I've gotta find him. He's going to be my dance partner for the night," she declared her mission for the evening, giving herself the once-over.

I really wasn't feeling the whole guy thing tonight. But I liked that Tasha was having fun.

I turned around and faced her.

"You look gorgeous, girlie," I said, moving a strand of her hair beautiful back into place.

She turned and smiled. "Thanks. So do you, Winks."

"You want a drink?"

"Sure do."

As we stepped back out into the party things were just as we'd left them.

"We are going to have so much fun tonight," Tasha grinned as we sashayed our way toward the crowded bar.

"First drinks are on me," she said.

"I got the next one round."

"Wow!" the bartender said as soon as we approached the bar. "I almost didn't recognize you. How's it going, Sidney."

I hoped she hadn't noticed me, but wasn't so lucky.

"Hey, Isabelle." I hated to speak. I didn't care how many drinks she'd hooked me up with in the past, or how cool she 'thought' I was.

"I like your haircut," she said.

I smiled, believing her a liar, then rolled my eyes when she looked away.

After Isabelle poured our apple martinis, Tasha slapped forty dollars on the bar, telling her to keep the change. I wanted to fill Tasha in on Ms. Isabelle, but didn't want to make it obvious. I gave her a funny look, then frowned at Isabelle when she wasn't looking again. Tasha looked confused. I frowned at her once more but she just wasn't catching on.

She picked up the two glasses and turned around, handing me one.

She rose her glass and said, "An apple a day . . . "

"Keeps the shrink away," I finished her sentence.

Tasha downed her drink in seconds, then, throwing money at Isabelle like she was playing the guitar at Grand Central, ordered two lemon drop shots, once again telling her to keep the change. Isabelle gave her speedy service, while I gulped down my appletini to keep up.

No sooner than my glass hit the bar, Tasha handed me a vial of sour, yellow tonic.

"Ready?" she asked.

I nodded before we threw our heads back and swallowed.

Tasha grabbed me by the hand as we made our way to the dance floor. Immediately, we were surrounded by two guys who'd seem to come out of nowhere. Mine was alright, but Tasha's looked like the *Chupacabra*. She didn't care, though. It was already "tomorrow", and later "today" she'd be back in Atlanta so she couldn't have cared less about what he looked like. She danced with him like he was the finest guy in the club, seeming to have forgotten about *Mission: Black Clothes*.

As the DJ spun the wheels of steel Tasha and I moved closer to each other, laughing and grinning as we bounced to the beat, making our dance partners jealous. She moved to her left. I moved to my right. She moved to her right. I moved to my left. We played peek-a-boo around their bodies, like they were props, until they looked at each other, wondering if we were even dancing with them at all.

Seeming full of steam, I could tell that Tasha was just getting started. I wasn't getting my money's worth at the gym, however, because after three songs, I felt completely out of breath.

Feeling as if I could pass out right there on the dance floor, I signaled to Tasha that I was going to the bar to get us more drinks. Still going, she nodded, gesturing that she'd be right there in that very spot when I returned. I nodded *OK* as I eased my way through the dancing crowd.

I journeyed back over to the scene of the crime where Tasha and I had killed our drinks, and leaned against the bar, waiting for Isabelle to serve up two more victims.

"Whatcha' need?" She put me ahead of at least four other people who had been waiting before me.

I leaned over and shouted, "Two apple martinis."

"You got it!" she shouted back.

I smirked to myself, thinking she had another thought coming if she thought I was going to give her a twenty-dollar tip like Tasha had. Trying to act all nice. She should've thought about her tips when she was talking all that trash. All I had for her was a *Thanks* and two dollars.

She came back in record time, delivering two filled-to-the-brim glasses of apple ecstasy garnished with umbrella-speared maraschino cherries and paper-thin apple slices that floated toward the bottom of the green pools like underwater crafts.

"Thanks." I sat twenty-two dollars on the bar and walked away.

I maneuvered my way through the bar area, careful not to spill our drinks. It was a challenge, though. Isabelle had really topped them off. The chunky crowd wasn't helping either. I had to duck and dodge dudes who were purposely blocking my way so that they could get my attention. Women who were bitchy about moving for their own reasons. And burly bouncers who gave everyone less room to work with. *"Dang, you're fine! Can I come with you?"* a guy called out as I cautiously carried the dainty glasses in my hands. Other women looked to see who he was talking to. *"I'll carry those drinks for you."*

"I got'em." I didn't even look at him. I just kept walking as if I had an unabridged dictionary balanced on top of my head.

I made my way through the archway that divided the main bar from the central dance floor. Men glanced, but I didn't have eyes for them. I was just looking for Tasha so that we could drink away the internal scars their kind had left us with.

Just as my feet explored the change in carpet color, a guy walked in front of me. Concentrating only on carrying the drinks, I eased under him in a gliding motion.

"Sidney!" he called out.

I turned around.

It was Mark.

"Oh," I said, uncomfortable in an instant. "Hey."

"I almost didn't recognize you." He sized up my haircut. "Nice look on you."

"Thanks," I said hesitantly, knowing he'd probably go back and exaggerate to Jared that he'd seen me in the club wearing a fade. At the thought of it, I gave the room a nervous scan.

"It's been a while. How are you?" Mark asked.

My head rotated from side to side, eyes shifting around the room.

"Fine," I said, holding the two drinks in my hand, ready to drop them if my eyes found what I'd hoped they wouldn't.

Mark followed my head with his, playfully blocking my view with side-to-side intercepts. "Who are you looking for?" he smirked.

"Huh?" My eyes met his, big and worried.

"He's not here," Mark said, knowingly.

My eyes asked *who?* but my mouth refused to take part in the deception. I was rendered silent.

"No one has seen him around lately," Mark added as he approached forbidden territory. "You know, I could tell that he was really crushed about you guys' break-up."

I brought the drinks close to my body, uncomfortably shifting positions.

"What happened to you guys anyway?" Mark wore a concerned frown that I refused to trust. For all I knew he saw Jared every day and knew better than I did what had happened.

Not wanting to talk about it I just shook my head.

"I don't know . . ."

"Well, he doesn't return my calls," Mark said as if to offer consolation. "It's been hard to catch up with him."

"Yeah, six doors down. That's a helluva journey. You wouldn't want to catch a charley horse on the way down. Right?" I rolled my eyes at Mark, who I felt was totally BSing me.

"Actually," Mark cut my eye roll short, "Jared sold his house. I haven't seen him in months."

My heart skipped a beat. I looked at Mark.

"He just, for all intents and purposes, vanished."

"Vanished with who? Janeyse?" I mumbled, annoyed, and fishing for information at the same time.

"Janeyse?" Mark looked confused. "Janeyse his college girlfriend?" He wanted me to specify.

"Really, Mark?" I gave him *a 'don't play dumb with me'* look. "Is that a remarkably common name where you're from?"

Mark's face changed. For the first time it actually looked serious.

"Well, no, it's just . . ." he hesitated. "Well, Janeyse passed away our first year of grad school."

My jaw dropped.

"Car accident. Back in 2005," he explained.

I thought back to the picture. It was dated the same year.

"I didn't know," I said, shocked.

I felt horrible. On top of that I was also confused. Jared had said that there was someone else. Janeyse was the only one I ever felt even remotely threatened by. If it wasn't her then who was it? Who did he leave me for?

I realized it must have been someone new. He'd been cheating on me. My whole night disintegrated right there in that spot.

Mark looked behind him, appearing rushed, like someone was waiting for him. I could barely control my disturbed face.

"Well, Mark, it was nice seeing you again." I prepared to walk away and digest the information he'd just given me. "You have a good ni—"

"Uh—Sidney." He grabbed my hand. I looked at his hand on mine. He let go.

"Um . . . I was wondering," he put his hands in his pockets and assumed a sheepish grin, "if maybe you wanted to go out sometime."

I looked at him, wondering what he meant.

"I mean, like, to dinner or something. Maybe dancing?"

Not believing my ears, I just looked at Mark like he was crazy.

Slowly, his expression turned from partially bold to appropriately embarrassed.

Speechless, I could only huff before walking away.

As I approached the room adjacent to the dance floor I saw that Tasha had found her guy in all black.

The two had apparently gotten acquainted, and were probably surprised to discover that they had an unlikely connection.

They smiled as they watched me walk up.

I approached expressionless, handing Tasha her drink.

"We've been waiting for you," Tasha grinned. She leaned in close to me and whispered, *"He wants to dance with you."*

"Wanna dance, Sidney?" Rico spoke for himself, wearing that deceptively-charming grin.

"Yeah." I took a quick sip of my drink. "On your grave. You drinking and driving tonight?" I asked, hopeful.

Rico looked surprised.

I grabbed Tasha by the wrist. "Come on. Let's go claim those seats before someone else does."

As I led her away Tasha looked back at Rico and shrugged. He lingered around for a while, watching us for a moment before heading off into the crowd.

As we approached the red velvet chairs Tasha wore an open mouth.

"Wow." She plopped down into the oversized chair and sat all the way back, her sangria pumps side-by-side. "That was harsh."

I tossed my purse onto the ice-cubed shaped table. "Yeah. And so was the way he dumped me. Or shall I say, *publicly shamed* me."

Tasha twisted her torso to look back toward the dance floor while I sat and took a sip of my drink, admiring my bumble-bee ankle boots and how cute they looked with my little black dress.

Tasha turned back around toward me, squirming in her seat as if she had a dress full of ants.

"You okay?" I asked, watching her wiggle.

She smiled and raised her drink. "I'm great," she said, then took a sip.

We both looked around at the carefree-crowd that swelled by the minute. Feeling both the music, and the drinks, I crossed my legs, swinging one to the beat.

Tasha, on the other hand, didn't look so relaxed. She uncrossed her legs, the bright pink spot on her outer thigh quickly fading upon the pressure relief, and looked as if her drink wasn't strong enough this round.

She sat up straight, clearing her throat.

"So," she said, "that's Rico, huh?"

"That's him . . . " I said, trying not to be uncomfortable with the fact that my best friend had found my ex attractive.

Tasha smirked. "Well, he's pretty obvious, isn't he?"

"What do you mean?" I began to squirm in *my* seat now. "Obvious how?"

"I mean . . ." she examined her drink, swirling its contents around as if she saw foreign matter floating around, "he's not necessarily the most committed-looking guy in the room. You know what I mean? But nice icing, though," she admitted while seemingly satisfied that what she'd saw in her glass was merely an optical illusion.

"Well, you're seeing a different side of him," I said defensively while secretly reflecting on how he was spreading the love around the room the night I'd met him. Tasha looked at me, almost knowingly.

When she looked away I eyed her, wondering if she had Mark potential, and would ultimately do me the way Jared's friend had just done him. Wondering if she *still* wanted to get with 'the cutie in all black'.

I switched my crossed legs, putting the left one on bottom duty this time.

"Because if he's obvious," I continued, "that makes me oblivious."

Tasha heard the defense in my reply, and saw the offense in my expression, even as I attempted to hide the latter behind my drink.

"Oh, no," she leaned forward, tapping me on the knee, "I didn't mean it like that. It's just, you know, he looks . . ."

She couldn't find a nice way to say 'full of it'.

My eyes located the subject of our debate as Tasha seemed to give up her search for an adequate adjective to describe Rico. Meanwhile, he was dancing the night away, carefree and cute. My leg kicked in agitation as I narrowed my eyes and lent him a contempt-filled stare. I forced down a swallow of my appletini that didn't taste so good when I watched him. I could feel my face turning red.

"I fucking can't stand his ass." I shook my head.

Tasha looked back toward the dance floor, seeing Rico's swaying body, as he quickly found a dance partner to twirl around in my face. While he pretended he didn't notice me looking at him I did everything I could to make him feel me. Directing every bitter thought his way, I telepathically tortured him. It began to work. His face looked preoccupied, and his body movements, unnatural. He knew I was loathing him from afar.

"What???" I lowered my drink, redirecting my eyes toward Tasha, who was giving me quite the look herself.

She shook her head. "Nothing."

I raised my drink back toward my mouth, hiding behind it while I watched Rico again, wondering how I could've ever been foolish enough to take him seriously. Tasha could see right through him within the first few minutes of their encounter. I couldn't see the real him in the nearly three months that we'd dated. It was embarrassing.

From the corner of my eye, I spotted Tasha watching me again.

"What, Tasha?"

She was acting strange.

"It's nothing," Tasha shook her head again, chuckling it off. "Well, actually . . ." she decided on second thought, but paused.

"Tasha. Seriously," I lowered my drink, "what is it?"

"Well, Sidney, it's just . . ." she hesitated again.

I widened my eyes and shook my head, asking her to spit it out.

"It's just . . . well, are you going to spend the rest of your life mad at Rico?" she asked with an incredulous tone that added 'you can't be serious, Sidney!'

I frowned. "What? What are you talking about?"

"I mean . . . 'On your grave'?"

"Uh-ohhhh. His looks aren't hypnotizing *you* now, are they?"

"Please!" Tasha batted her hand back toward the dance floor. "It's not about him. It's about you."

"That's right. And did you forget what he did to me?" I asked Tasha, who'd apparently suffered a sudden case of amnesia. It almost sounded as if she was taking up for him. "We *hate* him now, Tasha. Remember?"

Tasha scrunched her curls upward on the left side of her head, as she looked in the direction of the crowd.

"Well, why do we have to hate anyone?" she asked.

I sat back and looked at her, as I tried to figure out where she was coming from with all of this, and if I owed this unwanted lecture to that disgusting truth serum she was sipping on earlier.

"I mean, why can't we just chalk it up to experience?" she added.

She said *we*, but she meant *me*.

"Tasha, I really don't wanna have this conversation right now." I was disturbed by the very subject, and couldn't believe she'd come all the way here to lecture me on my hatred for Rico. She was my best friend. She was supposed to be on my side. I guess I had to remind her.

"Rico's an asshole, Tasha. Remember? An ass-*hole!* And you shouldn't care less how I feel about him," I told her, wondering how she couldn't jump at the chance to join me in my scorn for him.

"Sidney, I understand that. But don't you think it's time to—"

"Look, I can appreciate that you're all chummy now with Tara and everything. But there are just some things that are unforgivable. And the way he did me is one of them. I need you to understand that."

"Sidney, you act as if you're the only one who has ever been rejected."

"Between the two of us," I gestured back and forth with my hand, "I am."

I took a much-needed sip of my martini.

Tasha looked at me. "Sidney, I was rejected before I was even *born*."

Her seriousness erased the sarcastic grin from my face.

"Before I even took my first breath," she added.

I couldn't argue with that, nor would I try. But if I could, I'd say it was apples and oranges. Her father and Rico were precisely that.

"Sidney, I can understand you being mad at Damon. He was your first," she dared utter the D word. "But everyone else . . ." she shook her head, "it's called kissing frogs. What part of that don't *you* understand?"

"No." I shook my head, disagreeing. "Jared was not a frog."

"Sidney, if he's not here right now, then he was frog."

That drove a knife right through my heart.

"Why are we even talking about this right now, Tasha? This isn't exactly my idea of having fun. I mean, I feel like I should be lying down on a striped sofa while you sit there with a clipboard. Can I expect a bill after tonight?"

I didn't like this little counseling session we were having. And I really didn't like hearing her talk about Jared that way. Nobody knew our relationship the way he and I did. I guess even *she* had boundaries. And she'd just overstepped them.

"I'm just saying, Sidney," she wouldn't let up, "don't lose yourself looking for love."

"I'm not lost. I know exactly where I am, Tasha." I laughed annoyingly. "I'm in a nightclub having the most ridiculous conversation with my best friend right now, when all I want is to finish this drink, hang out a bit, and go home."

"But you've changed, Sidney. Don't you see?"

"Is this about Melvin? Because if it is, I told you, nothing happened."

Tasha exhaled in frustration. "This isn't about Melvin, Sidney."

"Then what is it about, Tasha?!" I raised my voice, feeling ambushed.

Tasha looked around and lowered her voice in an effort to convince me to do the same.

"Sidney, don't get so defensive." She leaned forward. "I'm only trying to—"

"*Sstzzzz! Ouch!*" I jerked my hand back in pain when she'd touched it.

Startled, she let go.

I put my tender hand in my lap, placing the other on top.

Tasha looked at me.

"I'm trying to help you, Sidney. You are the prettiest girl I know." She touched my face, trying to compliment a smile out of me, but it didn't work.

Her tone changed.

"Look, I'm your best friend—"

"*Are* you?" I gave her a look that said she wasn't acting like it.

Her chin wrinkled. "Yes. I am, Sidney. It's just, you say you want to get married, yet you go after guys who obviously don't. Yes, Rico's handsome. I admit it. He's physically flawless. But so is a cubic zirconium. It looks just the like the real thing. All sparkly and nice. But at the end of the day it's essentially worthless. It has no true value. Despite how nice and authentic it may appear, it's just fake a diamond in the end."

I just looked at Tasha as she continued preaching.

"Look, you win some and you lose some," she said. "But you certainly can't go around collecting enemies. I mean, look at you? What happened to my best friend? The person who taught me to be joyful and optimistic? The fun one? The happy one? What happened to her?"

"Life happened to me."

"*Life?*" Tasha frowned. "Sidney, you don't hold the patent on pain. Everybody has—"

"Excuse me." A guy approached from out of nowhere, unwittingly throwing himself into the crossfire. "Would you like to dance?"

"No!" I growled.

He jerked his head back. "Oh, well, that's fine," he told me, "because I was talking to her," he said, looking at Tasha, who sucked her teeth and waved him on impatiently, never taking her eyes off me.

He walked off, looking back at us like we were both in the wrong atmosphere for our attitudes.

Her train of thought broken, Tasha tried to pick up where she'd left off while I began to wish that one of us had taken him up on his offer.

"Sidney, I just don't want to see you hurt yourself over people who don't really even matter. People who won't even mean anything to you in a few years—or even a few months. I mean, come on. Would you have married *Rico?* After everything you told me, would you have really gone the distance?"

"That's not the point, Tasha."

"It's *not?*" she said, puzzled.

I didn't say anything. She'd caught me contradicting myself because I couldn't think straight with all of the surprise lecturing taking place.

"Look," she said with earnest eyes, "I know what he did to you was wrong—what they *all* did to you was wrong. But, for your own sake, you really have to learn to let things go. There are places, you know—awful places—for people who couldn't let things go."

"Let things go?" I choked on that bit of advice. "This from a woman who did a hundred on the highway just to ask a man who'd given her the finger if that was his IQ, or the actual size of his dick?" I reminded Tasha, who began looking more and more like a hypocrite to me.

Did she forget I knew her? Did she forget it was me she was talking to? I knew every secret. Every dirty little deed she'd ever done. I think she *was* catching amnesia.

Tasha tried to laugh it off, but I could see the frustration in her eyes. Somehow, though, she couldn't see it in mine.

"Sidney, that was almost eight years ago." She ran an agitated finger across the rim of her glass as I looked at her bitterly, still thinking about her Jared remark.

She wiped the condensation from the glass. "There comes a time in everyone's life—in *your* life— when . . ." she walked on eggshells, but crunched along anyway, "when you have to grow."

"Grow?" I leaned all the way back in my chair, completely blown away. Not even the plush velvet could put me at ease. I might as well had been sitting in *Old Sparky* himself, I was just as uncomfortable.

My stomach rumbled in grief as it absorbed the impact of her words. I couldn't believe this was my best friend talking. My *best friend*. Did she say *grow*? Is that what she thought of me? She didn't know what she was doing. She was pushing me off the ledge. My best friend was pushing me off the ledge.

My eyes watered. I couldn't even speak I was so choked up with emotion. I could barely look her in her eyes that tried to connect with mine.

Grow?

She'd tried to soften the blow with an empathetic smile, but it was no use. I knew what she was trying to say. She was telling me that I was unreasonable. That I was mean. Grumpy. Immature. She was telling me to grow the hell up!

My eyes forced themselves to look at her. They looked at her with a foreign glare. They looked at her like she was the most merciless assailant—the unexpected one. The one I never saw coming. Then I looked past her, over to the dance floor, only to see Rico shaking his rump like he hadn't a care in the world. The music failed to penetrate my ears as I took in the entire scene. Only sounds of resentment and discord filled my head.

I looked back into Tasha's face that was unchanged. That was, unbelievably, awaiting my expression of agreement. Concurrence. A nod that said, *'ya know, you're right'*. The total *opposite* of what I was feeling inside.

She didn't get it. I was sad. I was hurt. This was how I coped. Didn't she know *bitter* was the new *blue?*

I cleared my throat, finally able to catch my breath.

"Well . . ." I uncrossed my legs and stood up.

Tasha looked up at me with pleading eyes, waiting for me to say something.

I bent down and picked up my purse. "Maybe we've just *outgrown* each other, Tasha."

"Sidney."

"No. I'm done." I put my hand up, preparing to walk away.

"Sidney, wait." Tasha went for my wrist, but I dodged her reach. I didn't want her to touch me.

"Sidney, I've known you for so long. Exactly half my life. "I'm your sister. *Sisters Always Share Honest Advice*. Remember?"

It was one of the four acronyms we'd come up with for our twin tattoos. Of course I remembered. But she'd forgotten. She'd forgotten who we were. She'd forgotten everything.

I looked at her, and shook my head.

"That's precisely the problem, Tasha. You're acting *just* like my sister." My eyes watered. "And Lord knows I don't need another Chaylene in my life."

I pointed my boots toward the exit and walked away.

CHAPTER 35

I'd just walked in. The seat was still cold. And my boss was already on my back.

"Sidney, may I speak with you for a moment?" He didn't even give me a chance to sign onto my computer.

I stowed my purse away in my bottom desk drawer, tempted to slam it shut, and stood up.

"Sure."

Slowly, I followed him down *Cubicle Row,* as curious eyes emerged, and everyone wished they could've been a fly on the grey fabric wall of my boss's office. I didn't look at any of them as I walked the plank, two steps behind him.

I was definitely not up for any lecture he had to give me this morning, as I already had a pretty good idea of what our meeting would be about. My poor attendance had finally caught up with me. I'd missed several days in the past few months. It had become harder and harder for me to show up—for me to muster up the motivation. I just couldn't pull it off like I had been able to do in the past. It seemed, more than ever, that every little thing got to me. And just last week a member cursed me out, calling me every short word her limited vocabulary could conjure up. Language like that really had a way of freeing up my line. But no sooner than I'd let her go, there was yet another customer ready to unleash on me.

As we turned the corner into his small office, my boss gestured to the only other available chair besides his.

"Have a seat," he told me.

As instructed, I sat down in the hard chair that many of those in trouble before me had sat. It didn't mold to my backside with the same familiarity, but I belonged there just the same. I crossed my legs, folding my clasped hands over my top knee, and waited for his opening remarks.

"Sidney, I wanted to discuss your attendance," he began.

I simply nodded.

"I've noticed you've missed several days, and . . ."

Before he could even finish his second statement, my mind was on Tasha. I didn't speak to her the entire drive home Saturday night, and hadn't returned any of her calls yesterday. I was still devastated by her disloyalty. She was the one person I thought I could always count on—the one that would never betray me.

Grow? The haunting echo of her words replayed themselves in my head.

"Given the decline in your dependability, I felt it was important that we meet this morning. As you know, we frown on low attendance . . ."

I wondered why Tasha would hurt me like that. I thought we were best friends. This left me to question everything. To second-guess our entire friendship.

You need to grow. Her words pierced my heart like a sizzling scythe with every recollection of them.

" . . . When you are out, the team has to work that much harder to absorb the effects of your absence. This results in longer hold times, and increased numbers of abandoned calls, which, in turn, affects our stats, and reflects poorly on the center at the end of the quarter. It's not fair to your teammates. And it's not fair to our members whose premiums help pay your salary . . ."

What if Tasha were me? What if she'd been through what I'd been though? Would she be so quick to tell me what was immature? Would she be so quick to dispense the forgiveness she so adamantly urged me to? I just didn't understand. She was there through it all. She'd seen it. How could she forget? How could she forget all that I'd been through?

You need to grow! I just couldn't shake her hurtful words from my head.

"So, basically," my boss concluded, having my most divided attention, "you just need to grow!"

I snapped from my daze.

"What? What did you say?" I looked at him.

He looked annoyed. "I said . . . that I don't want to see this trend continue to grow."

"Oh . . ." I looked away, still out of it.

I couldn't think straight, much less hear straight. I hadn't had an honest night's rest in days. I felt like the walking dead. I didn't even put on any makeup this morning and was sure the dark circles under my eyes raised some suspicions as to my health and mental state. I wasn't even sure that my clothes matched this morning.

My boss looked at me, aware of the fact that my mind was miles away.

"I hope I see a renewed work ethic in you, Sidney."

I nodded. "Yeah . . . Renewed."

I leaned back in the chair, still zoned out. The minute traces of consciousness I had left could tell I was frustrating him. He looked at me disappointedly. But I couldn't snap out of it.

"Look," he removed his glasses, "you're one of the hardest workers here. I'd hate to lose you over something like this," he slipped in the obligatory threat.

I gave no reaction. I just sat there, daydreaming.

My boss opened his desk drawer, pulling out the legendary Corrective Action Form. I'd heard stories of them but had never laid eyes on one myself.

"Now," he hung his glasses back on his hook nose, handing me a pen, " I just need you to sign this form acknowledging that we've discussed your recent attendance issues and that you've made a commitment today to improve. This places you on a 30-day probation. In the event you miss any portion of your scheduled work day—and that includes tardies and early sign-outs—you'll be given a final warning, in which case if your attendance continues to be unsatisfactory you will be terminated," he spoke matter-of-factly.

I signed the form, pushed it back in front of him, and didn't say a word.

He looked disappointed by my lack of emotion.

"Okay. I'll make you a copy of this," he said.

I nodded, numb-faced.

He peeked over the rims of his featherweight frames. "Is everything okay?"

I nodded faster this time. "Yeah. Yeah, everything's okay." I uncrossed my legs and intentionally sat awkwardly, pretending my legs were two identically-charged magnets that repelled each other, hoping his discomfort would mean my dismissal.

It worked.

"Alright, well, thank you." He succumbed to my body language, trying not to look between my legs like the natural born man in him may have wanted to.

"Thank you." I stood up, pulling my skirt down.

As I walked out of my boss's office, Sarah jumped, then fidgeted around with some papers on her desk. She tried to act like she was working, but the unfortunate timing of her screen saver gave her up. The snoop hadn't struck a key in, at least, five minutes as the settings were all preset and required administrative access to change them. When the floating bubbles popped up on her monitor she quickly tapped her spacebar then looked at me with guilty eyes, hoping I hadn't concluded the obvious. I wasn't worried about her silly self. I had other things on my mind.

What a way to start the day, I thought to myself as I walked through the busy department, bypassing my desk and heading straight for the restroom. I knew my boss was only doing his job, which included making sure I was doing *mine*, but I really couldn't appreciate that fact right now. I resented him for not having ESP and knowing what I was going through.

He would've backed off if he had. I begrudged the fact that he simply couldn't look in my face and see what was going on. Forget what was coming out of my mouth. Just look into my eyes if you want the truth. Of course I wasn't okay.

I pushed the bathroom door open and went right to the sink. Turning on the faucet, I cupped my hands to collect some water, my face meeting them halfway. I cupped them a second time, splashing more water on my colorless complexion, trying to revitalize it somehow.

As I raised my head and looked at my reflection, dripping wet and tired, something inside my heart took a quick dip at the sight of myself. I didn't even recognize my own image. My hair looked awful. And the bags I unsuccessfully tried to sleep off came with me to work this morning. My eyelids were heavy. And my lips were chapped. I turned away from the ugly image and went into a stall.

As I sat there, giving little to no effort to the intended order of business, I still couldn't shake Tasha's words from my head. They merged with my boss's, and even fraternized with Rico's, uniting to launch a common attack against me.

What do you want me to do?

You need to grow!

Renewed.

I gathered up some tissue and wiped the tear that was tangled up in my eyelashes.

Other toilets flushed. Faucets turned on and off. Hand dryer-motors blew loud, then quiet again. And occasional footsteps made two-way traffic across the linoleum floor while I sat in the far right stall fully clothed, frozen in my thoughts.

"Hey," an upbeat voice followed the loud squeak of the swinging door.

"Hey, Sarah."

I quickly identified Pat's voice.

"So, what's the skinny?" Sarah asked.

"On what?"

"Sidney was in Steve's office."

My ears perked up when I heard my name.

"I think she's getting written up." I could hear the elation in Sarah's voice when she said it.

Pat sighed. "Yeah. I guess she's missed a lot of days lately."

I forced a silent, ear-clearing yawn in order to hear them better.

"Well, what's going on with her?" Sarah inquired.

Pat played dumb. "What do you mean?"

"You've *seen* her lately? She looks a mess."

"Well, she's been going through a lot," Pat came to my defense. "She's been really down ever since she and her boyfriend broke up."

"Whaaaaat?" A third voice following a flush joined the conversation. "You mean that fine hunk of man in the picture she's got on her desk?" Her voice went from surprised to hopeful.

"It's not there *anymore*." Sarah took delight in sharing that fact. "Why'd they break up anyway? Do you know?"

I knew Pat wouldn't put my business out there like that, especially to the enemy. I hung my head, shaking it in disgust, thinking what a huge gossip

Sarah was. She was clinging to her forties, yet didn't have anything better to do than talk about me.

"Did she tell you what happened?" Sarah continued fishing for information.

"Well . . . " Pat sounded like she didn't know what to say. "I think he left her for another woman."

My eyes squinted at the shocking sound of Pat sharing my business. I had only confided in her on Friday. It didn't take her long to cave.

"Don't tell her I told you, though," she said, the swift tone of regret accompanying her request.

"Oh my. What a shame," Sarah said, clearly with sarcasm.

"Well, she should've seen that coming. A man that fine? *Humph*. You're *asking* for trouble!" the anonymous voice said, finding my business just the boost she needed to get her through the day. They all got buzzed off my business, like it was some juicy soap opera instead of my life.

"Isn't that strange?" a raspy voice that sounded like it belonged in the facilities next door rather than in here with us ladies joined the conversation. The unmistakable hack that followed soon identified it as belonging to Margaret.

"What's strange?" Pat asked.

A faucet drowned out the conversation for a moment. I struggled to hear over the whistle of the pipes and the high-pressure splash of the water.

". . . I mean, you look at her and you think she's got it all together," Margaret was saying as I tuned back in, having missed most of what she'd said.

"Mmm hmm . . ." Voice #3 cosigned.

"Young. Pretty. Nice figure. College," Margaret listed. "Yet she doesn't seem to have it any easier than the rest of us when it comes to the opposite sex. It's like none of it even matters."

They all had something philosophic to say about my life. They all seemed excited by my misfortune. It was as if it made them feel good that I was feeling bad.

"It's like they say," the unknown voice said, "The only thing better than good booty, is *new* booty."

"Yep. And don't forget what they say about a pretty woman: *'somewhere, someone is tired of her'*."

"That's true," Sarah couldn't wait to agree. "Pretty women get dumped every day. You've gotta have something to back that pretty face up," she tried slipping in an insult.

"Yeah, but Sidney's a good person," Pat didn't let her, almost redeeming herself. "She didn't deserve that," I heard her say as the eight footsteps faded out into the hall.

"The hand is quicker than the *eye*—not the mouth!" I halted the woman who'd rattled off her member ID number to me like a Texan auctioneer. She either had way too much confidence in my ten-key abilities, or far too much caffeine in her diet. It wasn't quite twelve o'clock, and already there were ninety-three calls in the queue.

"Five . . . nine . . . five . . ." she went painfully slow just to spite me. I let her play her silly game until she was finally finished.

"Yes, ma'am. I'm showing that the claim was just paid today. You should receive your EOB in the mail in a few days." I tried rushing her off the phone. The ticker tape display was flashing out of control.

I put my phone in *Not Ready*.

When she hung up, without so much as a *thank you,* my phone dropped out of the lineup.

I took a deep breath and leaned back in my seat, sneaking a quick break. As I sat there rubbing my forehead red, I felt a headache coming on. The buzzing hum of the headset chatter that surrounded.

I looked around, seeing people wearing the same headsets as me. Sitting in the same uncomfortable office chairs as I was. And taking those calls, one-by-one, just like me. But I noticed that they weren't tapping their pens and kicking their feet in aggravation like I was. They weren't looking up, frowning at the call queue or massaging their temples. They all, every last one of them, seemed to be, simply going with the flow.

I looked over at Ruth, who was chatting away. She was starting to show. Her husband was pulling doubles at his job so that she could stay home once the baby was born. Dan was psyched about the free trip to Greece he'd won on the radio. He and his fiancée, who worked here as well, were using their full two weeks of vacation for the trip. Jenny's last day was Friday. She'd accepted a promotion at our corporate headquarters in Kansas. She was excited about the new management position, and people were already starting to kiss her butt, afraid she'd come back for their jobs as revenge for the torture they'd put her through.

Taking in everyone's joys, I felt so alone and unfulfilled. I rubbed the corners of my eyes before putting my headset back on.

I wouldn't be lucky enough to win the lottery but I'd *beat* the one in thirty-seven odds of receiving Mr. Miller's phone call. His irksome voice complaining on the other line was the final puzzle piece to the eye-watering day I was already having.

Squeeze. Squeeze. Tom Bomb's eyes and tongue popped out. *Squeeeeeze!!!*

"Why do I waste my time writing you people letters if no one is going to respond? Hello???!"

He was going on and on, complaining. I just sat there, listening.

"I mean, what are you people doing down there?"

Squeeze! Squeeze! My fist opened and closed as my thoughts blocked out his words. All I could do was think about was how everything in my life had fallen apart.

". . . And if you ask me I think that's a bullshit policy!" Mr. Miller said of his prescription cap and the policy that had limited his quantity of *Viagra*. "I mean, how is a person supposed to—"

"Have you ever stopped to think that maybe nature is trying to tell you something, Mr. Miller?" I interrupted his rambling.

"I beg your pardon?"

"Sir, you are seventy years old. Haven't you done enough damage with that thing already?"

I could only imagine how many hearts he'd broken with it. How many lies he'd told over it. And, most recently, how may letters he'd written just to keep it on life support.

Mr. Miller was furious with my line of questioning.

"Why, I've got a good mind to—"

"You may have a good *mind*, my friend, but that's not what you're calling about, now is it?"

I rendered him speechless. All that came out of his mouth were frustrated, surprised gasps for air.

Finally, he got his wind again.

"Young lady, I think you'd better—"

"Who *cares* what you think?" I rolled my eyes, inching my hand closer and closer to the *Release* button.

"I think your supervisor would."

"Then bother *him* about this!" I released the call, sending him back to the starting line.

There were one hundred and three calls in the queue by now. Giant, red, triple digits were flashing at me. I knew it would be at least a good twenty minutes before he'd get through to another representative to report me.

I pulled up Word and started a new document. Dating it, I tabbed down two spaces and began typing. Just as I'd struck a few keys, a shadow hovered over me.

"Sidney," Pat stood over my desk, "you ready to go to lunch?"

I glanced up at her for a moment before putting my eyes back on my monitor.

"How are the twins?" I continued striking keys.

"They're good," she sighed.

I looked up at her again. I still couldn't believe she was so quick to tell something that I'd shared with her in confidence.

"But I'm so exhausted." She shook her head like she was complaining, but I knew she was happy. She was loving every minute of motherhood.

I clicked the *Save* icon on my document, then pulled up my email and composed a new message, typing my boss's name in the recipient's field, before attaching the saved document. Once attached, I clicked open the document and proofread it: This hereby serves as notice of my resignation—effective immediately!

I listened to Pat as she described her new adventures in diaper-changing and bottle-warming. As she rambled on about the twins, I clicked *Send*, then reached down and got my purse from the bottom drawer, scooping up my personal items from my desk and shoving them inside.

As I rose from my seat, Pat, who, too busy talking, hadn't noticed my actions, stepped back, keys jingling in her hand. " Ready?" She smiled.

I smiled back, then leaned in and gave her a big hug. I felt her stiffen in surprise. Holding her a while, I could smell the sweet scents of milk and baby powder on her shoulder where the receiving blanket must've lay draped this morning.

I let her go.

Pat looked confused, but smiled anyway.

"What's up, Sidney? You okay?" she chuckled, still wearing that glow, even postpartum.

I reached down into my cubicle, grabbing *Tom*, who'd sat on top of the computer's tower, and handed him to her.

"Take care, Pat. Okay?"

Her mouthed opened in bewilderment.

"And enjoy those babies," I told her before walking out of that office for good.

CHAPTER 36

The interstate was mine. Not a single car's headlights chased my bumper. I drove into the murky darkness, the bridge lights paving my way as they bowed in a descending line of welcome. The air was crisp and light. The moon appeared patient, as if not to rush relief from the sun in the early morning sky. And the stars did not dim their lovely luminescence. Their twinkle retained their midnight glow as if happy to have my company.

I wasn't happy, however. I wasn't as happy as those stars, or as patient as that moon. I was restless, and miserable. I needed to clear my head. I needed to get to a quiet spot and empty out all the thoughts that were clogging up my brain.

I took the next exit.

Having my choice of any, I parked in the first space, unconcerned with my improper alignment as I was sure I'd have the beach to myself. I got out of the car, tucked the key into my back pocket, and made my way toward the sand.

It was dark.

Chillingly silent.

The beach didn't open to the public until seven, so, technically, I was trespassing. But I didn't worry about the security guard I saw sleeping back there in his truck near the restrooms. I could've come to perform a human sacrifice,and he would've been none the wiser in his unconscious state. I continued walking.

Reaching the sand, I took off my shoes, allowing it to force its way between my toes. It was cool like flour. Its grains, like fine porcelain. And like quicksand, I sank into its delicate pockets with every labored step.

Making my way toward the dark blue waters, erect palms waved in the whistling wind, enhancing the echo of the ocean's whisper. The morning breeze harmonized with the light-roaring tide that called out to me from the shoreline. Hearing the tide gave me chills. The sounds of small waves kissing the sandy shore sent a shiver throughout my body. I froze in my tracks, deciding on a spot.

The lamps from the lifeguard's post lent enough light to where I could see shipwrecked plankton, and seashells, lacing the shoreline. And what I couldn't see, I could smell. The fresh scent of beached barnacles and saltwater combined to create a smell that was purely marine. I sat, hugging my knees, crystallized earth engulfing my feet, and closed my eyes as I inhaled slowly, deliberately, filling my lungs with the purifying air that oxygenated my suffocating body. I didn't let my eyes distract me. I kept them closed in order to hear—to feel—the earth's heartbeat.

As the cool morning breeze whipped my naked limbs, just as time and experience had my heart, crisp winds combed through my hair, carrying with it traces of my thoughts. Quietly I sat, unfazed by the birds that seemed to resent my presence. They swarmed rebelliously as if the break of day belonged to them, and I was merely an intruder. Still I sat there absorbing the fresh ocean air that calmed me.

Tasha really hurt my feelings the other night. On the drive home, she went on and on about not understanding how someone so full of love could share her heart with hate. When did she get so Ghandi on me? And, most of all, when did she start judging me? I mean, maybe I *was* a little salty. Maybe I *had* changed. But if I had, I expected that she'd understand the path of my evolution better than anyone—not condemn me. After all, what was I supposed to do? Who was I supposed to become? How could she expect someone to keep smiling when they're getting kicked in the teeth? Was I to stay the smiling fool? Was I to keep pretending it didn't hurt? And who was she to judge me? To turn on me? How could she emotionally abandon me the way that she had?

Several winds blew. Hundreds of waves rolled in and out, playing tag with the shoreline, as the sun played hide and seek with me. I sat there, still waiting on the great gas giant to shine its spotlight on me and bring me some spiritual attention so that I could ask some questions. I wanted to ask God why he'd allowed me to go through what I had. Why He'd watched these horrible things happen to me when He knew that all I wanted was to share my love with someone who wanted to share theirs with me. *Love.* That was a basic human need with actual scientifically-proven mental and physiologically-essential benefits. Why would He deny me of that?

Didn't I matter? Was I not of flesh and blood? Why would He deny me love?

As dawn took its time, I raised my head and took in a deep breath. My eyes adjusted in the moonlight, sweeping the beach, noticing all the surface sediments on the huge, sand carpet. Rocks. Pebbles. Shells. Billions—trillions—within my sight. But I'm sure the beach was home to a number far beyond my comprehension.

As my mind faded them out of focus I thought back to Rico and the other night. How his looks gave him pick of the room. How he could get married *tomorrow* if he wanted to. Surely there was always some woman who'd flatter herself all the way to the alter. I thought about what he'd said to me at the grocery store, about not being ready for what I wanted to give. No one ever seemed ready. Not for me, anyway.

I began to think about Jared and how hearing Tasha speak of him in such a way stirred my emotions. Why did what she say about him affect me so? Why was I so protective of a love that, apparently, never truly was? It didn't make sense to me. Nothing did anymore.

I wiped my eyes that were starting to produce tears against my will, then looked back toward my car, parked in the darkness. Having ventured out so far I saw it with just as much clarity as I saw my own life.

My life was in total shambles. Nothing was going right. Nothing was as I'd intended it to be. And I felt so alone. I thought about my parents, and how I missed them. How far away I was from them. How I'd left them behind in New York. I began thinking about Damon and where *he* was in his life. I figured he probably had kids with his wife by now, and was as happy as can be. I wondered why he deserved that life. Why he deserved what I so desperately wanted after how he'd treated me. It wasn't fair. It wasn't fair that he was back in New York—living my dreams— while I was miles away from home, living out this never-ending nightmare. I wanted to be home. I wanted to be happy. I wanted all the things he probably had. And I resented him as I remembered my true reason for being here.

I'd never told anyone the real reason I'd left New York. It had nothing to do with the city, the climate, or new opportunities. It was Damon. Damon was the reason I'd left. He and I shared a secret. A secret that only I knew we shared.

That day, at his job, when Damon asked me how I knew about his wife being a stripper when I, supposedly, didn't even know he was married, I told him that I'd just found out earlier that day. That Collette had just told me that morning after he and I had spoken with one another. I sensed suspicion in his tone, and feared he'd call me a liar, and snatch the money right out of my purse. But I was prepared to stick to my story, and tried everything within my facial expression's power to convince him that it was the honest-to-God's truth.

Damon had studied me for a moment—a quick moment. Maybe a second and a half, as I stood there adamant and unwavering. He looked into my eyes. I looked into his. I was careful not to blink.

And that's when I saw it.

He knew. Damon knew I was lying. I saw it in his eyes. At that moment he'd just realized the truth about it all. The truth behind my coincidental with-child condition. At that precise moment he knew full well that I was lying to him.

Yet he let me take the money.

For weeks I tried convincing myself that it wasn't true. That I hadn't seen so clearly in his eyes what I knew he had known at that moment. His eyes. The way they moved. The way they shone. The way they blinked when he'd put together all the pieces of my pathetic plot and subsequently decided—at record speed—that it was still worth to him in order to preserve the anticipated results. He pretended. He pretended to believe me—to be fooled—just to get me out of his life.

For the first half of that moment, when he'd realized it, I was afraid. I was so afraid and embarrassed that I'd just been busted that I thought I was going to faint. But by the second half of that already-split second—when he quickly and ever so slightly adjusted his expression in order to allow me to assume the perceived victory—I felt the most sickening feeling of degradation in the pit of my stomach. There was no baby to bind him. No paternity suit to keep him up at night. No liability whatsoever. He was free and clear. Free and clear to walk away with his money *and* his freedom. So at the end of that moment—when he didn't walk away—at the crescendo of that historically-significant second of my life, I ended up walking away with his money, and he, once more, with my power.

Only this time he took my pride along with it.

After that I knew I could never look at him again. He knew how pathetic I was. And I certainly couldn't risk running into him and his friends in public. For the remainder of my time in New York I didn't go anywhere. I stayed in my apartment—a hostage of humiliation—harboring this secret that was too heavy for my heart. And was too large for my zip code.

As the memory of it all poured out of my heart, sticky tears covered my face. With blurred vision, my eyes, once again, swept across the shoreline seeing the fossils scattered around me. I wiped my face as I picked one up, thumbing off the sand. I held the shell in my hand, then looked around at the countless others, clams no more, but merely shells of their former selves. Plucked by predators—stripped clean and dry—they lay discarded, on display, until footsteps made them seashells, and time made them sand.

I brought the one I held closer to my face, studying the silver floor of the bivalve animal. I blew inside the shell and swept my finger across the smooth interior that felt like glass. I wondered if, like an oyster, its mollusk body had ever spun a pearl. If it ever produced such a precious jewel. Though a relatively rare occurrence I knew it was possible.

I'd once read that a pearl is an oyster's—or clam's —response to irritation. That when foreign matter invades its delicate inner tissue, the animal secretes a substance that hardens to form a barrier between it and the source of its irritation. This callus, this *pearl*, as we have named it, serves a protective purpose. Unable to expunge the irritant, the animal uses this pearl as a buffer—a biological bandage—to effectively comfort and protect itself.

But, at some point, I further read, the animal's body begins to identify the pearl as, yet, another irritant, creating a positive feedback cycle where the pearl, in turn, gets bigger and bigger. Consuming greater portions of the animal's body, the pearl, then, becomes a deformity. What was developed to help the aquatic animal, eventually hinders it. Now where is the mercy in that?

As my eyes began secreting a substance of their own, my breathing became short and sporadic, as I sat there in the sand. My eyelids grew heavy, and scratchy. Completely drained, I gave my face to the sand, every breath inhaling its burning-sharp grains. Tears continued streaming down my face—fleeing from my thoughts—rendering me too exhausted to ask the sky for anything at all. And when daylight finally swallowed the moon, I was paralyzed. And silent.

A clamshell on the beach.

CHAPTER 37

"Do you hate me?"

"What kind of question is that?"

"One that's long overdue," I said as I repositioned the phone against my shoulder. My skin was covered in sand. Itchy and dry. But somehow I didn't feel it as much.

"Of course I don't hate you. You're my sister," Chaylene's tone called me ridiculous.

"Then why do you do me the way you do? Why are you so nasty to me?"

I inevitably began crying.

Chaylene sighed heavily at the sound of my tears.

"Sidney, look, I'm sorry about what happened when you were up here that weekend. I was upset and I took it out on you. I shouldn't have done that."

"I'm not just talking about that weekend. I'm talking about my whole life, Chaylene. My whole life I've felt that you've intentionally mistreated me."

"What are you talking about?"

"You've been less than a big sister to me. You didn't let me hang out with you and your friends. You didn't let me borrow your stuff. You never took me—"

"Sidney, that's the natural dynamic of the relationship. You were my kid sister. Of course, I didn't want you hanging around me and my friends. But that was a long time ago."

"That doesn't make it right."

"I'm not saying it does, but what can I say?"

"You can tell me why you left. Why did you just leave me like that all of a sudden?"

"Sidney," Chaylene huffed, "you had entered college by then. And I was graduating. What did you expect me to do?"

"But you didn't even say goodbye." My voice rose for an instant, then tapered off in my sorrow. "You just . . . took off. "

"Dennis was starting a new job and—"

"Of course," I rolled my eyes on the other end. "You wouldn't want to miss Dennis's first day on the job. Such a special occasion. And we know how much *those* mean to you," I said sarcastically.

"Sidney, there's just a lot you don't understand."

"I understand that you left the family. I understand you didn't tell anyone what you were doing. I understand you just—"

"I was pregnant, Sidney."

What I had planned to say next got sucked right back down my throat at the sound of that revelation.

I was breathless.

Chaylene sighed heavily before continuing. "I couldn't tell Mom and Dad. I couldn't tell anyone. Not until Dennis and I were husband and wife. You know how Mom is: Marriage *first*—not the other way around."

"Pregnant?" I asked, confused. "I thought you said Jonathan was . . . "

Chaylene was quiet as I pieced it all together. I always did think my nephew was pretty big for a preemie. He wasn't six weeks early after all. He was right on time.

I didn't know what to say. When I'd asked the question I wasn't expecting something this heavy. I always thought her reason for leaving was because she was just sick of me.

"Sidney, I don't hate you," Chaylene said as if reading my mind. "I never have. But let's face it. You turned cold against me."

"What are you talking about?"

"Sidney, I remember so clearly. Ever since you came home from the hospital, you barely said a word to me. That was when our relationship went from normal to nearly nonexistent. Admit it. You blamed me. You blamed me for the accident. I swerved to miss that box in the road, and ever since you—"

"I don't blame you for the accident, Chaylene," I cut her off. "I blame you for not coming to see me. For letting me lay up in that hospital without so much as even a single visit from you!" I began crying again. "If I blame you for anything it's that!"

Having finally confronted her about it, my emotions were free flowing. Tears poured profusely from my eyes.

"Okay, Sidney," Chaylene's tone grew firm, "now I *really* don't know what you're talking about."

"My hospital room looked like a greenhouse! Tasha. Peli. Mom. Dad. Everyone came except you. Everyone cared but y—"

"Sidney, I *did* come to see you! Every night! Every single night I came and sat by your bed. What are you talking about? Don't you remember?"

I couldn't believe it. I couldn't believe she was lying about something like this. That she had the audacity to try to rewrite history—alter it to accommodate herself. Did she think I was stupid? I was sixteen, not four! I would remember if she'd came.

"Every night, when I got off work, I would come to visit you," Chaylene said." It was late. I know. And the medication had you so groggy most times, but you have to remember."

I grabbed my head. I felt like the room was spinning as Chaylene continued.

"I would rub pierced vitamin E capsules on your face, and hold your hand until you drifted back off to sleep. I'd sit with you for hours—sometimes until my classes the next morning. How could you forg—"

"Chaylene, you *never* came. Never!" I screamed. "You were absent at a time that I needed you most. You weren't there for me. You're my sister and you weren't there for me. You never came!"

"I did!" Chaylene insisted. I stayed with you all night. Every single night. I held your hand, and sat with you all night long. And I'd bring you gerbera daisies every time I came."

" No . . . " I shook my head. "No—that was Mom. *Mom* would sit . . ."

Just then my mind flashed back to Chaylene in that Chicago boutique's dressing room. The necklace. Grannah's necklace.

Blood rushed to my head.

I couldn't believe it. The necklace. The daisies. I thought it had been Mom by my side those nights, holding my hand in the dark when I was lonely and afraid in that cold hospital room. I thought she'd came *twice* a day. But it was Chaylene who'd came in the evenings. Chaylene wore the blue crystal pendant that soothed me to sleep. It was her all along. My sister.

My eyes began to sting as my memory struggled to recount the parts that, up until now, I could not. I remembered being in that cold hospital room, numb. The medicine took both pain and perception from me. Thinking back, it was those visits—*Chaylene's* visits—that pulled me through. Though I'd slept through the majority of them, waking up to the flowers and feeling the loving presence that lingered in the room, helped to speed up my recovery. I was certain of that. I just never knew that it was my sister's love in the air that I was feeling all along. That it was Chaylene.

"Daisies . . . " Tears streamed slower from my eyes. "That was you?"

"Yes," Chaylene whispered. "They were my favorite. I wanted to . . ."

She paused. For the first time I could feel her pain. I never imagined I'd be the cause.

"Chaylene, I'm sorry. The necklace. I thought . . ."

Chaylene sighed, finally realizing what had occurred. "Grannah's necklace. You thought I was Mom because of the necklace." I could hear the pain pouring out of her words. She sounded like she was about to cry. "All this time you thought . . ."

She couldn't finish. But she didn't need to because I felt the same hurt as she did at that moment. It was mind-blowing. Heart-crushing. To know that this mix-up, this chance case of mistaken identity and subsequent destruction of a relationship had stolen so much time from us, was almost inconceivable.

"I thought it was Mom, Chaylene. I'm sorry."

I cried harder. I couldn't apologize enough.

"I'm sorry. I'm so sorry, Chaylene. All this time. All this time I thought . . ." I couldn't cease my crying long enough to get my words out. Chaylene was right. I had held this against her all those years. I thought she didn't care about me. All the while, she thought the same of me. I couldn't believe how wrong we had both been. How much time we'd lost over this. It hurt. It hurt the both of us

And now, I wasn't the only one crying.

After crying and talking with my sister for hours about things I never thought we would, I realized that my entire perception of our relationship was, if nothing else, skewed. In my mind I'd formulated this one-dimensional, negative idea of what we were and *had been*, blocking out all the positive. There *were* good times prior to the accident. My resentment made me forget that. But, now remembering, I suddenly rediscovered a different Chaylene. The Chaylene I'd missed out on all these years. In just this one conversation I felt so close to her. And with the hot phone pressed against my ear I'd finally built up the courage to ask what I'd been wondering all along.

"Chaylene, can I ask you something?"

"Sure."

"What's going to happen with you and Dennis?"

Chaylene released a shaky breath, like she was fighting back more tears when she said, "We're going to divorce."

"Are you sure you want to do that?"

"It's not even about what I want to do anymore," Chaylene explained. "It's what I need to do. He cheated. He broke the vows. He betrayed me in a way he'd promised he never would."

"Do you think he loves you?"

She didn't answer right away, but eventually said, "Yes . . . I do. But whether he loves me or not is not the point," she said, sticking to her guns. "He hurt me. How do I forgive that?"

Chaylene had always been extremely proud. She'd starve to death if her enemy supplied the food. For her this particular situation was a no-brainer. Game over. Dennis lost. In her mind, it *had* to be this way. He *had* to lose. Even if it meant a tremendous loss for her as well.

I wasn't sure what to say anymore. I'd learned my lesson back in Chicago about sticking my nose too far where it didn't belong. Things were, apparently, much more complicated than I knew.

"Well, whatever you decide, Chaylene, I support you."

"Thank you, Sidney. You know it's been crazy trying to get everything together. I didn't realize how much stuff we'd accumulated over the years . . ."

As Chaylene went on to tell me about the plans she'd made with respect to the divorce and splitting up the property I found myself thinking about Jared. Even though my words seemed to have very little effect on Chaylene, they had opened up my own mind to a different perspective. A different way of viewing the situation regarding Jared and me.

At that moment I'd decided that I could no longer occupy space in the one body I had with hate, or heartbreak. I could no longer harbor resentment for Jared just because he didn't love me in the end. That truth was, that wasn't his fault. It wasn't his fault that he didn't love me. He'd only followed his heart, which, happened to lead him away from me. I realized I couldn't force him, or anyone else, to love me. Just as I could not be forced. Free Will gives one the right to choose. So who was I to resent Jared for exercising that right? He had done what he needed to do for himself. He'd made his choice. And I had to forgive him for hurting me in the process. It was the only way that I could really free myself from the pain I held inside only to my own emotional and psychological detriment. I had to love *myself* enough to forgive him for *not* loving me.

" . . . And my attorney says that I get to keep the house since . . ."

I swallowed and braced myself for what was to come as a result of my next statement. But I couldn't help it. I needed to be honest with her.

"Chaylene?" I interrupted her.

"Yes?"

"Chaylene, I don't believe in blanket second chances—I truly don't. I don't think everyone deserves a second chance. You don't give everyone a second chance to screw you over again," I prefaced. "But . . ."

"Yes?" Chaylene said when I paused.

"Well, I just think that when two people still love each other—the way you and Dennis obviously do—then anything is possible."

Chaylene remained quite as I continued.

"You were right that day. I do envy you. You have something most people want—including me—and that's true love. I most definitely envy that. But most of all, I envy your power. You see, you have the power to decide what happens between you and Dennis. You control that. And, I don't know, I just feel like if two people still love each other then the rest is kind of easy. I mean, if someone doesn't love you there's nothing you can do about it. Get off the ride and go home. But the only thing standing between you and the one *you* love . . . is yourself. That's a kind of power a lot of us wish we had."

"But why? Why should I forgive him, Sidney? I get ill just imagining the details."

Chaylene went on to share those details with me as she imagined them, as I, parched from my failed sermon, poured myself a glass of water then sat down at the table, clearing a space for myself.

The table was cluttered, as it had been for weeks, where bills and other junk mail had found themselves in the company of dirty dishes and unreturned items from the pantry. Using a grocery flyer as a coaster, I pushed more important-looking materials aside lest they get wet. Among the decidedly-important stack peeked out a white envelope with purple, calligraphy writing.

"Right. I understand . . ." I told Chaylene, letting her know I was still listening. Like anyone, she seemed to be more content when I offered my ear rather than my advice.

I pulled the envelope from the pile, noting the 2-week-old Indiana postmark. Holding it to the light, I saw what appeared to be a hand-written letter visible through its thin, paper casing. My heart skipped a beat when I noticed from whom it was sent.

I opened it.

Dear Sidney,

I know what my son told you. But I think you should know the truth . . .

CHAPTER 38

Dennis headed out as soon as *he got Chaylene's message. Though he'd initiated the call, just as he had numerous times before, this was the first time she'd actually responded with a return call. To him it was promising. It gave him hope.*

He drove, tempted to push the speed limit in the pouring rain, wondering what she had to say to him— in person, as specified in her message. What made her decide to invite him over after refusing to even speak to him for so long? Her message was vague, conveying nothing of her intent, just: 'It's me returning your call. Come by when you get this.'

Dennis knew he still hadn't signed the divorce papers Chaylene had drawn up more than three years ago. He was stalling. He hadn't even looked at them, and couldn't care less about the legalities of it all, or the division of the property. He just wanted his wife back. He certainly didn't want to sign anything that would make it official that it was over between the two of them. That would seal his fate. Chaylene would be a single woman again. A single, attractive *woman. The very idea of Chaylene ending up with another man just killed Dennis. He couldn't let that happen. His heart told him it was only a matter of time before someone stole his angel. Before someone else came along to claim what he'd lost. The thought made his foot apply additional pressure to the gas pedal.*

Dennis had grown obsessed with winning Chaylene back, especially since a couple years back, his friend told him that he'd seen her at a bar, flirting with several men, accompanied by a woman who could've doubled as her shorter twin. The knowledge of this did something to Dennis's heart that caused him to feel a piece of what Chaylene must've felt. If she felt even half as bad as he had having heard that, then he knew that, like him, she was suffering.

On that dark, rainy road, the anticipation of seeing his wife again was torturing Dennis. He hadn't seen her up close in so long. When he'd come by to pick up the kids, Chaylene made sure they were already dressed and ready to go before he got there so that there was no reason for him to sit in her living room, trying to steal glances of her, or read her emotional state. Chaylene wouldn't even come downstairs. She wanted to give Dennis neither the privilege of seeing her face, nor the opportunity to beg his way back into the house. That's how strongly she felt about divorcing him.

Dennis drove, heart thumping, palms slippery wet on the wheel, in a focused gaze. He couldn't wait to see her again. He was glad she'd finally called back, and was really hoping it hadn't been just to lean on him about those papers. He was tired of living without her. He was miserable waking up without Chaylene by his side. He was living in a two-bedroom apartment ten miles away. Alone. He never even had any company. There was no cause for gathering, or celebration. He had been mourning the loss of his one true love. Someone he'd undoubtedly let down.

Someone whose trust he'd hoped he could regain.
He'd prayed about it. Now he just hoped his prayers
had been answered.

He wanted to stop and get some flowers. But
Dennis, still uncertain of the nature of her call, was
apprehensive. All of their correspondence, all of their
communication had been through her attorney. He
hadn't spoken to her in so long that he no longer
knew how to read Chaylene's tone. Not the way he
used to. She hadn't responded to the many apologetic
letters and cards he'd sent. And the very fact that she
stayed upstairs told him that she wasn't the least bit
moved by them.

In fact, all of his attempts to regain Chaylene's
heart and companionship had failed. Even his most
extravagant. One day, believing it would be just the
thing to win her back, Dennis showed up to the house
with a $30,000 ring. A ring that most any woman
would've gladly accepted as the expensive heart-felt
gesture it was intended to be. But Chaylene wasn't so
easy. She rejected both Dennis and his wallet-
crushing peace offering, saying she didn't wear fake
diamonds. Dennis tried to assure her that it was,
indeed, real. That he'd paid a pretty penny for it, and
could show her the receipt if she'd requested. But
Chaylene explained to her confused husband that
without the love, loyalty, respect, and devotion that it
was supposed to symbolize, the diamond was, then, a
fake.

Chaylene said that too many women ran around
wearing fake diamonds gifted from untrue husbands,
lying about the quality and state of their marriages,

and that she refused to be one of them. Specifically, 'I'm not wearing some bullshit ring for anybody!' she'd vowed. Dennis had no choice but to return the ring, and himself, back to where they both came from.

As Dennis reflected on his numerous failed attempts at making amends, it saddened him to know that he'd hurt Chaylene that much. He knew a compassionate Chaylene. A merciful one. So her refusal, most of all to communicate with him, scared him in a way that nothing else had. He loved her so much, and now he was afraid he'd lost her forever.

How could I have let this happen? *Dennis wondered. They complemented each other well. They* completed *each other. Where he was hard, she was tender. When he was uncertain and afraid, she was encouraging and sure. At times where he was anxious, Chaylene was calm. He was sure he'd found his soulmate, and hoped there was still a chance for them to rekindle their love. Even if it wasn't exactly pure anymore. He hoped he'd only tarnished it slightly, as opposed to destroyed it. And he knew that this was his last chance to make something happen. To make her listen to him. This time, he would have to come 100% correct—no holding back—and tell Chaylene the truth: that she was his everything. And that, without her, his life had very little meaning.*

All that thinking made Dennis decide that flowers were probably a good idea. After all, what did he have to lose? He had nothing to lose and everything to gain. He looked out through the rainy windshield, and pulled his car over into the next shopping plaza he saw. To his luck, there was a floral boutique, tucked away between a dry cleaners and a tarot shop. Tempted to go in for a desperate reading, he coasted past the New Age shop, and continued toward the boutique with the flowers in the window.

The lights were still on. The sign was lit. Thinking this was already a good sign, Dennis got out of the car, fighting through the brutal rain, and ran inside the shop, hoping he'd find something nice to help him win back the love of his life.

"Good evening," the shopkeeper, folding gift boxes in the rear of the store, greeted Dennis upon his entrance.

Dennis nodded the same, then dashed over to the refrigerated floral display case. His reflection cast on the frosted glass door, he saw an array of flora— chromatic and beautifully-arranged bouquets—and immediately went for the two dozen, long stem roses in a sparkling crystal vase. He picked up the beautiful arrangement and headed toward the counter.

"Nice," the old man behind the counter said, smiling at the tall vase filled with sweet-smelling roses.

Dennis, preoccupied, reached into his pocket for his wallet, still wondering how it would all play out this evening. He hoped last night would be, indeed, the last night he'd ever have to sleep without Chaylene.

"Popular choice, too," the old-timer added. "I don't know one woman who doesn't fall head over heels for roses." He wiped his damp hands on his green apron, then began punching keys on the register. "Yep. If

I've learned anything in my seventy years, it's that all women love roses. All women."

Dennis looked up at him.

Dennis pulled up to the house within an hour of receiving Chaylene's message. He parked in the circular driveway, and remained in his car a moment, gathering his thoughts, and courage. He was tripping off the fact that he was so nervous. He and Chaylene had built this house together, and now he was scared to even go up and knock on the door. His stomach did somersaults, and his heart pounded, as he feared Chaylene would be just as cold and unwavering as she had been all this time. He feared this visit was strictly business. No intimate discussion whatsoever. No allowance for any last pleas. No chance for reconciliation.

Dennis sat in his car and felt his hands beginning to shake with anxiety. He couldn't control it. He clasped them together and took a few long, deep breaths to fill himself with the courage he needed to proceed. Finally, he unfastened his seatbelt and got out of the car, slowly making his way up the driveway.

Dennis walked like he was walking his last walk, his pace intentionally delaying his fate. The rain pelted him every step of the way with great force. But in a breath-holding stare, he continued up the driveway. Soaked were his head and clothing by the time he'd reached the tall, oak doors, but he stood there, warm from adrenaline and hope.

He pushed the doorbell.

As the bell's chime echoed in the uncertainty of the night, Dennis felt as if he had a drum in his shirt.

His limbs trembled with nervousness, and his stomach felt sick as he waited for Chaylene to answer the door.

Trepidatious breath filled his lungs as he realized that, in a few seconds, he would finally see the beautiful face of his wife. The face that had caught his eye many years ago across the busy college campus. The face that turned many heads but only smiled for him. The face he'd saddened and brought to tears. The face he longed to caress again, and kiss. Finally, he'd be able to look into the big beautiful eyes that had never ceased to melt his heart, and send signals of remorse and apology. He'd even be able to smell the mild, refreshing delight of her scent. He remembered how the smell of soap always seemed to cling to her skin all day like morning dew on a thirsty petal. Little memories like that made his heart race faster in the agony of the suspense until, finally, the lock clicked.

The door opened.

Standing there, soaked, Dennis's eyes slowly made their way up from his feet all the way to the face of Chaylene, who was standing there, staring at him, her eyes penetrating his spirit like the lightning bolts far behind him penetrated the sky. Dennis stood there spellbound and watery-eyed at the very sight of her.

Chaylene stepped aside.

Nervous, but never breaking his gaze, Dennis stepped into the foyer with feet that felt like boulders were strapped to them. Chaylene looked at him. Her eyes matched his, but Dennis, too consumed, didn't *notice. He was about to lose himself, but he held it together.*

From behind his back, Dennis produced a white box, offering it to Chaylene.

"Please, open it," he asked Chaylene, his nervous hands supporting the medium-sized box.

Chaylene looked at Dennis apprehensively.

He looked back with eyes that reiterated *Please*.

Chaylene lifted the lid from the box then quickly looked up at Dennis when she saw that it was empty.

"What you're looking at is my life without you," Dennis said before Chaylene could say anything.

He clutched the sides of the box, shaking his head to ward off the tears.

"I have nothing, Chaylene. My life is completely empty. And your love . . ." he still fought tears "is the only thing that can fill it."

Chaylene took the box from Dennis.

"I'm sorry, Chaylene. I'm so sorry I hurt you. I'm sorry I hurt *us*."

Chaylene kept her eyes inside of the box as Dennis's emotions seeping to the surface.

"I love you, Chaylene. Please. Please be my wife again. Please love me again. *Please* . . ."

Chaylene held the box and stared inside of it. In it, she saw her own life.

But she knew the choice was hers.

EPILOGUE

Mom wondered what was taking me so long. She couldn't start her plump and juicy peach cobbler without the nutmeg I volunteered to go get. She'd called me on my cell, telling me more people had just arrived, and inquiring on my whereabouts. She just didn't understand how hard it was these days to find an open store at 3 o'clock in the afternoon on Thanksgiving Day.

Spice in hand, I was finally headed home, glad to be back in The Big Apple. I decided to take the long way back, despite Mom's cobbler, so that I could cruise a bit and be alone with my thoughts before rejoining the bunch back at the house. There was a lot to think about. So much had happened in the past nine and a half months.

For starters, last weekend I had the honor of being maid of honor for the very first time. Bumping their wedding up a full year, Leann and Reggie tied the knot. I'd never seen someone look so beautiful in a wedding gown. Reggie was all eyes when he saw her coming down the aisle, veiled and gorgeous. And, for the first time as well, I saw the love in his eyes that Leann had seen all along. It touched me, seeing that. And, apparently, I wasn't the only one. Before they even got to their vows, the room was full of sniffles and wails. Leann's grandmother, front and center, led the symphony. Reggie was crying too. He could barely recite his portion of the vows, so overwhelmed by emotion. I was surprised by it all. I didn't know he had it in him. In fact, there were a lot of things I didn't know about him.

Turns out, Reggie was a tightwad with a plan. He'd been saving to buy a house for him and Leann all along, knowing since the first day they met that she was the woman who completed him. With his cash, and her credit, they were able to buy a nice little starter home, a fixer-upper that Leann, with her real estate connections, couldn't wait to tear into and renovate. Honeymooning in Aruba, she'd sent me a postcard, which I received yesterday. All it said was: *'Having so much fun we broke two beds!'*

I guess some things never change.

A couple of days ago I spoke to Kiana. She was so excited about seeing me in a few weeks. She was back living with her mom, who was ten months sober. It was amazing how much different Lorraine looked. Sobriety looked good on her. She'd sent me a picture of her and Kiana, and it was like I was looking at two completely different people. They both were happy, and shining with joy. I was happy for the two of them. So many positive things were happening in Kiana's life.

Kiana had made, both, the cheerleading squad and the honor roll. She had zillions of friends. And, to both our surprise, she told me that her favorite subject in school was math. Imagine that. Lorraine thanked me for being there for Kiana at times where she was unable to. I thanked her for allowing me to be there. It was due, in part, to Kiana that I was able to put my own life into better perspective. She was a young inspiration to me. An example of strength and endurance. She wasn't half my age but was twice as strong.

As for me, I was living back in New York, teaching kids and adults at *Deborah G.'s Dance Studio*, a new studio that opened up in the city, while also working on my dance degree. Given all that had happened, I had finally decided to take ownership of my life, and to do what I wanted to do all along. Practicality is fine. But I prefer passion. Dancing has always been that for me.

Speaking of passion, Mom and I had a heart-to-heart the day after Chaylene and I had ours. I told Mom that, though I knew her heart was in the right place, I wanted her to ease up on me about the husband thing. I knew she meant well, but that was pressure that I just didn't need. I told her that apple trees can take four to eight years to bear fruit, and that, if Mother Nature was patient, then why couldn't we be? Mom promised she wouldn't bring up the issue again. And I'd promised her that when I did find that special, together-forever someone, she'd be the first to know.

The sun rose from behind the clouds as I turned onto my parents' block. I saw Tasha's car parked in her parents' driveway. Still living in Atlanta, she was in town visiting for the holidays. I couldn't wait to see her later this evening.

After our quarrel that night at the club, Tasha showed up at my door, five days later, with two huge bags, and a great big hug, using two of her three-week vacation on mending our fractured friendship, cancelling her trip to Jamaica. As I was newly unemployed at the time, having quit my job, she and I spent the time getting to know the new us. Those days following our argument had been transformative ones for me.

Even though I didn't want to hear it that night, Tasha was right. I must've been crazy crying over losers like Damon, and Rico. Bringing myself down over guys who weren't even close to being worth it. And it was high time that I let go of the negativity that was only keeping me miserable inside while life went on merrily for others around me.

I couldn't believe how much time I'd wasted thinking about how a particular person treated me on a particular day. So many of my days were spent reliving disturbing moments of my life, mourning events that took place some time ago, hanging on to drama that didn't serve me. Letting it change me. My personality. My character. I hadn't dated Damon and Rico for two seasons *combined*, yet I'd devoted roughly two years of my life to their dishonor, hating them as I moved through a lesser quality life as a result. It was senseless to keep hurting over someone who wasn't hurting over me. To hate when I was the only one suffering. Tasha helped me realize that. And I appreciated that she wasn't my 'Yes Man' but, instead, my best friend. Even when it was uncomfortable to be.

But as for Damon, karma did eventually come and tap him on the shoulder. Turns out, his wife had some secrets of her own. Thinking he would be enjoying a leisurely trip with her to New England, he suddenly found himself seated in the greenroom of a certain television show, only to later be catapulted onto a stage and told that He is NOT the father!

Tasha DVR'd it, having been tipped off prior to its air date, and the two of us watched it repeatedly, eating popcorn and brownie bites, offering our viewer's commentary. It was pretty sad. But trust me, I didn't cry.

Chaylene was sitting on the porch, her hands stuffed in mittens and neck wrapped in fleece. When I pulled into the driveway she stood up.

As I unfastened my seatbelt my heart started beating funny again, but this time for a completely different reason.

I got out of the car, and, wearing a giant-sized grin, ran fast up the stairs.

"Chaylene!" I hugged her tight.

"Sidney!" She squeezed me back

We held each other genuinely for the first time in, what felt like, our entire lives. We had become so close these past several months. We spoke on the phone every day, sometimes for hours. It was such a wonderful feeling having my sister back in my life. I imagined it was one of the best feelings in the world.

"Here"—Chaylene let me go, feeling under her scarf—"I have something for you. I want you to hold onto this." She removed Grannah's necklace from around her neck, clasping it around mine.

I looked down at the shiny blue gemstone, rolling it between my fingers.

"Oh, my gosh. Thank you, Chaylene." I was touched to my very core.

She smiled.

"I have something for you, too," I told her, reaching into my coat pocket.

Chaylene covered her mouth and gasped when she saw what sat in the palm of my hand.

"My wedding ring!"

Dennis had given her a new one by now, but I knew this particular ring held sentimental value that was irreplaceable. There was no way I could've thrown it away, regardless of what my sister and I were going through at the time.

Two tears fled Chaylene's eyes as she looked at the, now, eight-year-old ring. It gleamed, as I'd had it cleaned prior to coming.

"My wedding ring . . . " she repeated, still in disbelief.

"Yes. *Yours*." I smiled as I watched her place it onto her finger with slight effort. "It's time I gave that back to you."

She nodded, wiping her wet cheek.

"Especially since I have my own now!" I flashed my 3-karat diamond engagement ring and beamed with excitement.

"I know! I know! I'm so happy for you." Chaylene yanked me into a congratulatory hug. We bounced up and down in celebration.

Later for that apple tree stuff. In five weeks I was going to be Mrs. Sidney Graham. Mom was so excited. She'd taken care of everything. It was almost like this was going to be *her* dream wedding. I let her run with it, green-lighting all of her ideas, even if I didn't particularly like them all. That didn't matter.

Because I knew that I was blessed to have her be a part of this. And those times I seemed to forget, Jared was there to remind me.   Sadly,   Jared's mom would be at our wedding only in spirit. Earlier this summer, after a year and a half of battling cancer, she succumbed to her disease and was now a beautiful angel in heaven. It was hard for Jared, not having his mother around to witness what would be such a special moment in his life. But I insisted she *was* around. This wedding had her name all over it. For it was because of her that Jared and I would wed at all.

In her letter, Jared's mom explained to me what he couldn't. She explained his thoughts and motivation the night he broke up with me. There *was* another woman. It was true. He didn't lie about that. But the other woman was her.

It was earlier that same week, when he'd left me, she explained, that Jared had learned of her cancer diagnosis. He was told by doctors that she had no more than a few months to live. The news devastated him. He suffered silently, resentful and bitter at a world that seemed to rotate without mercy. He'd lost his father during college, his girlfriend shortly after, and, just as unexpectedly, had been told he was losing his mother. To him, it seemed the world was taking away everyone he loved. And he just couldn't bear to risk another loss somewhere down the line. He began to feel that he needed to detach himself from the only other person he loved so dearly. And that person was me.

Jared's doing a lot better now, though sometimes he struggles. He asked me one day, *"Sidney, how do I say goodbye to my mother? How??"* I simply told him that he doesn't. That he never says goodbye to her. That saying goodbye to his mother would be like saying goodbye to his soul. It was impossible to do so. For he was given the light of *life* inside of her womb, and no one else's. I told him that he was still as connected to her now as he was when he'd grown and slept under her heart and lungs those many years ago. That she was a permanent part of him. And that he was a permanent part of her. They were spiritually destined to be together forever. Far beyond what he can see and understand right now as he mourns the physical loss of her, and that beautiful smile of hers.

I happened to see her beautiful smile every day, however, when I got to work. On the wall, in the main office of the dance studio that Jared had bought for me, and named in her honor, Mrs. Graham (aka *Deborah G.*) hung 8-feet high, in all her 1967 matte finish glory, for all dancers, current and aspiring, to pay homage as they danced their way toward their dreams. Just as I had mine.

Chaylene repositioned the necklace against my sweater as I looked down at its sky-blue sparkle.

"So now you've got your 'old', your 'borrowed', *and* your 'blue'—all in one," she said.

I looked up at her. *"Borrowed?"*

"Well, yeah," she said, wearing a stingy smirk.

I smirked too, thinking she couldn't blame me for trying.

"Now all you need is your 'new'," Chaylene smiled.

"Oh, I think I've got plenty of that." I squeezed her hand.

"Well, we better get inside," she warned. "Dennis is probably talking Dad's and Jared's ears off. You know, the whole proud Papa-To-Be thing," she rubbed her occupied belly and laughed.

"You're right," I agreed. "And I wouldn't want my little niece catching a cold for her birthday. *Isn't that right, sweet baby? Isn't that right?*" I bent down, talking to Chaylene's enlarged abdomen. "You think she'll hold off until the wedding?"

"I think she will," Chaylene said. "She knows how much being your matron of honor means to me."

I looked up at Chaylene.

"I love you, Sidney," she blurted out, her eyes watery and round. "I love you so much."

My bottom lip quivered as I leaned in and hugged her. "I love you too, Chaylene. I love you, too."

As I stood there holding my sister I realized that my virginity wasn't my power after all. The same was true of my desirability quotient, and relationship status. Love was my power. Friendship was my power. Family was my power. From these sources I pulled my greatest strength. A strength that would outlast any single moment, or person, in my life.

As for Love and I, we eventually made friends with one another. Once I'd realized that Love was never torturing at me, or wanting to ridicule me, but rather wanting me to truly get to know it, to understand it, and to see it already present in my life, then the two of us were just fine. So often Love, like Chaylene in my hospital room, falls victim to mistaken identity, or even downright impersonation. Sometimes when we think it's standing before us, smiling at us in all its six-foot-two-hundred-pound gorgeous glory, the opposite is true. We've been tricked by a wolf in Love's clothing. Other times Love simply goes unrecognized, unnoticed in the heart of an individual because it doesn't look like what we thought it would, or should. It doesn't match our fixed, unrealistic and, sometimes, excessively-superficial expectations. We grumble that it's absent from our lives when, in actuality, it's been there all along. We were just too unaware to see it.

Through my experiences I've learned that Love is not a lottery. It's not something you win. It's not even something you earn. It's simply quietly ever-present. Always available and visible in some form, waiting to be acknowledged. Appreciated. Love yearns to be recognized in its various forms and actions such as compassion, the willingness to listen and to seek understanding, and, of course, forgiveness. Love—*True* Love—is wiser than we know. And more sensitive than we can imagine.

So as it turns out I *had* grown over the years. In bigger ways than I'd expected. And now as I reflected on my past, I no longer looked back with regret. The past, exactly as it was, had been an integral part of my emotional, psychological, and spiritual development. Without it I wouldn't be the person that I was today, or *where* I was today. And right now I happened to like both. My journey, no matter how turbulent, taught me things that I plan to carry with me for my entire life. The past had been my teacher. My sculptor. It educated me. Shaped me. While *pain* was its byproduct *wisdom* was its masterpiece. And I was grateful to it, tears and all.

But while I've gained this newfound respect and appreciation for my past, I'm often careful not to over-appraise its significance, or misuse it by way of constantly reliving things in my mind. Instead, I leave the wounds closed. Sealed shut. Sure, I'll take the scars. But as for the feelings, the emotions, I leave those there, in the past, right where they belong. Because, by far, one of the *best* things about the past is that you never have to do it again.

1

424